Praise for Raymond Khoury

'A world-class writer of pure-bred thrillers' *Daily Telegraph*

'Khoury writes big, fast-paced thrillers . . . he's a craftsman whose muscular prose carries conviction' *Guardian*

'A high-octane rollercoaster ride of thrills and spills' *Irish Mail on Sunday*

'Rip-roaring action man stuff' *The Times*

'History, mystery, suspense, and action - Khoury knows the recipe for a good read' *Library Journal*

'High-octane thrills from a master of the genre' *Irish Independent*

'As hauntings go, this is one to freeze the blood' *Northern Echo*

Raymond Khoury is the internationally-bestselling author of the Sean Reilly novels: *The Last Templar, The Templar Salvation, Second Time Around (The Devil's Elixir), Rasputin's Shadow* and *The End Game* as well as two stand-alone thrillers, *The Sign* and *The Sanctuary*. Also an acclaimed screenwriter, his credits include the BBC Television series *Spooks* and *Waking The Dead.*

Find out more at www.raymondkhoury.com or follow him at facebook.com/lasttemplar

*Also by Raymond Khoury*

The Last Templar
The Sanctuary
The Sign
The Templar Salvation
Second Time Around (originally published as The Devil's Elixir)
Rasputin's Shadow

RAYMOND
KHOURY

# THE END GAME

An Orion paperback

First published in Great Britain in 2016
by Orion Books
This paperback edition published in 2016
by Orion Books,
an imprint of The Orion Publishing Group Ltd,
Carmelite House, 50 Victoria Embankment,
London EC4Y 0DZ

An Hachette UK company

1 3 5 7 9 10 8 6 4 2



All the characters in this book are fictitious,
and any resemblance to actual persons, living
or dead, is purely coincidental.

A CIP catalogue record for this book
is available from the British Library.

ISBN 978 1 4091 2953 0

Typeset by Input Data Services Ltd, Bridgwater, Somerset

Printed and bound by CPI Group (UK) Ltd, Croydon, CR0 4YY

www.orionbooks.co.uk

*For Eugenie Furniss, Jon Wood*
*and Mitch Hoffman, consiglieres and*
*friends from day one.*

# PROLOGUE

Kyle Rossetti felt the needle puncture his skin and slide deep into his lower back.

Again.

The pain was beyond compare. An electrical spasm ripped through his legs, but the duct tape holding him firm against the metal table caused the jolt to rebound back into the bone, then out again toward the surface of his skin in a cycle of reverberating suffering—or so it felt.

Eventually, mercifully, the agony subsided.

"How attached are you to the notion of being able to, let's say, run?"

The voice came from the man standing directly behind him. That he was a man was all Rossetti knew about his captor. Having not laid eyes on him at any point, he had no sense of what the man looked like. His voice was neutral, calm, but filled with purpose. His accent gave away nothing except that he was American, or had at least lived in America for most of his life. Rossetti shook his head—or would have done were it not for the tape holding it firm against the table—and silently cursed himself. Of course, the guy could be from anywhere. Anywhere at all.

"I can tell you permanent neurological injury is rare—at least it is when the needle is inserted by a doctor. Which, sadly, I'm not. The numbness, the tingling or the pain—they could be normal side effects of what I'm doing. Then again, they could all be signs of irreversible, permanent damage. You never really know. Unless that's the intention."

Rossetti already understood the perverse logic behind this particularly twisted method of torture. The instinct of a victim is always to struggle, to do absolutely anything to avoid the source of pain. With a three-inch needle stuck in your spine, you'll do pretty much anything you can to stay completely still, which means you won't struggle and you won't even consider trying to free yourself, even if that were possible.

That was assuming you could stay still and not react to the extreme pain searing through you.

The sweat that had pooled under Rossetti's torso felt cold and clammy. It was as if fear itself had seeped out through his pores.

"I'll ask you again, and if you don't give me a full and detailed answer, I'll close my eyes and start to move the needle around in there. Then we'll both be at the mercy of whatever power controls the random chaos of the universe."

Rossetti took a deep breath.

He was tough, by any standard. He'd covered numerous wars, including spending five months embedded with the Eighty-second Airborne in Afghanistan. He'd narrowly avoided death way more times than he could remember—or was even aware of, for that matter. He'd been threatened and bullied by lawyers, corporate stooges and government agencies. He'd stood before a congressional hearing and repeatedly refused to divulge his sources, even when threatened with a charge of treason. On that particular occasion, he'd ended up spending over four months in prison until his sentence was revoked on appeal. Writing about the experience—how he'd barely managed to avoid the drugs, violence and degradation that seemed to be commonplace in his country's correctional facilities, though exactly what they were supposed to be correcting, and how, seemed to have long been forgotten—had earned him a George Polk award, to add to his Pulitzer. He never thought of himself as particularly brave, though he had often been described as such by his colleagues and by those members of the public that still believed in freedom of the press and agreed with the notion of their government being held to account.

Right now, he needed all the bravery he could muster, although he already knew that it probably wouldn't be enough.

When he'd been grabbed from outside his TriBeCa apartment in the middle of the night and bundled into a van, it had been instantly clear to him that it had to be connected to the recent call he'd received. With a sinking heart and a lurching gut, he had realized that his source's instructions not to talk to anyone about what he'd told him, nor attempt any form of research—whether verbal or digital—had been not only well intentioned, but also very specifically designed to keep Rossetti alive. Not out of any sense of decency, but simply so Rossetti could share with the public whatever it was that his source wanted to get off his chest. And the same investigative impulse that had singled him out as the journalist most worthy of this scoop was the same impulse that had landed him here. And, he realized, would most likely lead to his demise. People didn't torture you intensely if they weren't already intending to finish you off afterwards.

The voice said, "I'll ask you one last time. Who contacted you? What did they give you? Who did you share it with?"

"No one. I swear. I told you everything I know. You think I wouldn't, given . . . this?"

"That's just not good enough, Kyle."

The man standing behind him pushed on the needle.

A supernova of pain lit up Rossetti's spine. The needle had, quite literally, hit a nerve.

The journalist howled, his eyesight clouding up from the tears. He was on the edge of fainting. Besides being comprehensively the worst thing Rossetti had experienced in his thirty-eight years, the pain was also the most terrifying as it carried with it the potential for the kind of spinal trauma that could cause paralysis.

Paralysis of exactly what, though, was a lottery.

He felt the air move against his bare skin as the man shifted on his feet. "You might need to find a new apartment. No way is a wheelchair going up those steps."

His torturer pushed the needle slightly deeper.

The pain was beyond excruciating and only started to subside when the needle was edged back, away from the nerve. As it did, Rossetti wasn't sure he could feel his feet any more.

He gasped with relief. "Please. Just say a name. Any name you want. I'll confirm it's him. Just . . . stop. Please."

The man sighed, then pulled out the needle. It clanged as he dropped it against the metal table. He then snapped off his gloves and let them fall to the ground.

He stood motionless, his breathing slow and steady.

Rossetti felt like a trapdoor had just opened beneath him, but he had yet to fall through. He knew it was the feeling you get when something really bad is about to happen, something you have zero ability to stop. He knew he only had a small window left. He knew that what he said now would probably determine whether he lived or died.

"I'm telling you the truth. I don't know who he is. Assuming it's even a 'he.'"

"The voice box?"

"Yes. He said he'd tell me everything at the meeting. Then he didn't show. That's all I know—I swear."

"But that's not everything, is it?"

Rossetti's mouth felt like the valley in Afghanistan where he'd watched a soldier bleed to death, and despite the warm air in what seemed to be a windowless room, his body now felt icy cold.

"It is, I swear. Just that—and what I told you he said on the phone about the janitors and the blind. But it's meaningless, totally meaningless. I didn't get any hits that meant anything."

There was the sound of a syringe drawing liquid out of a vial. Then two small, dull splashes as a couple of drops hit the metal table. The man clearly didn't want to risk injecting air into his victim's bloodstream.

Rossetti's mind raced with alarm, bouncing against conflicting thoughts, desperately grabbing at anything that carried a hint of comfort. He wondered if the man was going to try some kind of truth serum, but surely the man would have tried that first? He hadn't seen the man's face. Didn't that mean they weren't going to kill him? But why inject him then? He was already fully immobilized. Unless they were going to move him. But why move him unless they were going to take him home? Yes. That had to be it. They were going to take him home as if nothing had happened.

He'd forget the whole thing. Maybe leave the job altogether. Maybe it was time for a change. Maybe he and Samantha could finally have the kids she'd been yearning for since they got married.

His rampaging thoughts were interrupted by the needle as it jabbed into his neck and delivered the syringe's contents directly into his vein. He quickly felt a strange warmth flood through his body and, as his consciousness started to fade, he heard the man drop the syringe on the metal table then walk around it.

The journalist found himself looking into the man's face. There was nothing that unique about him, nothing vaguely memorable. It was like staring at an expressionless mannequin, a blank template for a male human specimen.

The man shook his head. “You got one hit. Just not the kind you were looking for.”

Rossetti’s eyes closed on the man’s cold, dead stare as he slipped into unconsciousness.

The next time he opened them, his entire body would be on fire.

# TUESDAY

# 1

*Allentown, New Jersey*

I really didn't want to be here. Then again, who would?

Three o'clock in the morning, me and my partner, Nick Aparo, in our unmarked SUV, parked on a dark street in the middle of nowhere, freezing our nuts off, watching, waiting for the go signal, making sure our target didn't vaporize before we nabbed him.

Don't get me wrong. This is my job. I do it by choice. I do it because I believe in it, because I think what we do, as special agents of the FBI, is important. And the guy in our crosshairs on this particular night deserved our full attention, no question.

It's just that I had bigger fish to fry. White whales, in fact, ones the Bureau couldn't know about. Ones I hadn't even been completely open about with Nick, either. I'm sure he could sense that something was still eating away at me. Ten years of sharing the line of fire with someone usually does that. If it didn't, you were probably in the wrong business. But he knew better than to ask. He knew that if I wasn't sharing everything, it was probably for his own good. To give him deniability, to let him keep his job and not face prosecution. Because to get to the bottom of the shark-infested sinkhole that had first sucked me in a few months ago, I'd probably need to break a law or two.

Nick got that—but he wasn't happy about it.

So we'd spent a lot of hours in strained silence as we avoided the whales in the room—well, the cabin of our Ford Expedition, anyway—and stared through the condensation-clouded windscreen and the snow flurries outside at the single-story house up and across the street, the one with the hypnotic, mind-numbing Christmas lights twinkling along the edge of its roof.

Whatever our target was doing inside his house, he was doing it in considerably more warmth than the poor saps sworn to bring him to justice. We were sitting in north of a hundred thousand dollars of customized FBI vehicle and the heated seats had still managed to conk out, leaving the two of us shivering like we were being continuously tasered. Running the engine while the whole street slept was not an option. Not unless we wanted to give our target a clear heads-up.

On the positive side, at least no one could see us. In terms of discretion, sitting in a snow-covered vehicle in a line of snow-covered vehicles was pretty much ideal.

The blizzard had stopped an hour ago, adding a more substantial covering to the inch that had refused to thaw. Now it was snowing again. This cold front was definitely winning in terms of historic meteorological bragging rights. I've got to admit: it was exhausting. The body burns up energy trying to stay warm, and at three in the morning, after several nights of this, I was running low on juice.

I watched my breath billowing out in front of my eyes as I zipped up my FBI parka, the cold metal of the zip reaching its endpoint against my nose. Any more coffee and there was zero chance of sleep when I finally made it home—in time to watch the sun rise as I zoned out against a deeply asleep Tess.

Nick, on the other hand, had no such concerns and was pouring himself yet another mug from the five-liter flask before sipping the steaming, bitter liquid like it had been lovingly made by his favorite barista. He looked ridiculous in his big, Russian-style fur hat, the flaps of which he had pulled right down over his ears, but nothing I said was going to make him lose it. At least he was watching the house with me and not sitting there flicking through an endless array of female Tinder offerings while subjecting them to the incessant vocal critique that usually accompanied his left- and right-swipes, which was his MO on previous stakeouts. Small mercies, I guess.

The subject of our impromptu igloo huddle was called Jake Daland. Daland was the founder and head honcho of Maxiplenty, which had taken over from Silk Road not long after we had shut that online marketplace down.

Daland had been on our radar ever since he'd set up his first torrent portal. As Hollywood and Washington got increasingly tough on those who wanted to watch their movies and TV shows without adverts and free from the epileptic buffering that still plagued most subscription sites unless you had a fiber-optic pipe to a main POP—or so the NYC field office's head geek, who couldn't utter two sentences without quoting *Community*, had put it—he'd handed the sites over to some underlings and gone underground, starting something far more insidious in the process: an anonymous barter site that would have made the communally minded blush. For its name, he chose a tongue-in-cheek twist on a Newspeak term from George Orwell's *1984*. He also came up with a neat twist to try and avoid the fate of Silk Road by avoiding financial transactions altogether—no cash, no checks, no credit cards, no Bitcoins. Maxiplenty was a darknet barter-only site, an online marketplace where you could do anything you wanted—get drugs, guns, explosives, launder money, or have someone murdered—provided you had something you could trade for it.

Daland wasn't making any money off those transactions. It was set up mostly as a sick, no-holds-barred, quasi-libertarian flip off to the government. You could only join Maxiplenty by invitation. Once you had successfully transacted your first barter, you were invited to subscribe to the online market, and this is where human greed got the better of idealistic nonconformism. The network had become a hub for the depraved—way beyond what Daland himself originally had in mind—while the subscription dollars began to flow in. The site had no overhead to speak of. As Maxiplenty grew, Daland remained in his rented house, spending next to nothing, late-night pizza his only indulgence. He'd obviously been paying attention to all those movies that made it clear that the criminals who stay out of prison are the ones who avoid conspicuous lifestyle upgrades and non-routine purchases.

When two of his users successfully swapped murders—a movie plot come to life, but with none of the embellishment at which Hollywood so excels—the US Attorney's Office decided that Daland was at least an accessory and, at worst, had procured both crimes. Several divisions of the FBI were now working together to take Maxiplenty down and lock Daland up. Courtesy of the two guys presently freezing their butts off, we already had signed confessions from both murderers. Getting Daland himself was nowhere near as straightforward. Maxiplenty used a sophisticated network of servers located around the world along with a seemingly infinite process of IP spoofing to disguise both the site itself and those using it. It had taken the techies at Quantico's Cyber Division lab weeks to secure enough evidence to ensure an arrest stuck. Evidence we now finally had, as of four hours ago. Which is why we were here, waiting for word that power had been cut to Daland's house before we stormed in.

We weren't alone. The whole team, including a couple of specialists from Cyber Division, was waiting close by, equipped with night vision goggles and, with a bit of luck, a little less frozen than us. The aim was to disconnect all the computer equipment—along with any battery backups—before we turned the power back on and began the bagging and tagging. I didn't want Daland to have the tiniest window in which to hit some kind of nuke switch and wipe his hard drives.

So here we were, poised, waiting for the engineers from Jersey Central Power & Light to tell us they were ready to hit the switch. They were fairly used to being called out at ungodly hours this time of year. The bad weather and overloading from seasonal light displays meant they had to be available 24/7. Still, it was taking longer than I expected.

"Heads up, Reilly," a voice announced through my earpiece. "Looks like it's feeding time at the zoo again."

"Got it."

I looked out through the near whiteout on the other side of the windows and saw the now-familiar pizza delivery car with half a plastic forty-eight-inch pepperoni sticking out of the roof glide past.

"*More* pizza?" Nick grumbled, peering out through the windshield. "How in God's name can he eat so much pizza and stay so thin? Bastard."

I turned to face him, a slight grin on my face. "Maybe he doesn't chase it down with a bowl of lasagna."

My partner was fairly legendary for his appetites, particularly when it came to Italian food and generously proportioned blondes. The former had provided something of a distraction when the latter ended up getting him divorced. Nowadays, he was happy to indulge in both, having finally come to terms with the court-appointed bi-weekly weekends with his eleven-year-old son. He'd also stuck with the spinning classes. I lost that bet, along with most of Twenty-six Federal Plaza.

"What's wrong with having a pizza as a starter? That's how they do it in Italy, you philistine."

I smiled. "Maybe he's got a gym in there."

His face got all bent out of shape. "At home? Alone? What's the point of that?

"The point of exercise being to meet the babes, right?"

"D-uh. But, hey, if I get to live a couple of extra years, that's cool too."

I shook my head, sadly. It was a now-familiar exchange enjoyed by us both, precisely because of its familiarity. When they say partners are like a couple, they're only half right in Aparo's case. Law enforcement tends to only see one partner at a time.

The delivery guy kept his engine idling as he hurried up to the door and rang the bell.

The snowflakes were getting meatier.

I adjusted the screen brightness on the laptop sitting at my elbow. Four video windows showed the feeds from the cameras we'd managed to set up on our target. I concentrated on the feed from the camera facing the house's front door, which was hidden inside a newspaper vending machine.

Jake Daland—elegant as ever in a short, silk kimono over a deep V-necked white T-shirt that exposed a mat of black chest hair—opened the door with the same calm, nonchalant demeanor. No stepping halfway through the door, no furtively peering to left and right. Zero interest in what was outside the house at all. Either he knew we were out here and didn't care, or—and though possible, it was by now fairly improbable—he didn't have a clue that he'd been under surveillance for weeks.

Daland took the pizza box and handed the delivery guy some money. The delivery guy seemed a bit thrown. They exchanged a few words as he struggled with his oversized puffer coat, fishing through its pockets, then shook his head, the cash in his outstretched hand.

"What's he doing?" Nick asked.

"Daland must have handed him a large bill and the kid doesn't have enough change."

Nick shrugged. "We're *so* on the wrong side of the law."

They exchanged a few more words, then Daland waved the driver inside. The guy went in and the door closed behind him.

Moments later, the delivery guy re-emerged. He was holding a gift-wrapped box from his most loyal small-hours customer.

Nick said, "Now he's giving the guy a Christmas present?" He shook his head. "I'm telling you, Sean, we chose poorly, man. Poor-ly."

The delivery guy got back in his car and drove away.

It was at that precise moment that my earpiece burst back to life. "We have a go. All teams: get into position."

Nick and I climbed out of the Expedition. We were wearing Kevlar under our FBI parkas, even though I thought it was highly unlikely we'd meet any armed resistance. Four SWAT members were already skulking up to the house's front door, while two other agents, Annie Deutsch and Nat "Len" Lendowski, climbed out of another unmarked vehicle and approached from the opposite direction. We had other men covering the rear of the house. The tech specialists would wait till the house was secure.

We fell in behind the SWAT guys. "One in position," I said into my cuff mike.

"Two in position," came the confirmation from the rear of the house.

"Hold," the voice in my ear said. A brief moment, then it came back. "In five. Four. Three." Two seconds later, the Christmas lights on Daland's roof snapped off as the power was cut.

We flipped down our night vision goggles and drew our sidearms as the SWAT team leader swung his battering ram through the door, but just as we were about to follow them in, an alarm burst to life inside me as my brain spontaneously highlighted something I'd seen as I walked up to the house.

Something I'd barely noticed out of the corner of one eye.

Lying innocuously by the edge of the curb, obscured by the shade of some parked cars, barely noticeable: a flash of red ribbon.

The Christmas gift that Daland had given to the delivery guy only minutes earlier.

I was electrified with the feeling that something was wrong.

"Nick! Car—now," I shouted as I pulled off my goggles and

stepped back, toward the sidewalk. I saw Deutsch and Lendowski looking at me, all confused, and just waved them on. "Go, go, go!"

They disappeared into the house as I passed the gift and jabbed a finger toward it, telling Nick, "The gift's a prop. He faked us out."

We hurried into the Expedition, Nick's face shooting me a sizeable question mark as I slammed the big SUV into gear and floored it.

We fishtailed away from the curb, with me shouting over the revs, "The delivery guy's still in the house. That was Daland who drove off in the pizza car."

Nick shook his head. "Bastard's got a couple of minutes on us."

The roads were covered with snow, but the four-wheel drive of the Expedition was rock solid as it ate up the miles. There were no cars driving around, not at that hour, and we soon hit an intersection. I stopped, clueless about which way to go.

"He knows he's burnt," I said. "Which means he knows everyone else is burnt too. So where's he going?"

Nick rubbed his face, trying to force his brain into gear. "Daland knows we'll be looking for the car and it's not the most discreet ride. He needs to ditch it, pronto."

"Yeah, but where? And swap over to what?"

The onboard satnav flickered through screens as Nick worked it. I couldn't wait for it to suggest some answers. I scanned the road's surface and could just about make out a set of thin tracks that turned left.

I followed.

Nick watched as I turned onto another residential street, then his attention went back to the navigation system. Thick walls of snow were now making it increasingly difficult to see where we were going. Even at full speed, the wipers were straining against the weight of the heavy flakes and the trail I was following was getting progressively more shrouded by the new snow.

We were going to lose him.

I adjusted the traction control. "He can't stay out in this. Either he's got somewhere to lay low nearby or he's got a fallback drive stashed somewhere."

Nick shook his head and said, "I can't see him having that much foresight. Doesn't seem in character."

I nodded. "A cab, maybe?"

Nick grabbed the car radio's mike. "I need the location of all twenty-four-hour cab companies around the target's house."

Moments later, the radio squawked, "Millpond Cabs, corner of North Main and Church."

The radio squawked again, another voice this time. It was Lendowski. "Daland's in the wind," he said. "The pizza guy is freaking. Daland told him he needed to avoid an angry boyfriend. Told him the angry guy's girlfriend was in the bedroom and gave him three hundred bucks. Reilly, where the hell are you?"

So it wasn't about change after all. Not that it mattered.

Nick nudged my arm and pointed urgently to the left. I swung the Expedition accordingly, heading west as Nick answered for us both. "We're closing on him. You and Deutsch secure the house."

"Already done. Power's back on."

"Are we good?" I asked.

"We've got several computers. The hard drives were already over-writing. He had battery backups, but tech disconnected them in time. I think we'll have enough once they've gone through data recovery. There's also a laptop, but its hard drive's been pulled."

I gunned the V8 engine, the four-wheel drive now winning a one-sided battle against the fresh snow.

The houses were larger now. Set farther back from the street.

Nick pointed up ahead. "Five hundred yards more, then we need to cross over North Main onto Church."

I was scanning every alleyway as we moved. I peered into a lot shared by a fitness center and a gas station. Nothing.

"Sean, right there!" Nick shouted as he opened his window to take a better look. I slowed the SUV to a crawl.

A narrow street ran about thirty degrees off our position. Almost completely obscured by snow-covered trees was the top of a giant pepperoni pizza.

I swung the Expedition to the left, ready to turn right in another fifty yards.

Nick gestured toward the fast-approaching junction.

A single vehicle was midway through a left-hand turn onto North Main Street.

As we got level with the vehicle, a Toyota Camry, I registered the

"Millpond Taxicabs" livery. The cab had pulled away before I could look inside.

I spun the wheel around, breaking hard. The Expedition skated a few feet in the original direction of travel, then completed the U-turn as the wheels regained traction.

"That's him."

Nick hit the siren as I swung the Expedition into the empty oncoming lane, accelerated beyond the Camry and swerved back into its path.

The cab's driver hit the brakes. Its wheels locked and the Camry slammed into Nick's side of the SUV, blocking his door.

I climbed out of the Expedition, pulled my sidearm, and edged around the front of the stationary SUV.

The shotgun-side rear passenger door opened and Daland emerged, both hands high over his head.

"Down," I barked. "On your knees!"

Nick had climbed over the seats and was now covering the taxi cab's driver, who had stepped out of the Camry, both hands in the air.

Daland dropped to his knees, shouting, "Easy with the guns! I'm unarmed."

I stepped toward him. "The hard drive. Where is it?"

"What hard drive?"

The taxi driver turned toward me, all panicked and jittery. "He threw something out the window as we turned out of Church."

Daland lowered his head, then turned toward the taxi driver, his face tight with anger. "They watch everything you do, every website you read, every keystroke you tap in. They know everyone you talk to, everything you buy. They own you. And you're no one. Imagine what they do with people who matter."

I held my position as Nick moved to cuff Daland. "Save the rant for your Twitter feed, Daland." I gestured at the taxi driver. "Show me."

He led as we jogged back toward the junction with Church, our footfalls crunching in the snow.

The radio squawked as I called it in. "Target secure, repeat, target secure. We'll meet you back at the house. And tell the pizza guy his car is safe."

The snow was falling heavier now and sticking to the ground with purpose, but it didn't take long. We found the hard drive, half-buried in the snow, by the base of a fence.

I brushed some snowflakes from my face, enjoying the sharpness of the freezing air as it hit my lungs.

It was good to be done with Daland. It always felt great to close out an assignment successfully. We'd done our part. From here on, the ball was in the DA's court. Right now, though, that familiar euphoria was tainted by something else, a foreboding about what I needed to get back to.

I looked up at the snowflakes, watched them cascade down onto my face which tingled under their gentle, cold stings, and shut my eyes.

The season, I sensed, really wasn't going to be particularly jolly.

## 2

*Boston, Massachusetts*

Dr. Ralph Padley was a creature of habit, or so he liked to tell himself.

To his wife, colleagues and students, he was a massive control freak with borderline OCD—and, more often than not, just a massive pain in the ass.

This last year, though, his finely orchestrated life had been thrown into chaos by something over which he had no control. That, combined with the absolute dread he felt at knowing that his days were now quite literally numbered, had only made him even less bearable.

The only person other than Padley who knew the origins of his near-pathological need for control was the psychoanalyst he had been seeing once a week for over a decade. When Padley was eleven—fifty-eight years ago almost to the day—he had failed to save his seven-year-old brother from drowning in a swimming pool during a family holiday at his grandparents' place in St. Augustine, Florida. He blamed himself. After all, he was the older brother who was supposed to take care of his younger sibling. His sense of guilt, according to his shrink, made psychological, if not emotional or practical, sense, but Padley couldn't help it. His nascent personality was more significantly affected by the fact that his parents concurred with his sense of guilt and decided he was indeed to blame. The failure of either parent to restart their son's heart—and both were family doctors—had seeded an idea that would later flower when Padley selected his specialism after his initial four years of study at Harvard Medical School.

Before the prognosis, before he'd started losing weight and his skin had taken on a jaundiced tint, Padley had stuck to a rigorous routine. Nowadays, as well as the regular weekly appointment with his shrink and Sunday mornings in church, he went swimming four times a week, attended a concert of classical music once a month and made love to his wife every other Saturday. This last routine suited his significantly younger third wife very well, as it meant she always knew when she'd be free to nip next door and unleash her libido on one of Boston's leading theatre critics, who despite a host of effete mannerisms and other evidence to the contrary—enough to convince Padley that his neighbor had zero interest in his wife—was most definitively not gay.

Padley was a Professor of Medicine (Cardiology) at Harvard, a post he'd held since 1985. As a surgeon, he'd saved many lives. He'd also taught many others who'd gone on to save even more lives. Over the years, he'd taken no small dose of solace in knowing that. He'd always considered it some kind of atonement for the other work he did, the work only a handful of people knew about.

The work that had the exact opposite effect on its subjects.

It had all started when he was in his early thirties, at a time he was deep into some potentially groundbreaking research in the field of cardiovascular pharmacology. His declared aim was to create a next-generation drug that could maintain a stable cardiac rhythm—a "pacemaker in a pill" that would, within a generation, render both pacemakers and beta blockers obsolete as interventions for heart attacks.

The world of medical research being as secretive and competitive as it is, Padley kept his work to himself. Five years and hundreds of lab rats later, however, his experiments took a wrong turn and he ended up creating the very opposite of what he was looking for.

The discovery first confounded then terrified him.

For a while, he struggled with what to do about it. He considered destroying any evidence of his work and forgetting about it. He knew the latter would be impossible and came close to doing the former several times, but he also found that impossible. The potential for his discovery was simply too powerful to ignore. He decided on another tack. Being a staunch patriot at a time when his country was embroiled in hot and cold wars all over the globe, Padley contacted the CIA. They promptly dispatched someone to interview him and turned out to be very, very interested.

The understanding was simple. He would be paid handsomely to continue to work covertly on perfecting his discovery and its delivery methods while carrying on with his official work at the university.

Not long after, the scope of his secret work was broadened.

He'd led a double life ever since. Compartmentalizing his life like that didn't present a problem for someone as maniacally organized as he was. It was actually quite a thrill to feel part of a covert, select group of people who were doing great things for their country. He enjoyed the meetings he was called to attend and, despite not knowing much about a couple of members in that group—not their real names, not a thing, in fact, about their lives—he'd felt a strong sense of kinship with them all and, by extension, with the agency.

Over the years, both lines of work had progressed successfully. Some groundbreaking research into hearts grown from adult stem cells had eventually put him squarely back on the medical map. Padley had found a way to grow cells that were capable of maintaining a stable electrical charge, without which even the most perfect artificially grown heart simply wasn't viable for use in a living human being. He resolutely failed to see the irony that someone with no sense of humor had spent his entire professional career to date working with what had been christened the "funny current", that is, the current that spontaneously occurs in the sinoatrial and atrioventricular nodes of the heart. Or to put it more simply, as he did to his students with a tone as patronizing as it was lacking in self-awareness: the electrical current that provides life to everyone in the lecture theater unless they're wearing a pacemaker.

His discovery appeased the faculty that had sunk over a million dollars into his earlier, "abandoned", pharmacological research. More than appeased, in fact, since they stood to make many times their investment from patents covering Padley's work.

So everyone was happy, except that Padley was still the dour control freak he had always been and his third wife had, much like her predecessors, still failed to achieve a single orgasm with her husband. Given that he'd never been able to bless her with children either, he at least had the decency never to question her burgeoning credit card purchases. Their lack of reproduction, though no longer a point of argument, had left a deep hole in his wife's soul—or so she put it—a hole that she filled with fundraising dinners and the aforementioned trysts with Boston's foremost theatre critic.

Less than a year before, however, everything changed. His whole world was upended by his test results.

He didn't have long to live.

The unwelcome, uninvited guest that was metastatic pancreatic cancer was also a very brutal and unforgiving one.

His emotive responses to it were unorthodox.

A life at the cutting edge of medicine meant denial was never going to be an issue.

The same applied to anger and bargaining—the very notions were beneath him.

Acceptance was already well anchored inside him—so well anchored that he refused to go through the rounds of chemotherapy that might slightly prolong his life. He didn't want to spend the time he had left either in hospitals or sick from the after-effects.

A sense of depression, however, did take root very quickly, and from that depression something else emerged: a fear of what awaited him in the hereafter, and an urgent, rapidly growing need for atonement.

Memories from years of covert operations and replays of hushed conversations were now vividly consuming his days and his nights. The faces of the dead, in photographs or newspapers or on television screens, accosted him at the most unexpected times, clamoring for attention and shouting out for retribution, while the disturbing, subconscious imagery of eternal damnation haunted his dreams.

Much as he tried to shake off this unfamiliar onset of guilt and regret, he couldn't escape it.

He needed to do something about it. He had to seek out some kind of forgiveness. He feared that he was well past redemption, even though he'd always been taught it was always a possibility if the intent was honest and pure. His wasn't necessarily so; it was driven by a very deep-seated, primal fear. But it was all he had.

He thought long and hard about what he could do. He didn't discuss it with anyone; not his wife, not his shrink, not even his priest. He would do this alone. If it wasn't possible to change the past, perhaps he could, at least, affect the future. But doing it would be tricky—and dangerous. And although he didn't have much time left to worry in terms of losing it, he clung, like many people who were suddenly faced with their impending death, to every day he had left.

No, he would need to be careful. And what he did had to be effective too, if he was going to have a chance at the redemption he sought.

His first attempt had proved disastrous. He'd thought he'd chosen well. The man he'd selected had solid credentials. But despite all the meticulous planning, despite knowing what he was up against and being aware of the capabilities of the very people who were now his enemies, Padley had failed. The person he'd reached out to was now dead. That man's death had, Padley was sure, come as a blessing after the torture he had no doubt been subjected to. But Padley's planning had at least been successful at one thing: it had kept *him* safe. No one had come after him. He was still free, he was still breathing. Which meant his precautions had worked.

He just needed to be even more selective in who he approached this time.

Days and weeks of mulling had yielded a handful of possibilities, but one of them stood out more and more with each deliberation. It even had, he thought, an elegant symmetry to it, which pleased his overly ordered mind.

He would make the call today, he decided. He'd be even more vigilant, more careful, than he had been the first time around. He'd use a different prepaid cell phone; one he'd also purchased for cash and that couldn't be traced back to him. He'd still use the agency-level voice changer for the call, the one he'd used on his first attempt. Most importantly, he'd be very, very clear in warning the man about what not to do.

After that, it would be out of his hands.

He'd just need Special Agent Sean Reilly to be as effective at his job as Padley had been at both of his.

# WEDNESDAY

# 3

*Mamaroneck, New York*

A gray-white union of sea, land and sky was barely worrying the drapes when consciousness seeped back into me. I twisted around and checked the time: noon. I know this sounds very decadent, but I'd only got back from Jersey just before six.

Nick and I had handed over to Deutsch and Lendowski shortly after five, a move that generated the usual sardonic, if unmerited, quip from Lendowski. I had plenty of time for Annie Deutsch. She was in her early thirties and usually wore that earnest demeanor shared by many ex-cops during their first couple of years with the Bureau, her face locked in an expression that looked like its wearer has been told they weren't allowed to smile ever again. She was attractive and single, two facts on which most of the discussions regarding her had quickly zeroed in. Lendowski, on the other hand, I could do without. Six foot two and pure muscle, he possessed a personality one would describe as belligerent—if one were being kind. He also had that holier-than-thou attitude that always made me suspicious, like it was a fine line between which side of the law he'd ended up on.

I'd given Nick a lift to Federal Plaza so he could retrieve his own car from the parking garage. Neither of us had much energy left for conversation. The city had looked coldly beautiful as dawn forced its way across Manhattan's skyline. A few Christmas lights shone in pockets of synchronized color, and it was enough to remind anyone who had forgotten that New York was still the greatest city in the world.

These overnights were actually a killer. As Nick climbed out of the Expedition, he reminded me to try and stay awake on the final leg. A couple of nights back, I'd very nearly fallen asleep at the wheel and had needed to pull over and grab an hour's shut-eye before driving home. Then I'd woken with a jolt at two in the afternoon, convinced that my alarm had sounded only moments before. Throw the body clock out of whack and the mind can do strange things. I was now looking forward to doing away with the Nosferatu schedule and getting back to a more normal, mortal routine.

Tess had driven my five-year-old son, Alex, to school and left me to finish off my fitful six hours. Miss Chaykin—we're not married—is my partner in everything but law enforcement, although that last bit was debatable, given our various adventures these last few years. I've never slept easy alone, and the past few weeks of night shifts and disrupted schedules had only served to underline how addicted I was to having Tess's warm body beside me.

We joked that, as a couple, this could be the closest we'd ever get to the sleepless nights and constant demands of caring for a baby, given that we hadn't had one together and were still debating whether having one now would be a good move. I was in two minds about that. It wasn't something I'd ever experienced. I'd missed the first decade or so of Tess's daughter, Kim, who was now fifteen, given that Tess and I only met a few years ago.

I'd also missed out on most of my own son's young life, given that his mom—someone I had a brief, but intense, fling with a few years ago—had neglected to tell me I was his dad until she and I had reconnected last summer. Not exactly your classic Hallmark family, but these days, I guess, few families are.

Kim was a great girl, more a fine testimony to Tess's single-parenting skills than to anything I had contributed since we'd all started living together. She and I got along really well. Much like her mom, she was impossibly headstrong and as sharp as The Bride's samurai blade, by turns delighting us with her growing independence and infuriating us with her dismissal of entirely reasonable boundaries. After the mortal risks I'd seen her mother take, survive, then thrive upon, I really shouldn't have been at all surprised. I even liked her boyfriend, Giorgio, a year older than her and a junior who already had Yale in his sights, despite their current sub-seven-percent admission rate. I'd once pictured myself pulling the *Bad Boys* routine on my daughter's boyfriend's ass, shotgun, wife-beater, and bottle of whiskey included, but the darned kid, clever and yet cool and sporty, had cruelly deprived me of any such pleasure.

Alex, on the other hand, still hadn't shaken off his demons.

But at least he and Kim had bonded pretty much instantly. To her credit, she had happily embraced the big sister role that had been thrust upon her, and seeing them together was a source of solace in the bittersweet world I seemed doomed to inhabit.

I threw on a T-shirt and some sweatpants and lumbered down to the kitchen. Despite still feeling groggy, it didn't take long for the Daland/Maxiplenty case to recede into inconsequence, shoved aside by the resurgent white whales that were crowding my mind. I guess I shouldn't be surprised. My globetrotting adventures with Tess had served to reinforce the notion that we're never done with the past. Or rather, the past is never done with us. It's just a matter of the correct key being turned in the right lock and all the secrets come tumbling out. And we can never know how we're going to deal with them until they're staring us in the face.

Shuffling into the kitchen, I could hear Tess in her home office, tapping away at her desk with the usual deft precision. It still took me twice as long as it should to file a simple report. I poured myself some coffee, glanced at the front page of the *New York Times* on Tess's charging iPad, then wandered, mug in hand, into the study, where my very own bestselling novelist/paramour was busy knocking out yet another page-turner.

She sat behind a very cool, huge aluminum desk that had been crafted from the tip of an old aircraft's wing; a gift from yours truly after her first novel hit the *New York Times* bestsellers list. Her eyes lingered on her screen as I sat down in an armchair facing her, coffee cradled in both hands. My attention was drawn to the rear of the house. The deck and small garden were, I now noticed, dotted with strands of miniature red and green lights. I gazed through the French doors, transfixed for a moment, then Tess looked up and smiled that radiant smile that always makes me give a conflicted and perverse thanks for the violent night when we first met.

She swung her long legs out from behind the desk. "Christmas lights and two thousand words already. Not a bad morning's work, huh?"

I smiled. "You're such a slacker. No lunch break for you."

She tilted her head and pursed her lips. "Actually, I figured we'd skip lunch and just head upstairs and you could help me choose which dress to wear Thursday night. Unless you have other plans?"

I was about to voice an objection—I mean, sure, we were going to be having dinner with the president. *The* president. At the White House. The dress choice was, I guess, important—and then, the look on her face as she'd said it hit a certain sweet spot inside my skull and I realized that this was code for something else entirely.

*Jeez, I love this woman.*

I titled my head, mock-studying her. "I did, but I know how much the holiday season means to you and the last thing I'd want is to disappoint you."

She flashed me a grin. "Hang on to that thought, cowboy."

I did have plans. I'd arranged to meet Kurt Jaegers in Jersey. Kurt was a white-hat hacker, a tech wizard who was helping me out privately, totally off the books. He'd asked for a meet, which could mean he had news for me, good news. I wasn't holding my breath, but I also had some new ideas on how he could help me with the white whales I was hunting.

Right now, all that could wait.

I needed to live a little first.

So, the white whales.

Not one, but two things eating away at me, chewing me up from the inside. Come to think of it, I'm not sure whale is the best metaphor here. Something like the alien from, well, *Alien*, the one that burst out of John Hurt's chest in the first movie, is probably a better fit.

For starters, I was still trying to track down the elusive "Reed Corrigan." Corrigan—real name, unknown—is the ex-CIA spook who had orchestrated the brainwashing of my son, Alex, earlier this year. A son I never knew I had, up until then. His mom, Michelle, was an ex-DEA agent I'd dated while on assignment in Mexico, before I met Tess. Michelle and Alex had got caught up in a sick plan to flush out a psycho Mexican drug baron nicknamed "El Brujo"—the sorcerer. The plan involved brainwashing Alex and using him as bait. Corrigan had worked on the CIA's mind control programs and had arranged to have some pretty disturbing things dumped into Alex's brain. The plan had gone seriously wrong and I'd got sucked into it. It had ended up causing Michelle's death and left me and Tess to pick up the pieces with Alex while Corrigan, whoever he was, was still out there somewhere.

I wasn't going to stop until I found the bastard.

Alex was now doing better, thanks to a shrink we'd been taking him to see every week. His nightmares had subsided, but they were still there, off and on. Moreover, the nasty things they'd planted in his mind about me were, I felt—maybe more out of hope than out of anything concrete—starting to subside. I didn't get the feeling that he was looking at me as apprehensively and fearfully as he often used to. We were tiptoeing our way into doing some normal father-and-son stuff, like me taking him to Teeball practice on Saturday mornings, but we still had a long ways to go.

To find Corrigan, I'd recruited Kurt to help me get into the CIA's files. When that didn't work, I'd resorted to blackmailing a CIA analyst Kurt had identified for me, a sleaze called Stan Kirby who'd been having an affair with his wife's sister. That exercise had mixed results. On the one hand, and totally unexpectedly, it turned out to be key in saving the president's life—hence our forthcoming dinner at the White House with the Yorkes themselves in a couple of days' time. On the other hand, it hadn't been much use in helping me get my hands on Reed Corrigan.

Kirby had dug up three case files that mentioned Corrigan, but they were all highly redacted and weren't much use.

One of them, though, kicked up the second whale, or alien, or whatever metaphor you feel works best here. That file, which concerned an operation called "Cold Burn" that Corrigan and Fullerton had been part of, also mentioned something called "Project Azorian." Not particularly ominous in itself, except that it then mentioned someone with the initials CR.

I knew the name Azorian. As a ten-year-old, I'd seen it on a printout on my dad's desk. It had sounded funny and caught my eye. When I'd asked him about it, he'd brushed it off as nothing important, and we'd joked about it being a good name for a comic book or sci-fi movie, à la *The Mighty Azorian*.

That wasn't long before I'd found my dad slumped behind his desk shortly after he'd blown his brains out.

My dad—Colin Reilly.

CR.

Seeing his initials alongside a mention of Azorian in the same file that concerned Reed Corrigan had jolted me like few things I can remember. First, my son, and now, my dad too? I was now even more determined to find this Corrigan, not just out of a burning desire to make him pay for what he did to Alex, but to find out the truth about my dad's suicide, if that's what it really was. I didn't know what to believe any more, and I had a strong feeling there was more to it. I mean, given what this creep and his crew were capable of, and given their abilities when it came to manipulating people, I was imagining all kinds of dark scenarios surrounding my dad's death.

It was all the more painful as I never really got a chance to know him. He was a tenure-track assistant professor at George Washington University, an expert in comparative law and jurisprudence, and he was consumed by his work. He wasn't the most gregarious or emotive person I had ever met, and he always seemed to have weightier things on his mind than hanging out with me. I don't think he was ever able to fully park the issues that fired him up or kick back and enjoy the simple pleasures of a family life. When he was home, he spent a lot of time in that study of his, which was off limits to this ten-year-old, not an unreasonable rule given the books and paperwork that were stacked all around it and my propensity to sow havoc. I do know he was well respected, though. A lot of people turned up to his funeral, men and women who, to me at the time, seemed like a very dour bunch of people, even given the circumstances.

My mom didn't talk about it much. Growing up, the subject of his suicide was off limits. Not that I asked much. At the time, all she'd told me was that, after his death, she'd discovered that he'd been depressed and was on medication. It was the most I'd ever got out of her on the subject. I don't think she ever really dealt with the grief or the sadness that he'd never told her about it. She just bottled it up, same as he had, I guess. Then, when I moved out and went to study law at Notre Dame, she remarried, moved to Cape Cod, and threw herself into her new life. We never talked about my dad after that. It was like her first husband had never existed.

I learned later that it's perfectly normal for a ten-year-old boy to repress the memory of his father's blood splattered against a wall—indeed, the first time in decades I had recalled the memory so vividly was when reading the redacted file from my reluctant CIA source about the man who had brainwashed my son. Mothers, however, are generally expected to ensure that the memory doesn't become buried too deep. On balance, maybe we both came out of it OK.

Thinking about my absent father also reminded me of how I wanted to always be there for Alex. My line of work, however, wasn't the most risk-free of occupations. It was something I needed to figure out.

One thing I didn't need to figure out, one thing I knew with absolute certainty, was that I would never forgive the man who subjected a four-year-old boy to treatment that was still beyond belief, even though I'd seen the results with my own eyes. Whatever it took, I was going to find him. Nothing would ever change when it came to Reed Corrigan and me.

Problem was, he was proving impossible to track down. The CIA was clearly protecting his identity, for reasons they weren't about to share with me. He was obviously a valuable asset, and I'd run out of options in terms of flushing him out.

Project Azorian also turned out to be a blind alley, both regarding Corrigan and my dad. Also named "Project Jennifer," it was the CIA's code name for an eight hundred million dollar operation to raise a sunken Russian submarine from the Pacific Ocean floor back in 1974. Howard Hughes had lent his name to the project to help with the cover story that the vessel that would raise the sub, the Hughes Glomar Explorer, was out mining manganese deposits. It had been one of the most expensive and technologically complex operations in CIA history—and one of their biggest successes—but the huge dossier about it was, in terms of what I was after, a dead end. I couldn't for the life of me figure out what the sub project had to do with my dad, or what it or my dad had to do with the CIA op called Operation Cold Burn.

The link with my dad, though, could open up some fresh possibilities. I'd asked Kurt to take another peek inside the CIA's servers to see if they had anything else on my dad. So far, he hadn't had much luck on that front either.

All of which left me with two final angles of attack.

One was for me to bully Kirby, the CIA analyst/Lothario, once again. Get him to fish for files about my dad, this time, see if following that trail instead would lead me to Corrigan.

The other was to talk to my mother and see if she knew more about my dad's death than she'd let on.

I really wasn't looking forward to either of them.

# 4

*Newark, New Jersey*

I walked across to the north side of Riverbank Park and waited, glad to be out in the open air and, for that matter, anywhere other than the inside of a Ford Expedition. Out here, most of the snow had already melted, though more was apparently due later tonight.

I'd crossed paths with Kurt Jaegers for the first time a few years ago when he moved up to the seventh spot on the FBI's cyber-crime watch list after hacking into the UN's server farm, using the same skill set I needed to track down Corrigan. He agreed to help me and hacked into the CIA's databanks after I promised him a get-out-of-jail-free card should he ever get arrested for something reasonably defensible. Kurt soon embraced the project with gusto, which surprised me. I was supposed to be one of the bad guys, as far as he was concerned—you know, big brother and all that. But Kurt and I connected. He had a good heart. I liked him, and I enjoyed hearing about the fantasy idealist world he inhabited.

For our meetings, Kurt always insisted on different locations and times to ensure that I hadn't been followed, even though I was pretty sure I was perfectly capable of doing this myself. His levels of paranoia weren't too outrageous, though, considering the people we were up against, although time was tight, me being due to meet Nick at Federal Plaza at four for the Daland post-arrest briefing.

I took a few steps toward the river and casually scanned through three-sixty. I was clean.

Kurt told me that he'd read a stack of books on fieldcraft and practiced covert techniques within MMORPGs—the "massive" in Massively Multiplayer Online Role-Playing Game, he'd assured me jokingly, was not a reference to his waist size. People overuse words a lot nowadays—everything is amazing, everyone's a genius—although in his case, massive was an understatement. But as he emerged from the tree line to the south, it was still bizarre to see the new, thinner Kurt. He'd lost a ton of weight—OK, maybe not an actual ton. I thought I could take some credit for him dropping so much flab. Our regular meetings not only got him out of the house, but also appeared to have given him a sense of purpose where previously, he had none.

Over the months he'd been helping me out, I'd gotten to know Kurt well. He'd opened up to me—probably more than he'd done with most people, I thought, given what he'd told me about his life. He hadn't had it easy, not that I'd imagined otherwise.

Throughout his school years, Kurt had been the butt of exceptionally cruel jokes—both verbal and practical—by a clique of particularly vicious girls. This systematic campaign had stemmed from his temerity in asking one of them to a dance at their fifth grade end-of-year party, a crime seemingly so heinous that he deserved to be punished for it till the end of his schooling.

By middle school, this clique had shared their hatred of Kurt with their meat-head boyfriends and his final two years of education had been off-the-charts intolerable. If it hadn't been for his Sony PlayStation, his dial-up modem and the trailblazing Internet chat rooms he'd joined as soon as they launched, he would have put an end to his miserable existence long before he'd had a chance to think through the long-term consequences of such a decision.

As with many other social outcasts, the Internet and the rapidly growing gamer culture it fed off ended up giving Kurt a reason to live. And like most hardcore gamers, he was a neophile at heart and wanted to see what would come next. He instinctively knew that games would become better, faster and more immersive and he wanted to be around as they did so. By the time he was twenty, he was as addicted to console games and the online world as he was to food, his treatment at the hands of the witches of East Brunswick having served to confirm his withdrawal from the world of women made of flesh and his dedication to those made of pixels.

If I didn't need Kurt myself, I'd probably have recommended him to our Cyber Division by now, but he and I had developed a routine and neither of us seemed to want to mess with it. Over the last few months, we'd worked together enough for me to mostly can my sarcastic instincts and accumulate no little respect for Kurt's doggedness. I also knew enough about the way things were going with surveillance and data-trawling capabilities, drones, high-powered mikes and micro-cameras to understand that one day, real-world agents would be almost entirely redundant. I just hoped that day didn't come until I had taken my pension.

Kurt was grinning from ear to ear as he ambled toward me, his gait still that of someone carrying the hundred extra pounds he'd recently shed. Maybe it was because of the holiday season. Christmas turned guys like Kurt back into Fifth Graders—happy ones at that. If it wasn't for keeping our meetings on the down-low, I fully suspect he would have been wearing a green knitted sweater that featured a reindeer.

Glancing from side to side, he covered the final few yards to where I was standing and gave me a small bow.

"*Kon'nichiwa, watashi no kunshu.*"

This was another of his tradecraft obsessions: routing our phone calls through Japan-based Skype accounts that he'd hijacked and never referring to himself or to me by our real names on any calls or texts. Which made no sense at all, given that we weren't even remotely Japanese. "Kurt, seriously. We're actually here, together."

"No names, dude," he said, flinching. "Come on. What if someone's tailing you and listening in on us?"

"I think I've got that covered," I said, then added, pointedly, "Kurt." With a juvenile half-grin.

He just brought it out in me.

He groaned, then gestured around him. "What do you think? Cool spot for a meet, no?"

"Pure genius." See what I mean? We all do it.

On the other hand, I did resist saying "Kurt" one more time.

Instead, I said, "You sure you haven't spent time at Quantico?" No way could I kill the sarcasm entirely. Especially when Kurt had me on a continuing tour of the myriad attractions of Essex County.

"Quantico, shwantico," he scoffed. "I'd like to see how long you and your guys would survive in the siege of Orgrimmar."

I ducked asking what that was—the cultural reference gap between us was beyond unbridgeable—and studied his face, then I scanned him up and down more carefully. Something else had changed, something other than the dropped weight: a general overhaul on the grooming front. Then it hit me. The Amazing Shrinking Kurt was chasing a female. As impossible as that sounded, I was somehow sure he was definitely on the prowl, and his upbeat manner made it clear he thought he was getting somewhere.

Not ideal, from a purely selfish point of view. Last thing I needed was for Kurt's mind to be diverted from the hunt.

I spread my hands quizzically. "Who is she?"

Eyes wide, Kurt pulled back his head for a second. "What? No!"

"Come on."

"How'd you—?" Then his grin returned and he wagged a puffy finger at me. "Oh, you're good. You're like so totally in the zone."

I tilted my head, my expression egging him for an answer. "Spill."

"You're gonna love her. She's great. And she's solid, a real asset for the team. She's going in deeper than I ever could."

I felt a stab of bile in the back of my throat. "'Going in?' What are you talking about? You told her? About us?"

Kurt backed away a couple of steps. "Relax, dude. Hear me out. She doesn't know who you are, doesn't know why we're looking for Corrigan. But she's got skills, man. *Real* skills."

I took a deep breath and calmed myself down. Kurt was no fool. He also wasn't having much success in penetrating the CIA's servers beyond what we already knew. Maybe he did need help. I was well aware that hacking government agencies had become considerably more difficult since the exploits of Chelsea Manning and Edward Snowden. But this was a dangerous game to invite someone to play.

I gestured to an empty bench. We both sat, Kurt edging away till there was a couple of feet between us.

"OK, so . . . who is she?"

Nervously, he crossed and uncrossed his legs. "She's called Gigi. Gigi Decker. Here . . ."

He took out his smartphone, swiped his finger across its screen to unlock it, and handed it to me. Its screen showed a full-figured and surprisingly attractive redhead who was—presumably, knowing Kurt's interests as I did—dressed in the garb of some kind of World of Warcraft character.

Gigi was clearly screensaver-serious.

He reclaimed the phone. "Lady Jaina Proudmoore. Archmage of

Kirin Tor. That's her real hair, by the way." He added this last part with genuine pride.

"I can see what you mean by solid. She seems totally . . . reliable." I can't really raise one eyebrow, but if I could, it would have been up.

Kurt looked offended. "Hey, when she's not in Pandaria, she's one hell of a hacker. I mean, truly outstanding. She's hacked the CIA's D-bases deeper than anyone I know. And the cool part is she's ideologically neutral. She hacks because she can."

"And to impress you, of course."

He beamed. "What can I tell you? I'm a catch."

I rolled my eyes, but my mouth smiled. He really was a lovable son of a bitch. I hoped Gigi wasn't about to break his heart, and not just because that would screw us both.

"OK, so she's amazing." Clearly, I need to retract my grumpy earlier criticism about contemporary word use. "So what did she find?"

He grimaced. "Well, it's good and it's bad."

My entire body tensed in anticipation. Maybe our search was finally going to move out of park. "What do you mean?"

He closed the space between us. "She went in and snooped around the user records and protocol logs related to the terms I'd been using in my searches around both Corrigan and your dad and came up with nothing. Then she went in again and went deeper. Still nothing. Then a couple of days later, we tried again, only this time, the logs and the user records themselves were gone. Everything that had data links to our target folders. Gone. I mean, up until now, they've been changing the access codes as per standard operation procedure at Langley. But in the last week, they've modified the protocols and wiped dozens of files."

He gave me that knowing look, the one loaded with portent.

I already knew the answer, but I asked anyway, "So they know we've been looking?"

He nodded, his eyes even wider with conspiracy.

"I'm having a hard time seeing anything 'good' here, Kurt."

"Well, yeah, agreed, that part's not great. But there's more. Gigi, she doesn't give up easy. And this was like a challenge for her, like they'd thrown down the gauntlet. So she goes into overdrive and starts trying all kinds of things, including this little trick of hers. She tries misspelling Corrigan in her trawl. She thinks laterally like that, you know?" He paused and nodded, more just to himself, grinning with admiration, savoring the thought. "And she got a hit. One with an 'm' at the end, as in, Corriga*m*."

"You're kidding."

"I'm telling you. She says it was more common than you'd think before spellchecking technology closed that crack."

He went quiet again. Kurt had this irritating habit of pausing to build portent. Maybe he'd watched too many badly written TV shows and it had affected the cadence at which he spoke.

"And . . . ?"

"She found a reference to Reed Corrigam—with an 'm'—in a deep archive. It was in a report from the *Direccíon de Inteligencia*—the DI, Cuba's intelligence agency."

I knew what the DI was, but I didn't want to burst his bubble. We at the Bureau had been known to butt heads with their operatives in Miami. Instead, I just said, "Makes sense. They would have been operational in El Salvador back then."

Kurt nodded, then looked around suspiciously, gave our surroundings a second pan-and-scan, then pulled some folded papers out from his pocket and handed them to me. "It's all in here. It talks about a meeting a DI guy had with Corrigan. It says there was a leak from the DI, and the DI agent is only referred to by his initials, but it mentions the name 'Octavio Camacho' as well and I googled that. The hit that seemed most promising was this guy," he said as he flicked through the printouts before pulling out a particular page. "He was a Portuguese journalist."

"'Was?'"

"Yep. Camacho died in 1981."

I flicked back to the report about the meeting. It had also taken place that year—a couple of months before Camacho's death.

I could feel my shoulders drop. "That's it?"

Kurt's face followed suit. "So far. But she's still at it. She's trying to hack some digitized archive backups. The encryption-compression algorithms aren't as secure as those for live data. At least not for Gigi when she's in the zone." He brightened at her name. The guy was totally lovestruck. "But maybe you'll come up with more on the Camacho front. Maybe you could check with Portuguese Intelligence, see if they've got something on Corrigan."

"Or Corrigam."

He smiled. "Exactly."

I wasn't thrilled. It wasn't much—not much at all. Just another dark alley with an insurmountable brick wall at its end.

Kurt read my face. "Dude, we'll find something. She will, anyway. I know it."

I shrugged. "All right. Do me a favor. Check on something else for me."

"Shoot."

"You remember our little Casanova down in DC?"

Kurt gave me a curious look. "Our man Stan?"

"Exactly. See if you can find out what his calendar looks like for Thursday."

He scratched the top of his ear with his thumb. "This Thursday? The day after tomorrow?"

"Yep."

"Thursday was Stan's booty night."

I said, "I'm wondering if it still is."

He nodded slowly to himself, the ear-scratching slowing down too. "No problemo. Easily done."

"Great. Thanks." I tapped the printouts as I stood up. "I'll let you know what I find."

"Cool," he said as he got off the bench too. "I'll say hi to Gigi from you."

I gave him a chastening scowl.

He said, "Dude, lighten up. It's Christmas."

I took a couple of steps, then turned back toward him.

"Treat her right, Kurt. She seems like a keeper. But don't let her push it too far. I don't want either of you ending up in an orange jumpsuit or as permanent houseguests of the Ecuadorian embassy. Not so soon after you've found each other."

Kurt beamed and patted his heart. "Thanks, man. Truly. I'm just . . . thanks."

"Don't push it, Jaegers. My Christmas spirit only extends so far." I turned and walked away. I couldn't resist a smile as I headed back toward the Expedition, but I felt deflated. The Kurt route—now the

Kurt and Gigi route—was going nowhere. Once he got me the info I needed about Kirby, I thought I might have to set him loose. I'd miss him—but this was getting us nowhere, and it was putting him and his archmage, whatever that was, at risk.

I was getting into the Expedition when my work BlackBerry rang.

I checked the screen. There was no number appearing on it. It was a private caller.

"Agent Reilly?"

I froze. The voice was cavernous and artificially monotone. Whoever it was was using some kind of electronic voice changer.

Never a good sign.

# 5

In these situations, my mind immediately goes to Tess, Kim and Alex.

I don't know why. I don't usually deal with psychos or serial killers. The cases I normally work on rarely have the kind of personal angle that can spiral into a vendetta against my loved ones or me. But right there and then, I thought of them. And it sent a spasm of worry through me.

I just said, "I'm listening."

"Are you interested in justice?"

"Look, I'm sorry, but it's really hard to take that question seriously when it's coming from a Darth Vader voice box."

The man paused, then said, "I know things, Agent Reilly. Things you need to hear. Things I need you to do something about. Things people are prepared to kill for in order to keep quiet. The question is, are you up to it? Are you ready to put your life on the line to get the truth out?"

I didn't know what to make of this. We get these whackos more frequently than you'd think, but they usually call the Bureau's switchboard. Special Agents' cell phone numbers aren't easy to get hold of.

I said, "I don't know what you've heard, but that's kind of the job description where I work. Who are you? How'd you get my number?"

"What I know, what I want to tell you about, goes way back. It involves a lot of people."

"OK, I'm going to hang up now, because we've hit our quota of big reveals this month as far as the Kennedy assassination goes, and—"

He interrupted me. "One of them was your father. Colin Reilly."

That got my attention.

I paused and caught my breath. "What do you know about my father?"

"The truth. Look, I'm prepared to give you everything. All the information you need, proof to back it up. I've kept a record of everything and I'll give it to you. But I need to know you'll make sure it gets out."

I tried to stay calm. I was fully aware that I was probably being played, but whoever it was was pressing some pretty hot buttons inside me. "You didn't answer my question."

"You know I won't. Not now, not like this. I'll tell you everything, but we need to meet."

"I need to know a bit more before I agree to something like that."

"No, you don't."

"Sorry. This conversation is over." I went silent, feigning I was about to hang up—but he called my bluff and stayed on the line without calling out in panic.

After a moment, I heard him cough—a weird, jarring sound, when it comes out through a voice box—then he said, "Let's not play games and let's not waste each other's time. I can't stay on this call much longer. All you need to know is, this is on the level. It's on the level and I need you. I need you to hear the truth—about your dad, about the others, about Azorian . . . just meet me."

Azorian. He knew about that too.

It could be a trap, of course. It could be Corrigan preparing my painful demise. But then again, if he'd wanted to kill me, he could have done it already. I wasn't exactly living la vida Salman Rushdie.

"Where and when?"

"Tomorrow. One o'clock. Times Square. By the Duffy statue. You know where it is, right?"

"Of course."

"Come alone. I won't show if I think you've got anyone else there. And, Reilly? Keep it quiet. I'm saying this for your own good."

"Oh?"

"The last person I reached out to—the only person I tried to tell about it—he's dead. And I'm sure it wasn't pleasant, not that death ever is, but—burning to death in his own home because of some electrical fire? A few days after I called him? Give me a break. And it's not like . . . I mean, I told him not to look into it, but some of these guys, it's just in their blood. They can't help themselves."

“Then why not cut the whole charade and come in to Federal Plaza? We can protect you.”

His voice stayed calm. “No. You can’t.”

“You’d be in federal custody. My custody.”

“No. The people I’m going to tell you about—they’re very powerful. And they’re on the inside. That’s why I need you to hear it all first. Alone. So you can think about what you’re going to do about it before they can shut you down.”

Something about his tone sounded convincing. Even with the voice box, the fear was palpably there.

“OK,” I said. “I’ll be there.”

“Good.” Then the line went dead.

## 6

*Ocracoke, North Carolina*

"We have a problem."

Gordon Roos frowned as he settled into an armchair on the wide deck and looked out over the sleepy, small harbor. Steam rose from the mug of coffee he held in his other hand, vaporizing in the crisp evening air.

He took a sip, then said, "We always have problems. So what else is new?"

"It's Padley."

The Outer Banks hardly ever saw snow. A couple of winters back, they'd had several inches, which was all the more notable for its idiosyncrasy. Roos didn't mind it. He liked the added privacy it offered. Since his move to Ocracoke, he was even more remote than in his previous house further up the coast, and it was exactly how he liked it—as long as he could hop in and out efficiently, and fast. His car rarely left the island. He kept a Cessna Skyhawk single-engine prop plane at the small airport, which was little more than a runway with a small, unattended cottage for a terminal. He also kept a sixty-foot sport fisher in the harbor, but that was purely for pleasure.

He loved the winters here. The late fall tourists were long gone, leaving the island to its few hundred year-round inhabitants. His house was part of a small cluster of buildings on the south-east side of Silver Lake harbor, all of which were occupied by locals. On one side was an artist. On the other, a folk musician, of a style that Roos found rather pleasing—which was fortunate, given the man's proclivity for late-night sessions. The neighbors mostly kept to themselves, though they always shared a drink at Christmas, a tradition that Roos found he enjoyed much more since his wife had left him. They'd never had kids, and his parents were long-since dead, so he had zero obligations at this time of year.

He had been looking forward to a quiet holiday season—reading, taking the sport fisher out into the Gulf Stream for some bluefish tuna, and bringing in the occasional paid companion for an overnight or two of carnal bliss. Then the call had come in on his encrypted satphone. Only one person had the phone's number. Edward Tomblin had been Roos's decades-long colleague at the CIA, though unlike Roos, Tomblin was still at the agency. Tomblin was also Roos's closest—and perhaps his only, in the true sense of the term, at least within the limitations of their line of work—friend. And Roos knew his friend well enough to read the gravity in his tone.

He asked, "Say again?"

"The leak? With the reporter? It was Padley. He's going off the reservation—or, more like, he's lost his fucking mind."

Roos took a moment to process it as he sipped his coffee. He felt the pleasing sting of the hot liquid as it hit the back of his throat and jacked his sharp mind into even more focus.

"How do we know this?"

"He made a second call. We only caught it because it was to someone on an active watch list."

"Who?"

"Oh, you're going to love this. Reilly. Sean Reilly."

The sting turned venomous.

"What did he tell him?"

"Not much. Just that he has stuff for him. Information. Records—of everything. Stuff he wants Reilly to go public with. Stuff that includes his dad. The doc's playing it smart, though. He's using a prepaid and a voice changer. He also avoided using any keywords we would have picked up. We only fingered him after we ran the recording through our red list and got a match. I guess he doesn't know we have decryption software for any voice box he can get hold of in this country."

"Or anywhere else, for that matter."

"I was being modest."

So they'd gotten lucky. They would have missed the call if they hadn't been monitoring Reilly.

Reilly. God damn Reilly, again.

Roos put that particular sting aside. "Padley, of all people? Why? And why now?"

"He's dying."

"What?"

"We ran a full sweep on the prick after we ID'd him. Turns out he's got pancreatic cancer. Aggressive and metastasized. He's terminal. Doesn't have long."

"Jesus."

"That's clearly on his mind, too."

Roos let out a long breath, then took another sip. He'd been in the game long enough that he already knew what they'd need to do. The thought still displeased him.

He liked the doc. Sure, the man had some irritating idiosyncrasies. Today, people would even consider him borderline Asperger's. But they were all control freaks in their own way. The nature of the business demanded it. Lives were often at stake—especially their own. You learned early on that the only person you could definitely rely on was yourself.

But this—this was a shock. Padley had come to them. He'd never wavered in his commitment, never questioned the tasks he'd been assigned, even when he wasn't given all the information, information that may have made him question things. To turn like this, to sell you out, for—what?

"So this is about redemption?" Roos asked. "The good doc wants to repent so he can get on the guest list at the pearly gates?"

"That's what it looks like."

Roos nodded to himself as he took in a lone sailing yacht that was motoring into the harbor. "OK," he said. "I don't see how we have a choice here. I'll get the Sandman to take care of it."

"No point bringing the doc in for a chat and showing him the error of his ways, is there?"

"What's the point of that? He's dying anyway. I almost feel bad that we're saving that backstabbing little shit from all the crap that's waiting for him. I watched my dad go through it . . . Hell, if you ever see me about to go through something like that, do me a favor and stick the Sandman on me."

Tomblin chortled. "It would be my pleasure."

It was Roos's turn to chuckle. "Asshole."

"What about Reilly?"

"What about Reilly, indeed."

Roos had wanted to deal with Reilly a few months ago, after

they found out he was gunning for "Reed Corrigan"—Roos's code name on some of the projects he worked on with Tomblin, back when Roos was still an active agent. Tomblin had counseled him to wait. Reilly turned into even more of a pest when he got involved in the Sokolov affair and prevented Roos from getting his hands on the fugitive Russian scientist who'd managed to give both the KGB and the CIA the slip, the incredible—and outrageously dangerous—technology he'd invented, and the monster payday that would have ensued. Then the son of a bitch went and saved the president's life and Roos had to back off, big time.

He wouldn't back off now.

"I think he's item two on the Sandman's to-do list."

Tomblin seemed to demur the length of a breath, then said, "Agreed."

"Especially now. Reilly can't be allowed to interfere this time. But we just need to be careful with him. He's a slippery bastard."

"Reilly's girl—she's a handful too."

"The novelist?"

"Yes. We need to make sure she doesn't have a bone to chew on after it's done."

"Sandman hasn't let us down yet."

"True," Tomblin said. "But like you said—she's like him. Resourceful."

"From the daily logs, he doesn't seem to be sharing everything with her, correct?"

"Yes. The bastard's keeping us in the dark too, but at the same time, it just might end up being what keeps her alive."

"If she decides to turn into a pain, we'll just have to deal with her then," Roos told him. "In the meantime, keep me posted. And better get our lapdog up to speed too. Maybe he'll finally start earning that retainer we're paying him."

"Agreed."

Roos clicked off and looked out. The yacht was reversing into its slot. He kept his gaze on it, judging the skipper's maneuvering.

For any mere mortal, the news was more than unsettling, but Roos had seen a lot worse. He wasn't about to change any of his plans. He would finish his coffee, take another look at the weather forecast, then go for a walk along the dunes, like he did most every evening. He was even considering getting a dog. He'd had one when he was a boy, but his father had shot it just before they'd moved to the city.

If he did buy a dog, the only person who was going to shoot it was him. And then only to spare it the years that Roos had no intention of suffering through himself. He figured he had fifteen good years left—twenty if he were lucky—quite enough for the useful lifespan of a purebred.

He smiled at the years of uninterrupted leisure stretching out in front of him. He firmly believed he'd earned them many times over. And nothing—nothing, especially not Sean Reilly—was going to interfere with that.

# 7

*Lower Manhattan, New York City*

We were all at the Beekman, one of our favorite haunts, a family-run Irish pub that purportedly served the best pint of Guinness in the entire city. Not that I would know. I was enjoying my second ice-heavy Coke, the decision not to drink having already earned me an hour of slating from the more old-school agents.

Our boss, Ron Gallo, hadn't even bothered to show. No surprise there: the Assistant Director in Charge of the New York Field Office was the kind of leader who thought getting down and dirty with the troops would lower him in their estimation. As if that were possible. He and I had little time for each other anyway. I don't know if it was due to his particularly poor management skills, although he ticked all the boxes: anger fits, hogging credit, going back on his word. He just exuded that smarmy, insincere, politically astute career focus that made me picture a weasel every time I saw his elongated, narrow-eyed face.

I was still weary from all the overnight stints in New Jersey, for sure—that, and that damn phone call. It was still weighing heavily on my mind when I felt a hand on my shoulder and turned to find myself facing Special Agent Annie Deutsch. I knew only rudimentary facts about her due to her being the most recent addition to the office. Right now, she was smiling, the cocktail in her left hand and the general camaraderie around us having obviously served to loosen her attitude. I feared for her around Nick. Although she was a petite brunette and thus didn't conform to his usual bombastic type, he'd commented on her attractiveness a few times already.

"Agent Reilly?"

"Agent Deutsch."

I detected the stirrings of a smile. "It's Annie."

"Sean."

Her eyes sparkled with that same elusive combination of intelligence, wit and lightly worn acceptance of a sure-fire ability to attract attention that I found so appealing in Tess.

She leaned in and whispered, close to my ear. "I need to get away from Lendowski. He seems to think I want his tongue in my ear."

I looked around. I could see Lendowski laughing loudly a few feet away from us, his leer locked on Deutsch. "Why me?"

I was only half joking.

Lendowski's often-embarrassing exploits with the ladies were widely known within the Bureau, mainly because he insisted on sharing them with anyone who would listen. He made Nick look like a monk. Lendowski had narrowly avoided at least three sexual harassment charges, and he always seemed to emerge looking like the victim, which was no mean feat for a guy who wouldn't look out of place on the WWE Network. He also loved to gamble, maybe even more than he loved annoying women.

The question seemed to throw her a bit. She hesitated, then said, "Because you're standing here." She paused again before adding, "And because of how she describes you."

"Huh?" I had no idea what she was talking about.

"You're Jim, right? Mia's knight errant?"

I shook my head and chortled. "Oh, Jesus." It was going to happen eventually, but the longer time passed without it happening, the more I had started to believe that it wouldn't.

Once she had heard that Tess was a bestselling novelist, it wasn't much of a leap for her to deduce that the male hero of her first two books was modeled in some way on Tess's very own man of action. The hazing about this was merciless with each new book, especially since Jim Corben had a goatee and lived on a cattle ranch when he wasn't traveling the globe on archaeological adventures at the behest of a mysterious secret society.

"Well, for starters, I'm no cowboy."

She tilted her head to one side. "And I ain't no buckle bunny either." Her faux-Texan accent was pitch-perfect, then Lendowski planted a hand on her arm.

"Mind if I cut in?" he said. "Annie and me were just talking, but she somehow got waylaid when I went to the bar." He flashed us a big, overly toothy grin. How many teeth did this guy have? "Get it? Way-laid?"

She gently removed his paw as he laughed at his ingenious

crack. "Len, how about you just lay off instead?"

He threw me a half-drunk wink. "They just love playing these games, don't they? It's all about the tease with these chicks. You should have seen how her eyes lit up when I told her 'endow' was the root of my family name. Isn't that right, babe?"

He went to put a hand on her waist, but she swiveled round so that he grabbed a handful of air instead.

He laughed and tried again, this time getting hold of her with both hands and attempting to maneuver her away from me and over toward the bar and a couple of his SWAT buddies.

The last thing I needed was Lendowski as an enemy, but he was clearly the worse for drink and I could tell that Deutsch's patience was running thin. But I also knew she realized that if she got on the wrong side of him—especially while they were partners—he was likely to set her career back some, or indeed stall it altogether. I, on the other hand, was part of the furniture and had enough goodwill aimed my way to ride out any macho posturing the big lug felt he might need to inflict upon me.

I moved in, grabbed his wrists, and firmly removed his hands from Deutsch. Then, as low as I could say it and still be heard, "Go back to your buddies, Len. Next round's on me."

He swung around viciously and his fist made the air move enough to create a piercing whistle in my left ear as my head jerked away from the blow.

Deutsch judiciously lurched backwards as I feinted the other way to avoid the follow-up, then Lendowski charged into me. I'd already vacated the space at which he was aiming so he hit a couple of suited Wall Street bankers instead.

He disentangled himself, pulled himself upright, and swung a right hook at my head, but overbalanced. All I needed to do was apply the slightest additional momentum to his leading shoulder to send him crashing to the floor—which I did.

Staggering to his feet, he cracked his knuckles and cricked his neck like the stereotype into which he had already fallen. He even gave me the thousand-yard stare, but somehow I resisted the urge to laugh, a reaction that would have done far more damage to our professional relationship than repeatedly punching him in the face.

It was all threatening to turn very ugly, but as Lendowski prepared to charge me again, Nick appeared and grabbed him from behind and said, "Yo, time for a break, big guy." He ushered him away.

I remembered that Nick and Lendowski used the same gym, and I hoped that they'd built up enough of a rapport for Nick to be able to reason with the guy.

Deutsch moved back toward me. "Thanks. Mia's a lucky girl."

I laughed at her insistence on using the name Tess had given her fictional alter ego. "That's what I keep saying." I decided against relaying this message, Tess definitely not being the kind of woman who enjoys being complemented on her choice of man by an attractive—and available—professional female colleague. Especially not one who was showing no sign of trying to find someone else to talk to.

We watched Lendowski nod grudgingly at Nick, then head out of the bar.

Annie said, "How does a Neanderthal like that manage to keep his badge?"

"Your mind's clouded by alcohol. He's actually a very charming individual. If you'd only give him a chance."

She eyed me curiously for a second, like she wasn't sure if I was being serious, then her expression brightened and she actually laughed—a first. "Now why couldn't they partner me with someone like you instead?"

"You've got to earn me, Annie."

I immediately regretted opening my mouth—even more so given the curious, but not turned off, look in her eyes.

"Earn you. Now that's an intriguing prospect."

"And that's my cue," I said, with a smile. "Seriously . . . just ride it out. They'll reassign you, I'm sure. They're not blind."

"I hope they do—I might not hold back next time."

"Just make sure you've got plenty of witnesses around."

I waved at her, turned and headed for the door. I stopped to tell Nick I was going home, then left. It was getting late and I was physically and mentally exhausted. We all were.

Outside, I saw Lendowski leaning against a wall in the alleyway that ran alongside the bar. At first I thought he was throwing up, but then I realized he was talking on his cell, which probably meant his bookie had called with more bad news.

I gulped a lungful of cold air and stuck out my hand for a taxi so I could reclaim my car from the Federal Plaza parking garage. In less than an hour, I'd be back in my castle, cuddled up with my fair maiden.

Lendowski had sobered up the second he'd heard the voice on the other end of the call, a voice that, although not that of his bookie, filled him with the same level of dread.

He owed his bookie about sixty thousand dollars, and he had no idea how he was ever going to pay it all back. They'd threatened him already, and the fact that they didn't bat an eyelid about doing that to an FBI agent left him under no illusion about how serious and unforgiving these people were. They had him sweating—not an easy thing to pull off with Nat Lendowski. Then, a couple of months back, he'd taken a call from someone else who knew about his debt. The guy had offered him five hundred dollars a week just to keep tabs on Reilly. Nothing too elaborate. He just wanted Lendowski to let him know if Reilly did anything odd or disappeared for any length of time without explanation.

Lendowski made no real effort to earn the money, but continued to collect the envelopes of used bills from his apartment building's laundry room every other week. He could have used the money to pay down the debt, but instead he gambled it—and lost. Which meant he was now at the guy's mercy as well as that of his bookie.

When he'd answered his cell, the guy cut to the chase.

"Hey, Len. It's time to start earning your keep."

Len scowled. "What do you want me to do?"

"Reilly," the man said. "Stay close to him. Imagine your life depends on it."

With a sinking feeling, Lendowski realized this wasn't going to be particularly easy, especially following what had just happened in the bar. But at least he could offer something.

"He's on his way home. I know he's got some big social engagement out of town tomorrow night. Heard him talking to his partner about it. He's taking his lady."

"OK. Good. Anything else, call me immediately."

The caller hung up.

Lendowski pocketed his phone, then turned and emptied his stomach against the wall.

# 8

*Mamaroneck, New York*

The mystery call still had me in its thrall.

I was in two minds about what to make of it. There was a chance it was genuine. The man's pitch sounded real. On the other hand, I couldn't ignore the possibility that I was being played. Either way, I had to go to the meet. There was no way I wasn't going, despite the usual complications, including the main one: I couldn't tell Nick about it, and he'd probably sniff it out and start hassling me about what I was hiding. It would also be safer having him there, but I'd started this thing on my own and I wasn't about to jeopardize his career over it this late in the game. I also couldn't risk spooking the caller if he was indeed genuine and had something of value to say.

I was lying on the bed, deep in thought, wondering about it all, while in front of me, Tess was busy pulling out one outfit after another from her wardrobe and parading them for my opinion.

"What about this one?" she said as she gleefully presented me with a long, shimmering bronze dress that flared out at the bottom. "You said you liked it when I wore it to that gala at the Institute." Her expression then clouded with thought just as fast as it had brightened up. "Then again—do you think the guest list at the White House might have anyone else who was also at that gala besides us?"

I raised my eyebrows and nodded positively, though evidently not with a lot of enthusiasm. I mean, by dress number three, I was fresh out. I went with the failsafe response: "They're all great. Besides, whichever one you choose, you know you're going to be the hottest girl in that room."

OK, I knew that wasn't going to cut it, and it didn't. Tess just gave me that deadpan look that signaled a lot of hard work ahead for me to make up for it and said, in her best ironic French accent, "You have such a silky tongue, Monsieur Reilly. No wonder women swoon over your every word."

"It's my cross to bear," I replied before heading out to the kitchen. "You want a beer?"

"Sure thing, my suave Casanova."

"I'm assuming that means you want foreign?"

"Moi?"

I smiled. "One Bud, coming up."

I hit the fridge, took a long chug, then sat down at the kitchen table and mapped out tomorrow in my mind.

I had to be at Times Square at one. I didn't think it would be a long meet, and that's assuming Darth showed up at all. The guy sounded so jittery it felt like anything would spook him.

On the other hand, he could show up and turn out to be the real deal. If so, I might try to convince him to come into custody, which, if he did, would obviously wipe out our little DC excursion. I could already picture how cheerfully Tess would take that.

She was all excited about our mini-break. She'd arranged for her mom, who lived up in Westport, to come down and look after Kim and Alex while we were out of town. It would be just the two of us, shacked up in a nice hotel room in the capital. Which would be great. Having to miss it would be bad. Then again, my covert meeting could go all wrong and morph into something nasty and intense, which was a different worry altogether.

I needed to be at Penn Station at two for our Acela Express down to DC I was already going to be on thin ice with Tess once I told her I'd be ditching her at Union Station and meeting up with her at the hotel later. That would be tight too—I'd be jumping in the rental car that was waiting there for me and driving out to have my chat with my favorite philandering CIA agent before joining her in time for the star-studded Christmas dinner.

That wasn't a conversation I was hugely looking forward to. I'd felt bad about blackmailing Stan Kirby the first time and it hadn't exactly endeared me to him either. He'd probably blow a gasket at having me show up again, and at his house for that matter, but I didn't have any other choice. A phone call wasn't going to have the full effect, not if I wanted to convince him to look into what the CIA's servers had on record about my dad. I couldn't show up at his office. And Kurt had called to tell me that his snoop into Kirby's digital footprint showed that his Thursday evening trysts with his sister-in-law seemed to have ended, and that he drove home from Langley straight after work pretty much every day. Maybe my intervention had put him back on the straight and narrow. Or maybe his mistress had just got bored with his sorry ass. Who knows. Still, I couldn't afford not to go out and see him. The dinner invitation to the White House was timely, a great opportunity to slip away and have my little chat with him without raising too many flags.

I decided it wasn't hugely productive to keep mulling over it any more. I just needed to get out there and see how both events would play out. Right now, the best call was to get back to the bedroom with Tess's beer and make up for not fawning over her overpriced selection of haute couture.

I didn't get much of a chance to fawn. Within moments of me handing Tess her beer, I saw her eyes move away and get hooked on something by our bedroom door.

I followed her gaze to see Alex standing outside the door, his face tense with worry despite clearly being half-asleep.

"Oh, baby," she said warmly.

She started to get off the bed, but I stopped her and said, "I've got this."

I turned and padded over to him, slowly. He just watched me in silence as I dropped down to one knee in front of him.

"Hey," I said softly, giving him a kiss on his forehead. "What's going on, champ? It's very late."

He stared at me, his lower lip curled out and quivering a bit, his big brown eyes brimming with anxiety.

He didn't need to tell me what was going on. This wasn't the first time he'd had a nightmare.

"Come on," I said as I lifted him up and hugged him against me. "Let's get you back to bed."

I glanced back at Tess. She gave me a pained half-smile and a small nod, and I carried him into his bedroom.

"Story," he mumbled, clinging to me tightly.

I melted a bit. Despite the anger coursing through me at what he was going through, what they'd done to him, at least he was now letting me comfort him, and not just Tess.

It was such a bittersweet feeling—enjoying holding my son

tight against me, feeling him cling to me like this, his protector, his dad—but at the same time wanting to pound the guys who did this to a pulp.

"OK," I told him as we cuddled up in his bed. "What are we in the mood for tonight? Some gobblefunk or that clever mouse and his big, toothy friend?"

Alex smiled.

I melted some more.

"Gobblefunk," he murmured.

"Good call," I said, and raised my hand for a high five, which he gently tapped back before rubbing his eyes with tight fists in that glorious way kids do.

We cuddled up and sank together into the wonderful world of the Big Friendly Giant. Alex's breathing got louder and slower, his little snores a symphony to my ears, a balm to my tired senses.

Once I was sure he was comfortably asleep, it was hard to extricate myself from that lovely cocoon and move back to our bedroom, but I needed to. I had to get some good zees in.

Tomorrow was shaping up to be a day of a complication or two, at best.

# THURSDAY

## 9

*Boston, Massachusetts*

Dr. Ralph Padley woke at seven, as he had every day since moving into the East Broadway brownstone seventeen years ago.

Until his body had turned on him, he had enjoyed starting his days there. The purchase had proved an exceptionally wise investment, as the area was now quite the equal of the Back Bay or South End—his meticulous research having, once again, paid off. As per his rigid habit, he showered, dressed, scraped a dusting of snow and a thin layer of ice from his windshield, then drove to the Starbucks at the corner of Beacon and Charles. Regardless of what he was going through, regardless of the aches and weaknesses, he would stick to his routine as long as he could. It would be his small revenge over what fate had decreed for him.

He walked under the string of Christmas lights hanging inside the faux-classical entrance and joined the short line. Beyond the Ionic columns that met the plaster-molded ceiling, there was a seasonal warmth, though Padley was entirely oblivious to the imminent holidays. More than ever, he vehemently believed that any feelings of joy generated inside retail outlets was nothing more than a cynical exercise in marketing.

Despite it all, Padley felt good today. Apprehensive, certainly. Fearful, even. But deep down, he felt hopeful. Today, he would trigger a sequence of events that, while highly dangerous, would—if successful—lay the foundation of his quest for salvation.

Handing his Harvard University travel mug to his regular morning barista, he ordered his regular morning drink—an Earl Grey Tea Latte—into which he poured a generous splash of cold half-and-half at the milk station. He noticed that the thermos was running rather low, but by good fortune held the exact amount of milk for his beverage.

Sipping his drink, he drove along Beacon and turned left into Clarendon, parking just before the intersection with Boylston

Street. He took his gym bag from his car and walked the hundred yards to the Boston Sports Club.

He entered the BSC—or at least attempted to—at the exact moment that a slim man wearing a fedora tried to do likewise. After the socially acceptable number of "sorrys" and an immaculately polite "no, excuse me," the fedora-wearing man deferred and stepped aside, eventually following Padley inside the building.

This exchange caused Padley to wonder why men no longer wore hats as a matter of course. His grandfather had always worn a Homburg and had told the young Ralph that a man's choice of hat said much about him, but as young Ralph had still been somewhat conflicted about what he wanted to say about himself, he had chosen not to wear a hat. He now had something to offer the world, something of which he could rightly be proud, and wondered whether it wasn't the time to choose a form of headwear. As things stood, he favored an ivy cap, perhaps in corduroy or wool—anything but Harris Tweed, he mused, thinking it would definitely send out the wrong signal—though he reserved the right to change his mind and opt for something more flamboyant.

He changed, draining the final few drops of his latte as he placed his gym bag inside the locker, then headed straight for the basement pool, which was twenty-five meters long with three lap lanes. At this hour, on a weekday, there was plenty of space for him to swim a hundred lengths of the fluid, rhythmic crawl that had many younger men watching in admiration.

He slipped into the water.

He did a couple of lengths, enjoying the feel of the water sliding around him, feeling the adrenaline light up his body.

Then he felt something else.

A twanging sensation in his chest.

Having self-administered every possible test for heart function many times over, he dismissed this and powered on toward the end of another length.

As he came out of a perfectly executed flip turn, he felt a sharp pain in his left ventricle.

His ability to self-diagnose offered him a brief, albeit illusory, moment of control. But as he passed the ten-meter line, he realized with no little surprise that he was in ventricular fibrillation.

*Impossible.*

He couldn't breathe, and gasping for air only made him inhale a lungful of chlorinated water. He was helpless. His entire body, including his head, was now under the surface.

At the edges of his perception, Padley felt the water being displaced as a lifeguard dived into the pool. Within seconds, he was being dragged toward the pool's edge, where another lifeguard helped pull him out of the water.

The first lifeguard began CPR, but Padley had by now retreated into his oxygen-starved brain and was entirely unaware of what was going on around him. He knew he was now asystolic, which triggered the thought—absurd though it seemed—that the research he had entrusted to the CIA all those years ago had somehow come back to him with interest.

With his body now lost to him, his mind experienced a second moment of clarity as he at last realized that for several years now, his wife had been screwing his neighbor behind his back.

As his heart became still forever, its current, or the dearth of such, only "funny" now to an absurdist, Ralph Padley smiled inside at how beautifully circular was the nature of his death.

Indeed, if he had been able to tell anyone, he would have said he was quite convinced he saw his brother's angelic face before everything went dark and he entirely forgot who he was and how he fitted into anything at all.

# 10

*Times Square, New York City*

One o'clock came and went, and no one turned up.

When I say no one, I don't mean it literally. People were there. Tons of them. It seemed like nothing short of a serious hurricane could keep the hordes away from the chaotic maelstrom that is Times Square, anytime of day or night. But of all the people there, no one approached or made contact with me.

Which surprised me.

My instincts had been pulling for the guy to be real, either way: whether he was a deep throat, or bait. Either one could help me find out more about my dad and Corrigan. I'd somehow reached the conclusion that it was going to happen, and I was leaning toward him being the real deal and genuinely having some critical information to share with me. And if that was the case, and he hadn't shown up, it would mean two things: either he got spooked, or someone got to him first.

I mean, I was there. I got there early, scoped the place out. It was packed, as always—in fact, more so. This close to Christmas, it gets even crazier than normal. The square, particularly that part of it, the pedestrianized area by the TKTS tickets booth, was like a condensed mini-Vegas, heaving with people, music, car horns, monster LED screens and neon lights, a relentless assault on the senses, which pretty much summed up most of Manhattan these days. I ended up standing there for over half an hour, scanning the area while my eyes and ears suffered its total onslaught. And in the midst of all that chaos, between the daze of wide-eyed tourists, harried locals, gawkers, hawkers, Elmos and Captain Americas and guitar-playing rhinestone cowboys, it was almost impossible to tell if anyone was watching me. Which was one of the reasons why Times Square was a favorite for unorthodox meetings like this. That, and the multiple routes through which to slip away.

By one thirty, it was time to move on. I checked my phone yet again. Nothing. And it was a thirteen-block walk down to Penn

Station, where Tess and our Acela fast train to DC were waiting for me.

Seated on the bleachers above the TKTS booth while feigning to surf through an iPad, Sandman observed the federal agent who was waiting for the meeting that wouldn't happen.

The iPad was a great prop for this kind of surveillance. Despite the cold and despite the swarm of activity all around him, everyone there, it seemed, was lost in some kind of handheld device, teleported to some alternate social realm—even those who weren't sitting alone. This new norm was actually quite a boon when it came to shadowing targets. It gave operatives like Sandman something to do with their hands. Sandman knew that was something aspiring actors always worried about. Many years and many deaths ago, he'd taken an acting course. Not that he ever wanted to be an actor. He just knew it would help him be more convincing while in character. He'd inhabited many personas in the course of his work and, despite all those kills, he was still a faceless ghost that hadn't appeared on a single police report or sketch artist's portrait.

His attention focused on Reilly, he casually scrolled through the pages of *The Huffington Post*, his default site. It always gave him a perverse thrill to glance at the opinions of people who thought that what they expressed in blogs and comments had any impact on what actually happened. He knew the real power in the world was beyond the reach of these naïve souls. He had probably done more to affect the flow of recent history than all of the site's bloggers combined.

Another of Sandman's targets was about to fall asleep forever.

He'd altered his look for the occasion, as he frequently did. Today, he sported a short black beard, some thick-rimmed glasses, and a beige Gant cap over a thick navy blue reversible jacket and faded jeans. He knew how to pass unnoticed, how to keep changing positions while keeping an eye on his quarry. He was a master at surveillance, so much so that not even a well-trained, talented agent would spot him.

Reilly, he was sure, hadn't.

No one had made contact with the FBI agent. No one slipped him anything, old-school style. There had been no dead drop, no manila envelope or memory stick passed to him by some slippery contact.

Which was good.

It meant Padley hadn't reached out to Reilly from the grave. Not yet, anyway. From here on they'd need to make sure that if he did, whatever he'd intended to give Reilly wouldn't see the light of day. Not that they had any reason to think Padley had anything to reach out with. Sandman had stuck around long enough to watch Padley's wife hurry out of the house when the call about his drowning came in. He'd sneaked in and searched the doctor's home office and come up empty-handed. He'd need to do the same at the doctor's office, as soon as he got a chance. Their contact at the NSA had already gone through Padley's hard drive, both at home and at work, and found nothing.

He watched as Reilly checked his watch and scanned the busy square again.

Still nothing.

As he studied Reilly, he wondered how he would ultimately choose to terminate the man. The agent was young, fit, outwardly healthy—and attuned to outside threats. It was an interesting and challenging assignment, to be sure. Unlike Padley. That had been a cakewalk. Sure, the doctor was being careful. But he was old, and although he didn't look it or act it, at death's door. And the cancer would have killed him anyway. Not that he felt he needed any self-justification, but Sandman knew he was simply bringing forward the inevitable. Indeed, that was all he ever really did, for any of his victims—hasten the sleep from which one never wakes.

A job description that, curiously, fitted his code name, even though it wasn't how it had originated.

His buddies in Third Battalion, Fifth Marines had christened him soon after their deployment to the Gulf in December 1990. Not only did he seem to thrive on the hot desert sand but, through some accident of genetics, he hardly needed any sleep. It was as though he were the one who made the others fall asleep—and so he became known as Sandman. It was a jokey, light-hearted nickname at first. When he soon demonstrated how effective he was as a killing machine out in the field, the nickname took on an entirely different connotation. And much later, when he embarked on his current work, it was a handy code name to have: rather than being distinctive and unique, it had many common associations in popular culture and parlance, which was useful in an age of pervasive keyword voice and data surveillance.

After three years in the Marines, followed by six years in Delta, he had been recruited by a private contractor. They had offered him several different paths. He quickly found his feet as a civilian, and was soon being hired out to a long list of government agencies and private companies.

He loved the independence, the raw freedom, of being his own commanding officer in the field—in his case, the ultimate urban guerilla theatre of war.

Sandman watched Reilly walk off and tucked in behind him.

It was time to find the right opportunity to execute the second part of his orders.

# 11

*Arlington, Virginia*

I left the rental on North Highland, to the east of Lyon Village Park, just south of the tennis courts where the trees provided almost total cover. The temperature had hit zero, but there was no snow on the ground or forecast for the next few days. Which was lucky. Any snow and the drive from Union Station to Kirby's neighborhood would have been a hellish nightmare of unintended donuts and stalled Priuses.

I was as low-key as I could be without attracting undue attention in this upscale neighborhood. Underneath the woolen cap and winter parka I could have been anyone as I followed the curve of Twentieth Street North and walked around Lyon Village Community House with its colonial-style bell tower. I could see the Lee Highway behind a low cluster of pristine apartment buildings. It was the tail end of the route I drove to get here.

Passing a small, well-maintained parking lot before skirting a small cluster of trees and bushes, I turned left onto North Harvard Street.

The houses were large here. Between four and six bedrooms, worth anything upward of one and a half million apiece, easy. But there was a strong atmosphere of tradition and neighborly feeling. Of course, there was as much moral compromise here as anywhere else. Had to be. It was just better concealed.

As I turned in to Twenty-first Street North, I could see the gabled roof of the three-story house that I knew belonged to Kirby. A Stars and Stripes hung from the flagpole that stuck out from the central gable, same as it did on the Google Maps Street View when I'd checked out Kirby's address that morning.

There were lights on inside and I assumed his wife and kids were already back home. Kirby himself was due to arrive back in the next half hour, or so Kurt had concluded after a thorough trawl of the Kirby family's recent credit card statements.

I stepped off the sidewalk and walked over to a group of trees at the edge of a large lawn. Standing within them, I was pretty much completely camouflaged. The lawn rolled up toward a large, Dutch-style house, which stood across the street and a couple of houses down from the gabled house.

My watch showed twenty after six. Not long now.

I did a quick three-sixty sweep.

The street was quiet apart from a young couple pushing a baby buggy back home after a bracing walk around the block—probably with the intention of sending the buggy's inhabitant to sleep.

No security lights that I could see. No cameras either. The residents obviously trusted their neighbors to be vigilant.

It wasn't long before a dark blue Lexus sedan pulled around the corner. As it turned right onto the driveway of the gabled house, the garage door started to swing open, its mechanism activated from inside the car.

The driver remained inside his vehicle for a moment.

I broke from behind the trees and started to walk briskly toward the open garage door.

Kirby finally climbed out of the Lexus, a shopping bag clutched in his left hand, his keys held between thumb and forefinger.

The garage door started to close.

Kirby opened the rear passenger door and leaned in to retrieve something with his right hand.

I sprinted quietly to close the final few yards, ducked under the open garage door and dragged the first thing I saw, a plastic box of rollerblades, level with the frame, blocking the safety beam and ensuring the door could not close.

Kirby, his head inside the car, hadn't heard me enter the garage. He ducked out of the passenger door and straightened, a bouquet of roses in his right hand.

When he saw me facing him all the blood drained from his face. "What the hell are you doing here?"

I gestured toward the flowers. "Making amends?"

I could see him wrestling with his instinct to blow up in my face. After a moment he seemed to relax, choosing level-headedness over righteous indignation.

"What are you doing here?" he hissed. "I told you I never wanted to see you again."

The garage door had already tried to swing shut then opened again.

"I need you to do something else for me."

From inside a navy blue Chevy Malibu parked less than twenty yards farther along the street, Sandman was listening through a long-range directional pipe microphone. Accompanying visuals were provided courtesy of a sniper's scope.

He had been surveilling Reilly ever since the agent's aborted meeting with Padley. The train journey from New York City to DC had been uneventful. As advised, there had been a car waiting for him at Union Station, its key in a magnetized case stuck to the underside of the chassis. The car had been parked in such a position as to allow Sandman to tail his target as he left the station.

The moment it was clear which house Reilly was interested in, he sent the address via encrypted email to one of his employers' data geeks. The surprising response, less than a minute later, told him the house belonged to one of their co-workers, a career analyst at the CIA named Stan Kirby. The man had spent twenty-five years at Langley and was currently a senior intelligence analyst with Level 2-B clearance. Despite two disciplinary warnings for timekeeping, he still had full benefits and was due the company's top-tier pension package.

Sandman focused on the sound coming through his earbuds as Kirby gave his reply.

"Something else? No. Fuck you. You said we were done last time."

"I know, and that was what I'd hoped," he heard Reilly say. "But something new came up, and I have no choice."

"No choice, no choice," the analyst mocked. "Don't give me that crap again. You love doing this."

I tensed up. This wasn't going well. "I don't. But I'm willing to do what I need to do to get answers."

"Yeah, well, screw you. Screw. You. I'm done with this bullshit. You wanna tell my wife, go ahead. Hell, her sister was the best thing that happened to me—until you ruined it."

I held his scowl, then shrugged and pulled out my phone. "Fine. That's the way you want to play it."

I feigned dialing a number, then brought the phone up to my ear.

Kirby's face sank. "What are you doing?"

"Calling your wife. That's what you want, isn't it?"

He dropped the flowers and shopping bag and leapt at me, his hands swatting at the phone. "Are you fucking nuts? Hang up. Kill the god damn call."

I brought the phone down and stared him down.

"What is it this time?" he asked, beaten down and angry.

"My father. I want to know what the agency has on him."

Sandman had already guessed at the history here. The agent had blackmailed someone inside the CIA. He had his own personal mole there. And that presented his superiors with a problem. If Reilly had been fed classified information relating to anything that involved them, he was a direct threat. Especially seeing as the call from Padley would have confirmed for the agent that there were layers he had yet to peel back.

"Your father?" Kirby said. "Who the hell is your father?"

"Colin Reilly. He's dead. He died in 1980. There's a mention of him in one of the Corrigan files you got me."

Sandman shook his head at Reilly's impetuous nature. In the morning, he fails to get hold of information he thinks might unlock an impenetrable mystery, and by the evening he's attempting to reactivate a relationship of coercion from which he'd already got out completely clean. It was exactly the kind of reckless behavior that was liable to get you killed.

The reckless behavior that presented Sandman with an opportunity he couldn't pass up.

He hurriedly typed another encrypted email:

*Kirby fed classified files to Reilly. Find which. Reed Corrigan + Colin Reilly namechecked.*

He pressed send, pulled out the earbuds, placed the scope, mike and buds on the passenger seat and climbed out of the car, pocketing his handset as he straightened. He'd already thought out how to deal with Reilly while having Kirby at their mercy until they'd found out everything they needed to know. At that point, Stan Kirby would meet a tragic, but entirely accidental, end.

Sandman walked toward the open garage.

I watched as Kirby racked his brains as he knelt down and picked the bouquet of flowers off the garage floor.

"I don't remember seeing any mention of him."

"It was only his initials, CR." I said it louder than I meant to, my frustration boiling over.

"Pipe down, will you? She'll hear us." He set the flowers on his car.

I could hear the desperation in his voice and see the dread in his face as he pictured everything he thought he'd resolved about to unravel. I was in no mood to cut him any slack.

"Same exercise, different name," I told him. "Get me everything on file about my dad and we're done."

He scoffed. "Why am I having a déjà vu here?"

There was the faintest sound behind me. I spun to find a gun pointed right at me. The man holding it wore a black unbadged baseball cap, which along with the thick-framed glasses he had on pretty much obscured his eyes. A short but full dark beard covered the lower half of his face and his hands were sheathed by black leather gloves.

The guy was a pro.

I watched as he took in the entire situation in one sweep, then raised his left hand and pulled on a red plastic T-bar suspended from the garage door by a short rope, thus disengaging the door from the motor and ensuring he couldn't be shut inside.

I glanced over at Kirby. He seemed thoroughly spooked. He didn't know him.

The bearded man finally spoke, addressing me first and waving his gun as a conductor's stick.

"Reilly, take out your gun and put it on the ground. Easy."

So he knew who I was. That told me most of what I needed to know right now. I paused for a couple of seconds, assessing the immediate situation, then slowly took out my Glock and placed it carefully on the garage floor.

"Stan, bring it over to me. Pick it up from its barrel. Two fingers. Gently."

Kirby complied and handed it over to him. The bearded man took it carefully, also from the edge of its barrel, then he moved his hand so he gripped it the right way around, but by the tip of his gloved fingers.

Like he didn't want to wipe my prints off it.

"Stan, do you have a gun in the house?"

"Yes. In the bedroom. It's in a lockbox."

The man thought about it for a second. "Not very convenient, Stan. Not when the guy who's blackmailed you before comes back to threaten you again. Comes to your own house and asks you to break the law and commit high treason. This armed motherfucker walks into your garage without invitation and waves his gun in your face to make you betray your country. What do you do, Stan? Do you just sit back and watch? Or do you do something about it?"

Kirby just stood there, nailed to his spot, like a silent pressure cooker on the verge of blowing.

"I'll tell you what you do, Stan."

The bearded man aimed my own gun at me.

"You jump the bastard and you kill him."

# 12

"Makes sense, doesn't it, Stan? Besides, I don't see how you have a choice here. You've got a family to protect. You don't want to spend the rest of your life in a supermax prison, do you?"

Kirby looked like he was about to have a full-blown heart attack. The bearded man kept my gun pointed directly at me, clearly having decided that Kirby represented zero threat.

"Take a breath and answer me, Stan, because in about ten seconds I'll just shoot you both where you stand and let your friends at Langley worry about cleaning up this mess. The mess you put them in."

Kirby's eyes lit up. I could see him processing: the agency knew about everything. Somehow, they knew that he'd leaked the files to me, and there was something in them so dangerous that the leak had to be plugged indefinitely. But they were offering him a way out. A way to keep his job and his pension. All he had to do was kill me.

"They'll kill you too," I told him. "He's already got the narrative they're going with."

Kirby glared at me. "What the fuck am I supposed to do? You see many choices here?"

The bearded man told Kirby, "So we're good with how this is going to play out—?"

In the split second that his eyes flicked across to Kirby, in the heightened intensity of that instant that consumed everything else just before a kill, I launched myself at him.

No choice. I wasn't going to just stand there and let them kill me at their leisure before polishing up their storyline and figured if I was going to get a bullet either way, anywhere in my torso would be preferable to my brain.

I had two guns to contend with, and aimed each of my hands at one of them. My right hand locked on his gun, my left hand on my Glock, my torso slamming into him in tandem with my head butting into his skull.

A shot exploded from his gun as he reeled back, my hands still locked on his. The noise jolted us both for a nanosecond, and I had no idea where it landed. We struggled as I tried to knee him, but he blocked it with his own leg and shoved me back, regaining the momentum. I had to keep him close, I couldn't let him free himself and back away, not even with one gun, so I kept my hands firmly gripped around his and I tried to wrangle my gun out of his hand—

Which is when the second shot burst out, this one from my gun, and then it all went haywire. I managed to twist his wrist enough to loosen his grip on my Glock, and as it fell out, I heard Kirby grunt and thud down to the ground just as a scream of "Stan?" came from somewhere inside the house, a woman's scream. In that frenzied moment, the distraction was just enough to allow the bearded man to pummel me across the temple with the grip of his own gun.

The blow hit me hard—real hard. I felt my teeth rattle against my jawbone as the blow connected. I struggled to stay on my feet, but I was weakened. We struggled some more, with me trying to muster any strength I had left to keep my grip locked on his gun hand and keep it aimed away from me. Then an alarm started blaring, the house's alarm, I figured—Stan's wife, hitting the panic button. It was like a tiny burst of smelling salts to my battered senses, and I used it to counter-attack and tried to headbutt him, only he saw it coming and avoided it. It was a gamble that left me exposed and he made full use of it, pounding me with a hook that connected squarely against my jaw. I blacked out for a second as my legs gave way under me and regained some partial sight just as I hit the ground, my unprotected skull cracking against the hard floor. I was at the edge of consciousness. I could feel the blood seeping out down my forehead from the first blow, and through foggy eyes, I caught sight of Kirby lying on the floor, a few feet away from me. The bullet had hit him through the cheekbone, and from the bloody mess at the back of his head, I could tell that it had gone straight through his brain.

I looked up and saw the bearded man pointing his gun down at me.

Then the woman yelled "Stan!" again.

Sandman heard it too and figured he had only seconds to get out.

His mind moved lightning-fast. He'd wanted Reilly dead, but he couldn't shoot him with his own gun. He quickly scanned the floor around them looking for Reilly's Glock, but before he could find it, his eyes locked on the casing from the shell fired from his own gun. The woman yelled "Stan" again, her voice much closer this time. He had a second or two to get out of there if he wasn't going to have to kill her too, an option he quickly discarded as too messy. He bent down and retrieved the casing. It wasn't as clean as he wanted it—he didn't have time to recover the stray bullet—but under the circumstances, it would have to do.

He then ducked through the open garage door and slipped away briskly, heading toward his car.

As the wail of the house alarm egged me back to consciousness, I felt my head. My beanie was soaked through on one side, courtesy of a fast-spreading patch of fresh blood. As I dragged myself onto my knees, the internal door to the house swung open and Kirby's wife stepped into the garage, a handgun clutched in her hand. She screamed "Stan!" as she saw her husband lying dead on the floor, then looked at me and swung the gun at me, her hands shaking.

"What have you done? Stan! Oh my God, Stan?"

I was still on my knees, getting up slowly, my vision blurred, my head pounding, but I raised both hands as defensively as I could.

"Please, don't shoot. It's not what it looks like. Please, listen to me. I'm with the FBI."

Sobs were heaving through her body as her face contorted and went from confusion and fear into wild rage—and I could see she was about to pull the trigger.

I was now on my feet and I faltered back a step, then another, hesitantly, my hands still way up and wide apart.

"Listen to me—"

She looked completely terrified, but one thing I knew was that an adrenalized shot with no aim at all was potentially far more lethal than a considered shot with a wayward aim.

She fired.

The bullet whizzed past my cheek, so close I was sure it took a few skin cells with it.

I wasn't going to risk a second one. I turned and ducked as I bolted through the garage door, willing my legs back to life.

I staggered toward my car, but quickly had to stop—a neighbor had stepped out of his house and had a phone in his hand. Then I heard the first police siren—coming from the direction I'd parked my rental. The neighbor must have called 911.

I lurched right and changed tack.

I veered off the street and ducked up the driveway of a neighboring house, cutting through to its back yard. I crashed through some bushes and over a patch of grass, heading across two back gardens toward another house at the end of the street, all the windows of which were dark. Within minutes, there'd be a police chopper in the air above me with a search beam sweeping the neighborhood.

I had to get far from here, fast.

I remembered the apartment buildings behind the Lee Highway and the parking lot for the residents beside them. No gates or fences. By now, most of the residents would be home and not going anywhere until morning.

Left hand clutched to my head in a vain attempt to staunch the bleeding, I swerved around the house, hoping there weren't any motion sensors on the property.

At the side of the house, I clambered over a fence, crashing to the ground on the other side as my legs gave way. My vision was still blurring from the concussion and there was blood running into my left eye. I rolled down a steep bank, plowing through seemingly endless lines of bushes as I careened downwards over a thick layer of wood chips, finally coming to a stop against a tree.

My recollection had been accurate. I was lying about a hundred yards from the unsecured parking lot beside the low apartment buildings behind the Lee Highway.

More sirens sounded, no more than a quarter mile away. I shook my head, pulled myself upright and staggered like a wounded animal toward the small lot, already scanning the vehicles for one old enough to be hot-wired.

# 13

*Washington, DC*

"Sean. Me again. Just a little heads up, baby—the car's picking us up in ten minutes. Ten. Minutes. You do remember why we're here, don't you? That casual pizza evening at your buddy's pad on Pennsylvania Avenue? At the . . . where was it, exactly? Oh, yes. I remember now. The White House!" The last three words were more yelled than said. Then, mock-cheerfully: "Call me, sweetie. This better be good. Historically good. Bye."

She clicked off, stabbing the iPhone so hard to end the call that she almost cracked the screen with her nail.

It was the third message she'd left him.

She stared at herself in the hotel-room mirror yet again, scrutinizing every inch of her appearance: the hair, the makeup, the jewelry, every fold of her dress, her shoes, right down to the pedicure on her toes.

Perfect. Immaculate. In her humble opinion.

Just one thing missing: her date for the big night.

It had happened before, sure. Maybe not on such a huge occasion. But he'd done a few no-shows. His job was like that. The unexpected had to be expected sometimes. She knew that.

But this felt different. Ever since the summer, ever since that whole affair in California and Mexico, he'd been keeping things from her. She knew that too. And it had worried her. She'd asked him about it, not too often, just when it felt like the right time to do so, when she felt he was a bit of a softer target than normal. And she'd failed. He'd kept insisting there was nothing going on. And now, this.

She was worried. There was no way to convince herself otherwise. You developed an instinct about these things; about the person you loved and were sharing your life with. And right now, her instincts were on the boil.

*Where are you, Sean?*

*

I saw my phone light up with Tess's call, but I couldn't bring myself to take it. I was still groggy, my brain still frazzled by the frenzy I'd just survived—and escaped.

I didn't know what to say without worrying her, scaring her, implicating her—I had to think things through.

I knew she was probably already beyond worried. No call, on a night like this—she'd have gone through frustration, through fury, and on to worry.

I hated putting her through this. But I couldn't do any better. Right now, I had to keep moving, and think.

Keeping my eyes on the road, I pulled the cover off the back of my phone and dug its battery out.

And kept heading north.

"Tess, it's so lovely to meet you," the first lady said as an aide introduced them.

Tess shook hands with her before turning to President Yorke, who asked, "So where is that barnstorming man of yours then? We were expecting the two of you?"

She felt immensely awkward standing there, an awkwardness that had started long before she'd reached the Southeast Entrance. The setting alone was intimidating enough, in the best of circumstances: Christmas dinner at the White House, hosted by the most powerful man on the planet and his wife. Not exactly a casual cocktail party, by any means. Throw in the fact that you were turning up alone, without your partner—who was the reason for the invitation in the first place—and without being able to give any convincing answer for why he wasn't there, and we're talking Richter-scale jitters of unease.

Henry "Hank" Yorke was coming up to the end of his first term, but the prospect of a whole year of monster campaigning that was about to kick off within weeks didn't seem to faze him. Tall and charismatic, he was in his late sixties, not as young as the country's more recent presidents. Still, he was in fine physical shape, and with the country enjoying a period of economic stability and no bruising foreign wars, he seemed as reasonably assured of a second term as any president ever was.

President Yorke and his wife, Megan, typically hosted a whole series of social events in the month that led to Christmas. Their social secretaries and their staff had been busy for weeks, planning the cocktail parties and dinners, cutting and pasting their way through the lists of donors, lobbyists, bloggers and reporters, government staffers and foreign diplomats and all kinds of supporters or notable achievers of every kind, making sure the guest lists were well balanced and well matched, vetting them again and again to make sure no personal slights or diplomatic faux pas would ensue. Tonight's event, though, was no six hundred-guest whirlwind tour of the White House's various reception rooms. This was a more intimate seated dinner in the State Dining Room—intimate, as in eighty people seated at eight tables of ten. Not as easy to get lost in the crowd or hide the embarrassing, empty seat at the table.

"Yes, where is he?" the first lady asked.

Tess just smiled uncomfortably, and all she could think of saying was simply, "I honestly couldn't tell you," with an embarrassed, half-laugh.

*I'm making excuses for Sean with the president!* She shuddered inwardly.

"I was so looking forward to meeting him," Megan Yorke said. "Hank's told me so much about him, and we owe him so much, of course. I haven't had the chance to thank him." She turned to her husband. "I still can't believe you didn't tell me what really happened that night or that you'd met with him until after Agent Reilly was back home in New York. I mean, I was there, too, wasn't I?"

Yorke gave her a practiced smile and nodded, expertly hiding any reaction to her gripe. "Sweetheart, we needed to make sure the threat was fully contained. I didn't want you worrying unnecessarily."

They both owed their lives to Reilly. No one could argue that. As Tess flicked a quick glance around the room, she wondered how many of the people around her had been there that night earlier this year, at the White House Correspondents Dinner at the Hilton hotel in Washington, the night a rogue Russian agent came close to causing a historic bloodbath. Yorke and his wife, along with most of their senior staffers and a star-studded list of guests, were saved from a horrific death, which was why Reilly had been invited to this dinner. Tess had debated not coming at all if he didn't show up, but she'd decided one of them showing up was marginally less rude than both.

"You know how it is," Tess said, forcing a smile to crack her tensely locked facial muscles. "He's probably out there chasing down some psycho while we're sitting here enjoying this very lovely Merlot."

"I don't know how you can take it in your stride like that," the first lady said. "It's so admirable of you, not even knowing where he is half the time, I imagine. At least when Hank here was still at the Agency, I gave up making any kind of social plans knowing how many times he'd stood me up, but at least I knew where he was and I knew he wasn't in danger since he was a desk jockey," she added with a small laugh and a sideways, playful glance at her husband. "Your life must be—well, I don't envy you. It can't be easy."

The president, whose route to politics and the White House had begun in intelligence, where he ultimately ended up running the CIA, nodded calmly in agreement. "I'm sure whatever it is he's doing, we're probably lucky he's doing it." His expression turned a bit more serious and he seemed to be studying Tess more closely. "You know, a lot of people aren't thrilled with his way of handling things—I've had more than a few calls about him—but I just tell them to back off. If anything, we need more guys like him. So whatever the reason he can't be here is fine with me. And at least we got to meet you."

She and Reilly had been placed at a table by the gingerbread White House, which she was told was something they crafted every year. It wasn't long before the hosts and their guests were all seated and enjoying a first course of chanterelle mushroom soup with goat cheese fritters. Reilly's empty seat stared at her from across the table. By the end of the meal, she felt like a wreck. Three times, she'd suffered the chastising eyes of the table companions who'd noticed her sneaking a glance at her phone under the table, but her screen was clear of any notifications. Reilly hadn't called or messaged her.

A profound sense of worry was crippling her.

*Where the hell are you, Sean?*

# 14

*Lower East Side, Manhattan*

The cushioning on the armchair was about as soft as a bale of reclaimed metal, but I still felt like I was going to drift off any second.

My head was pounding—as much from overexertion due to grinding over the events and my options at this point as from the blow from my gun.

I checked my watch: five after two. My host was out late, even for a weekday, obviously enjoying having his life back after the circadian confusion of the past few weeks and no doubt busy converting the endless stream of Tinder matches into flesh-and-bone conquests. I just hoped he'd come back home instead of staying over with whatever buxom free spirit he'd graced with his fickle presence.

I'd hot-wired a vintage Honda Accord and driven it into the city, where I'd left it in a parking garage. Coincidentally, and weirdly, I found a dead ringer for Nick's fur hat on the dash, which I "borrowed" —the warmth it offered my still-fragile head trumping its questionable aesthetics.

I'd walked the five blocks to the familiar apartment building. Imitating my partner's gruff voice, I'd told a furious random resident via intercom that I'd had too much to drink and forgotten my house keys and after they'd reluctantly buzzed me in, I'd picked the lock of the rent-controlled sublet in which I was now squatting.

It was unlikely my host would be feeling particularly hospitable when he arrived home. Being either sound asleep or unconscious would in all likelihood make things even worse, so I forced myself to yet again methodically go through everything that had led up to this night. Even in my addled state, I knew that something might land differently, trigger a new memory or provoke the kind of tangential thought process that could lead to fresh insight. Two hours later I was drifting on a thick cloud of despair, exhaustion, throbbing pain and borderline concussion when I heard the apartment door squeal open.

I tried to stand, but my head felt like an anvil. I crashed back down into the armchair as Nick walked into the room and switched on the light.

His jaw dropped as he spotted me—the beaver still on my head, a thick stream of dried blood plastered to the side of my face and a fine coating of rock salt down the length of one trouser leg.

"What the fuck . . . Sean?"

"So you don't know already?"

"What are you talking about?"

My voice was weak. "No, I just thought . . . they would have called you by now."

He went to fish his work BlackBerry out of his pocket. "My phone's on silent. It's been a big night, I mean . . ." He hesitated a bit, like he was unsure about what to say, then added, "Tinder booty call, you know how it is—"

Then he saw the screen.

"Shit," he grumbled. "Eleven missed calls." He raised his eyes and studied me, then any remaining light dimmed right out of his expression. "What's going on?"

"Sit down, man. Just . . . sit down."

I finally told my partner everything.

The whole messed-up story, starting with my first encounter with Kirby. I didn't give out Kurt's name, though. I figured I owed him his anonymity, and Nick didn't pick at it. Instead, he just sat there and listened, shaking his head but holding back his unspoken disapproval and saying nothing until I was done. Then he just sat there in silence for what felt like a hell of a long time.

He finally took a long, haggard breath, leaned forward, and looked me squarely in the eyes. "You need to hand yourself in, Sean. It's the only way. Every second you're not in custody just makes it look worse."

"No. No way." I was too burnt out to elaborate.

"It's the only way. At least then, you have a chance they'll believe you. You have to do it. Spill the whole story. The blackmail, the files. Everything. You know how it works. If everything you say is true, which we know it is, if it can all be verified, which I can make damn sure of, then maybe there's something just north of a snowball's chance in hell that your version of the past twenty-four hours will be believed as well. Or at least considered till evidence is found to support it."

In my mind, the chances of that weren't even worth considering.

"No," I said. "Look, they've been protecting this Corrigan all along. For whatever reason, they don't want him found. They'll claim he never existed and bury me." It sounded much worse now that I was voicing it. "I need to find him myself."

"Right, because you've been so stunningly successful at it so far?"

I lost it. "What do you want from me, Nick? Look at me. I'm fucked. You want me to just serve them up my head on a platter?"

"Jesus, Sean," he shot back. "Listen to yourself. You don't know what you're saying."

"We were struggling for the gun when it went off," I yelled. "My prints are all over it. His wife saw me. Me—no one else. Just me."

"There wouldn't have been a struggle if the guy in the beard wasn't there," he yelled back. "It was self-defense—"

"Which is impossible to prove if I can't wheel in the beard to back up my story."

"You think you're in any fit state to be doing anything? I mean, look at you. It's a miracle you're not laid out on a sidewalk somewhere." He took a breath, studied me some more, then his tone calmed. "It's got to stop, Sean. You've got to stop with the lone vigilante shit. I need my partner back. I need my buddy back. I've watched you get totally obsessed by this Reed Corrigan, and . . . you've changed, man. All these secrets . . . And your focus isn't there any more. Your mind used to be one hundred percent on the job, but ever since last summer . . . You're always disappearing off on your own, doing Christ knows what."

"We got Daland, didn't we?"

"We got Daland because however much your attention is elsewhere, you're still a damn good agent. Nothing will ever change that. But look where it's got you. I mean . . . Christ!"

I was too tired to argue, but I heard the edge of desperation in my own voice. "You think I'm enjoying it? You think I'm happy my partner is down on me the whole time? I can barely concentrate on anything without that bastard popping into my head. It's the same thing at home. Alex may be OK—better, at any rate—but I'm still back there. Every time I look at him, I think about what they did to him, and it just . . . I can't let go, Nick. And now there's my dad, too . . ." I tailed off, took a couple of deep breaths. "I need to know what happened to him. And I have to do it alone. More than ever."

"What if you find something you don't like, something you were better off not knowing?"

"What do you mean?"

"I mean, what if your dad was in bed with these guys and really did kill himself out of guilt?"

"'Guilt?'"

"Maybe. Who knows. Maybe he was part of something nasty and he couldn't live with that. I mean, what do you really know about him, Sean? Sometimes some doors are best left unopened. I sure as hell wouldn't want to know about everything my dad was up to after he left us."

I was too incensed to even begin to answer him, but even in my worked-up state, I couldn't dismiss his words entirely. All I could bring myself to say was, "He wasn't part of anything nasty. He was a good guy."

Nick shrugged, calmer now. "Yeah, well, I hope he was, buddy. I really do." He sat there and just stared at me, nodding his head slowly, deep in thought.

"OK," he said. He nodded again, to himself, solemnly, then pushed himself to his feet. "I'll go make us some coffee."

I leaned back and closed my eyes, eagerly anticipating the caffeine hit. I hadn't been sure that Nick would see things my way, but I had to keep pushing. We were partners, after all.

I must have dozed off because I woke as Nick walked back into the living room, a steaming mug of coffee in each hand.

"Should have stayed the night with Rochelle." He placed his mug—bearing the deeply ironic slogan "Husband of the Year"—on a low table in front of a battered sofa. "She offered, you know. But there I was thinking I needed a clean shirt for the morning. Big mistake, huh?"

He turned to hand me one of the black-and-white FBI mugs from the White House gift shop, a gift from yours truly.

"It's been a night of big mistakes," I muttered.

Then, just as I took the mug, he grabbed my wrist, cuffed it and pulled the other end down toward the metal arm of the chair. The mug smashed against the hardwood floor, splashing scalding hot coffee across us both.

Using his downward momentum against him, I tried to wrench his arm all the way toward the floor so I could lock my free arm around his neck and pull his gun with my cuffed hand, but he knew exactly what I would try and was already exerting counter pressure in an upward trajectory—enough to bring the open cuff level with the metal tube. He closed the cuff with his free hand and stepped back.

"What the hell, Nick? What are you doing?"

He looked straight at me—his expression tense and apprehensive as I did the obligatory struggling gesture with my cuffed hand. The cushioning may have been past its comfort date, but the metal frame was rock solid.

"Nick," I blurted. "Don't do this."

"I'm sorry." He was quite deliberately echoing my earlier reply.

"I'm getting closer," I rasped. "The shooter who followed me to Kirby's house must be working for Corrigan. And they don't want me to find out the truth about my father. Why else would they act now? They could have killed me anytime."

"Sean, listen to yourself. 'CR'? That could be anyone."

"What about Azorian? I told you. I saw it on his desk—"

Nick exploded. "That was a zillion years ago, for Christ's sake! How can you possibly be sure you remember it right? And anyway, say there is this big conspiracy, say you find out something bad happened to your dad. What then? Then you have to find out who was involved. And why. And then you need to punish them. Just like with Alex. There's no end to that journey, Sean. And you want to do it all by yourself. Without me, without the Bureau. On the sly. That's just nuts, Sean. How in God's name can you not see that?"

I was about ready to explode myself, but I took a breath and looked my partner right in the eye. The whole set up was so absurd that I'd resolved not to share it with anyone, but the time had come for full disclosure.

"Look, there's . . . there's something else. I didn't tell you because he said not to tell anyone. So they don't get killed."

"What are you talking about?"

"Some guy called me. I don't know who. Electronic voice modulator, prepaid, the works. He told me he had information about my dad. He said he would tell me the truth. We arranged to meet but he didn't show."

"Are you actually hearing yourself? And this 'deep throat' . . . you're saying he didn't show up. Meaning you went to the meet alone. Without me to back you up. And maybe grab the guy and bitch-slap the truth out of him. That's just—that's great, Sean. Just real clear thinking there."

"I didn't want to get you sucked into this."

Nick raised his hands and shook the air with them. "So you decide to head down to DC to blackmail Kirby into getting you that information. Just like that. You see what I'm talking about, right? This isn't an investigation, Sean. It's one burnt-out, revenge-obsessed agent on a mission to self-destruct." The veins popped on his neck as he yelled it. "So this is my intervention, OK? I'm not going to let you do it. Not for my sake—I mean, forget me. I'm irredeemable. But for Tess and Kim. And Alex. Hell, and for you, 'cause I love you, you dumb fuck." He held my gaze, then plunked himself back down heavily on the sofa across the room from my armchair.

He pulled out his phone. "You're going to hand yourself in."

I shook my head. "No, Nick. Don't . . ."

"You're giving yourself up. Right now."

I watched him unlock his phone. "No. Listen to me. You think I'll be safe with the cops? These guys want me dead. Put me in some holding cell and they'll get to me."

"We're not going to the cops. We're keeping this in house. I'll take you down to Federal Plaza. We'll go over the whole thing with Gallo, step by step. Then we'll decide what the hell we're going to do."

"They'll get to me. Anywhere in the system and they'll get to me."

"Not on my watch."

He took out his phone and hit dial. He waited for several seconds, then said, "Boss? Sorry to wake you. Yeah, it's about Reilly."

A beat, then he rolled his eyes. "Let me get a god damn word in and I'll tell you."

I could hear his teeth grinding as he listened to the Assistant Director in Charge ream him out.

"He's here, with me," he finally put in. "He wants to hand himself in, but only if you can guarantee FBI custody." A pause, then, "OK. We'll be waiting."

He ended the call.

I felt like someone had unloaded a cement mixer in the pit of my stomach. "What have you done, man?"

"I'm saving your life."

I shook my head with despair. "You think Gallo, of all people, will honor that?"

"You're one of his. I think the ADIC will do whatever it takes to give the Bureau a chance of containing this cluster fuck. And I'll be here to make sure of it."

"They won't give us Corrigan. Without him, we've got nothing."

"You saved the president's life, Sean. Maybe it's time we called in the big guns."

"Even then, you'll come up empty handed, trust me."

"You should have a little faith, Sean."

"I'm all out."

There was nothing left to say. We just sat there in silence and waited for the callback from Gallo. We were both clearly running different scenarios through our rattled brains, because Nick then broke the silence and said, "If the Bureau doesn't get anywhere, we go to the press."

I shrugged. "If I'm not dead by then."

"Let me worry about keeping you alive. You think about what you're going to tell Tess."

Her name hit me even harder than the pistol whipping. Everything frittered away as my head filled with images of my family. Maybe Nick was right. Maybe my resolve to find out what happened to my dad so I could let go of the past was stopping me from seeing what effect the present was having on Tess and our kids and putting our future at risk.

Either way, I'd be dealing with it from inside an FBI interview room.

Nick's phone rang. He picked up, listened, then said, "OK. We'll meet you there in an hour."

He turned to me. "Gallo's coming in." He then reached over and handed me his phone. "You need to call Tess. Then you need to find yourself a good lawyer."

# 15

*Washington, DC*

"Sean, what the hell's going on? The FBI says you're wanted for—"

I heard some shuffling movement on the other end of the line, like someone was taking the phone from her, then a male voice said, "Agent Reilly? This is Tom Murray. DC field office. Where are you?"

So they were there already.

I was fully expecting it, but still. It was an easy trail. My gun. My prints. My rental car, in my name. Train tickets bought together. A quick call, maybe to the house or to the office, would have shown us being in DC for the big dinner. A hotel check would have kicked up our reservation.

The dinner. I wondered when they'd got to Tess. Before, after or—ouch—during.

"I'm in FBI custody in New York. I've handed myself in to Special Agent Aparo. Can you please put Tess back on the phone?"

Saying it there and then—it felt odd that I couldn't say what my instinct would have made me say, which was, "put my wife back on the phone." I felt a small tug at the pit of my stomach about that. Maybe it was something I ought to fix. Assuming she wanted it. Assuming it would still be relevant. Assuming we still had a life together to look forward to.

"You'll pardon my being a bit of a stickler about this, but I'll need some confirmation of that first."

"Hang on."

I passed the phone to Nick, told him what he needed to do. He spoke to Murray for a minute or so, explained the situation. Gave him the reassurance he needed. Then he handed it back to me.

"Sean?" It was Tess's voice. "What's going on?"

Hearing her like that, weary and worried—not easy.

"It's . . . complicated."

"Don't give me that. What's going on?"

I had to smile to myself. She was tough, and I needed to remind myself that, whatever happened, she'd be in my corner. "I'll tell you the whole story when I see you. Long story short, someone got shot and they've made it look like I did it."

"Which you didn't, obviously."

"Obviously."

"OK, so there's nothing to worry about," she said, maybe more to seek out some reassurance for herself.

"It'll be fine," I said. "But until that's sorted out, I thought—" and here, I glanced at Nick, who was watching—"it would be better if I handed myself in so no one got the wrong idea."

She went quiet for a moment, probably realizing how out of character that was for me.

"Good," she just said. "Hang on."

I heard her ask the agent, "Are you charging me with anything, or am I free to go?"

"Go where?"

She was firm. "Where do you think?"

He demurred, then said, "Let me make a call."

She came back on the line. "I'll take the first flight up. I should be with you by eight."

"No," I told her. "Go to the house first. I'll have Nick meet you there. They might want to send people over to have a look around and you should be there. I wouldn't want your mom to have to deal with that on her own."

"She can handle it, Sean."

"I don't doubt that," I said. "But still . . . go home first. Then come into the city once they're done."

"Are you sure?"

"Yes," I said, the prospect of having my own house searched by an ERT crew curdling my insides. "Tess, I'm—I'm really sorry about all this. I really am. But just . . . bear with me. We'll ride it out, you'll see. OK?"

"Of course," she said. She paused, like she wanted to say more, but couldn't.

“Get some sleep,” I finally said. “Tomorrow’s probably going to be a long day for us both.”

“I love you,” she said.

I echoed the feeling, then hung up.

# FRIDAY

# 16

*Federal Plaza, Lower Manhattan*

So here I was, in a room I was all too familiar with, only this time *I* was the guy sitting at the bare metal table and cut off from the outside world by a steel-and-glass door and an eight-digit passcode.

It wasn't even dawn yet, but we'd been at it for over an hour. Just me, Gallo, and Nick at this point, in the austere, windowless twenty-third floor interview room at Federal Plaza. The forty-one-story building that forms the western edge of Foley Square was the hub of the law enforcement and judicial machinery in Manhattan. It had also been my home away from home for over ten years. Now, it was my jail. I can't really say I ever pictured that happening.

I hadn't lawyered up, although I knew I might well have to bring one in soon. The cameras, which were located high up on opposite walls, were switched off. Gallo had agreed to that, but not before putting up some stern resistance, which was all for show, of course: he knew keeping our initial conversation off the record covered his ass as well as mine and he needed to get a better handle on what he was dealing with before deciding how best to tackle it.

The thrust of my argument was simple. Why would I kill Kirby? He'd helped me the first time around, and I needed his help again. Gallo's cynical response was, I had to admit, one that was hard to bat away: by my own admission, I was charged up, I was desperate for answers; maybe I pulled my gun to threaten him. Maybe he charged me in a fit of rage. Maybe we struggled for the gun, and he ended up dead. And that was aside from the far-from-inconsequential admission that I had admitted to blackmailing an employee of the CIA into passing confidential files to me.

I was getting a taster of how hard it might be to convince a neutral third party about the mystery man in the beard. Of course, Nick and the guys in DC would rake the area for witnesses or CCTV footage that might back up my claims, but frankly, short of a video recording showing him along with what actually happened in that garage, I couldn't see how that was going to help exonerate me.

This wasn't looking good.

Also, it hadn't been as easy to keep Kurt's name out of it as it had been with Nick.

"How'd you ID Kirby as a soft target?" Gallo had asked.

He may be a prick, but he's not a dumb prick.

I'd ducked the unspoken question with Aparo. I needed to duck it again now. "I asked around."

"What do you mean, 'asked around?' Who?" Gallo's ego didn't take kindly to being deflected like that.

"That's not relevant right now, all right? I needed someone with access and I asked some people and his name came up. Can we move on?"

It took a couple of more to-and-fros, but we grudgingly did.

Gallo's expression darkened gradually the more I spoke. It was like his eyes were receding into a couple of abysses deep in his skull with every word. I was under no illusions that this was due to any concern over me. It was all about him, obviously. How his lack of oversight could have allowed this to happen, especially seeing as he knew from day one that I was trying to find Reed Corrigan and was getting stonewalled by the CIA at every request.

This risked sinking him too, perhaps not as badly as me, but still—for someone like Gallo, any impediment to the sacred career path was a major disaster.

Which is what Nick and I were banking on. And Nick adroitly steered Gallo to the conclusion we wanted. Whether or not he'd go through with it was another matter.

Throughout all this, an angry cocktail of emotions concerning my partner was roiling inside me. Even though I understood where he was coming from, I was still uber pissed off at how he'd railroaded me; on the other hand, I appreciated how clear-minded and committed he was during all these initial proceedings. I've always chided him for his cynical outlook on life, a perspective I'd dubbed "pragmatic nihilism," as in: life is pretty much bullshit, so you'd better be fully present in those exceptionally rare moments when good stuff happens, because otherwise it's just completely remorseless bullshit. This wasn't good stuff in any way and I know he wasn't enjoying it in any way, but he was totally present and in my corner. But I could see that, even with all the best will in the world, this probably wasn't going to be enough.

Especially not when the CIA decided to join the party.

They arrived at around seven thirty, two of them.

Showtime.

Annie Deutsch and Nick brought them in before she left again, giving me a glance and a little nod that spoke volumes about the confusion and concern swirling inside her. The door closed, sealing us in, and curt introductions were made. The clear alpha among the two was called Neil Henriksson. He was tall, slim but solid, had carefully trimmed hair that was somehow more beige than blond, and an expression that seemed locked in disdain mode. I could just imagine how much fun he had to be around the house. I didn't register the name of his minion.

As they were sitting down, Henriksson said, "OK, Special Agent Reilly, let's start from the beginning, shall we?"

Gallo just turned to them calmly and said, "Special Agent Reilly has taken the Fifth and won't be answering any questions without the presence of his lawyer."

Henriksson's expression shifted dramatically—as in he panned his head around by forty-two degrees.

"Excuse me?"

Gallo said, "You heard me."

The ADIC was going to try to keep me under his roof. Again, not out of any sudden outpouring of empathy for me. It just gave him more to bargain with in terms of limiting the blowback to his CV before giving me up. And it gave me more time to think and figure out what my next step should be.

Henriksson didn't miss a beat. "Maybe you don't quite grasp what we're dealing with here. This isn't a run-of-the-mill murder investigation. This is a matter of national security."

Nick piped in and asked, "How so?"

"Agent Reilly is wanted for questioning in the murder of an employee of the CIA. An employee with significant security access."

"And how is that a matter of national security?"

"Reilly may be working with elements whose aims are as yet

unknown. We need to understand what we're dealing with and whether or not there has been a breach."

Nick nodded sympathetically, then said, "I understand. On the other hand, they might have had a falling out over some chick." He couldn't have said it more flippantly if he tried. Then he added, "Unless you know something more specific you're not sharing with us? Maybe about someone at the agency who goes by the handle of Reed Corrigan? You know, the one this office has put in more than one request about, only to be told he doesn't exist?" He paused for a second, then before Henriksson answered, he said, "Oh, wait, sorry, I know—you can't, 'cause it's classified. Right?"

Henriksson's spine straightened as his gaze bored into Nick. "Like I said, this is a matter of national security. My instructions are to escort Agent Reilly down to Langley where our people and the Arlington County CID can question him."

"He's not going anywhere," Gallo said.

"The man is believed to have shot an employee of the Agency with B-2 clearance," Henriksson fired back. "We need to understand what happened and contain any potential security breach. Urgently."

"Look, I'm with you on this," Gallo replied. "We're on the same side, remember? But my hands are tied. There's due process involved. Right now, all we have is Reilly handing himself in and saying someone tried to kill him. That's all we have right now. He's offering to tell us exactly what happened once his lawyer's around, which should happen sometime this morning. We can't even arrest him yet, not without a formal indictment. You have one?"

Henriksson's jaw tightened visibly, then he said, "Not yet."

"Not to worry. I've got the DA coming in shortly."

"The murder took place in Virginia."

Nick said, "Yeah, but he's up here, isn't he?"

Gallo added, "We need the paperwork sorted out. Until that's ready, our hands are tied. We can't process him—or release him."

Henriksson took a breath, like he was deciding whether or not to share something—or at least wanting to give that impression. Then the jurisdictional tussle resumed. As I watched them argue, my mind took a step back and I couldn't help but take note of how they perfectly encapsulated something I'd noticed years ago regarding the vast distance between the country's agencies and their employees. More often than not, law enforcement seemed to attract passionate races like the Italians and Irish, fiery emotion-driven extroverts with inferiority complexes who shared an unshakeable moral sense bound-up with Catholicism—whether devout or lapsed—and an idea of society rooted in the extended family and a realism that meant being open to people's better nature, even while accepting that humans are fundamentally flawed. The intelligence agencies, on the other hand, seemed to attract a far colder type: Northern Europeans like Henriksson—introverted, dour Puritan ideologues possessing a self-hating superiority, who see family as a tortuous chore to be endured and society as little more than a paranoia-inducing crowd of sinners who need to be permanently spied upon and are, even when under 24/7 watch, still sinning in their minds.

I also started to get antsy, like this wasn't going to work out how Nick imagined. I started to think that I might have to find my own way out of here, which wouldn't be easy—except that I knew the place inside out. Which meant that although I knew how virtually impossible it would be to escape, I was probably as qualified as it gets to find some minute weakness and exploit it.

Gallo and Nick stood their ground and won—for now. I wasn't going anywhere yet. Henriksson and his minion were led out by Gallo while Nick stayed behind.

"You must be starving," he said. "I'll get you something."

I nodded, wearily, "Thanks." I wanted to also thank him for fighting for me, but I was still smarting from his bringing me in. Then my tiredness fell away long enough for me to remember what I needed from him first.

"Forget the food for a second," I told him as I checked my watch. "Tess should have landed by now."

"She's coming in, right?"

"Later, she's going home first," I said, then I pointed up at the cameras. "Are they still off?"

Nick nodded.

I dropped my voice anyway and leaned in. "I need you to do

something first. I need my laptop secured. I don't want anyone tampering with it."

"You want to call her and . . . ?" He didn't need to finish his thought aloud.

"No." I kept my voice down. "I don't want her implicated in any way, I don't want to give anyone any cause to hassle her." I looked at him.

"What, you want me to . . . ?"

"I want you to keep it safe. We can do this officially. I'll give you my formal consent to search my house for evidence. Go there on the basis that you're bringing her in. Talk to her; tell her what's going on. Try to give her some reassurance. And take care of that too."

He held my gaze, then nodded. "OK."

Despite everything, despite the hurricane of conflicting emotions raging inside me, I had to admit it was a bit of a relief to have him there, as my partner, knowing the whole story, looking out for me. I missed having my partner riding shotgun alongside me. I missed this.

Maybe, one of these days, I'd forgive him after all.

# 17

*Ocracoke, North Carolina*

"I just heard from our people in New York. They're playing hard ball," Tomblin informed Roos over their encrypted phones.

Gordon Roos was fuming, but, as always, he never showed it. He was too busy moving chess pieces in his head, anticipating reactions and counter-reactions and deciding on how best to handle the crisis that had mushroomed around them.

At least they knew more than they did before the screw-up in Arlington: Reilly had found himself a weak link inside the CIA and had leaned on him to help him find Roos. That leak was now plugged, and Reilly was being blamed for it. That wasn't a bad result at all. But having Reilly in FBI protective custody—that was far from ideal.

"We need to get him out of their hands fast," Tomblin added, "shut him up before someone starts taking his blabbing seriously."

"Or we take care of him while he's in there."

"That's the other option. Riskier, of course."

"Do we have any assets in place?"

"A couple of promising candidates," Tomblin said.

Roos knew he could count on the man's judgment. Edward J. Tomblin wasn't just Roos's partner back when Roos was an active agent, as well as his oldest friend. He was also a very capable man, one of a handful of top-level CIA employees to have survived six administrations.

They had both been recruited by the CIA straight from college in 1969 and immediately sent with the legend of medical aid workers to the self-declared Republic of Biafra, where they had forged an unbreakable bond in the ocean of blood that had engulfed south-eastern Nigeria. Although their individual reactions to the atrocities they witnessed there were different—Roos experiencing the first flush of the kill-or-be-killed mindset that had defined him from that point on, while Tomblin established the Zen-like detachment that would serve him equally well, but with fewer heart attacks—both had emerged with the absolute conviction that they could survive anything.

In the forty-odd years since their first posting, this had indeed proved to be true. Together they had survived the final few months of the Vietnam War, the killing fields of Cambodia and Angola, followed by a few years at the spearhead of the Cold War, where they'd first used the two code names of "Reed Corrigan" for Roos and "Frank Fullerton" for Tomblin.

It was around that time that the Janitors were born. They'd achieved so much with that small, covert unit, work they were proud of. Work that had kept the nation safe. And then, after 9/11, their paths had diverged. While the country's intelligence agencies came under fire, smaller conflicts were brewing and boiling over around the planet. Roos saw the potential to bail on the political infighting and cash in on his connections and expertise by going private. He started hiring himself out to various governments and corporate interests and raked in serious fees.

Tomblin, on the other hand, was less of an adventurer and preferred to weather the storms and stay at the agency. He did well. In fact, he hadn't possessed an official public job title since 2005, which was when the CIA's National Clandestine Service was first created in the aftermath of 9/11 and the Iraq War. The NCS didn't do "public." It was the covert, deep-dark arm of an organization that wasn't exactly an open book itself, and followed an even more aggressive approach to keeping the nation safe. Under its official remit, it had "the national authority for the coordination, de-confliction, and evaluation of clandestine operations across the Intelligence Community of the United States," meaning it could pretty much do anything it wanted. As the NCS's Deputy Director, Tomblin oversaw five of its main divisions. This included the Special Activities Division, which conducted both overt action such as paramilitary raids and assassinations in denied areas, and covert action such as PSYOP—Psychological operations.

And it was because of one aspect of PSYOP—namely, mind control, something they'd both been involved in years earlier, in CIA programs such as MK-Ultra—that they were both in this mess.

Because of a young boy's father who just won't let go.

Roos had brought this calamity down upon them all—on

himself, on Tomblin, and most of all, on the man who initially put together and ran the Janitors unit, the man who stood to lose more than either of them.

"All right," he told Tomblin. "I'm expecting an update from Sandman within the hour. Let's review then."

"OK." Tomblin paused, then said, "Reilly has several pressure points we can use, Gordo. And we know how much he treasures them. Especially the woman and the boy."

Roos smiled inwardly. "That's exactly what I was thinking."

# 18

*Mamaroneck, New York*

Maxed out on caffeine in a vain attempt to counteract a night of maximum stress and zero sleep, Aparo arrived on the tree-lined street on which Reilly and Tess's house stood and parked his Ford Taurus in front of the three Evidence Response Team vehicles.

He climbed out and went to talk to Max Goodman, the Special Agent in charge of the ERT, who was emerging from a GMC Yukon parked a little farther down the street.

Aparo waved as he approached. "Just give me half an hour, OK?"

He'd called Goodman and asked him to wait till he arrived at the house, making it clear that the inhabitants were a Bureau family and that, right now, his partner wasn't guilty of anything except fleeing a crime scene.

Goodman shook his head. "You said wait till you arrive, and you're here now. We need to go in."

Aparo lowered his voice, trying the conciliatory approach first. "Look, Max, the lady only stepped off the red-eye an hour ago. Let me go in first and talk her through it before your guys go storming in."

Goodman wasn't impressed. "You shouldn't be anywhere near this case. You're his partner for Christ's sake! Now get out of my way so I can do my job."

Aparo put a hand on Goodman's arm. "Come on, Max. She's got her mom and two kids in there. A teenage girl and a five-year-old boy. Isn't that the same age as your kid? How'd you feel if you were in their place? You wouldn't want your kid going through something like that, would you?"

Goodman didn't reply.

"They'll be heading off to school in a few minutes," Aparo added. "That's all I'm asking."

Aparo knew this was the moment it went one of two ways. Either Goodman felt a sizeable stab of sympathy when he imagined his boy looking on as armed storm troopers went through his family home from top to bottom, or the mere mention of the guy's son in this context risked further harsh words at best, or a fist swung at his face.

Goodman went quiet for a moment then said, "OK. Go. I'll wait till the kids are gone."

Aparo hid his smile with an earnest expression of sincere gratitude. "Done. I owe you. And do me a favor, keep the guys out of sight until the kids are gone."

Tess had arrived home about half an hour earlier, her stress levels off the chart. The Evidence Response Team vehicles were already parked out on the street, though Aparo had texted her to say that no one would try to enter the house before he got there himself.

Her mom was already well into the school routine, with both Kim and Alex finishing their breakfast while Eileen made their lunches. Right now, the kids were oblivious to the events of the past twelve hours. Although Tess knew this couldn't last, she wanted to see Reilly face to face before she decided what to tell them. Her mom, on the other hand, knew something was wrong the second Tess had called her from La Guardia to say she'd landed—way earlier than expected. Eileen had lived through enough of Reilly and Tess's misadventures to know when to ask and when to stay quiet. So far, she hadn't asked, but Tess could read the worry simmering behind her stoic expression.

As Tess tried to help with the lunches—despite her mom trying to brush her away—the doorbell chimed.

She froze, then forced herself to snap out of it. She gave her mom a knowing look. "I'll get it."

She glanced at the kids as she headed out of the kitchen. Alex was oblivious, his concentration locked on the box of cereal. Kim, on the other hand, seemed fully aware that something was very wrong. Her questioning eyes followed Tess out of the room, but much to Tess's relief, Kim seemed to grasp her mother's unspoken desire to not discuss it just yet.

Feeling sick to her stomach, Tess went to the door and looked through the spy hole.

Aparo. Alone.

She opened the door and let out a breath of relief. "Nick."

He stepped inside.

She spotted the ERT guys outside as she shut the door behind him. The sight rattled her and her voice went shaky. "What's going on, Nick? What the hell is this?"

He stepped closer and took her in his arms for a big hug, patting her across the shoulder. "We'll get through this. It's going to be fine."

She pulled back and nodded, wiped her face, then motioned for Aparo to follow her into the study, where she closed the door after them.

Aparo remained standing. "I need Sean's laptop."

"Why?"

"He wants it out of here so no one messes with it. I can't do it, though. I didn't walk in with anything. Can you carry it out? The ERT guys will be watching us leave, so it needs to look casual."

Tess looked at her MacBook Air, open on the aluminum desk.

"We've got identical machines. Different specs, but same on the outside. I'll just say it's mine if anyone asks."

She went over to a large set of drawers and pulled out another MacBook Air, which she slid into a pink slip case. Then she closed the open laptop and put it in the drawer.

As she stuffed the pink slipcase into her leather shoulder bag, she heard her mother say, "We're off."

"Hang on."

She stepped out of the study, found Eileen, Kim and Alex in the kitchen. Avoiding her daughter's scrutinizing gaze, Tess put on her best carefree smile.

"See you later, guys. Soak up that knowledge."

"Mom—" Kim said, but Tess cut her off.

"I'll see you later, baby," she said as she leaned in and kissed her on the temple.

"Where's Daddy?" Alex asked.

Tess glanced down at him. Curiously, he seemed worried as well. It was almost like he could also sense the tension, which, given his age, surprised Tess.

She bent down to his level and straightened the collar of his coat. "He went straight to his office, but he said to tell you he misses you a lot. Both of you. Now go on, or you'll be late."

She gave Alex a kiss and watched them all head out into the garage, then she hurried back to the study.

"OK," she told Nick, "talk to me. What the hell is going on?"

"The guy Sean's been after all this time? The guy that had Alex brainwashed?"

"Reed Corrigan."

"Yeah. Sean won't accept that Corrigan is a ghost. He's still trying to find the bastard. That's why he went to see that guy in Arlington—the guy who got shot. His name was Stan Kirby. He worked for the CIA."

Tess's eyes went wide. "Sean's accused of killing a CIA agent?"

"As things stand, yes. Well, not exactly—Kirby wasn't a field agent. He was an analyst."

"But he didn't do it, right?"

"Of course he didn't. And we're going to help him prove that. We're going to do everything we can to find Kirby's real killer. And I'm going to do everything I can to find Corrigan, because finding him may be the only way to prove Sean's innocence. Everything else is on hold as of last night."

A sense of utter dread chilled her to the core. "Sean couldn't find him, Nick. What makes you think you can?"

"Sean was doing this alone, on the side. I'm going to use something Sean didn't—the entire resource of the Bureau. I'll even go see the president if I have to."

That last sentence leapt from Sandman's earpiece and anchored itself firmly inside Sandman's mind.

Aparo could turn into another problem, he thought.

He was parked around a corner a hundred yards down from Reilly and Tess's place. As he listened to the conversation taking place in the house, Sandman could just picture Tess Chaykin's mind racing. He didn't have video—cameras, even the tiniest pinhole ones being used for covert surveillance nowadays, had been deemed too much of a risk, in terms of detection. Someone with a keen eye like Reilly might spot them. Audio, on the other hand, was much easier to conceal and yielded the same results.

"So Sean's been digging into this the whole time?" she said. "Since he brought Alex to live with us?"

"Yep," he heard Aparo reply.

"And he didn't tell you?"

"No. And believe me, I asked. I asked a lot."

"Why wouldn't he tell you?"

"To help me keep my job. And maybe keep me out of prison. Same goes for you, I guess."

"Why?"

"He was leaning on Kirby. The guy was sleeping with his wife's sister."

"Charming."

A sentiment with which Sandman concurred.

Aparo didn't comment. Instead, he added, "He's had someone helping him out, but he won't say who. Any ideas?"

Sandman listened as Tess thought about it, his senses alert to a key piece of the puzzle possibly dropping into his lap—then Tess said, "No."

Sandman frowned. Still, a couple of major gaps in Reilly's backstory with Kirby had been filled. And he thought he knew where he might find the rest of the answers he was looking for.

Tess let out a tired breath. "I knew something was eating him. All these months . . . I thought it was this stuff about his dad."

"That's part of it too. Or at least Sean believes it is. He's got it into his head that there's a connection between Corrigan and his dad. He thinks maybe Corrigan had something to do with his dad's suicide."

Tess couldn't process what she was hearing. It was all so farfetched. As a plot for one of her novels, she would have dismissed it out of hand. But she also knew that reality often trumped fiction—that there are things that happen in real life that are so bizarre and unexpected they'd never allow for the suspension of disbelief necessary to retell them as a story.

"I need to hear it from him."

"Of course. That's where we're going."

"OK. Let me grab my things."

She retrieved her iPad from the kitchen and picked up a more formal jacket from the closet in the front hall. And as she headed for the front door, Tess felt a combination of dull fury and desperate sadness. Anger that the man she loved had needed to conceal all this from her—even if it was to protect her—and sorrow that she hadn't been able to help him deal with his frustration and uncertainty.

She would do all she could to help now.

They left the house together, Aparo waving his thanks to a tall guy in shades and an FBI windcheater.

She climbed into Aparo's car and left her house to the mercy of the Evidence Response Team.

Sandman heard his encrypted phone ring as he watched Aparo's unmarked drive past him.

"Are you still at the target's house?" the voice asked.

"Yes. His woman and his partner just drove off."

"There's another player. We need to find him."

"I'm on it."

"We need that laptop."

"I figured as much. Engagement protocol?" Sandman asked.

"The partner is expendable," the voice informed him in an even tone.

"The woman?"

"Optional."

"Copy that."

Sandman cut the call, fired up the engine, and pulled away from the curb.

# 19

The pit of Aparo's stomach was yelling at him.

He hadn't eaten since he'd shared a Chinese take-out delivery with his latest playmate, food they had burnt off shortly afterwards by a couple of hours of mutual cardio workout. And much as he'd enjoyed that, much as he was looking forward to seeing her again, he was glad he'd turned down her offer to spend the night, as it meant he'd been there in his partner's hour of need.

He turned to Tess. "I haven't eaten since yesterday. Anywhere we can stop for me to grab a bite?"

"There's a nice café just after the CVS up ahead. They do decent take-out sandwiches."

A quarter of a mile later, Aparo pulled into a parking space.

"Can I get you anything?"

"I'm good," Tess replied.

"Did you eat this morning? It's probably going to be a long day."

Tess shook her head. "I'm OK, thanks."

"A coffee at least?"

She smiled. "No, Mom."

"O-kay."

Aparo climbed out and walked toward the café.

He reached the door just ahead of a guy in a fedora and a heavy winter coat who was heading in too. Aparo nudged the door open behind him so it didn't swing back into the man's path.

The place was clearly popular. Many of the small tables were taken by singles or duos, several of them working at their laptops. Aparo went straight to the counter, where three people were ahead of him. He glanced at the list of offerings as he waited his turn, then ordered the special: sausage and tomato omelet in a baguette, with a large coffee, black.

"Double quick, please," he said as he handed a ten dollar bill to the ponytail/goatee in the black T-shirt behind the counter. "And keep the change."

He stepped aside to let the guy in the fedora order.

As he waited, he scrolled through his messages and emails. His inbox was heaving, but there was nothing there that couldn't wait till he was at the office.

His attention was diverted by a waitress behind the counter who was holding out two brown-paper bags. "Bacon on rye . . . and an omelet baguette."

Aparo reached for his order, but as he took it, the guy in the fedora reached across him, knocking Aparo's bag to the floor.

"Oh Jeez, I'm sorry," the man said, shaking his head with clear embarrassment. He stooped to pick it off the floor, fussing over it, muttering "I'm such a klutz sometimes," as he brushed it down before turning to face Aparo and handing it back to him. "I'm really sorry. Let me buy you a replacement."

Aparo glanced at it. The sandwich was longer than the bag, it's edge poking out of it. It might have touched the floor, but barely. Also, time was an issue. He was in a rush to get to Federal Plaza. "No, it's fine."

"You sure?"

"Sure."

The man relaxed a touch. "OK. Sorry, again." He touched his hat in an old-school gesture of deference.

Aparo waved him off with a "No problemo," took his coffee from the outstretched hand of the waitress, then left the café, bag already open and baguette on its way to being chowed down.

By the time he got back to the car, half the baguette was already in his belly.

Tess couldn't resist sending her mother a text to see how the kids' school run had gone.

The message was pointless and Tess knew it. She was just taking a momentary break from the bigger situation looming over her and finding a touch of solace in obsessing over the mundane. Her mom had, predictably, fired back one of her signature replies, informing Tess that everything was miraculously fine and that she was looking forward to a nice mug of coffee with her as soon as her circumstances allowed it. Her mom hadn't used quote marks around circumstances. She hadn't needed to. Tess saw them anyway.

She watched as Aparo climbed back into the Taurus with a coffee in one hand and an open sandwich bag in the other. He was wolfing it down.

"Hungry much?" she asked.

"Just what the doctor ordered," he just about managed in between mouthfuls as he put the vehicle into drive.

They hopped onto I-95 and joined the stream of traffic heading south toward the city.

Tess's mind was all over the place, exploring all kinds of scenarios about what awaited her and Reilly. She didn't say much, and Aparo was busy polishing off the baguette and the coffee.

They'd been on the interstate for about ten minutes when Aparo winced. She'd noticed it after she spotted him scrunch up the bag and throw it over his shoulder onto the back seat. It was a habit she imagined was common to all FBI agents due to long hours spent on stake outs but one she'd managed to talk Reilly out of, at least when it came to the family car.

Aparo grimaced with pain.

"You OK?" she asked.

"Heartburn." He balled his fist and slammed it into his chest, moving his left shoulder up and down in an attempt to alleviate his discomfort. "I think I've got a bottle of water in the back somewhere, can you pass it over?"

"Sure." She bent around and rummaged through the clutter on the back seat and found an half-empty bottle. She handed it over just as Aparo clutched at his chest with his left hand and gasped.

"Jesus! Are you all right?"

His right hand was still firmly on the wheel.

"Yeah. It's nothing. Just zero sleep, an empty stomach, stuffing my face and—"

He moaned as his head lolled back against the headrest and his right arm went slack, sending the car swerving into the passing lane.

"Nick!"

Tess grabbed the wheel, fighting to steer the car back into the center lane. An SUV blew past to their left, barely missing them.

"Jesus! Nick! Wake up!"

She yanked the wheel too fast, causing the Taurus to bounce off a semi speeding past on the inside lane and hurtle across back toward the median divider. A cacophony of squealing brakes and panicked horns filled her ears as the car cut across a flatbed truck, clipped a compact and bounced off it.

Tess watched in horror as the compact careened back into the inside lane, slamming into a panel van that had swerved to avoid them.

There was no way she was going to reach the brake pedal. She swung the wheel away from her and the car flew across the lanes again and into the divider. Sparks flew from the screeching interface of car and metal, but the vehicle was still traveling too fast.

Glancing over her shoulder to see if the cars immediately behind her were anywhere close, she slammed the Taurus into neutral and pulled the handbrake.

The car fishtailed as it began to slow, noise and smoke filling her senses before it finally came to a stop about a hundred yards farther on.

Tess screwed up her eyes and breathed a sigh of relief, then turned to Aparo. He wasn't breathing. The driver's door was wedged against the divider. A trail of damaged cars and trucks littered the highway behind her, and to her right was a now-slow stream of traffic, all of it trying to avoid the pile up that was now blocking the inside lane. There was no way for her to get out of the car safely.

She reached over the prone agent and released the lever to throw his seat back, then clambered onto him and started CPR.

"Nick! Wake up! Do you hear me? Wake up!"

Aparo didn't move.

She tried again.

Some air hissed from between his lips, but there was no gasp or cough to signal that he'd started breathing for himself again.

She raised her right first and hammered it down onto Aparo's chest. Then again.

"Come on!" She pounded, again and again.

With no result.

# 20

Tess's heart broke as the deepest of all primal instincts told her that the man sitting beside her was now gone, and never coming back.

She rolled off Aparo and fell back into her seat, her head throbbing from where it had slammed against something during the mayhem.

Up ahead, a grey sedan had pulled into the lane in front of her. Its driver, a man with short hair and a thick coat, was already walking back toward the Taurus. There was something vaguely familiar about him, but her mind was too flooded with stimuli to be any clearer than that. Within seconds, he was near by her door and looking in.

"Are you all right?"

She stared at him, still shaken and dazed, and didn't answer at first.

"Miss? Are you all right?"

He yanked against the door handle, but the door was locked. He pointed at the inside of the panel.

"Can you unlock the door? Miss?" He was mouthing the words more clearly now, like he thought she couldn't hear him. "You need to unlock the door."

His words sank in and she pulled the door handle. The door creaked open.

The man helped her out. "What happened? Are you all right?"

"I don't know," she stuttered. "He just—he just stopped breathing." She was on the brink of tears.

"Let me have a look," he said, ushering her away from the door so he could climb inside the car.

Tess didn't move. She was still in shock and couldn't peel her eyes off Aparo's still body. Then a thought cut through the haze and she pulled out her phone to dial 911.

"Miss," the man was saying. "Can you step aside?"

She raised her gaze at him, his words at the edge of her consciousness—and she nodded. As she moved aside to let him past and her finger was about to hit the call button, she heard a siren behind her. A Highway Patrol car speeding down the empty passing lane toward them and pulling up just behind the mangled sedan, the lights on its roof rack still flashing.

She watched the uniform step out of his car, then noticed the man beside her step away from her and head back to his car. He turned to glance at her as he walked off, gave her a little knowing nod, then got in his car and drove off.

"You OK, miss?" the patrolman was asking.

She turned, nodded, and, still foggy-brained, called Federal Plaza.

Deutsch was listening to Gallo and Lendowski argue about Reilly's gun and the prints report that had come in from the DC Field Office when her desk phone lit up.

It was the switchboard. "I've got a call here for Agent Reilly," the operator said. "What are we doing with his calls?"

"Put it through."

Deutsch didn't recognize the voice at first. It was a woman, and her tone was urgent. "I need to speak to Sean. This is Tess. Tess Chaykin. Something terrible's happened. Please."

Deutsch's spine tightened. "Miss Chaykin, this is Agent Deutsch. What happened? Where are you?"

"I'm . . . I'm somewhere on I-95. We were on our way down to Federal Plaza, Nick and me, and—there was an accident. Nick, he's—he's dead."

Deutsch felt the blood literally drain from her face and she just froze, the surreal words echoing inside her without finding purchase. After a moment, she barely managed to ask, "Nick's dead?"

She could hear Tess's voice break as her weak reply came back. "He's dead. I'm right here next to him. He's—he's gone."

It can't be, Deutsch thought. It can't—and yet, it was true. Just like that. It had to be. Tess was not a flake.

Aparo was gone.

"Jesus," Deutsch managed, "but—how? I don't—"

"He just—I don't know, it's like he had a heart attack or an embolism or something. He just went. Just like that. He was driving, and—we hit the barrier."

"What about you—are you OK?"

"I'm all right. I wasn't hurt. But I need to speak to Sean. Oh my God, Nick's son. We need to tell Lisa."

"Hang on."

She looked up, and through eyes that seemed resolutely unwilling to focus clearly, she saw that Gallo and Lendowski were still locked in heavy discussion. She cupped the phone's mouthpiece.

"Hey," she called out to them, then shouted, angrily, "Hey."

They both turned, visibly surprised by her outburst.

She sat there in silence for a moment, still processing it and not quite sure how to say it. When she spoke, her voice was so quiet it was almost inaudible.

"It's about Aparo. He's . . . he's dead."

She saw their expressions cloud up, gave them a second to let it sink in, then added, quickly, as she held up the phone, "I've got Tess Chaykin on the line. Reilly's wife—his partner," she corrected herself. "She was with him. They were in a car crash. She's in shock and she needs to talk to Reilly." She focused on Gallo. "OK if I take him the call?"

Gallo looked at her, confusion lining his face, as he steadied himself against Lendowski's desk. Then he said, "Sure. Go ahead."

She nodded, told the operator to transfer the call to her cell phone, and rushed toward the interview room.

She was at the keypad when her cell phone rang. She took the call as she keyed in the code, trying to keep her voice even, to stay professional. "Miss Chaykin? I'm passing him over to you, hang on."

The doors slid open. Reilly—she still couldn't get used to calling him Sean—was in his chair, scowling at the wall.

"I've got Tess. Something awful's happened."

Reilly rose to his feet and grabbed her cell phone. "Tess?"

Deutsch watched as he listened, his eyes filling with disbelief, then horror, then the unmistakable glistening of tears.

## 21

I felt like every muscle in my body was trying to rip its way out through my skin.

A raging, boiling centrifuge of blistering anger, bottomless grief and creeping dread had me unable to form a coherent thought beyond that brutal, soul-crushing realization, much less decide what to do next.

The doors slid open and Lendowski came in with a coffee and a sandwich.

"Gallo told me to bring you this," he said. Because, of course, he'd never have done it without clear instruction from a superior. Like I didn't know that.

He placed the coffee mug and sandwich down on the table.

I asked, "Any news on Nick?"

I could see him adjusting his attitude—partners were sacred, even if you had good reason to hate one half of said partnership. Plus he and Nick were gym buddies.

"Were"—not "are."

Surreal.

"Still waiting on the postmortem," he said, "but it sounds like he had a heart attack."

I pulled the coffee toward me, tore off the lid and took a gulp, the burning sensation at the back of my throat dulling the deeper, more intractable pain, which had needle-sharp tentacles smothering every nerve ending.

I took another sip, fuming at the idea of his pointless death.

"He treats his body like a dumpster all these years, then, what, six months into this new gym routine and being more careful with his food, this happens?"

Lendowski shrugged. "When your time's up, it's up, right?"

I shook my head in disbelief. I'd heard about guys dropping dead after over-exerting themselves after years of doing nothing and it had always struck me as somewhat absurdly ironic. This was beyond absurd—it was just cruel.

Lendowski scratched his head. "You knew him much better than I did, but like you said, all that junk food, zero exercise and chasing tail, not to mention a high-stress job and a dick for a partner . . . It'll catch up to you."

He couldn't resist the dig, and he smiled as he said it, unwilling to fight over Aparo's corpse.

I wasn't willing to do that either. "Not now, Len. All right?"

He seemed taken aback, then just said, "Sure."

He turned to go, then turned back. "He was a good agent. The Bureau was built on guys like him."

I nodded. "Yep."

"There but for the grace of God, you know what I'm saying?"

I just shrugged and Lendowski keyed in the code and left the room.

I was hungry, not having eaten since the train ride down to DC, which was—how many hours ago? I'd lost track. Still, I couldn't face that sandwich. Nick and I had been partners for more than ten years. Apart from all the life-and-death situations we'd been in, the times we'd saved each other's lives, I'd also lived through some great times with him, lots of laughs, lots of long late-night chats, as well as suffering with him through his personal hardships—the problems in his marriage, the women, the divorce . . . and now it was all over, just like that. A friend, a partner, a vibrant man with a hearty appetite for life, a father, an eleven-year-old son's dad, gone in the blink of an eye. Snuffed out.

Hard to accept.

I know, we're all heading that way. The only question is when. I thought of Nick's son, Lorenzo. Eleven years old. A year older than I was when my dad died. I knew what he'd be going through. I'd need to try to be there for him, when—if—I ever managed to get my life back on track. Lisa, his ex-wife, would need our help too. Despite everything, they'd still spent fifteen years together, twelve as husband and wife, eleven as parents, and that doesn't go away, not unless there was a major hurt involved, and there wasn't. She'd be hurting now, I was sure. It just made me angrier that I was in here, not there, with them, helping them through this.

Selfishly perhaps, it also made me think about Tess again. About our life together. About Alex and Kim. About whether or not I was really living the life I wanted.

The twister spinning inside me was throwing out all kinds of wild thoughts. What I still couldn't get my head around was the timing of the shooter appearing in Arlington, as in: why kill me now? That had been their plan after all. Kirby was just collateral damage—fortunate collateral damage, at that. I mean, I'd been chasing after Corrigan for months, so why had it taken him this long to deal with me? Kurt and I had been treading water. No, something else must have forced Corrigan's hand, and if that thing was mission critical enough to decide to send me to an early grave, it was unlikely anything would be allowed to screw with the plan—meaning they still needed me dead.

Even with Corrigan's reach, his design was beyond the resource of one man. He had to have help beyond feet on the ground, someone inside the CIA. The question was, how many of them was I up against?

When it came to colleagues, the preference among spooks seemed to be either long-term allegiances or selling them out for short-term advantage, with nothing much in between. Corrigan's inside man at the CIA could even be "Frank Fullerton," his partner back in the day, according to the files Kirby had given me—or whatever his name really was. Kurt and I had got nowhere with Fullerton either. Maybe it was worth putting Gigi on his trail.

And then, something that had tugged at the back of my head since Deutsch had handed me her cell almost an hour earlier, started to crystallize more fully.

My "deep throat" not showing up at Times Square. The bearded man at Kirby's. The CIA at Defcon One over an analyst, meaning they knew he leaked the files. And yet they'd waited until now to do something about it. What had changed?

The call from my "deep throat."

That had to be what had them spooked. But he hadn't yet given me anything.

Maybe they thought he had.

And then Nick dies. Just after he swore he was going to leave no stone unturned and push the Bureau into doing everything it could to help me. This made him more dangerous to them than I was, and two questions were clawing at me: one, could Corrigan have known just how dedicated Nick now was—I closed my eyes, *had been*—to tracking him down, and two, could they have killed him?

Impossible.

But the coincidence in the timing was hard to ignore.

I mean, if they'd poisoned him somehow, it would show up in the postmortem. But if they did, if they could kill Nick that easily, what was to stop them killing me where I sat? Especially without having him to look out for me?

I stared at the coffee, then at the sandwich, and decided to leave them where they sat.

I had to get out of here.

Deutsch could see the accident scene up ahead.

The whole southbound carriageway was closed and would be for at least another hour. Surprisingly, it seemed that Aparo was the only fatality, though she'd heard that occupants of a few of the other vehicles involved had suffered some superficial injuries and one broken leg.

She left her car at the cordon, flashed her badge and hurried toward a cluster of smashed-up vehicles, Highway Patrol cars and ambulances, one of which headed off noisily as she approached, ferrying more injured to the ER at White Plains Hospital.

A striking woman with curly blond hair was sitting on the tailgate of a Westchester EMS ambulance, an ice pack against her head. An EMT had just finished checking her over and a state trooper stood a few feet away, talking into his radio. It looked like he was waiting to take the woman's statement.

From the author photographs on the dust jackets of her books, Deutsch knew this was Tess Chaykin—and she could see why Reilly had fallen for her. Even after living through the past couple of hours, there was a poise and self-possession about her that seemed almost otherworldly. A poise she needed to regain herself.

She showed her badge to the state trooper. "Give me a couple minutes, will you?" The trooper nodded, and Deutsch walked over to the woman. "Miss Chaykin?"

Tess looked up, and Deutsch immediately noticed her warm green eyes. She pictured her and Reilly and felt a quiver of jealousy, then chastised herself as she remembered that the woman's partner was languishing in a holding cell and suspected of murder.

"Tess," the woman replied.

Deutsch held out her hand.

"I'm Annie Deutsch. We talked on the phone."

Tess shook her hand. "You're the agent with the jackass for a partner, right? At a bar the other night."

Deutsch found the stirring of a smile. "Yes. Reilly was very . . . chivalrous. How's your head?"

"Sore, but the EMT says it's not a concussion."

"That's something."

An uncomfortable silence settled over them for a moment, then Deutsch asked, "Where have they taken Nick?"

"He's on his way to White Plains," Tess told her.

Deutsch nodded, staring into the distance, following the ambulance's ghostly wake. "They'll need to do a postmortem."

Tess looked crushed, the finality of Aparo's death clearly still hitting her hard.

Deutsch asked, "What happened?"

"I don't know. One second he was fine, then he just . . . went." She paused, then said, "I need to see Sean."

"I'm here to drive you back, but before we go," Deutsch said as she gestured at the waiting patrolman, "they need you to give a statement."

Tess nodded, then repositioned the ice pack on her head. "I'll make it quick."

It wasn't the best plan I'd ever come up with, or the safest.

In fact, it was definitively one of the craziest, most borderline demented ideas I'd ever thought up.

Right now, I had nothing else.

So I took a deep breath and called out for Gallo.

Two minutes later, a junior agent who's name I couldn't remember brought me a phone and sat across the table from me to wait till I was done.

I called Tess's cell. She answered immediately.

"Sean?"

"Are you OK?"

"I'm fine. Sean . . . God, it was horrible. I can't believe he's—" I heard the dam burst and she started to sob.

I let her feel it for a few seconds.

"Tess, I'll see you soon. Annie's going to bring you over. OK?"

"Lisa . . ." she said, referring to Nick's ex-wife. "Someone needs to tell her. And Lorenzo . . . my God."

"I'll take care of it," I told her. "I'll call her. You've been through enough for now."

"OK," she said, her breath catching.

I gave her a moment to regroup. I needed her to get what I was going to say.

"It's all just," I finally said, "crazy. It's like the stars are aligned against me lately. Like what you were saying, the other night. About karma and our past lives. Remember?"

I heard Tess hesitate and was silently willing her to get it—given that we hadn't talked about anything like that anytime recently.

*Please, Tess. Focus. Be my wingman on this.*

"Of course I do," she said.

*Good girl. Great girl.*

"Maybe I did something in the past that I'm paying for now. I mean, how else can you explain all the crap that's been happening to us?" I paused, more to add a bit of drama for the junior agent's benefit than out of need. "I wish I could go back and find out. You know what I'm saying?"

It took her a couple of seconds, then she said, "You think that would be useful?"

She was reading me.

"I think it would. Big time." I thought I'd add an extra hint, just to make sure. "It's like what Nick always used to say—"

I heard the confusion in her tone. "What?"

Almost imperceptibly, I slowed my words, subtly altering my tone—not so the junior agent could notice any change, but enough that someone I'd spent thousands of hours with would notice.

"He used to say: 'Close, but *no cigar.*' Well, that's me right now. No cigar. And with Nick gone, I need every *grain* of help I can get . . ." I slipped straight back to normal speed and tone. "I need that cigar, Tess. Doesn't have to be a whole cigar—just a couple of puffs, to give me hope." I paused. "You understand what I'm saying, right?"

I could hear the cogs in her brain engaging, spinning around and clicking into place.

"You know where that expression comes from, don't you?" she said, her voice shaky. I knew this was all for Deutsch's benefit, because Tess was now—I hoped—covering for the fact that she knew exactly what I was trying to tell her. "They used to hand out cigars as prizes at fairgrounds. Back when the games of strength were for grown-ups. So when you slammed the giant hammer down on the metal plate and the bell didn't ring, the guy would say 'Close, but no cigar!'"

"You should put that in your next book."

"Maybe . . . OK, I'll see you shortly—I just need to go back to the house first. I . . ." her voice softened and got a bit muffled, as if her mouth was closer to the phone now. "I need to change. I kind of messed myself up during the whole thing. Do you mind if Annie drives me home first?"

I felt a small twinge of relief as I pictured her saying that while looking at Deutsch, who'd be nodding sympathetically.

Relief—and hope.

She'd definitely got my message.

# 22

Tess kept her nerves in check as Annie Deutsch swept the Chevy into the employee entrance by the small playground at Federal Plaza.

She'd never done anything like this before—anything that could land her with some serious jail time. She tried not to allow the possibility any room to breathe, and kept pounding it back every time it did a Whack-A-Mole on her. She needed to do this.

*Reilly* needed her to do this.

She followed in Deutsch's shadow as the agent escorted her through the busy lobby and across to the line of bulletproof doors that protected the FBI's separate set of elevators. There, Deutsch fast-tracked her through the metal detector and a quick handbag search at security. The pills did trigger a curious pause, but given everything that had happened, it was perfectly normal for her to have some headache capsules with her.

They rode the elevator up in silence, then Tess followed as Deutsch led her through. The floor was quiet, though there were still several agents at their desks. With each step, she felt her strength draining away. It was all becoming more real and more irreversible. She couldn't help but worry if any of it was going to work, and had to suppress a strong urge to turn around and high-tail it out of the building. It was a bad enough risk for Reilly, but she knew she was potentially compromising her own freedom and any chance that Kim and Alex would have of her being around for the next few years. But then she flashed again on all the times that Reilly had saved her life—from the trunk of the car at the Vatican; from the explosives-laden vest in Turkey; from drowning when De Angelis sank the dive boat in the hell of that biblical storm. She owed him this, no matter the cost—and she owed herself the chance of being with the man she'd chosen, both of them free from the terrible weight that was transforming Reilly into someone she barely recognized.

Within minutes, they were at the door of the interview room.

Through the glass, Tess glimpsed Reilly, sitting there in the bare room. He sensed her and looked up, and their eyes met. A gale of mixed emotions rushed through her: a short-lived elation at finally seeing him, being within reach of his arms, his lips, his solid embrace, that was quickly eclipsed by the paralyzing visceral dread of seeing her Reilly, her Special Agent, her uncompromising champion of law and order, locked away like some petty criminal.

Deutsch was about to punch the keypad and usher Tess in to Reilly's interview room when a heavily built man Tess had never met decided to butt in.

"Hold on there, Annie," he said, obviously addressing Deutsch. "I assume this is Reilly's other half?" He looked at Tess. "Miss Chaykin, right?"

Deutsch's fingers hovered at the keypad while Tess studied him, her instincts telling her the guy was bad news.

He put out his hand. "Nat Lendowski," he said. "But everyone calls me Len."

Lendowski. So this was the cretin Reilly had talked about, the guy who'd harassed Deutsch at the bar.

Tess shook his hand warily.

"I'm sorry we're meeting under such grim circumstances," he told her, "but I'm glad you're OK."

Tess nodded politely. "Thanks."

Lendowski indicated the interview room with a flick of his head. "Bet he'll be happy to see you. It's been a long night."

"Been long for us all," Tess replied. She glanced at Deutsch, sending her an unspoken prompt to move along and get her to Reilly.

"OK then," Deutsch said as she turned and started pressing the keypad—

Lendowski interjected, "Hang on, you're not letting her take that in with her, are you?"

Deutsch stopped, and she and Tess turned to face him, momentarily confused.

He was pointing at Tess's handbag.

"Excuse me?" Tess said.

"Your handbag," he told her. "You can't take that in with you."

Deutsch held both palms up, irritated, and said, "Len, for God's sake, are you serious? She was cleared by security—"

"Annie," he interrupted her, firmly. "He's being held for questioning. About a murder."

"His partner just died," Deutsch countered, her tone sharp. "She was in the car with him."

"Irrelevant," he replied. "Security protocols still apply. You remember *them*, don't you?" He wasn't bothering to mask the condescension in his tone.

He kept his gaze on her, and waited.

Tess turned to Deutsch. "It's not a problem."

"No, this is ridiculous—"

"Annie. It's fine," Tess insisted. She peeled the strap off her shoulder and handed her bag over to Lendowski. "I assume it'll be safe with you?"

"I wouldn't be too sure," Annie put in, scowling at her partner.

"I'll guard it with my life," Lendowski grinned.

Tess nodded, then spread her arms out wide, so they were horizontal. "I suppose you're going to want to frisk me too?"

Lendowski went rigid, visibly taken aback by the unexpected offer. Tess just stood there, teasingly, one eyebrow slightly raised, her arms spread wide, her stare locked on him, challenging him, totally serious about it.

She watched as Lendowski's eyes jumped over to Deutsch and back, a flicker of nervousness. He opened his mouth slightly, a lag between that and the words coming out. "No," he said. "That won't be necessary."

"You sure? Protocol and what not?" she goaded him.

"That's fine," he said, somewhat sheepishly.

"OK then." Tess turned to Deutsch, a minuscule glint of victory brightening her face. "Can I see him now?"

"Of course."

Deutsch punched the code in and the door clicked open. The two women stepped inside.

Reilly was already on his feet, and Tess didn't wait for an invitation. She brushed past Deutsch and flung her arms around Reilly's neck, pulling him into a tight embrace and kissing him on the mouth.

"Tess, please," Deutsch told her. "No touching."

"Oh, baby. It's so good to see you," she said as she pulled back, ignoring Deutsch's comment and keeping her arms still around him. She cupped his face with her hands, held them there for a moment, then slid them together behind his neck.

"Thank God you're all right," Reilly told her.

"It was horrible, Sean. Just horrible."

She kept her arms around his neck. Which earned her another rebuke from Deutsch. "Tess. You need to step back from him."

Tess glanced back at her. "Yes, yes, I'm sorry."

She needed to move fast.

What Deutsch couldn't see, what Tess made sure she couldn't see, was what her hands were doing.

Rummaging into the fold of the cuff of her shirt.

Pulling out the two gelatin capsules she'd hidden there during her quick visit to the house, the ones she'd hastily emptied of whatever supplement they contained—turmeric, was it?—before refilling them with the brownish powder she'd taken out of the stainless steel vial Reilly kept tucked away behind a loose panel in his cupboard, the vial he'd brought back from Mexico.

The vial she and Reilly referred to as the "cigar tube."

"*No cigar.*"

The two capsules were now tucked inside her right hand. It was time to pass them to Reilly.

She slid her arms down and took both his hands in hers. "We're going to beat this, right? We're going to get you home soon?"

"Tess," Deutsch repeated. "Come on."

"OK," Tess said, and complied—but not before she'd slipped the two capsules to Reilly.

She sat down in the chair and Reilly did the same in his. Deutsch stayed standing, to one side.

"I'll be home soon. We're going to beat this," Reilly said, his tone calm and reassuring.

"We need to get you a lawyer. A good one. Anyone specific you want to use?"

Reilly glanced at Deutsch, a finger pointing up at the cameras. "Did Gallo agree?" he asked.

Deutsch nodded. "Just while she's in here, yes. They're off."

Reilly acknowledged her reply, then carried on talking to Tess. They talked about Aparo's ex-wife, and Reilly told her he'd spoken to her, told her what had happened. He asked Tess how their own kids were doing, then he filled her in on what had happened since they'd parted at Union Station, told her what had preceded it, repeating his story yet again. They talked about how and what she would tell the kids, and what she'd say to her mom. And throughout it all, the one thought Tess couldn't suppress was wondering about whether or not what Reilly was about to attempt was going to work—or whether he'd survive it.

She didn't want to leave, because leaving meant he would go through with his plan. But after a while, she had to. They both knew it. But before she went, she had to take the role to its conclusion, for Deutsch's benefit. The less they suspected something was going on, the more chances Reilly had to get away with it.

"You couldn't let it be, could you?" she asked him.

"What, let the bastard get away with it?"

"He already has—don't you see that? You're the one who's about to be charged with murder and he's . . . he's a ghost. A mirage." She tried to fake anger, but it was sadness and fear that were now searing through her. "You still don't even know his real name."

She knew they were both walking a tightrope here. It was fortuitous that something they shared was exceptional self-control. Indeed, it was one of the things that first attracted her to Reilly—his immense self-discipline and single-mindedness. But unlike most other positive traits, it was one that could go catastrophically wrong.

His anger as real as hers, though, she knew, similarly controlled, Reilly slammed the table with both fists, but stayed seated.

"Everyone keeps saying leave the past behind, but it's the past that defines us. It makes us who we are and shapes what we become. I don't want my life controlled by the bad things that happened when I was a kid any more than I want Alex's future affected the same way. But the only way to stop that happening is to confront it head on and deal with it before it does that."

"Alex, and Kim . . . they need a father, not an avenging angel."

"It's not vengeance, Tess. It's justice. They're not the same thing."

“Maybe not, but one often pretends to be the other. Especially when it’s the obsession of one man.”

Her eyes were flooding—with anger and hurt, but also with fear.

It was time to go.

She got up, looked over at Deutsch. The agent understood and nodded.

Tess turned to Reilly, bent down and hugged him again, burying her face in his neck.

“Don’t do anything stupid,” she whispered in his ear. “I need you with me. Always.”

“I’ll see you soon,” he replied. “Promise.”

“You’d better,” she said. Then she kissed him, hard and desperate, before tearing herself away and leaving the room.

## 23

I checked my watch—0300 hours.

They'd let me keep it, but only after humorless expressions in response to my joke about the timepiece's frustrating lack of Bond-style garrotes or lasers. I'd be waving it goodbye once I was processed formally and once I was in the system that way, it would be much, much harder to get out.

I had to make my move tonight.

I was lucky to still be here, in a holding cell at Federal Plaza for the night. This wasn't standard procedure, by any means, but by the time Gallo received the formal indictment, it was too late for me to be processed by the Marshal's Service, interviewed by the Pretrial Services Agency, and walked across to the new federal courthouse at 500 Pearl Street which loomed over the classic, hexagonal state courthouse on the east side of Foley Square for presentment before a federal magistrate judge. Best they could manage was to escort me up to the twenty-sixth floor to be photographed and fingerprinted before bringing me back down to the interview room. I needed to be lodged overnight before being taken to be arraigned in the morning. Normally, they would have shipped me over to the MCC, the Metropolitan Correctional Center just across the square, behind the courthouse. But the facility was perennially overpopulated, and whoever was pulling the strings would have ample opportunity to kill me while I awaited my arraignment, with a menu of wide-ranging options: false-flag terrorist, corrupt guard, white-power psychopath or just some poor schmo blackmailed into doing their bidding. I felt it would be much safer to be under this roof for the night, and Gallo grudgingly agreed to keep me there. Everyone was too shaken up by Nick's death anyway, so it was all put on hold until tomorrow. Which suited me fine.

I was moved to a holding cell and given a blanket and a pillow to soften up the hardwood bench.

Not that I cared about any of that.

My mind was totally elsewhere. Mostly thinking of Nick, of course. He was still there vividly inside my head, and I kept finding myself thinking I could ask him to help with this or that before reminding myself that he was gone. I guess it still hadn't sunk in fully.

Mostly, though, it was in the context of what I was about to attempt.

I still had the two capsules in my hand, aware that the more I moved, the more likely it was that I looked like I was concealing something, even in the middle of the night.

Lendowski—I'd seen the agent through the open doors when Tess had left—was probably half-asleep in his chair, but I couldn't risk being seen acting in any way that appeared suspicious. Protocol was to monitor the holding room's audio and video, so even if Lendowski was dozing right now I knew he could easily be wide awake at any moment.

Tess knew where I'd hidden the small stainless steel vial I'd kept in my possession after that nightmare we all went through in Mexico last summer. We'd talked about it a lot, as she was—no surprise there—fascinated by what it contained, the only known sample of the raw, unprocessed drug that countless people had died fighting over, from the adventurer-chemist who had discovered it, to El Brujo, the drug baron who wanted to unleash it on the world.

Good times. Not.

In a tranquil space, the raw drug was supposed to bring about visions that were either genuine memories of that person's past lives, or images at once so timelessly primal and so deeply personal that this was the only way to rationalize them, the alternative being an experience so unbelievably irrational and so threateningly surreal that the mind simply had no way to frame it.

I still wasn't one hundred percent sure exactly where I stood on the matter. One thing I did know, though, was that taking the drug now, in my depleted and exhausted state, would wreak havoc on my body and my mind. I just couldn't see any other way out.

Leaning back in the chair, I carefully took apart the capsules, then I moved both hands up to my face, palms level with my mouth, like someone trying to rub wakefulness into a head that was already more than half-asleep. I popped the capsules into my mouth then swallowed hard, barely managing to force the hard gelatin shells past my esophagus.

My guess was I'd just ingested about a gram of the drug. Thankfully I hadn't tasted it much as I'd swallowed them fast, but what I did taste was vile, somewhere between burnt cabbage and a dog food concoction Purina had rejected. I quickly found myself fighting the urge to gag.

I sat perfectly still, trying to regulate my breathing, waiting for the effects to take hold.

It didn't take long.

Within a few minutes, I felt the urge to vomit. I forced my chin down onto my chest—if I threw up now, the drug wouldn't have time to work and I'd be staying exactly where I was. I clamped my mouth shut and held my breath, willing my stomach to accept the alien mixture. I released the breath as slowly as I could, letting the air escape from my nose while keeping my mouth firmly closed.

I waited as long as I could, then sucked in a lungful of air. My stomach felt like it was trying to expel a barrel-load of psychotic piranhas and I twisted on my chair, trying to resist the urge to stand up and give my insides more space to flip about.

Obviously the drug still had some potency, though exactly what it would do to me next was anyone's guess. I was bargaining on the compound's deeper hallucinatory aspects not kicking in first, giving me a window in which I could put the drug's physiological effect to good use.

I gasped involuntarily from a vicious pain in the back of my throat, a sensation like multiple bee stings. Swallowing hard, I felt like I was finally winning the battle against my stomach's attempt to empty itself.

My extremities had started to perspire. I could feel my palms becoming clammy and beads of sweat starting to pop on my forehead. My temperature was definitely on the rise, even if I was keeping my bile down for now.

The table came up to meet my chest as I doubled over in agony, my abdomen feeling like it had just been slammed by a Lee Mazzilli bat swing.

I couldn't help but yelp from the pain. My throat was burning now, my mouth dry. I felt like I was going to pass out.

If it was going to happen, it needed to happen now.

I started pulling against my cuffs, rattling the chain against the table while forcing my entire body back against the chair.

Staring directly at a camera I filled my lungs then shouted as loudly as I could, "Hey! Hey! I need some help in here!"

The gamble that I'd already absorbed enough of the drug to screw up my metabolism would hopefully pay off, because it was time to eject the contents of my stomach, with maximum choking for full effect.

I relaxed my entire body, focusing everything on the roiling in my stomach and the nausea at the front of my head.

Bile shot out of my mouth as my stomach tried to expel the foreign matter that had only landed there a few minutes earlier.

I balled up my fists and smashed them down against the top of the table. Then again. And a third time.

"Hey! Help me! Anyone!"

My stomach sent a geyser of bile up through my throat and out of my mouth.

I thrashed against the chair, no longer knowing how much of my behavior was natural and how much was for show. I was close to losing the ability to control the situation and that would render the entire plan useless.

From the corner of my eye, I glimpsed the doors slide open and Lendowski run in, closely followed by Deutsch. The rapidly receding part of me that could still think straight noted that this was in my favor.

"What the hell?" Lendowski grabbed my shoulders and pulled me up off the table, ensuring that my airway was clear. I wasn't even aware that I'd slumped forward, but my lungs burnt as I gasped for air. I'd clearly been well on the way to asphyxiation.

"Nice try, buddy, but I'd expect more from you than the old two-fingers."

I gulped down some more air before trying to speak. "I'm not! I'm burning up, Len."

Deutsch stepped toward me, grabbed my face and peered into my eyes. "His pupils are blown and he's running a serious fever."

I fought the intense nausea so I could watch Lendowski's reaction.

"Bullshit. He's fine. Aren't you, Reilly?"

I tried to speak, but all that came out was a loud moan.

"He's made himself barf, that's all it is. It's what all those beanpole models do in the john at restaurants."

Deutsch stood to face her partner. "He needs medical attention. Now."

I retched again. Nothing came up this time, but my insides felt like they were being ripped apart.

I tried to stagger to my feet, but there wasn't enough give in the cuffs and I crashed back down into the chair.

Deutsch was shouting now, "We need to call 911."

"Forget it."

"Len, listen to me. He's in really bad shape and he needs help right now."

I could see Lendowski fuming inside. "Fuck this!"

"It'll be faster to take him ourselves. Presbyterian is less than two miles away. Come on!"

Deutsch uncuffed me, then lifted me upright and grabbed my waist with her right arm, flipping my left arm up and around her shoulders. She was deceptively strong for her size. She glared at Lendowski. "Help me lift him."

They dragged me toward the door, then Lendowski stopped to wipe some vomit from his jacket.

Deutsch turned back, wondering what the hell was going on. "Move!"

Lendowski walked over to the exit and keyed in the code. The doors slid open. I could hear him speed-dialing Gallo. It would take the ADIC at least forty minutes to make it back to Manhattan, so at least I'd be spared his gloating if I failed.

Taking my other arm, Lendowski helped Deutsch march me down the corridor toward the elevator.

Lendowski was finally starting to show some concern. "Jesus, he's shaking like he swallowed a jackhammer."

Deutsch leaned in toward me. "Just breathe, Sean. Breathe."

My whole body was flip-flopping between a lightness that felt like my skin was filled with helium and heaviness so extreme that

I was convinced I would literally sink through the floor and ooze from the ceiling of the floor underneath.

I could feel myself starting to drift out of consciousness. The last thought to crawl across my mind as it shut down was simply this:

*This isn't going to work.*

# 24

I came to with a jolt as Lendowski shoved me into the back seat of his Explorer. Deutsch followed me inside, pushing me upright so I wouldn't choke to death.

It must have been only a couple of minutes, but it felt like hours.

Somehow my head felt absolutely clear—like on those rare occasions when your body is allowed to wake up when it's ready, rather than when your smartphone demands it. But it was much more than that. A lucidity I'd never experienced, as though I were at once inside the moment and outside it, looking in.

*Maybe this is going to work after all.*

Multiple signals hit me at the same time:

My wrists weren't cuffed. Deutsch was right-handed, but she was sitting to my left, directly behind Lendowski. I smelled like a bum. I was about to make things ten times worse than they already were.

Deutsch was thrown backward as the Explorer lurched into drive. She muttered a curse under her breath and fastened her seat belt.

I allowed my head to loll forward.

My left wrist felt Deutsch's forefingers as she tried to find my radial artery.

"His pulse rate is too damn slow. Hurry!"

The vehicle bumped up the ramp and screeched out onto Broadway.

I focused on my breathing, ensuring it was as shallow as I could make it without becoming light-headed.

My temperature had dropped, but I was so soaked in sweat there was no way Deutsch could know this.

I gave thanks that Lendowski had decided not to use the siren. Traffic was sparse on the snow-dusted streets and the icy sidewalks were empty. All a sound-and-light show would have done was attract attention.

We sped south past City Hall Park, my left hand slowly edging its way toward Deutsch's sidearm.

When I looked up to check she hadn't noticed, it wasn't Deutsch I was staring at, but a skinned corpse with pale blue eyes. Its limbs abnormally elongated. Gills either side of its chest and what looked like a long bony fin pressing into the seat from its flayed back. Brackish water seeped from the gill slits.

*What the—?*

I scrunched my eyes shut till my eyeballs ached. When I opened them, I was looking at Deutsch again.

The drug was supposed to make you relive scenes from your past lives. Supposed to—because the only one who had told me they'd experienced it firsthand was the cartel boss El Brujo, admittedly not the most reliable of attestants given how warped his brain had to be after a lifetime's kaleidoscope of drugs. If it actually worked, I'd been hoping for something more along the lines of finding myself in Renaissance Italy or maybe even a romp as a Templar during the Crusades.

This was . . . different. It seemed to be taking me much farther back, maybe to some kind of primordial state of existence—or it was just mining the deepest, dormant trenches of my imagination.

I went through my options, hoping the crazy-ass visions would abate for a few minutes. I could point a gun at Deutsch, but there was a sizeable chance Lendowski would simply call my bluff, which would do me no good at all as I had zero intention of seriously harming either of them.

Aim at Lendowski first and Deutsch was liable to attempt to reclaim her gun, which could get very messy indeed.

I needed the vehicle roadworthy, but I quickly realized I had no option but to crash it.

Something was tugging at my ankle. I looked down into the footwell. A mess of disgusting super-sized leech-like creatures—only leech-like because they appeared to be covered in thick fur—were crawling over each other in a mad rush to attach themselves to my legs.

The urge to stamp down on the sickening aberrations was so strong that I actually felt my right leg lift off the floor, before I wrested control back from my reptilian brain and returned my foot firmly to the Explorer's carpet, from where the leeches had retreated.

This was going to get worse before it was going to get better. Plus we were closing in on the hospital. It wouldn't be long before we got there.

Screw it.

It was time to make my move.

As Lendowski swung the vehicle left off Park Row into Spruce Street, I balled my right hand and drove it hard into Deutsch's stomach, simultaneously grabbing her regulation-issue Glock 23 with my left and, in one continuous motion, swinging it full force against Lendowski's head, knocking him out cold.

He slumped forward. The Explorer bounced up onto the sidewalk between a couple of trees and slammed into the side of the Pace University building.

Deutsch was almost upright again, but I already had her cuffs—which she wore cop-style—off her belt.

"Hands. Now," I ordered.

"What are you—?"

"Now, Annie."

Her eyes burnt into me. "You're making a big mistake. Sean, listen to me—"

I cut her off. "I've got no choice."

For a moment, her pride got the better of her. I could see it in her eyes—fight was getting the better of flight—but her expression quickly changed to one of reluctant acceptance as she held out both hands. I clamped one of the cuffs on her right wrist and kept firm hold of the other end.

"Out."

She exited the vehicle and I followed her out the same side.

"Help me with him."

I took Lendowski's handgun out of its holster and tucked it into my trousers, then we dragged him from the driver's seat and propped him against one of the trees.

From the corner of one eye I glimpsed a wild-eyed ape sitting in the tree, dark blood oozing from its mouth as it chewed on the lump of torn flesh it was holding in one hand.

Although I was still just about able to distinguish between reality and my increasingly disturbing visions, with each passing minute I could feel more of my awareness pulled toward the world of the drug and away from the here and now.

I shook my head violently as I clamped the open end of Deutsch's cuffs to Lendowski's left wrist, grabbed his phone, his badge holder and his wallet, then turned to Deutsch. "Your cell."

She handed it to me as I returned Lendowski's wallet to him minus the bills. I kept his FBI creds, figuring they might come in handy since I didn't have mine any more.

"Sean, don't do this."

"I don't have a choice."

"Of course you do.

"I didn't kill him, Annie."

"Then let us find the guy who did. Like Nick said, we've got to have each other's backs."

"The people I've pissed off, maybe *they* killed Nick. And they'd go through all of you to get to me. I can't risk that."

I saw surprise light up her face regarding what I said about Nick's death as I said it. "It's our job, Sean."

"It's my fight."

I turned away from her, amazed that she was still willing to engage with me after what I'd just done.

Although there was little chance she'd be able to drag Lendowski more than a few feet, I went back to the Explorer and retrieved the cuffs from the glove compartment where I knew Lendowski kept them.

I cuffed Deutsch's left wrist to Lendowski's right so that the two of them encircled the tree, then removed his tie, balled it up and stuffed it into her mouth.

"Sorry about the punch—and about this."

She shook her head in resignation.

I climbed into the Explorer, hoping it still drove.

There was a crunching, shearing sound as I reversed away from the concrete wall, down off the sidewalk and back onto Spruce, then a wet squeal of tires as I sped away.

# 25

I guessed I had minutes before the shit hit the fan. I had no idea how long my current state would last, and no clue whether the next phase would be a hundred times worse. My body appeared to be following my commands even though it felt like I was moving in slow motion. If I was indeed moving as slowly as it appeared, I'd be back in custody before dawn.

That was the worst case scenario. What I was hoping for was that I threatened both the FBI and the CIA with such monumental embarrassment that they'd try to keep a lid on my escape, at least till morning, when everyone had been interviewed and a decision had been made about who to blame. I also bargained on Corrigan staying out of the way—at least till it looked like they weren't going to find me on their own. I had a whole lot to do before then.

I stripped the batteries from both phones and dropped the pieces out of the window as I turned right onto Gold, passing Lower Manhattan hospital, our original destination, then turned right onto Fulton. I could see 1 WTC up ahead, its shimmer brilliant in the darkness.

The Explorer skidded in the snow as I turned into a blind alley. I killed the engine, climbed out and checked the back, looking for anything I could use to cover my vomit-stained clothes. I was grateful for the cold weather as I laid eyes on his winter parka, along with a spare suit he kept in there and a holdall for his gym stuff. I also saw his flashlight and grabbed it too.

Parka on, hood up, suit, flashlight and both FBI-issued Glocks stuffed in Lendowski's holdall, I started to walk back down Fulton Street. I knew there was a twenty-four-hour parking garage about five hundred yards south of Gold Street and I was hoping that I'd be able to hotwire at least one of the cars left there overnight.

I jogged up the ramp of the multi-level building, scanning to the left and right for a car old enough not to be controlled by a computer. As I moved my head, everything started to warp and buckle—like my field of vision was spread across a sheet blowing in the wind. Leeches were squirming under the cars. I heard a pounding sound behind me. I turned to see the feral ape from the tree. It was bouncing something off the bonnet of a Toyota Corolla. I moved closer, edging around the vehicle, and saw my father's severed head, its blood-matted hair gripped in the ape's hand. His eyes—still open—looked exactly as they had when I found him sitting at his desk with his brains blown out.

My instinct was to continue on, but somewhere from deep within came the urge to take the head from the ape—to stop it inflicting any more pain. I felt myself moving toward the Corolla as the ape continued to smash the head against the bodywork, its movements growing ever more manic. I was less than five yards out—close enough to see the individual hairs on the ape's skin—when instinct won. I turned and dragged myself away, heading for the up ramp.

By the third level, I was again gasping for breath. After a couple of minutes spent doubled over, the visions again receding, I straightened up and saw what looked like an early nineties Caprice over in a far corner. If it was indeed a Caprice, then it was likely it could be trusted. It wasn't by random choice that so many police departments chose the vehicle before it was usurped by the Ford Crown Victoria.

As I dragged myself toward the car, a searing light flashed behind my eyes. I felt like I was plummeting down a bottomless well. I tried to shake my head clear but my vision was blurred. I forced myself to keep walking toward the car.

My eyes cleared and I found myself standing directly in front of the Caprice. I smashed the rear right-hand window, opened the door, and eased myself inside.

The steering column cover came off easily and I started to fish for the ignition wires.

A shooting pain ran up my spine as I leaned into the steering wheel, but my fingers had already found the right ones.

The engine sprung into life.

My pupils felt like they were the size of pinheads. My field of vision had been narrowed to about twenty degrees, but I managed to steer the car down the ramp, crashing through the barrier and out onto Fulton. I took a left on Pearl and got onto the FDR, my autopilot following the route I usually took back to Mamaroneck. Traffic was sparse but steady and I kept my speed down and tried to drive as though I didn't have a psychoactive drug doing cart-wheels in my veins, but I quickly discovered I needed to pull over. I managed to get off the FDR at Houston and wormed my way through a couple of deserted streets before pulling into a free spot and killing the engine.

I needed new ID and a change of appearance.

I needed to get hold of Tess without putting her in jeopardy.

But first, I needed to sleep off the primordial demons running amok inside my head.

# SATURDAY

# 26

*Federal Plaza, Lower Manhattan*

Nat "Len" Lendowski was having a lousy day.

Actually, lousy might be just a touch off the mark.

He was so pissed off he was looking to rip someone's head off. Ideally, Reilly's.

His bruised head was still hurting from where the agent had cold-cocked him with Deutsch's gun. To add insult to injury—literally—Reilly had taken his gun and his badge, cleaned his wallet out of almost a hundred bucks and taken a spare suit he kept in the back of his car before leaving him out on his ass in the street, handcuffed to Deutsch, their arms daisy-chained around a tree. Then came the final affront: sitting in the twenty-third floor conference room at seven in the morning, on a Saturday, and getting reamed out by Gallo in front of the whole office and a couple of stone-faced CIA douches for letting Reilly escape.

"The two of you, get your butts out to Reilly's house," Gallo barked at him and Deutsch as he concluded the debriefing. "I don't want to see you back here unless he's with you. Preferably with him wearing the handcuffs this time."

It was understandable that the last thing Lendowski needed right now was to have another bodily orifice drilled into him. But it was unavoidable. Failing to make the call would only make things worse.

As they stepped out of the elevator and made their way to the garage, he told Deutsch, "I'll see you down there in a minute. I need to use the john."

He watched her disappear out of the lobby, angled away from the flow of people coming in and out of the building, then pulled out his replacement BlackBerry and dialed the number.

The familiar voice picked up after four rings. "Congratulations," the man said, his dry tone heavy with sarcasm.

"Fuck off," Lendowski replied.

"Oh, feeling a bit precious, are we?"

"He got the jump on me," the agent spat back. "It wouldn't have happened if that useless bitch they've got me with knew what she was doing."

"The thing is, it *did* happen, and I need to know what's being done about it."

"We're going to stake out his house, but he won't show, of course. He's not that dumb."

"A fair assumption."

"We're up on his cell, but he's not going to use it. We're putting up a van outside their house as we speak, in case he makes contact some other way."

"No all points then?"

"No."

This seemed to please the man. He said, "They want to keep it under wraps."

"Seems that way," Lendowski replied. "Not that it makes any fucking sense. We should have every last pair of eyes looking for his mug out there. Must have been those two Agency dickheads' doing."

"I'm sure your boss's bosses don't want this hitting the news channels either. It's not exactly something you want to advertise. You should be grateful for that. You'd be the one on center stage."

The comment didn't pass unnoticed. The man had never said who he was working for, but he seemed well in tune with the community's internal politics. "You think I give a shit?" Lendowski countered. "I just want to see that dickhead locked up."

"In one piece?"

The question caught the agent out. He paused, wondering about that. "I'm easy on that one."

"All right. You'd better get out there. How long's your shift?"

"Open-ended," Lendowski said with a self-mocking grunt.

"Find him," the voice said. "And let me know the second you do."

Deutsch waited for Tess to pick up her phone while keeping an eye on the garage elevator.

"Come on," she whispered. "Pick up!"

It wasn't a conversation she wanted to have with Lendowski anywhere near her.

Tess picked up.

"Tess? Annie Deutsch. Can you talk?"

"What's going on?"

"So you haven't heard from him yet?" Deutsch asked, listening carefully for clues in the response.

She thought she heard a sharp little intake of breath in the brief pause before Tess answered.

"Heard from Sean? What do you mean?"

"He gave us the slip last night."

The intake, and the break, were more significant.

"How?"

Deutsch wondered about that question. Was Tess Chaykin genuinely surprised? Or was she just playing the part? Given what she knew about Tess, given what she knew about what she and Reilly had been through, it wouldn't surprise her if Tess had something to do with his escape. She'd been to see him, after all—although under Deutsch's supervision. It would reflect even worse on Deutsch, she knew, if Tess had used that meet to somehow help Reilly pull it off.

She filled Tess in on what happened, briefly, then, aware that Lendowski might appear at any moment, got down to the reason for her call.

"He's going to call you, Tess. You know it and I know it. Somehow, he's going to make contact. And I can't stress enough how important it is that you do the right thing here. You need to try to convince him to hand himself in—"

"You know he's never going to do that," Tess interjected.

"I know. But you have to try. Hard. And you have to be seen to be trying, Tess. We're talking aiding, abetting—you know the drill. I want to keep him safe. But I want to keep you safe too. I also want you to put me in touch with him. Just me. Tell him to call me. Give me a chance to talk to him, see what he wants. Maybe broker a deal for him to come in. Will you do that for me?"

Standing by the counter in the kitchen of her house in Mamaroneck, Tess went quiet as she chewed over Deutsch's words.

"I can tell him," she finally offered. "I don't think it'll do much good."

"You have to try," Deutsch said. "Please. For his sake. Get him to talk to me."

"I'll try."

"Good. You have my number."

After she ended the call, Tess steadied herself against the counter. She felt a dizzying cocktail of elation and dread as the ramifications of what had happened sank in.

Reilly was out. He was free again, which, on its own and unencumbered by the bigger picture, was a huge relief—only the bigger picture was massively worrying. He was a fugitive, a suspected murderer, with all the considerable resources of law enforcement on his trail.

Her legs felt like she'd just run a marathon, but she still found herself padding through to the front of the house and tilting the slats of the plantation-style shutters so she could peer out the living room window at the street outside.

It was quiet. This early in the morning, especially on a crisp cold day like today, was when Westchester County was—for her—at its peaceful best. She took in the deserted lane, quite a change from the ERT circus it had hosted the day before. Stalwart patches of snow dotted the front lawn while a thin dusting of it clung obstinately to the bare branches of the big oak tree by the driveway.

The surveillance team was, no doubt, on their way.

She stood there in silence, enjoying the calm before the storm. The kids and Tess's mom were asleep—no school on Saturday—blissfully unaware of the drama the day would inevitably bring. She'd need to tell them, of course; she'd need to look at their faces and watch as each word she uttered chipped away at their innocence and replaced it with fear and worry.

As she watched a lone starling hop along a low branch, she became aware of a ball of anger inside her gut, and she could feel it growing at an alarming rate no matter how tightly she tried to subdue it.

The anger she was fighting right now felt oddly similar to what she had experienced when her marriage to Doug—Kim's father—had first begun to unravel, even before the inevitability of his subsequent affair and the divorce that quickly followed. You didn't need your partner to screw someone else in order to feel betrayed, and the way she felt about Reilly's total inability to let go of the past, or at least be honest with her about the intensity with which it was consuming him, was uncomfortably mirroring how she'd felt about Doug, back when she still cared.

It was a bizarre irony of human nature that only love could underpin such extreme feelings of anger and betrayal, and that was the big difference in the two situations. By the time she found out about Doug's affair, she had already fallen out of love with him, his deception simply providing the end of a chapter and the promise of new horizons, rather than the beginning of a chapter filled with circular resentment and claustrophobic bitterness. This was very different. Despite the anger, she was more in love with Reilly than ever, which only made all the conflicting feelings churning inside her harder to calm.

She wondered where he was, how he was doing, and what he was thinking right now.

Yes, he'd definitely be in touch.

And she couldn't wait to see him.

## 27

By the time I first became aware of a semblance of daylight around me, I had no idea where I was or what time of day it was. All I knew was that I was shivering. A lot.

I had the vague, disturbing conviction that I was in the cellar of El Brujo's hacienda in Mexico, where I'd been held and force-fed a drug that was meant to extinguish my soul for all of eternity. That was quickly dismissed in favor of our house in Mamaroneck and then for my old bachelor pad in the city. My mind—struggling for handholds on a sheer climb—finally settled on a West Hollywood hotel room in which I'd spent two weeks the summer I turned nineteen. I'd taken a Greyhound to Los Angeles and, within a few hours of arriving, I'd been struck down by a flu that was so virulent that I'd had to find myself a bed and spent all the money I'd saved for three months in California on two weeks in the Econo Lodge on Vine. I barely ate for a week and couldn't move for almost ten days. A pretty young Mexican maid named Rosita had taken pity on the poor sick guy from Chicago, checking on me at the beginning and end of every shift to ensure I was still alive and bringing me bottles of water and left-behind pizza slices. When my fever finally broke, I was so exhausted that I'd had to spend another three days in the hotel recuperating. Finally feeling well enough to venture out, I'd summoned up the courage to ask Rosita to dinner. She'd smiled kindly and told me she was engaged, though still waiting for her betrothed to save up for the ring she'd chosen.

I'd had enough dollars left to catch a Metro bus to the Greyhound terminal, from where I took the first bus back east.

My mother never asked what had happened and I'd never shared it with her. Instead, I got a summer job as a clerk at the Forty-second Precinct of the Chicago Police Department before moving to Indiana to begin my law studies at Notre Dame.

As I lay there between sleep and waking, feeling nineteen but knowing I'd traveled a very long way from who I was back then, it struck me that even though I rarely thought of that connection, those three months on Addison were probably instrumental in my later decision to apply to the Bureau. There was something about the camaraderie and sense of moral purpose at the precinct that was deeply satisfying, the idea that not only could you intend to make a difference—however small—but that you actually could make society a better and safer place.

As the Bureau came into my head, so did everything else. Clarity gradually seeped back into my mind and my surroundings fell into focus. I wasn't at the hacienda or chewing on leftover pizza. I was curled up on myself in the car I'd stolen, wrapped up in Lendowski's parka and using his suit as a makeshift blanket, and I realized that the shivering was simply from the cold, which was reaching me with little resistance since I'd smashed one of the car's windows. I rubbed my arms as I tilted myself up, slowly, hesitantly, my eyes stinging, my fingertips buzzing with a mild electrical current, my head pounding like someone had pimped out my skull with a subwoofer.

I'd never taken psychedelics like LSD, or any hard drugs for that matter, so I didn't know if I was experiencing a normal comedown. If I was, I couldn't imagine how people actually got a kick from doing these kinds of psychoactive drugs. The endless, mind-numbing all-nighters we'd pulled last week outside Daland's place were suddenly a fond, idyllic memory by comparison.

I stepped out of the Caprice and looked around. I realized I was in the East Village, on Third Street, close to its intersection with Avenue C. I needed to get something hot inside me, ideally something loaded with caffeine. I pulled up the collar on Lendowski's parka, then remembered it said FBI on its front breast pocket and across its back, so I quickly shrugged it off, turned it inside out, and pulled it back on. A couple of minutes later, I was basking in the warmth of a small coffee shop, my hands toasting on a big mug of heaven. Each sip seemed to jump-start a bundle of neurons in my frazzled brain, and once the egg platter starting working its magic, I was starting to think maybe I'd gotten away with this. My body seemed to have ducked any permanent damage from the drug, though it would take years before I'd know for sure if my mind was as lucky. For now, at least, I was a reasonably sentient being once again. Which wasn't ideal, given that the events of last night, and the bigger picture, came galloping back. I think I might have preferred to stay in wonderland.

I needed to get in touch with Tess, let her know I was OK. I also needed her to help me with a couple of things, but I had to figure out how to contact her safely. I was sure the Bureau would have a Stingray van parked outside the house, and besides not wanting to be caught, I didn't want to get her into trouble. I thought about it while I worked on a second mug of coffee, then came up with what I thought was a halfway decent plan. I'd need to buy myself a cheap phone and a couple of prepaid SIM cards.

To say my options were narrow would be a gross understatement, but while I was still out and alive, I figured I had an advantage. I already knew more about Corrigan than made him comfortable and there was a good chance that thanks to Kurt or Kirby or my elusive deep throat, I might have some information I was as yet unaware of—information he didn't want me to have. I thought of Kurt and how all his paranoid fieldcraft suddenly seemed not quite so crazy. In fact, along with my unwillingness to share any details with Tess, it had probably saved his—and Gigi's—life.

On the other hand, I wondered if it had all cost Nick his life. The thought hit me like a black hole of sadness, consuming me from the inside. I raised my mug slightly and gave my dead buddy a silent toast.

"I'm sorry," I said under my breath.

As I set the mug down and stared into its murkiness, one thing was clear. There was no way I was going to prove that I was innocent. Not without signed confessions from the perpetrators. My only course of action was to find the man pulling the strings and secure evidence that I'd been framed.

I nodded to myself, slowly. Nothing had changed when it came to the big picture. It was still brutally simple.

I had to find Corrigan.

*

Sandman ground over the curious text message as he stared at himself in the mirror while he shaved.

He'd spent the night at a hotel, thinking he would take the time to recharge. He'd been on the go ever since the whole affair had gone into overdrive: flying up to Boston to take care of the doc, then back to the city to pick up Reilly's trail at Times Square, following him down to DC and on to Kirby's, then the altercation at the CIA analyst's house after which he'd lost Reilly. He'd spent a sleepless night staking out the agent's home, only to then discover the agent had turned up in FBI custody. Shortly after, however, he'd had to take care of the agent's partner but failed to retrieve the laptop. He'd welcomed the night's break to have a shower, a decent meal, and a hard think about what his next move would be, knowing Reilly was locked away in federal custody and beyond his reach.

And then the encrypted message had come in, informing him Reilly had escaped.

Kudos, he thought. Impressive move, all the more since Sandman still didn't know how Reilly had managed to pull it off. The information he'd received was still sketchy—Reilly had somehow faked being sick convincingly enough to be taken to a hospital.

Sandman wondered if Reilly had had inside help. He'd need to look into it, find out who had been escorting him at the time of his escape. Perhaps that thread might lead back to Reilly now that he was in the wind—if the thread that had popped up on his screen in the form of a cryptic text message didn't pan out, a text message that had been sent to Tess Chaykin's iPhone and snagged by the Stingray van that was now parked near Reilly and Chaykin's house.

The FBI had been using Stingray technology for years. The system, which mimics a cell phone tower, was fitted inside an unmarked van and was able to pinpoint the exact location of all mobile devices within its range and intercept all conversations and data coming in and out of any targeted phone. The Bureau didn't need a wire tapping warrant to deploy Stingray; instead, they used it under the authority of "pen register" orders—otherwise known as "tap and trace" orders—which were very easily granted by the courts since they only required "probable cause" under the Fourth Amendment. These orders were only supposed to allow investigators to collect metadata such as a list of the numbers communicating with a suspect's phone. The fact that Stingray could also eavesdrop on conversations and read message traffic was an innocent, but fortunate, bonus.

The SMS had come in from a throwaway and the SIM was no longer in use. It didn't have a history to mine, either. It had come to life for less than a minute, just enough time to type in Chaykin's phone number, add in the short message, and hit send. The SIM would be under heavy watch, but it was pretty evident to Sandman that it would never be used again.

The meaning of the message, on the other hand, was far from evident.

I'M OUT AND OK. NEED U TO BRING SURV PACK. TONIGHT @ MONASTERY

Sandman was intrigued.

Surely Reilly had to know Chaykin's phone would be under watch, her SMS messages monitored? And asking her to bring him his "survival pack" would risk getting her picked up and charged—assuming they could prove that she knew the message came from him and that she actually met up with him.

The question was: what did Reilly mean? Where was he telling Tess Chaykin to come meet him?

The FBI team watching the house was still working on figuring it out, but so far they didn't have a conclusive answer. It was too vague and could refer to too many places. It wasn't a priority for them anyway. All they'd need to do was follow Chaykin when she left the house. She'd lead them straight to Reilly.

Sandman intended to be there when the meet took place. Reilly needed to be silenced before he could be taken into custody. If necessary, he knew he could get assistance from the FBI agent his employers had on their payroll, but he preferred to do it alone. Reliability was never an issue when he was operating solo.

He stared at the words on his screen, trying to divine their hidden message. He went over everything he knew about Reilly and Tess. Then he went wider. He looked at the file he had been given about those close to him, starting with Aparo—and an unexpected association flew off the screen at him. Something that, to him, seemed like the obvious solution.

Sandman nodded with satisfaction. It would be dark soon. He needed to make a move if he was going to get there before Reilly.

# 28

*Mamaroneck, New York*

Skulking by the window of her bedroom, Tess peeked out at the sleepy, tree-lined street as the early darkness of winter settled in. She could see the unmarked sedan parked outside the house, across and slightly down the street, and knew Annie Deutsch and her partner were in it. She could also just about make out the Comcast van one house further away and knew it was the Stingray monitoring vehicle they often used in these situations—which was why she was intrigued by the text message that she'd received.

Much earlier that day, as she was leaving Federal Plaza, she had already been wondering about where and when she would meet Reilly. She knew that, if all went well, he would make contact soon after he was out. He'd want her to know he was OK and that the capsules had done their job. She also figured he would need her help. His reckless text message had seemed out of character until Kim had come into her bedroom with a curious question and it all fell into place.

She turned away from the window and edged over to the bed, on which sat Kim's denim backpack, the one she'd personalized with small pyramid-shaped studs. She had packed it with Reilly's jeans and Timberland low boots, a pair of thick socks, underwear, a winter shirt, a small vanity case she'd been given on an overseas flight that included a shaving kit and toothbrush, and the stash of cash—two thousand dollars' worth—they kept in the gun safe for an emergency. She'd also put in Reilly's personal handgun, a Glock 19, and a box of rounds.

She glanced at her watch. It was time to get ready.

She could hear a blissfully oblivious Alex laughing to the antics of *Despicable Me 2*—still his default movie—with his grandmother downstairs in the living room, and guessed that Kim was probably sulking in her bedroom, gorging herself on an endless stream of Snapchat messages and Instagram likes while preparing herself for the aborted fun night out at the movies with her boyfriend,

Giorgio, and, probably far more distressing, the imminent, if temporary, loss of her prized phone.

It had been hard to convince Kim to help her, but she couldn't see any other way around it. She needed to leave the house undetected, and she needed transportation that wouldn't raise suspicion. Kim and Giorgio had arranged to go out to a movie, and it had presented Tess with an opportunity she couldn't pass up.

She hadn't yet told her mom or Alex about Reilly's predicament—not about his capture, nor his escape. She decided she'd wait to see how tonight played out before doing so. Kim, on the other hand, now knew something was seriously wrong. When she'd come in to Tess's bedroom to tell her about the weird message she'd received, Tess had closed the door behind her and led her into the bathroom. Talking low out of paranoia regarding long-range listening devices, she'd whispered her instructions to her daughter. Once she'd thought up the rest of her plan, she'd then told Kim about it, but hadn't said any more than what she needed to say to get her daughter to play ball. It hadn't been easy. The repeated hushed protests about missing out on her date were hard to put down. Eventually, though, Kim had grudgingly agreed.

Presently, Tess had to get into gear.

She went downstairs and announced that she was going to run a bath and get some "me time," all while avoiding her mother's dubious, probing look. She said she'd make herself a bowl of granola afterwards and left her mom to sort out dinner for just herself and Alex, since Kim was about to head out to a movie and, most likely, a pizza, with her boyfriend. Tess then headed back upstairs and began setting the scene.

She filled the bath, leaving the door open so the sound of the running water percolated downstairs. While it was running, she hastily put on Kim's oversized tan parka, her signature beanie, snow boots and thick polka-dotted scarf, then she checked herself in the mirror. It was odd to see herself dressed like that, though there was nothing shocking about it. It was hardly an embarrassing MuDAL moment—yet another of the hip acronyms Kim had taught her with a roll of the eyes, Mutton Dressed As Lamb. Not in that garb. Had this been summer, things might have been different, but she was too covered up for the cold to feel even a tinge of a Peter Pan Syndrome moment—another one of Kim's useful lessons.

Once she was done, she switched on the speaker system by her bed and selected a calming Coldplay playlist on her iPod. She then turned off the bedroom lights, dimmed the lights in the bathroom, and, after checking the front of the house for any signs of life from the window, she waited.

Right on cue, Giorgio's old Jeep pulled up outside.

She grabbed the backpack and stepped into the hallway, where she called out to Kim.

"Honey, G's here."

"OK," came Kim's halfhearted attempt at an enthusiastic reply.

"I know it's Saturday night, but don't be back too late," Tess said out loud as she took the stairs down to the front hall. A wall shielded her from the couch and the TV, and she tensed up for a second as she reached the door, hoping her mom didn't get up or come out of the kitchen to say goodbye to her granddaughter. She was clear as she stepped outside, the hood of Kim's parka pulled over her beanie.

She did her best to imitate Kim's teen gait as she made her way down the path to Giorgio's waiting car. Without glancing back toward the FBI sedan or the van further away, she climbed into the car.

Giorgio's face went all wide with surprise. "Mrs. Chaykin?"

"Just drive, Giorgio."

"But—"

Tess shot him a firm look and pointed ahead. "Drive, will you? I'll explain later."

Giorgio put the Wrangler into gear and pulled away from the house. Tess hazarded a discreet glance back, although given the darkness and the steam obscuring the rear windshield, there was little chance the agents staking out the house were going to recognize her.

She allowed herself a small smile. It had worked. No one was following. She nodded to herself, pleased at how she'd been inspired by both Reilly's recounting of Daland's arrest and the fact that she still had the physique to pull this off. It helped that Kim was now less than an inch shorter than her own five foot seven.

She stared ahead, heart pounding at the thought of being able to feel Reilly's arms around her again shortly.

From the unmarked sedan down the street, Lendowski watched Tess Chaykin's daughter climb into the Jeep and head off.

Deutsch had already run the plates while the car idled outside the house. The information had matched the data coming back from Stingray, telling them the car was the girl's boyfriend's.

"Dad's on the run and wanted for murder and she's going out on a date," he said with disdain. "Kids today. Christ."

"Maybe she doesn't know," Deutsch said.

Lendowski just let out a sarcastic shrug for an answer.

His target was still inside the house. As he kept his gaze fixed on it, he wondered if Reilly would really be stupid enough to try meeting with Tess. You didn't need to be Sherlock Holmes to know about the astonishing number of fugitives who were caught simply because they made contact with family members.

His BlackBerry vibrated. He glanced at the screen's caller ID. He glanced at Deutsch and gestured back at the van with his thumb as he picked up. "What's up?"

"Something's off. We think she's on the move."

Lendowski didn't get it. Why the hell would they be tracking the girl's phone? "I know, I just saw her leave."

"Chaykin?"

"No, numbnuts. The daughter."

The Stingray operator in the van clarified. "Not the daughter, doofus. Chaykin herself."

"Negative. I've got eyes on the house. Chaykin's still at home. That was the daughter."

"Then how do you explain the stream of Facebook and Instagram messages flying back and forth from her laptop?"

Her laptop? "What about her phone?"

"It's powered down. We can't track it."

Which didn't make sense. Why would the girl switch off her phone? What teenager did that—ever?

Lendowski scowled as he realized what had happened. The bitches were playing him.

"Hang on." He turned to Deutsch. "Something's wrong." He

thought fast. “Check the house, see if Chaykin’s still inside. I’m going after the boyfriend’s car.”

Deutsch didn’t argue. “Damn it,” she muttered as she hurried out.

She’d barely slammed the door shut before Lendowski was powering away from the curb.

Sandman was sitting in the darkness of Aparo’s apartment when his encrypted phone vibrated with an incoming text message.

It read:

CHAYKIN’S ON THE MOVE

He deleted it, then settled back into the uncomfortable armchair that faced the front door. As he checked the silenced handgun in his lap, he ran through his plan once more, making sure there were no wrinkles.

The location Reilly had chosen to meet his woman was going to be a boon. After all, Sandman mused, what better place for an agent to commit suicide than the apartment of his recently deceased partner? A death for which, in his delusional, troubled state of mind, he could conceivably blame himself.

# 29

It didn't take long for Lendowski to catch up with the Jeep. Mamaroneck was a small town and there weren't too many options if one was aiming to leave it. North or south on the Boston Post Road if you wanted a slow amble, or the thruway if you were on any kind of schedule. Most people going anywhere took Mamaroneck Avenue up to the thruway's on-ramps.

He caught up with the Jeep just as it was turning onto the Post Road and stayed well back, not wanting to give his quarry any chance of knowing he was there. Then he remembered his cash-only employer and what he'd been asked to do. As the Jeep turned left onto Fenimore, he pulled out his phone and dialed the number.

As before, the man answered promptly. "What's going on?"

"I'm on Chaykin's tail," Lendowski told him. "She's on her way to meet Reilly."

"We know," the man said. "We have an asset waiting there."

This surprised Lendowski. "Waiting? Where?"

"In the city. Where the meet is going to take place. It should be taken care of before Chaykin gets there."

This didn't fit. "The city?" Lendowski asked. "That was the message in the text?"

"Correct."

Something was definitely off. "She's not heading into the city."

"Say again?"

"She's not going into the city," Lendowski said. "Look, if that's where she was going, she'd be jumping on I-95 or taking a train in. And I can tell you she's not doing either. She's turned off the road that leads to both of them as we speak."

The voice hesitated, then asked, "You're sure about this?"

"I'm on her fucking tail," Lendowski fired back. "She's going somewhere else. Somewhere local, by the looks of it. This road leads nowhere."

"We could have a serious problem here," the man growled. "All right. Stay on it. I might need you to step up. I'll call you right back."

Which was timely, as Lendowski now had a call waiting from Deutsch.

"She's gone," Deutsch said, her voice breathless. "They faked us. You got them yet?"

Lendowski thought fast. He was alone, following Chaykin, who was likely to lead him straight to Reilly. His employers—who seemed to have deep pockets—sounded like they were in a bit of a panic. The bit about him stepping up to the plate was still ringing in his ears.

He thought he might have an opportunity here.

"Nothing yet," he told Deutsch, thinking he should buy himself some time. "I'll call you as soon as I have anything."

"I'll put out an APB on the Jeep," Deutsch said.

"No," Lendowski countered. Last thing he needed right now was interference. "Let's not spook her yet. She could well lead us to Reilly. I'll find her. Just give me a bit more time."

Deutsch audibly hesitated, then said, "OK. Call me the second you know, either way."

"You got it." He hung up.

In Aparo's apartment, Sandman was livid. "Is he sure? How reliable is he?"

"He's a Fed," Roos replied. "The guy knows what he's talking about. You can't get there in time, can you?"

"Up to Westchester? I'm an hour away, easy. Depends on when and where they're meeting." He cursed under his breath, pissed off at how Reilly had played them.

"OK," Roos said. "Get up there. I'll keep you posted."

Lendowski saw the Jeep's brake lights flare up and watched as it pulled into the CITGO gas station just before the thruway's overpass. He pulled over and killed his lights. Tess got out, then the Jeep came back out of the station, pulled a U-turn and headed back toward him. As it drove past, Lendowski's phone rang again. It was his off-the-books employer.

"OK, here's the deal, Len. We've got no assets nearby and it's likely they can't get to you in time, so we're going to need you to take care of this."

Lendowski saw Tess now walking away from the station, heading north along the quiet lane. "What do you mean?" Even as he said it, Lendowski knew what the man was going to ask him to do.

There was silence for a moment, confirming that Lendowski had indeed guessed correctly. Then the voice said, "Fifty thousand."

Lendowski climbed out of the car, feeling a spike of unease at what he was hearing—and thinking. "For your Reilly problem to go away permanently? That's what we're talking about, right?"

"I knew you'd see things our way, Len."

The strangest mixture of elation and abject terror at what he was contemplating now raced through him. "I'm not sure about this."

"Come on, Len. We need you to do it. And you could do a lot worse than be on our team."

"You realize what you're asking me to do?" He was now following Tess, staying well back.

"All I'm asking is for you to take advantage of the unique situation you're in. Think about it. This'll wipe out what you owe your bookies—something the Bureau doesn't know about, right? Like the IRS and those wads of cash we've been handing you?"

The threat was implicit. The bastards weren't content with cajoling him into playing ball. They had to resort to threatening him. Well, screw them, he thought. Them, and Reilly. He'd turn this to his advantage, big time.

He steeled himself, greed now pumping adrenaline all through him. "One hundred. Two if she needs to go too."

"I don't have time to play games with you, Len. And I'm not the Sultan of Brunei either. One hundred I can do. Just him or both of them, that's up to you. But it has to be clean, either way."

"One fifty."

"Len. Take the deal. It's the clever move, trust me."

Shit.

Still—this was still a big payday. Tax free, one shot, done.

Time was pressing.

Lendowski's thoughts were ricocheting all over the place as he tried to make sure he had all the bases covered. "But how? I don't know who you are. How're you going to get me the money?"

"Check your bank balance on your phone. We're wiring in half as we speak."

He shouldn't have been surprised they knew where he banked, but the notion still made him feel sick to his stomach. "Bank account? No, fuck that. Cash only. I can't have a deposit this big show up like that."

"Don't worry about it, Len. We'll swap it for cash once it's done and clean it up as an honest mistake. It won't be an issue. In the meantime, it's yours. Consider it an advance."

He was screwed. They knew enough about him already to get him kicked out of the Bureau, if not put behind bars. And it wasn't as if this was about someone he liked.

His face set in a scowl that could force water through ground coffee at espresso pressure, he relented. "Deal," he said. "I'll call you when it's done."

He hung up, knowing he'd need to explain his absence and his radio silence to Deutsch later. A problem with his car, maybe. Then there was another, more significant problem. His backup gun—a clean Sig P226 with the serial numbers filed off—had been concealed inside the spare of his Explorer when Reilly had driven off with it. He hadn't yet had time to retrieve it.

He thought he might just have to kill Reilly with his bare hands.

# 30

*New Rochelle, New York*

I'd made it as far as Baychester before the urge to close my eyes had become overwhelming. I'd pulled into the Bay Plaza parking lot, smeared a couple of handfuls of halite-dirtied snow across each license plate, then slept in my stolen Caprice for a couple of hours, this crashing-out-in-cars thing was becoming far too much of a habit for my liking.

The physical exertion and adrenaline-fuelled nature of the previous few hours seemed to have conspired to mean that, instead of experiencing IMAX-style waking visions of my past lives, I was in fact sound asleep.

Presently, I was sitting in the darkness off Pinebrook Boulevard and reminiscing about happier times, specifically the time Tess was screaming at the top of her voice: "It's all crap. I'm going to smash this laptop to pieces so I never have to write such appalling trash ever again."

Happier times, indeed.

Tess had been beyond frustrated. She'd been working on her second book and had written herself into a corner. I had saved the day by shutting down the laptop before it was permanently retired and making Tess join me on a brisk walk.

It was obvious that Tess could tell a story—the sales figures from her first book had made that clear—but the sea change from archaeologist-adventurer to desk-bound author had meant that Tess had some pent-up adrenaline to burn off. The bi-weekly Bikram yoga clearly wasn't cutting it and sometimes cabin fever got the best of her. So I took her to the only trail I knew in the area and walked her from one end to the other and back again, something she now did every week on her "Zen walk," occasionally alternating with other routes to keep things fresh.

Am I a great partner, or what?

The Leatherstocking Trail was a gorgeous haven of woods and wetlands, and the strip I was talking about, the southern section of the bigger, fifteen-mile-long Colonial Greenway loop, was where Tess let off steam instead of taking it out on a thousand bucks' worth of MacBook.

Several of the roads that ran roughly north-south through the east-west trail gave easy access to it, which meant that, overall, the trail was a flawless way to expose a tail or physical surveillance, being no more than two hundred feet wide in most places and giving no consistent cover. Even better, the overcast weather meant that drone coverage would be difficult to pull off unnoticed—assuming they even knew we were here—which, I hoped, wasn't the case.

Tess and I knew each other's thought processes well enough for me to be pretty sure that she would hit the trail from somewhere near its eastern end, maybe at Fenimore, and walk west, while she would expect me to approach from the opposite end, which was exactly what I was about to do. If we needed to make a quick getaway, then either car would be an option.

I had been waiting in the Caprice for about twenty minutes and was now as sure as I could be that I was alone. I grabbed the flashlight and one of the Glocks from Lendowski's holdall—his or Deutsch's, I had no way of knowing which—climbed out of the car, crossed Pinebrook, and struck out along the trail. After about a thousand yards, I passed the sign stating that I had crossed from New Rochelle into the town of Mamaroneck.

There was barely enough light for me to see my way without the flashlight, the combination of dull moonlight and light pollution from the town revealing islands of snow in a sea of thick foliage made up of ash, maple, oak and other trees that were beyond my limited knowledge of upstate flora. The only other thing I knew was that there was poison ivy dotted along the trail. Given how swimmingly everything had gone these last few days, I decided I wouldn't be surprised if I fell face-first into some before the night was out.

I figured it would take me no more than twenty minutes to pick my way to the center of the trail, which was where the Sheldrake River forked. This was the part of the trail farthest from an intersecting road, and therefore a perfect place to meet. I hoped Tess would think the same.

With my line of sight constantly flicking between the ground and the trail, I continued eastwards.

When I reached the only intersecting road between where I had left the car and the river, I checked in both directions before continuing on my way. Ten minutes later the trail opened out into its widest and most isolated area, where it crossed the easternmost of the two river forks.

I slowly skirted the perimeter, eyes and ears alert for any sign of movement. Apart from assorted nocturnal creatures, I was alone. I concealed myself behind a cluster of trees on the north side of the area and waited.

After another five minutes I heard the faint sound of someone approaching from the east. Less than a minute later, the sound resolved into clearer footfalls. Then Tess appeared. Alone and carrying what I recognized to be Kim's denim backpack.

She stopped and turned to look back the way she had come, ears straining for any sound behind her.

There was nothing but silence around us.

I watched as she moved into the clearing and waited, then I stepped out from behind the trees.

"Tess." As low as I could say it and still be heard.

She swung her head, saw me, and walked around the edge of the clearing toward me, her pace picking up with each step.

We closed the ground toward each other in seconds, then fell into each other's arms, Tess having dropped the backpack to the ground.

"Thank God," she whispered.

We stayed like that for a long time. The only thing either of us needed right then and there was the warmth of the other's body.

We finally broke apart.

Her face flooded with concern. "You're OK, right? The drug? You're OK?"

"It did the trick," I said. "The jury's still out on any long-term effects." Then I looked her up and down, and the garb sank in. "You're Kim?"

She half smiled. "I may decide to stick with this look. What do you think?"

"As long as you don't go getting tats and piercings all over you, young lady," I said, wagging my finger.

"We should stop. This is getting creepy."

"Agreed."

I waved at her attire. "So Kim—she helped you with all this?"

"She didn't just help—she gave up a date with Giorgio for it." My face obviously telegraphed my confusion, so Tess added, "He dropped me off."

I smiled. Kim—Tess's mini-me—she was key to why we were standing here. I gazed at Tess's eyes, which appeared dark in the bleak light, but which I knew to be exactly the same shade of green as Kim's.

"She's everything that's great about you."

She thought about this for a moment. "And Alex has none of your obsessive traits. Yet."

I nodded. She was right, of course. But none of that mattered. Right now, I was just so damn happy to see her. And I couldn't have done it without Kim. Or without a silly dad-lesson I'd insisted on one rainy Sunday afternoon a couple of years back.

I'd wanted her to learn Tess and my cell phone numbers, as well as our home number, by heart. I'd explained to her that just because no one knows anyone's number any more didn't mean that everyone has suddenly become immune to losing things. I mean, seriously, who remembers anyone's number these days? Lose your phone when you're out and it's unlikely you'd know how to contact anyone because your phone now functions on behalf of—and often instead of—your brain.

So as decreed by Kim, the three of us had memorized each other's phone numbers, her flawless logic being that if she had to learn our numbers, then we should have to learn hers too, an argument she had won at the time by pouting till we agreed. And had just won again, uncontested, since I was able to send Tess the fake text message from a burner phone that didn't have her number stored in it.

It was the other message, though, that had led Tess here.

I had decided to contact her indirectly, and thought of a couple of options. One was to go through Kurt, then something better dropped into my mind. I found an Internet café and created a fake Facebook account using some photos I'd cut and pasted off some of Kim's friends' profiles, then used that to post a comment on a recent photo of hers. The comment had to get through her rapid-fire fingers and her ruthless indifference filter, and it needed to tell her it was me, without announcing it to the guys in the Stingray van. So I'd used a name that was bound to get her attention.

One of the first times I met Giorgio when he and Kim started dating, I lightheartedly referred to him as Georgie Boy, which went down like a lead balloon. I had intended it as a term of endearment, channeling a nickname Jerry used for George on *Seinfeld.* I mean, it wasn't like I was calling him Boy George or cracking any lame Armani puns. I'd explained its origin and, given that I get a bit evangelical when it comes to the *Seinfeld* canon, I'd talked about George's other nicknames, most notably T-Bone and my favorite, Art Vandelay. Still, the resistance was noted, and "Georgie Boy" only rarely saw the light of day. I was still waiting for the day I'd be able to sit through box sets of the series with her, but there always seemed to be another *Pretty Little Liars* hogging any available viewing time she had.

So "Georgie Boy" had put a "Like" on one of Kim's photos, along with a comment that asked "How's Stacy's mom?"—a reference to a song we liked and joked about—with a winkie face. It had taken a couple of minutes, but when she'd replied—presumably after showing it to Tess—"She's got it going on, Art!" with a laughing emoticon, I knew she'd got it. So I commented back, "I can't mow her lawn! How about a quickie on the Zen walk instead?" with a tongue-out emoticon. She'd replied "8OK!" with two of the tongue-out faces.

"'A quickie on the Zen walk,' Georgie Boy?" Tess smirked. "I dunno if Kim's ever going to forgive you for that."

"Hey, it did the trick, didn't it?"

She nodded, then her expression darkened. "What's going on, Sean? Where do we go from here?"

"I'm going to find Corrigan and prove that his guy killed Kirby. It's the only way."

She studied me, then just nodded. I guess she knew we were

past the point of arguing about this. She gestured toward the ground. "I got what I could."

"Maybe you and the kids should go to the ranch—" I was referring to her aunt's place in Arizona.

"No way," she cut me off. "You need me here. But your guys have the house under watch 24/7. Where are you going to stay?"

"I have no idea."

"Maybe with whoever's been helping you?"

A loaded question, by the looks of it. No point denying it now. "Nick tell you?"

She nodded.

Which reminded me of something I needed to know. "What else did he say? When you saw him?"

"What, at the house?"

"Yes, before the . . . before the accident?"

"He said you wanted your laptop safe."

I nodded. "Where is it now?"

"I brought it back to the house after the accident. I hid it in the loft. I figured the ERT guys had already gone through the house, so it was safe there. I mean, I didn't know where else to put it. Should I have brought it?"

"No, that's fine. I just didn't want them to have access to it to either track down the guy helping me out, or plant stuff on it. What else?"

"He told me everything you told me at Federal Plaza. About Corrigan, your dad, Azorian."

"What else?"

"That's it. He just said he was going to do everything he could to help clear you. That with you in custody, he'd use the Bureau's weight to get to the bottom of this with the CIA. Maybe even ask the president to help." She studied me, then asked, "Why are you asking me this?"

"I don't know. It's just . . . him dying, the timing if it."

He face scrunched up with concern. "You think he was murdered?"

Before I could answer, we both heard it.

The snap of a branch.

Then silence again.

Tess motioned for me to take Kim's backpack. "Go. Just go."

"No." I jabbed a finger at the trees to my right and hissed, low, "Hide. Quickly."

Tess sprinted away as I reached for the gun tucked in the small of my back—

But before I had it fully out, a figure emerged out of the trees and came rushing at me, fast, with what looked like a gun in his hand. In a flash, he'd plowed into me, knocking us both to the ground, his left hand locked around my right forearm. Driving a knee into my gut, he levered himself upward and threw a couple of lightning jabs at my head with his gun hand, dazing me enough to let him force the gun from my hand.

He picked up the gun I'd dropped and stood up, tucking it into his belt holster and pointing his weapon directly at me.

"Get up, asshole," Lendowski spat.

I shook my head and tried to focus my eyes, but what I saw made no sense. For one thing, he was alone.

"Where's Deutsch?"

His expression went all weird and wry. "She couldn't make it."

And then all at once, disparate little observations fell into line. The call outside the bar. The gambling. The unusual levels of interest in my routine. His being here, without Deutsch.

They'd got to him—and now he was going to do their bidding.

"Len. Don't."

He just shrugged. "Don't what?"

"Think about what you're doing. They'll never let you live."

"Shut up." Beyond the tension and the anger in his voice, I detected some fear, like he wasn't totally comfortable with what he was about to do.

It was an opening, a vein to mine.

"They'll own you," I pressed. "And when they don't need you any more, they'll put you down. You know that, right?"

He didn't want to hear that. Instead, he shoved the gun in my face. "Enough. Call your bitch, get her back here."

"Len—"

"Call her."

I held his glare for a second, then said, "Go screw yourself."

He grabbed my jacket and pulled me to my feet, looping his left arm around my neck, his right hand holding the gun to my head.

"Tess!" he bellowed. "I know you can hear me. You have five seconds to join us." He started counting them down, loudly.

I heard the faintest sound behind me. Lendowski was still counting, so I hoped he hadn't heard it. Maybe Tess was working her way around us.

I yelled as loud as I could to give her cover, "Don't! He'll kill us both, get out of here—"

Then I heard the crunch of her feet, and Lendowski must have heard them too, and in the moment he tried to decide what to do, something slammed into the back of his head, a rock or a branch—I couldn't tell. All I felt was the side of his skull bouncing off the back of mine, but he managed to stay on his feet. Down, but not out, he was already spinning around and taking aim at the trees, his left arm still choking me.

I shouted, "Stay down!" as I drove my right elbow as hard as I could into Lendowski's side, then wrapped my right leg around his and pushed him over, bringing us both down.

As we hit the ground, his left arm loosened enough for me to roll to my right, trapping his right arm flat so that he couldn't fire the gun.

"Tess! Run! Now!"

I thought I heard her take off as I balled up my left fist and slammed it against Lendowski's right wrist. His grip on the gun loosened, and it fell away. I tried to grab the gun as I simultaneously rolled off him, but he landed a barrage of vicious blows to my midsection with his left before dragging me back from the gun, kicking me in the gut, and wrapping both hands around my neck.

I knew he was far stronger than me and would probably be able to take anything I threw at him, especially with him knowing I was weakening by the second, so I put every ounce of strength I had left into forcing myself upright so Lendowski didn't have gravity to help him.

Kneeling on the frozen ground, Lendowski behind me, his thumbs digging into the back of my neck, I hoped that Tess was using the time to get back to her car and away.

I could feel myself starting to slip into unconsciousness—a state I had spent far too much time skirting in the past few days. I had to fight it with the idea of needing to ensure Tess, Kim and Alex were safe. But I couldn't. His grip was too strong, and I was helpless. As I started to fall into a deep ocean of inky blackness, I thought about my dad. Maybe I'd find him. Ask him face-to-face what drove him to take his own life, when every cell of my body still wanted to live.

A loud sound reverberated through the dark water, turning everything upside down.

Suddenly the water was thinner. Lighter.

I was no longer sinking fast, but rushing toward the surface.

I felt the cold air against my face as I burst back into consciousness.

Tess was standing over Lendowski, the gun in her right hand, her whole body shaking with shock.

Lendowski lay on his side, stone cold dead. A big chunk was missing from the side of his skull. The blood oozing from the gaping hole appeared black against the dirty snow, spreading in slow motion as it seeped into it.

I pulled myself to standing, covered the ground to him, and pulled his gun from its holster and tucked it into my pants. Then I moved to Tess, put an arm around her and gently eased the gun from her grasp. She was shaking, a lot, her faraway gaze locked on Lendowski.

"Tess. Tess. Listen to me. It's going to be OK."

She didn't answer. She just nodded, nervously.

"You weren't here, all right? You were never here." I leaned back a bit so I could look her squarely in the eyes. "Neither was Kim."

She looked down at Lendowski's corpse, still shivering. "I'm glad I was."

I pulled her in and kissed her on the forehead, keeping her close, keeping my lips on her cold skin, feeling her veins throbbing away under my fingers. After a few long seconds, I pulled away and went back to his prone body. I fished through his pockets and pulled out his BlackBerry, which unsurprisingly was turned off. I stuffed both guns and his phone in the backpack.

"You need to go home. Before anyone finds him. I'll drive you into town."

"No. I'll be fine. I'll make my way back. You need to get out of here."

I shook my head. "I don't want you walking through the trail on your own. I'll drop you where it's safer. Then, just go home. They'll be wondering where Lendowski is. Anyone asks, you went out for some air and a think. That's it. You stick with that. You never saw me."

She didn't move. "What are you going to do?"

I looked down at Lendowski's body. "Find the bastards who paid him to kill me."

She placed a hand on my arm—her eyes locked on mine, grasping at anything. "He tried to kill you. Doesn't that prove something?"

"They'll just argue he was here to arrest me and I gunned him down."

I could hear the desperation in her voice as she pleaded, "You could come back with me. I'll sneak you in through the backyard, then you could go up into the loft space."

"What, and watch DVDs while you sneak me up some energy bars and a milk cartons?" I threw a weak smile at her. "Go home, Kim. It's dangerously close to your curfew."

"How can you find them when everyone's out looking for you?"

"I'm going to even up the odds. Don't worry. I've got an advantage here. I know how this game is played."

She threw her arms around my neck and pulled me in for a kiss. After a minute or so, I gently peeled off her. I reached into the backpack and gave her back the gun she'd brought me, along with the box of ammo. "Keep it near," I told her as I put away the one she'd use on Lendowski. "I seem to be building up a collection of FBI Glocks." Then I took a fresh burner phone from my jacket pocket and handed it to her. "I'll call you on this. I dialed my number from it, so it's stored in the call log. Call me if you don't feel safe for any reason."

"I won't feel safe till you're in the clear and back home with us."

I nodded. There was nothing I would have liked more. “We’re going to get through this, Tess. I promise.”

She looked at me for few seconds, then nodded back.

I nodded again, then started to drag Lendowski’s body toward the tree line.

# 31

*New York City, New York*

Across the street, I could see the nightclub that Kurt had designated as our latest meeting place. All manner of leather-garbed, tattooed and pierced night creatures were standing outside, smoking. It didn't look like where I imagined Kurt would spend his Saturday nights. Maybe Gigi was broadening his horizons.

After ensuring that Tess was safely ensconced in a cab and heading home, I'd left the stolen Caprice in a parking garage near White Plains station and taken a train into the city. Kurt had been out with his gal when I'd texted him, and he didn't seem at all pleased that he had to interrupt their date for an urgent powwow.

I'd changed into the clothes Tess had brought me, ditching Lendowski's suit and parka in an alleyway dumpster beside an Italian restaurant. I'd given the discarded items a generous coating of week-old pasta sauce to dissuade anyone from reclaiming them while on a high-calorie dumpster dive. I'd also taken the holdall that now carried the three Glocks and the stuff Tess had brought me and shoved it into a dark, tight spot behind it, making sure no one saw me and figuring it stood a reasonable chance of still being there when we left the club.

Satisfied as I could be that there was no one watching the place, I crossed the street and headed for the entrance, angling my face away from the CCTV cameras bolted to the building's facade. I was well aware of our intel-gathering agencies' capabilities when it came to finding a needle in a haystack, and I knew that, from here on, I'd need to avoid any kind of camera or even a phone call if I didn't want the monster servers that picked through anything they could sink their claws into to get a lock on my trail.

Before I could get through the door, two hundred and fifty pounds of bouncer blocked my way. "Wrong door, buddy."

I held up the denim backpack. "I need to change. The wife hates this side of me. Had to sneak out."

He thought about this for a moment then nodded me in,

grudgingly. "Go on." As I stepped past him, he called after me, "You'll have to tell her eventually, you know. One way or another, secrets always find a way out."

Everyone's a guru.

I maneuvered myself through a murder of Goth girls—some of them looking no older than Kim—and went inside.

Time to really screw up Kurt's evening.

Strobing lights and bizarre electronic music pummeled my senses as I made my way through the dark and sweaty catacomb-like space. I found Kurt and his new friend seated at a small table at the back, away from the frenetic dance-floor crush. They were both dressed in full costume, but the clientele was so freakish they fit right in. I was the one who looked way out of place.

Kurt, dressed in a red tie, high-collared white jacket and blue cape, smiled weakly. "We were on our way to a *Final Fantasy* all-nighter at a pop-up cinema. No time to go change and not too many places we could go to dressed like this. Gigi suggested we meet here."

Gigi looked at him quizzically, then struck a coquettish pose—chin resting on the backs of her hands. "Not Gigi. Lumina." She flashed me a grin. "From *Final Fantasy Thirteen*. And he's Cid. Cid Raines."

So she was also averse to using real names.

Terrific.

Lumina—pink hair, black bodice reining in her hard-to-ignore chest, pink-lined sweeper tailcoat, short feathery skirt and black mid-thigh stockings—looked me up and down. "So this is the Fed?"

Kurt nodded, looking intensely uncomfortable. I assumed he had filled her in while they were waiting, and while I wasn't massively comfortable with it, I didn't really have time to worry about such subtleties.

Even here, with the sound system at less than full tilt, no way was anyone going to hear what we were saying, so I decided to dive right in.

"Kirby's dead. And the evidence says I killed him."

Kurt's face lit up. "Jesus. What happened?"

I gave him and Lumina a brief overview—from my arrival at

Kirby's house to my escape from Federal Plaza. Keeping with my recent theme, I omitted the parts that featured Tess.

Gigi listened intently, unfazed—which surprised me. Kurt, on the other hand, looked more and more uncomfortable.

I got to the end and shrugged. "So here I am."

Gigi gave me the raised eyebrow. "To kill one government employee may be regarded as a misfortune; to kill two looks like carelessness."

I smiled. It was my fault. My own natural flippancy was obviously infectious. "Oscar Wilde. Nice."

Gigi smirked with unexpected appreciation.

Kurt said, helpfully, "His wife's a writer. She's—"

I shot him a withering look. "I did manage to read a book or two long before I met her."

Gigi grinned. "I have to admit I lost it myself with my adorable panda when he told me who you were, but this is all magnificently fucked-up. It's like you guys are living some old-school ARG."

Kurt gave me the eye roll. "Alternate Reality Game, dude."

Gig swatted him and said, "He knows that." Then she turned to me, all serious now. "What do you want us to do?"

"I'm not sure. Anything new with our search?"

Gigi said, "The CIA servers started running some kind of purge two hours after I started snooping around about the black ops you were interested in. I backtracked through the commands on the relevant server and it definitely wasn't an automated systems procedure. Someone went in and told the archive to overwrite anything connected to those ops. From the way the instructions are configured, I'd say someone didn't want their trail visible to the sys admins, which means the purge is outside standard data policy."

My head was spinning, and not just from the music. "OK, so you're saying you've hit a wall?"

Her mocking expression emasculated my question. "No wall's impenetrable, G-boy. I've left some anonymous botnets running. They mimic multiple internal searches of the SCI database. I've asked them to trawl for anything connected to the files. They'll come home to mama. But that might take a while."

“A luxury I don’t have.” I felt deflated. “I don’t have anyone else to turn to. And I need to start fighting back.”

Kurt held his hands out, defensively. “Dude, seriously, we can’t—”

“I don’t mean it like that, relax. But maybe there’s stuff you can help me with.”

“Such as?” Gigi asked. I didn’t sense resistance in her tone or her expression. More like excitement.

“Listen to the chatter. See if my name comes up. This is a CIA and FBI situation, and it seems like they’re keeping the whole thing hushed up—for now. I’m thinking neither agency wants to look inept, and it’ll be much easier for whoever’s after me if the cops aren’t in the way.”

Still in something of a daze, Kurt nodded. “Sure. OK. I guess.”

Gigi put a reassuring hand on Kurt’s arm. “We can do that. It’s *this* guy they want. Now go get us some drinks because you’ve heard all this before while I need vodka.”

Kurt got up and headed for the bar, and I asked Gigi, “What about that reporter? The Portuguese one in the Corrigan file?”

Gigi leaned in toward me. “Octavio Camacho. I looked into that.”

“He died shortly after the meeting with Corrigan in which he was mentioned, right? Back in 1981?”

She nodded. “Yes. In a rock climbing accident. On top of being a hotshot investigative reporter, he was also an avid mountaineer. The coroner’s report found death by misadventure.”

“That’s it?”

“Well, that and some scattered references about him on the DI’s servers, but they’re heavily redacted. He was definitely someone of interest for a brief period of time. Before he died.”

She gave me a knowing look. I didn’t disagree.

“No other hits on Corrigan or Corrigam or any other obvious misspellings?” I asked.

“Nope. And nothing else in any CIA or DI files—or at least not in the ones I could get into before the purge started.”

Kurt placed a White Russian and a couple of beers on the table and sat down. I was so bummed out I picked up my beer and almost downed the whole thing in one chug.

Gigi gestured to Kurt, who handed me his beer as a chaser.

I was warming to her.

She crossed her legs, flashing me way more thigh than a happily monogamous man should ever catch sight of. "Where are you going to stay?"

I was already halfway through Kurt's beer. "I don't know. Some crappy motel somewhere."

"No way. You're coming home with me. I've got plenty of space."

Kurt looked utterly crestfallen. "Hang on, hang on. Serious?"

"The man needs a pad, Snake."

I looked at them, totally lost.

They caught it. Kurt said, "Snake Plissken?" Still nothing. "Kurt Russell's character? *Escape from New York*? No?"

Clearly, I was going to need a translator around these two.

Kurt turned back to her and said, "I haven't even stayed over yet." There was a clear whine in both his expression and his tone.

Gigi laughed. "Hey, can't have Mommy getting too lonely, right?"

His face fell even further.

She elbowed him in the side. "Chillax, Snake, I'm only messing with you. You can come too. And who knows . . . Maybe—"

I threw up my hands. "Stop. Please."

Kurt's expression went back to the guileless smile I had always found so appealing. It was clear my appreciation of Kurt's many qualities had company, though there were certain qualities that would need to stay silent in my presence for this to work.

Gigi downed her White Russian and stood up. While she was taller than I expected her to be, her feathery skirt was so short I had to look away. My eyes caught sight of five guys and what looked like a drug sale going down in a dark recess of the club, away from the bustle. The negotiations seemed heated and for a second it looked like it was going to get nasty, then they settled down and got back to business. I had to remind myself to stay cool and can my instincts since I couldn't do anything about it anyway, so I looked away, trying to find something less burdensome on which to settle my gaze, only to be drawn back to my freaky friends and the micro skirt.

Gigi grabbed Kurt's arm, pushing him toward the door. "Come on, Cid. Lumina's feeling frisky."

As I trailed in their wake, the idea of being someone other than who I really was seemed immensely appealing.

# SUNDAY

## 32

*Federal Plaza, Lower Manhattan*

Seated at the conference table, Deutsch didn't think it was possible to feel angrier, sadder, more tired or more frustrated than she did at that precise moment. It was twenty-hours since she'd last sat in that same chair, twenty-four hours since her boss had chewed her out publicly in front of the same collection of grim faces. Déjà vu all over again, except for the fact that Lendowski wasn't at the table—or anywhere to be found, for that matter.

They'd found his car parked by a gas station a few yards away from the thruway's overpass. There was no sign of foul play. His work cell phone was missing and turned off, its battery pulled—meaning there was no way to track him. There was no one at his home, either.

Gallo had driven into town again and was chairing the emergency proceedings for the second day running, and on a Sunday morning at that. The two CIA liaisons, Henriksson and his silent partner, were also back in the room, as were four other agents from the New York field office that Deutsch barely knew.

"We know Reilly left the city in a car he stole from a parking lot on Fulton Street shortly after he escaped custody," one of the agents said. "A 1994 Caprice Classic. We've got the car heading north on the I-95 at around two thirty in the afternoon yesterday, so around twelve hours after his escape. We don't know what he did in the meantime."

Deutsch noticed Henriksson studying her impassively and knew her face must have looked like thunder at the renewed mention of Reilly's escape. She tried to shrink into herself in a vain attempt to disappear from the room.

"We have another couple of street camera sightings in and around Mamaroneck last night. Nothing after that. So either he dumped the car or—"

Henriksson seemed to lose patience and interrupted. "We're wasting time. We all know what happened. Reilly drove up there to see Chaykin. They met somewhere, Lendowski stepped in and Reilly got the jump on him. Whether Agent Lendowski is still alive or not is the only question here, although given we haven't heard from him yet, my guess is he's no longer around to tell his side of the story."

Deutsch jolted to life. "Hang on a second—that's a pretty big assumption to make with no evidence."

"Oh?" the CIA agent asked, his tone chillingly calm. "You have a more likely scenario about where your missing partner is?" His sardonic emphasis on "missing partner" was hard to miss.

Deutsch tried her best not to look like a jackrabbit trying to stare down an eighteen-wheeler. "No, but—why didn't he call in his position or ask for backup?"

The robotic Scandinavian wasn't going to be deterred that easily. "Maybe he didn't get the chance. Maybe Reilly jumped him before he had a chance to call it in."

"But why didn't he—"

"What?" He cut her off firmly. "Reilly already assaulted you and Lendowski once. It's not like he has an aversion to using force. And if I may offer some advice here, Agent Deutsch—I wouldn't go out of my way to defend an agent who escaped while under your expert custody. It might make people wonder." Without giving her a chance for an indignant rebuttal, the CIA agent turned to Gallo. "We need to bring in Chaykin. She knows what happened. We need to question her."

Gallo glanced at Deutsch, frowning, then swung his gaze back on Henriksson. "I agree, Chaykin's lying to us. I mean, that whole story she gave Agent Deutsch about her feeling trapped and needed to clear her head—it's total bullshit. No question. But we can't prove otherwise and we can't just wheel her in here based on conjecture. Her lawyer would have a field day."

"Then don't give her a chance to lawyer up. In case you've forgotten, this is a national security matter. In fact, we wouldn't be sitting here today if you'd handed Reilly over when we asked you to instead of giving in to his Fifth Amendment bullshit."

Gallo adjusted his position in his seat, visibly uneasy with where this was going.

"Reilly's history here might be checkered, but it's only checkered in terms of his unswerving commitment to getting the job done. And I don't appreciate your coming in here and—"

Deutsch slammed her hand down on the table, harder than she had meant. The noise succeeded in gaining her the attention of everyone present. "He's not a killer," she said.

Henriksson looked at her like she'd sprouted a second pair of eyes. "You do realize he's wanted for murder?"

"This isn't some crazy psycho we're talking about, OK?" She glanced around the table. "You know this guy. You've worked with him for years. I mean, Christ. Doesn't that count for anything around here?"

She looked around the table. She seemed to have struck a nerve.

"Look, I agree," she continued. "Tess Chaykin probably did give us the slip to see him. I can't see any other reason for it. But I don't think Reilly is a cold-blooded murderer. There's more going on here. You must know that."

She hazarded a glance at Henriksson and felt like slapping that narrow-eyed, immutable expression off his face.

He ignored her outburst and turned to Gallo. "I don't think it's advisable to keep Agent Deutsch on this case. I think her perspective is, at the very least, skewed by her—"

It was Gallo's turn to interrupt. "You know what? It's not your decision, is it? The last time I checked, the FBI wasn't a wholly owned subsidiary of the CIA. So how about you rendition your ass out of my bureau and leave this case to us, given that this is a domestic situation which, I think, just happens to be outside your agency's remit?"

Deutsch sat back and breathed out, zoning out of the tail end of the confrontation.

# 33

*Richmond, Virginia*

Roos guided his Cessna Skyhawk through the low-lying clouds and landed at Chesterfield County Airport without difficulty. The bad weather that currently had the East Coast in its grip was giving Virginia a break, and his time in the air was only marginally longer than the two-hour flight to which he had become accustomed.

Ten minutes later he was in a rental car on his way up the Richmond Beltway toward Midlothian.

He and his old partner had felt the need to discuss the current crisis face to face. They'd met at the golf club many times; it was a convenient midway point for them both, as far by plane for Roos as it was for Tomblin to drive to from his home further north in Virginia and his day job at CIA headquarters in Langley.

While in the air, Roos had exiled the call, the one that had awakened him well before he had planned to get up, from his mind. Instead, he allowed himself to savor skimming the frothy blanket of clouds below him, totally cut off from the complications of the world below.

Now that he was back on the ground, the facts as he was aware of them had rushed back into sharp focus, and they required his urgent attention.

He took the Midlothian Turnpike into an area to the west of Richmond which had morphed from having originally produced the very first commercially mined coal in what would become the United States to becoming home to several golf clubs. In the decades that he had known the area, the last remaining forests had almost entirely given way to suburban sprawl, leaving a couple of small parks and the lush, undulating hills and managed woodland of the clubs as the only reminder of how the land had looked. This continuing spread of subdivisions—and the highways that serviced them—was one of the prime motivating forces in his move to the Outer Banks and then later to Ocracoke, the simple fact being that the island had extremely limited capacity for development along with a community that understood the raw beauty of their environment.

Salisbury Country Club had genuine history, something he always looked for when selecting a location where he would regularly spend even the smallest amount of time. The clubhouse, built along Colonial lines in the 60s, had replaced the original eighteenth-century hunting lodge which had burnt to the ground in 1920.

Roos waved to the valet as he pulled up to the clubhouse. Although he came here fewer times with each passing year, he was still well known by the staff, and they kept the formalities to the barest minimum whenever he was here. The club was civilized enough to have no need for security cameras, except at the perimeter, the member vetting process alone being enough to ensure this would suffice. None of them would be signing in or out. If anyone asked, none of them had been here.

The door swung shut softly behind him as Roos walked into the largest of the wood-paneled private rooms. A large oil painting of Thomas Jefferson—who had saved the property from being confiscated by the British when its owner was captured coming back from Scotland on revolutionary business—hung over a massive stone fireplace, which took up most of one wall.

Edward J. Tomblin was sitting in a burgundy leather armchair drinking tea. He wore a dark brown tailored corduroy suit, handmade loafers and a forest-green V-neck sweater over a cotton shirt that appeared to be at least ten years old. Along with his Yale University tie, his attire made him look more like a college professor than one of the most powerful men in the intelligence community—a position few people who met him would suspect, as he exuded the kind of easygoing authority that had always perfectly complemented Roos's more intense manner. As befitted his position, though, Tomblin was a very shrewd operator. He had the influence and inside knowledge to move between the agency's often warring factions and always come out on the side that appeared to have won, even if it hadn't. Running the National Clandestine Service was the culmination of his career-management skills. The only step up from there would be running the whole agency, which was a remote but not an inconceivable possibility.

Tomblin looked up from his tea. "I'm not sure I approve of what they've done to the back nine."

Roos sat down on the floral-patterned couch to the right of his friend. "I'm not sure someone with a handicap that has to run into triple digits is entitled to an opinion on that matter, Eddy."

Tomblin snorted. "Maybe, but I still have to look at it every time you drag me down here. Are you going to join us for Christmas this year? Mary was asking."

"As she has done every year since my divorce," Roos replied. "It's still no. Regretfully, of course."

"Of course. I'll pass it on."

A waiter brought Roos the coffee he had ordered, then left again. Roos glanced around the room as he took his first sip. There was no one seated within earshot. The large room was silent except for the crackle of logs in the huge fireplace.

"This is a total clusterfuck," Tomblin said. "How the hell did Reilly get out?"

"We don't know. They said he got sick so they were taking him to a hospital when he made the break."

"What about your inside man? Is he still missing?"

Roos nodded. "Last time we spoke, he was trailing Reilly's woman. He thought she was going to meet with him."

"So Reilly took him out."

"Looks that way."

"That's what happens when you use a non-vetted asset." Tomblin thought about it. "We need to find his body. It only makes Reilly look worse. In case."

"Screw the body. We need to take Reilly out. That's all."

"Does Sandman have any leads?"

"Nothing at the moment. But Reilly'll resurface. He has to."

Tomblin said, "At least the Feds are taking our lead on this and keeping it shuttered. But we need to shut him down before we lose that window."

"I'm down with that, as the kids say. What about the penetration attempts? Have they stopped?"

Tomblin didn't seem alarmed at all. "No. Someone's still trying to break into our servers. Looking for you. This guy's got a real hard-on for you."

"And that's supposed to make me feel better?" Roos cursed the day he'd accepted to help out an old friend at the DEA with his offbeat plan to bait a major Mexican drug baron—a favor that had first put Reilly on his trail.

"Reilly's got someone helping him. Whoever it is, they're very good. Not many people out there with that much talent. If we can backtrace their location, it'll lead us to him. We can't let this get any further, Gordo. No more screwups. Any of this comes out and . . . you want to spend the rest of your years behind bars?"

"It's not going to happen." Roos struck the arm of his plush chair with each word.

"We need to put Reilly down. Fast."

"Have you put the Fort on him?" he asked, using his preferred nickname for the NSA.

"As of this morning," Tomblin said. "I got one of our guys there to set it up quietly. Full spectrum, priority one. We've got a lot of videos and recordings for the cameras and voice taps to work off, which helps. He's bound to turn up soon."

This pleased Roos. He knew how pervasive the NSA's reach into surveillance camera networks was and how effective their face recognition software—to say nothing of voice-match monitoring of phone lines and keyword tracking. "Who gets the alert?"

"Just you, me and Sandman. We're keeping it in the family."

"Good."

"Speaking of family . . ."

Roos set his mug down. He sensed there was more at play here.

"I'm worried about contagion and our favorite brainiacs."

Roos knew where this was going. He just shrugged. "They were always going to be a weak link. That's why we've have them on such a tight leash."

Tomblin leaned in. "They're civilians, Gordo. They're old. And they're not like us; they didn't join up for the cause. They're scientists who more or less stumbled into this. They gave us their expertise out of, I don't know, a sense of duty, an intellectual curiosity, maybe for the thrill of it . . . but at the end of the day, they're still civilians. With all the vulnerabilities and failings that entails."

"And we can't risk that any more."

"Padley had his Road to Damascus moment and decided to clear his conscience. The three of them—they talk to each other. Especially Padley and Orford. They were close back in the day. How do we know it's not a feeling they all share? How do we know one of the others won't do what Padley did?"

"Won't try to do, you mean," Roos corrected him.

Tomblin brushed the comment away. "I think we should clean house."

Roos let the notion sink in. He'd already considered it himself, but thinking about it and *doing* it were two different things. He knew these people. He'd worked with them for years. They'd done everything asked of them, without fail.

And now they'd have to die. Simply because they were a security risk.

Roos let out a small chortle. "You want the Janitors cleaned up? Not all of them, I hope. I'm kind of partial to sticking around a bit longer so we can enjoy these little chats before I embarrass you out on the course yet again."

"You know what I mean," Tomblin told him.

Roos nodded. "OK. We should start with Siddle. He's the more clued-in of the two."

"Sandman's going to have his hands full."

"It's what he does. Let's finish our tea and head out. I'll send him instructions from the first tee while you go through your mulligans." Roos studied his old partner. "Did you tell Viking what's going on?"

"No need," Tomblin said. "We can take care of it."

Roos nodded and leaned back into the couch. He could see two problems. One was that Sandman was indeed going to be a busy man. The other was not so much a problem as a subtle alarm going off deep in the folds of his experienced brain: he needed to make sure any blowback from this whole mess didn't end up catching him in its blaze.

Ex-partners and old friends counted for a lot, but every

relationship had its breaking point, and he knew things were getting stretched unbearably thin. Beyond the fact that they would all end up in prison if this thing ever blew up, some of his old partners had even more to lose if that ever happened.

He'd need to watch his back from here on.

# 34

*Chelsea, New York City*

I woke to the sound of Gigi busying herself at a kitchen range which occupied the center of the large loft. The sofa bed in one corner of the huge open-plan space was surprisingly comfortable and the low partition walls around it, though far from reaching the high ceiling, made the contained area feel like a separate room. The main bedroom had proper walls and a suspended ceiling, though I was still pretty sure I'd heard Gigi's muffled wails of ecstasy during the night.

We'd taxied back to her place well after midnight, after I'd retrieved the holdall. Gigi had insisted we stop for some Thai food on the way back and, seeing as I was her guest, I could hardly tell her otherwise. I also needed the nourishment.

Without turning on the main lights she'd gestured to the corner, told me to make myself at home, then pulled Kurt toward the bedroom. I unfolded the bed, opened a couple of the screens, took off my boots and jeans, fell onto the bed and was asleep in under a minute.

"Hey, you want bacon with your pancakes?"

By the sounds of it, breakfast was definitely going to be better than a motel muffin loaded with enough preservatives to survive into the next millennium.

Gigi's head peered around one of the screens. "Wanna keep me company? I gave Kurt a major workout last night, so I doubt he'll be up for a while."

The wink only made it worse and I shuddered. "Gigi, seriously. Way too much information."

She gave me a curious look, the mischief never buried too deep. "But you're happy for him, right? I mean, I can tell you like him. When he told me about you, I thought you must be using him, but he was adamant that you were a team."

"I'll deny it if he asks me, but yes, I am fond of Cid. Or Snake. Or whatever avatar he's using today."

"Good. Because I'm kind of fond of him too. And I wouldn't want anyone messing with him. He's a doll. And a surprisingly generous lover—not many of those around, let me tell you."

I gave her the look.

"OK, OK, sorry." Her expression shifted, her eyes now probing me. "Tell me something. You promised my big boy a get-out-of-jail-free card in exchange for helping you out. Which, let me tell you, while he's with me—he ain't gonna need, I'll make damn sure of that. But regardless—you're not in any position to help anyone out now that you've joined the dark side, are you?"

She was right. But I wasn't going to encourage it. I needed her and Kurt in my corner. I just looked at her, and said, deadpan, "And your point is?"

She just stared at me, not moving a single facial muscle, just expressionless. Then she burst into a big grin. "I'm just messing with you. Hell, I'm happy to do it just for the fun of it." She pulled her face back and headed toward the kitchen area. "Come on, Squidward. Your feast awaits."

The loft took up the top floor of a six-story, early twentieth-century building a couple of blocks east of the highline. From what I saw when we arrived late last night, it looked pretty iconic with its elaborate brickwork and beaux arts touches. The living space was huge and bright, even on a cloud-dampened day like today, enhanced by the light from the full-height windows at the front and the glass doors that lead to a small, private garden-like terrace at the back that was further enhanced by a commanding view of the Empire State Building. I glanced down from the window of my enclave. The street was lined with high-end furniture stores and quirky fashion showrooms, all with big logo-bearing flags outside marking their territory. Directly across from the building was a restaurant whose name I recognized, one of those big, trendy brasseries that are always packed. Gigi was clearly doing very well for herself, which I was curious about.

I pulled on my jeans and ambled out into the open space. It was dominated by a massive steel table at its center that was covered in stacks of every flavor of personal computer, server and router imaginable but only a single Mac. I guess that was yet another thing Kurt and Gigi had in common—a hatred of all things Apple.

A high-tech, glass-fronted cabinet stood along the sidewall, lights blinking asynchronously across the faces of the shiny new kit bolted within. I had no idea what any of it did, but I assumed that some of it was what enabled Gigi to roam the Internet undetected.

"Careful," she said as she appeared from the kitchen. "That's some highly tuned machinery you're looking at."

She explained that it was her gateway to the digital world, and I quote, "running across multiple fiber connections and defended by myriad firewalls, each and every IP packet bouncing both internally through spoofed IP subnets then externally through POPs at random and constantly changing locations around the globe and back again before reaching their destination."

I just nodded like I even understood ten percent of it. I glanced around, took in the space and the technology, and told her, "Nice."

She gave me a curious glance. "I know, right? And I bet you're wondering who's paying for it all?"

"I wouldn't presume," I said with a smile.

"Just another classic tale of a black-hat hacker turned corporate security consultant. I tell banks how not to get compromised. In return, they pay me considerably less than if I were hacking their firewalls and moving funds into my own account, but it's still some serious green and at least I don't have your cyber-crime buddies on my tail. And yes, I've done that, though I never kept a cent. It was just a thrill, but the whole thing's got a bit boring, which is why I'm enjoying all this black ops stuff Kurt and you are into."

I was happy to hear it was all legal. I was rapidly becoming a fan of Kurt's gal and, although she was still breaking into all kinds of secret databases—a lot of it for me—I was glad she wasn't involved in anything else that could land her behind bars.

I followed her to the gleaming white island around which the rest of the kitchen was arranged. An industrial-strength laptop was open at one end, so I sat at the other. Gigi was wearing an oversize Metallica T-shirt and track-pants, her hair scrunched up pineapple-style. Without makeup or a costume, she still looked pretty damn good. Maybe even more so. Kurt's toast had definitely landed jam side up.

Gigi set down two plates piled with pancakes, bacon and fruit, then brought over a cafetière and two white china mugs.

She pushed the plunger down and poured us some coffee. She took a sip from her mug and started tapping away at her laptop keyboard.

I asked, "Anything overnight?"

"You're extremely hot right now." She realized what she'd just said and blushed, something I wouldn't have guessed she was capable of. "I'm talking about the chatter. You're not my type, though."

"Duly noted." I steered the conversation back on track as I dug into the pancakes. "FBI? CIA? Any others?"

She smiled. "All of them. The NSA has been particularly animated. Everyone's asking how a killer got himself invited to dinner at the White House. Somewhere, I suspect, heads are about to roll."

I shook my head sadly. "I never did get Angus Beef with the truffle-scented Merlot sauce."

"All served on official White House china," Gigi added.

"Of course."

"Wow. That sucks." She pointed at my plate. "Try the bacon. I fry it in maple syrup. It'll run rings around that Angus Beef any day."

"I don't doubt that for a second." I took another sip of coffee and bit into a strip of bacon. I was impressed. She saw the look on my face, and it clearly pleased her.

"You'll be glad to know that the cops have been told to back off," she added. "There's no BOLO. No all-ports. No all-agency alerts."

"Nothing about a missing FBI agent?"

"Not that I saw." She set her mug down and fixed me squarely. "So . . . what do we do now?"

I finished my mouthful. "There was something else. This guy called me. Like with a proper, 'deep throat' vibe. Not the movie," I added. "I mean, not *that* movie."

She grinned. "I kind of got that."

"He told me he had information for me. Stuff he wanted me to put out there. A record of something he was involved in. He said that the last person he reached out to got burnt to death. Said he told the guy not to look into it before they'd met, but he did. Said it was in his blood and that he couldn't help himself."

That seemed to get some wheels turning. "You have any idea who your source was?"

"He never showed. The way things are going, he might be dead too. But the guy he talked about, I'm thinking he could be an ex-cop, maybe a private investigator."

She put down her fork and started tapping away at her laptop's keyboard.

"Let's see . . . died, fire, news, in the last—what, month maybe?"

I nodded.

She went back to work. "Limit results to US news sites . . . OK." Her eyes were scrolling down the screen, totally fixated. "Greensboro woman dies saving her three kids in a house fire, guy dies jumping into a fire at Burning Man . . ."

This went on for about a minute, then her face lit up. "OK, try this one on for size. Kyle Rossetti. Writes these big investigative pieces for *The New York Times, HuffPo, Vanity Fair*—quite the action man. Embedded with the troops in Afghanistan, did a big piece on the Deepwater Horizon oil spill that earned him a Polk award. Hot, too. The good kind, I mean. Check him out." She flipped the screen around so I could see his head shot. Yes, I had to concur: the man had a rugged face and a gaze that pretty much conveyed the extremes of human behavior he must have witnessed.

"And?"

She flipped the screen back, and the edges of her lips turned south. "Electrical fire in his apartment, a condo at 113th and Adam Clayton Powell Jr Boulevard. He burnt to death. About two weeks ago. Wife's a nurse. She was on night shift." She stabbed a strawberry half with her fork and looked over at me. "These guys really don't like reporters."

"Can you find the coroner's report?"

She chortled. "Please." A few clicks later, she was there, her eyes scrutinizing the screen like laser scanners. "'Accidental Death.'" Her fingers were soon away again, rapid fire, stopping only long enough for her to fast-read something, then she was off again. I was awed by the coordination between her fingers, eyes and mind, her ability to assimilate and filter through information at warp speed. "Of course there's several blogs claiming he was murdered for something he was writing about. CIA, Mossad, Putin. The usual suspects."

I gulped down some coffee, thinking about what to do next. "Who was the fire investigator?"

"Dan Walsh. A fire marshal out of Battalion Twelve. That's with Engine Thirty-five on Third Avenue."

"Can you get me his home address?"

Gigi gave me a mocking stare. "You really need to get with the program, G-boy."

I smiled. "Duly noted. Again." I finished my last mouthful of pancake and set my fork down. "OK. Will you see what else you can dig up about Rossetti? I need to shower. I have a fire marshal to visit."

"On a Sunday? Is nothing sacred to a rogue FBI agent?"

I had to smile at that. Then I remembered Lendowski's phone. "Can you get into a locked BlackBerry?" Before she gave me a look that could wipe the data off a terabyte array, I added, "An FBI BlackBerry."

A beatific expression lit up her face. Clearly I was about to make this a Sunday worth remembering.

# 35

*Mamaroneck, New York*

The scene outside Tess's house was markedly busier. Two local patrol cars had joined a second FBI sedan now parked along her street. The Stingray van was still close by, of course, but they'd moved it an extra block away to try and attract less attention. Gallo and Henriksson had at least managed to agree on that single point: the need to keep the story quiet and avoid letting the press and the blogs get hold of it. Because of the controversy over the rampant eavesdropping and the failures in recent foreign policy, the intelligence community was already trying to live down a constant barrage of criticism. The negative publicity of an FBI agent murdering a CIA agent was something they were both keen to avoid.

Annie Deutsch was back outside the house, leaned against her car, oblivious to the cold. After the big meeting earlier that morning she'd had a private sit-down with Gallo in his office and, after thanking him for his support, she'd lobbied hard to be reassigned to keep tabs on Tess, despite the fact that she and Lendowski had already failed at that task once. Gallo had initially resisted but he'd ended up relenting, willing to accord her a chance to redeem herself and find out what happened to her missing partner.

Four agents, assisted by members of the local police force, were canvassing the area around where Lendowski's car was found. They'd yet to yield anything useful.

Deutsch had yet to confront Tess. Even though she knew Tess had lied to her after she'd come home last night, she needed to get through to her. She needed Tess to feel Deutsch could be trusted. She didn't know what was going on, but she was sure that Reilly would need help, and she had to do everything she could to make sure she was there to offer it if—or rather, when—that time came.

She was thinking about how best to approach Tess when a number she didn't recognize lit up the screen on her phone. It had a Virginia area code.

She took the call with her customary, "Annie Deutsch."

"Agent Deutsch? Alejandro Fernandez. Virginia DFS, Manassas. I was told you're taking Agent Aparo's calls?"

It took her a couple of seconds to process what he was referring to: Virginia's Department of Forensic Science. Aparo's work cell had been rerouted to the switchboard at Federal Plaza, as had Reilly's. She didn't know where Manassas was.

"Yes, that's right."

"I'm calling with the lab results on the second bullet. Agent Aparo had asked me to keep him in the loop."

"I'm sorry—the second bullet?"

"From the shooting in Arlington?"

Deutsch straightened up. "I wasn't aware of this."

"The bullet from the body, that one's conclusive. It matches up to the Glock we found at the scene, the one registered to Sean Reilly. We recovered a second bullet, though. It was embedded in the wall of the garage. You weren't told?"

"No."

"OK. I assumed you'd want to know."

Deutsch felt her pulse race. "Of course. What did you find out?"

"It's fresh. Recent. Could easily have been fired around the time the shooting took place."

"What else?"

"Not much. We don't have a casing, and the bullet was too badly damaged by its impact to give us anything we can run through the database. One thing, though. It wasn't from the same gun."

A burst of adrenaline flooded through her. "You're sure?"

"Absolutely. Reilly's gun was a Glock. This slug's a forty-five. I've sent it over to the CFL in DC, but I doubt they'll find anything we couldn't."

Deutsch thanked him and told him to keep her appraised of any further developments. She hung up and was still thinking about how much a second bullet could help Reilly's case when a passing car distracted her momentarily.

She turned instinctively as her eyes were drawn to it. It was a white Toyota Prius with a single occupant, a man with a shaved head and thick, black-rimmed glasses. She couldn't see him clearly, but the impression she got was of a rather effete man. He slowed a bit as he passed—basic human curiosity, she assumed—glancing at the house and the uniforms outside before driving on.

Sandman's eyes registered every detail as he took in the scene outside Tess Chaykin's house.

His mind working like a 3D scanner he mapped out the house's relative location to its neighbors, its entrance and driveway, the positions of the law enforcement vehicles watching it. He was even sure he glimpsed Tess Chaykin at her window, looking down at her new reality.

He noted the FBI agent he'd read about in the most recent report Tomblin had sent him, Annie Deutsch. They had her phone on special watch now in case the CIA liaison's read was correct and she had more vested in the case than she'd admitted.

He thought of ways to apply more pressure on Reilly. Chaykin was the obvious soft target, of course. So were Reilly's son and Chaykin's daughter. He already knew where they went to school, knew the ideal spots on the likely route they would be taking every morning. School would soon be out for the Christmas holidays, but for the time being, he had that option if he needed it.

He wondered about Deutsch. Was she a potential pressure point too? Not as powerful, to be sure. But it was a possibility.

He turned the corner and drove away, headed for the café where he'd slipped Aparo his final condiment. The omelet baguettes looked to die for, he mused, enjoying his little joke, and he was famished.

It was there that he received an email alerting him to two new assignments, there that he first started imagining how he would kill the highly talented Marcus Siddle and the slightly creepy Ralph Orford.

# 36

*Queens, New York*

I drove out to Queens in Gigi's BMW 4 Series convertible, which she'd offered to me without even blinking.

I checked my face in the mirror—exhausted but presentable—before climbing out of the BMW and walking across the street.

The fire marshal who signed-off on the coroner's report on Kyle Rossetti lived in a 20s Astoria semi, from where it would take no more than thirty minutes to drive across the East River to the Twelfth Battalion building on Third Avenue.

A couple of traditional wooden sleds lay on the postage-stamp front yard. The noise of joyfully shrieking children mixed with the slap of snowballs finding their target drifted from the rear of the house. They sounded happy. I hoped I wouldn't have to apply too much pressure to get the information I needed.

The doorbell chimed as I pushed the button. I looked around the inside of the porch where several sets of ice skates were neatly arranged. From the number, colors and sizes I guessed they had three kids: two girls under ten and a teenage boy.

I was still gazing at the skates—wondering whether my entire family would ever go skating together again—when the door opened and a slim woman with freckles and warm brown eyes looked at me inquiringly. I figured she was in her mid-thirties. She was dressed in lazy-day sweats and wore her straightened mousy-blond hair in a loose ponytail.

She scrutinized me for a couple of seconds before asking, "Can I help you?"

"I hope you can. I need to find your husband. It's important."

"He's at the basketball court." She gestured. "Three blocks east."

I must have looked skeptical.

She shook her head. "I know. In this weather. It's nuts. But he shoots hoops every day, no exception. Says it keeps him sharp, so I'm not going to argue with him. Because in his line of work, if you're not sharp, you're dead."

I nodded in recognition, which she immediately read. "You a cop?"

"FBI."

"I hope he can help you." She turned to go back inside but turned back again. "Wait a second . . ."

She reappeared a minute later with a large thermos flask and a couple of mugs. "I made him some soup. You can share it with him."

I took them from her, thanked her, and left.

The basketball court was an unfussy concrete square boxed in by a twelve-foot wall of chicken wire. It backed up against a thicket of bare trees. Although some of the court was still under three inches of snow, the area inside the three-point line had been cleared. Dressed in baggy sweats, a tall African-American guy was playing one-on-one with an imaginary opponent, his breath misting in the freezing air.

He danced clear of the phantom defense, bounced the ball and released a shot. The ball dropped through the hoop without touching the rim.

I flashed my badge, hoping that my assured technique would preclude closer analysis of my ID. "Nat Lendowski, FBI. Just need five minutes of your time."

"On a Sunday? Would you have pulled me out of church?"

"I don't know."

He gestured to the court. "Well, this is my church. Come by Third Avenue tomorrow, I'll be happy to help."

I held up the thermos flask. "Your wife said I should bring this."

Taking a step toward me, he studied me for a moment, then shook his head and smiled. "OK, tell you what. If Janette wants you here, that's good enough for me."

He gestured to a wooden bench on a patch of snow-covered grass beside the court. The snow had been cleared from the bench; a thick winter coat slung over the back.

I passed the flask to its owner. "You investigated a fire. A condo at 113th and Adam Clayton."

He handed me a mug of steaming soup then poured one for himself. "Sure. Journalist by the name of Kyle Rossetti. Poor guy burnt to death. What's your interest?"

"We think he was working on a piece about Maxiplenty."

"The crime Internet thing?"

"That's the one. We have the founder in custody, but he's lawyered up and locked down." I took another sip of the soup. "It's good."

"Yeah, who needs more, right? A wife you still want to live with, kids you can be proud of, a job to come home from and food in your stomach."

I nodded, agreeing with everything he said, but still knowing I'd never be able to enjoy any of that till I dealt with my white whales.

Both of them.

The next part was a gamble. I knew it would sound plausible—and I suspected Walsh had better things to do than check it out for himself.

"We know Rossetti wrote about Maxiplenty. We're thinking maybe he uncovered more than he published. And maybe that made him a target."

Walsh screwed the top back on the flask. "Everything burnt. Files, laptop, everything. Unless he had cloud backups or documents stashed away in a safety deposit box, you're not going to find anything."

"You're sure it was an accident?"

"Absolutely. No evidence of foul play." He read my expression, cause he then said, "You seem disappointed."

Which I was. I didn't see the point in hiding it. "Kind of. It sends me back to square one."

He thought about it for a second. "Look, everything about the case is consistent with an accidental death: Melted insulation and carbon build up from arcing inside the light switch—that's a spark crossing the air from one piece of metal to another. It was only a matter of time before it got hot enough to start a fire. Stacks of books and papers close by. Flat battery in the smoke alarm. We think he was probably asleep on the sofa when it started. Maybe he got up and tried to deal with it, but his clothes caught fire. Guys from Engine Fifty-eight found him on the floor, maybe he tried to roll himself out."

I mulled over his words, then asked, "Say you wanted to burn someone to death, make it look like an accident. How would you go about it?"

He nodded, his eyes lingering on the distance. In his line of work, this was the case far more than it should be. "Off the record?"

"Sure."

He shrugged. "First, you'd need an apartment building which didn't have an AFCI—an arc fault circuit interrupter—in place of the standard circuit breaker."

"And Rossetti's building didn't have that?"

"No. We advocate everyone uses them, but there's no law to enforce their use. It's also easier with people who think they're too busy to stay on top of their smoke alarm."

I shook my head. Strike two.

"Then all you'd need to do is swap a switch somewhere in the house for one you've already messed with. Would take no more than a couple of minutes. Then, to be one hundred percent sure the fire takes hold, you'd use an ignition agent. Someone who knows what they're doing would know which one—maybe ethanol—where to place it and how much to use. Too little and the fire may not catch. Too much and you leave an ILR—ignitable liquid residue—then we'd know it was arson."

At the level at which Corrigan operated, I figured all of this was perfectly possible to accomplish—and all without leaving a trace. Another thought hit me.

"Did you see the tox report?" I asked. "Anything in his body that could have slowed him down? Something to make him unaware of the fire till it was too late?"

"No. Nothing. Not even alcohol. If there was something, that didn't leave a trace either."

I had nothing more to ask. "Thanks for your time."

Walsh stood. "Good luck and sorry I couldn't be more help. I'm gonna head home. Promised the kids we'd make a snowman."

He took my empty mug and added it to his own on top of the flask, stooped to pick up his basketball and left me sitting on the bench, feeling more and more certain that Rossetti was murdered—wondering how many more people Corrigan had killed in "accidents."

As I stood, my burner rang. It was Gigi.

"Rossetti's editor died two days after him." Before I could ask, she added, "Heart attack."

The two words just speared right through me and nailed me to the ground, right in that spot, as Nick's face—not breathing, but lifeless, still belted into his seat, as I pictured he was when the car was finally at rest—came storming back into my consciousness.

# 37

*Chelsea, New York City*

Gigi rolled her eyes. "Come on. Not every premature death is part of a conspiracy."

We were back in her loft, seated around the kitchen block—Gigi, he-who-must-not-be-named, and me. Gigi's fingers were dancing flittingly across her keyboard as she talked, while Kurt's were scrolling through pages on an Android tablet.

"Right now, I'd be more surprised if he did die naturally," I said.

"I called up the newspaper while you were on your way back. Said I'd met him at a TED talk I saw online that he'd been to and that he'd asked me to give him a ring when I was next in town. Anyway, long story short, the guy was a heart attack waiting to happen. Not exactly slim, never did any exercise beyond walking to the office and back from his apartment in Murray Hill and taking the elevator down not once but twice an hour to have a smoke—yep, like a chimney, since he was in high school. Also, beaucoup coffee. Throw deadlines and dwindling circulation and ad numbers all newspapers are facing these days . . ." She let her words trail off and gave me a knowing look.

"What about my partner?" I asked. "He lived on junk food, didn't exactly have the most stress-free of jobs?"

"Possibly indulged in erectile assistive pills," she interjected, half-asking. To my questioning look, she hastily added, defensively, "You said his libido was running amok since his divorce, and given his age—"

"I don't know, maybe," I said, cutting off the rest of her analysis. "I do know he was living healthily since his divorce. Eating better, hitting the gym most nights, cutting down on the alcohol."

"Even worse." Gigi stood up, crossed to the wall-mounted machine and started to make coffee. "You hear these stories all the time, people changing their lifestyle so fast their body can't keep up."

"So he's a likely candidate if he's living like a slob or if he's cleaning up his act? You can't have it both ways. Plus he had a buddy who was a trainer and who was overseeing his workouts. I remember Nick complaining about wanting to look better—there was some girl he liked and he wanted the weight to come off overnight—but the guy wouldn't let him."

Gigi and Kurt exchanged a quick glance—the subject was maybe too close to the bone, given the new and improved Kurt. Then Gigi turned to me and said, "Reilly. Read my lips. *No es posible.*"

"How do you know that?" I countered, getting frustrated. "You're not a doctor."

"I'm not, but—look, if you could kill someone by triggering a heart attack at will, don't you think we'd have read about it by now? I mean, at some point, someone somewhere would have used it and gotten caught doing it and it would have made a lot of noise." She waved her hands. "We'd know about it."

Kurt lifted his eyes from the tablet. "You're talking about doing it by, like, slipping someone some kind of drug? That would show up in an autopsy, surely?"

"What if it doesn't? What if these bastards have developed something that doesn't show up? Remember, this isn't some two-bit outfit we're talking about. This is spook central."

That quieted them down for a moment. "You'd have one hell of a cool murder weapon," Kurt said.

I couldn't get that idea out of my mind.

But it was more than that. Camacho, the Portuguese reporter, dies in a climbing accident back in 1981. Rossetti, the investigative reporter, dies when his apartment goes up in flames. His editor then dies from a heart attack, as does my partner.

How many others have died to keep secret whatever it is these people don't want uncovered? And what is it they don't want us to know about? Was that the reason the CIA was protecting Corrigan and shielding him from me? What was he part of? And what's the connection to Camacho that goes back more than thirty years?

The same year my dad died.

"OK," I said. "We need to try and figure out what Rossetti and his editor might have known. What can you do?"

Kurt glanced at Gigi. "We can look at both their digital footprints," he said. "Have a look at their emails, see what they might have searched for online. Phone records, too. Might get a movement trail from their phones too, see where they've been hanging out."

I went silent for a second. What someone with the right skills could do nowadays, the amount of information they could dig up about our lives—it still boggled my mind. I don't know that the guys at our Cyber Division could do any better.

"Great, let's do it. I also need to talk to a heart guy. Someone at the top of his game. I need to know if this is possible."

As he tapped his screen, Kurt said, "I kind of figured you would. There's a whole bunch of major cardiologists in this city, but here's a guy I thought looked interesting." He flipped his tablet around to show me. "Waleed Alami. He's at NewYork-Presbyterian—its Ronald O. Perelman Heart Institute, to be exact."

I perused his bio. Great credentials, to be sure. Looked gregarious, younger than I'd imagined, maybe in his late-forties, with a full head of swept-back hair and thin-framed spectacles. "Why him?" I asked.

"Well, he's a top cardiothoracic surgeon but he's also a big cheese in cardiac arrest research."

There had to be more. "And . . . ?"

Kurt gave it up with a slight grin. "He's got this cool Frankenstein machine to revive people who get heart attacks. I figured being cutting edge, you know, having an open mind . . ."

I nodded. "OK. Sounds good." I checked the big clock on the wall. It was four in the afternoon. I didn't think Alami would be at the hospital today. But I knew how I could get him to meet with me on a late Sunday afternoon. It was a small gamble, but I didn't think he'd call the office to check if "Nat Lendowski" really was with the FBI—or still alive, for that matter.

Before I called him, I needed to make another call. I didn't want to waste one of my throwaways, which I knew I'd need to discard if I used it now.

I turned to Kurt. "I need to make a call. Untraceable. Can you set me up?"

"*Hai, mochiron,*" he said with a little bow.

I gave him Deutsch's number and he did his usual party trick of putting it through a VPN'd fake Skype account that was billed to the credit card of some random woman in Japan. Moments later, Deutsch picked up.

"Are you still outside the house?" I asked without an introduction.

"Reilly!" she exclaimed. "Where are you?"

"Is Tess all right?"

"Yeah, she's—well, she's OK right now. She's in the house—I think. I mean, I can't be sure any more, can I?"

I didn't rise to the bait. "I need you to look into something. Are they doing an autopsy on Nick?"

She went quiet for a breath, then said, her tone soft, "I don't know, but . . . I'd expect so, given how he died, no? Why?"

"Tell the ME to look for anything that shouldn't be there that might have caused it."

"What do you mean?"

"I don't know," I told her. "Just get them to run a full tox on him. Make sure they look for anything unusual—anything that could bring on a heart attack."

She paused again—clearly, she wasn't expecting any of this. "You think he was murdered?"

"It's a possibility."

Her tone went low, muffled, like she was cupping the phone for privacy. "Shit. Who—and why?"

"I'm looking into it. In the meantime, do me a favor. Keep it to yourself. Just ask the ME yourself and get him to call you directly if he finds anything unusual. And Annie?"

"Yes?"

"Stay alert. Keep Tess and the kids safe. And keep yourself safe too. These guys don't mess around."

I could hear the tension reach her throat. "Reilly, we should tell Gallo. If you're right, we need to—"

"No. If you say something, they'll know we communicated and they'll take you off the detail and I want you there. I want you looking after Tess. Plus I don't want to put you at risk by having them think you might know something you don't. OK?"

She thought for a beat, then, without sounding overly convinced, said, "OK."

"Annie, you're going to need to be super-vigilant. Don't take anything for granted. Don't trust anything—not a phone call, not a badge—without checking it through."

"I hear you," she said.

"We're going to get those bastards," I told her. "Every last one of them."

I hung up, wondering if I believed my own words.

A thousand miles south, Sandman exited the United Airlines Airbus that had brought him down to Miami. He picked up the waiting rental car and drove off, feeling a familiar tingle, the one that preceded the adrenaline spike of a well-executed kill. He sensed a clean, strong bite there, one that could well lead to his quarry. He'd be getting that spike sooner, of course, here in Miami. He wouldn't be there for long. Then he'd fly back to New York and, with a bit of luck, he'd finally put the Reilly saga to bed.

# 38

*NewYork-Presbyterian Hospital, Manhattan*

I strode across the limestone oasis that doubled as the reception area of the Perelman Heart Institute, my footsteps echoing across the vastness of its five-story atrium. A muzak-free ride up the elevator later, I was on the fourth floor and being ushered into the office of Waleed Alami, MD.

In keeping with his gregarious bio pic, he was very welcoming and didn't scrutinize my creds, only giving them a cursory glance. In truth, only the guys who had something bad to hide ever did. I felt bad lying to him about who I was, but I didn't have a choice. We shook hands and I thanked him for coming in to talk to me at such short notice, and on a Sunday too. I then told him I was investigating some recent deaths and asked him, straight up, if there was a way for someone to commit murder by giving someone else a heart attack besides using the old movie trope of scaring the crap out of them.

"That does really happen," he said. He wasn't smiling or taking it lightly in any way, which didn't surprise me. In my experience, guys like him who were at the top of their game never did when discussing their field of expertise. "Are we talking heart attack, or cardiac arrest?" he asked. "'Cause you do know there's a big difference, right?"

"I don't, but—either one, if it's fatal," I said.

He thought about it for a moment, then decided he needed to take me through the basics.

Like most people, I guess, I had assumed both were synonymous, but he explained how they aren't at all the same thing. A heart attack is a circulatory problem and occurs when the blood flow to part of the heart is blocked. Over time, coronary arteries that supply the heart with the oxygen and nutrients it needs to keep doing its job typically get blocked by fatty deposits—plaque—and the clogging eventually leads to heart damage. The injury can lead to electrical conduction defects in the form of blocked beats or disrupted electrical circuits. Surprisingly, he told me the heart usually didn't stop beating during a heart attack. Some heart attacks, though, did lead to cardiac arrest.

The latter is different. It, and not the proverbial "heart attack," is the leading cause of death in our country, and it's very prevalent—over a third of a million out-of-hospital cardiac arrests in the US alone each year. It's an electrical problem, meaning it's triggered by an electrical malfunction in the heart that causes an ineffective heartbeat. The heart's pumping goes haywire, the brain, lungs and other vital organs get starved of blood and the victim stops breathing. Death occurs within minutes if CPR, or a defibrillator, aren't used.

"It sounds to me like what you're asking about is an SCA—a sudden cardiac arrest, when the heart just suddenly and unexpectedly stops beating."

"Yes," I said.

"Well, the heart has an electrical system of its own. It's not like other muscles in the body that rely on nerve connections to get the electrical stimulation they need to function. The heart has its own battery, it's called the sinus node and it's in the upper right chamber of your heart. This is what controls the rate and rhythm of its heartbeat. If something goes wrong with the node or with the flow of electric impulses through your heart, you get an arrhythmia, which is when the heart starts beating too fast or too slowly or not at all. In the worst of these cases, your heart comes to a sudden stop—sudden cardiac arrest."

I asked, "So is there something that can disrupt these electric signals—something someone could be given without knowing it, in one shot, one dose, not over time? Someone who's in good health, who doesn't have any kind of underlying heart disease?"

"Well, arrhythmias that cause cardiac arrests don't just happen on their own, but they can happen to people who don't have any pre-existing conditions."

"How?"

"Stress. Strenuous exercise—you've read about young athletes who suddenly collapse in the middle of a game. An electric shock."

I shook my head. "No. I'm talking about something like a drug, a pill—an injection, maybe. Some kind of toxin. One shot."

Alami shrugged. "Well, an overdose of cocaine will do it. Or a bad reaction to any number of illegal drugs. You could also have a drug-to-drug interaction that could lead to a fatal arrhythmia. It could be a number of things."

I shook my head again. "It needs to be something that won't show up in an autopsy."

Alami's expression shifted. I felt like he was suddenly a bit wary, even suspicious, of me.

I raised my hands defensively. "Doc, please. I'm only asking because I'm trying to understand if it's possible. 'Cause if it is, there could be a whole raft of murders that have gone unnoticed. And the people behind them need to be stopped before they can use it again."

He studied me for a moment, his expression clouded. "Well, if someone has come up with something like this . . . I can't imagine." He thought some more. "Undetectable in an autopsy? That rules out a lot of compounds."

"But do you think it's possible?"

"I come from a school of thought that believes everything is possible. Whether or not we've discovered it yet, that's the question."

"Where would you look?"

He thought about it for a few seconds. "There are compounds that could trigger a bad reaction that might not be detected in an autopsy because we already have them. It's just a question of how much is there, I suppose. Something based around calcium gluconate, maybe. At a much higher concentration than normally found in the body, it's conceivable that it might create an electrolytic imbalance. Or potassium chloride. It's in a lot of prescription drugs, and both potassium and chloride are present in the body. A spike of potassium could trigger ventricular fibrillation, which could lead to cardiac arrest, like they sometimes use in state executions. But again, the difficulty is in figuring out what the right dose is, being able to concentrate it into a small enough dose so it passes unnoticed when you're administering it, I suppose . . . and figuring out how to not have it break down and get absorbed into the body quickly so it doesn't show up in an autopsy. We're talking about much, much higher concentrations than you'd normally find."

"But if no autopsy were performed there wouldn't be any obvious external signs anyway, right? It would just look like a cardiac arrest."

"Yes." He had a worried look on his face, like it had sunk in. "You really think someone's doing this?"

"More so than before I walked in here."

He went pensive for a moment, then said, "Is there a recent victim? Someone you suspect this might have been done to?"

"Yes."

"And is an autopsy being done?"

"Yes."

"Can you get me in to see the body?"

"You're not a coroner. I don't know."

"Get me in. Let me have a look and run some tests of my own. The best way to figure out how it's being done—if it's being done—is by examining the body."

It made sense. Of course, I couldn't arrange it, not in my current persona non grata status. But I couldn't tell him that. Not yet, anyway. "OK. I'll see what I can do. In the meantime, will you think about it some more and let me know if you come up with anything?"

He let out a dry chuckle. "You think I can help it?"

I shook his hand and thanked him for his time, then I said I wasn't carrying an extra card, you know, it being Sunday and all. It didn't look like it worried him in the least. I gave him my burner's number and the office line at Federal Plaza. It was a risk, but I had to give him a working number in case he did come up with something, and it would have been odd not to give him the office number too. I hoped it wouldn't come back and bite me in the ass.

As he was showing me out, he said, "Next time you get someone you think this was done to, get the paramedics to bring them here as fast as they can. To the cardiac care unit, not the ER."

"Why?"

"Maybe we can help where others can't."

I wasn't sure what he meant, then I remembered what Kurt/Cid/Snake had mentioned. "Someone at the office said you had some kind of Frankenstein machine?"

He chortled. "Hardly. Come, I'll show you."

He led me to a medical ward and onto an OR that was unoccupied, and showed me a wheeled trolley that was packed with equipment—several monitoring readouts, pumps, and all kinds of tubes running between them. It looked like a robot someone put together in their garage.

He patted it. "This is it. And it doesn't need lightning to work." His face barely cracked into a smile, which was probably as much as I was going to get out of him today. "It's an ECMO. An Extra Corporeal Membrane Oxygenation. Since we've been using it, we've had twice the success rate of other hospitals in bringing people back from 'death.'" He used air quotes on that last word.

I didn't quite understand what that meant. I mimicked his quotes. "'Death?' You're dead or you're not, no?"

"It depends on what you mean by 'dead.' That's a whole other discussion . . . what I can tell you is, based on my research and after talking to a lot of people who we and others have brought back after their bodies were considered 'dead,' when any monitor you hooked them up to showed zero life in their bodies or brains—many of them had clear recollections of those lost hours. Their consciousness was still there, even if their brains didn't exhibit any signs of life—at least, none that we can detect. We can't explain it, neurologically. But it's a fact."

I would have loved to tell him about what I'd experienced over the summer in Mexico with Alex and El Brujo and how open-minded I'd become on the subject of our souls and their ability to transcend time and live beyond our physical bodies. But now was not the time for it.

"The thing is, at some point," he continued, "you, me, all of us—we're all going to experience cardiac arrest. That's ultimately the cause of death for most people. Usually, it's because something else in the body fails, maybe from an advanced cancer, and the heart is overstretched without getting what it needs to keep pumping. But if it happens when the rest of the body has the ability to keep going, which is very common, then the minutes and hours after your heart stops are critical. And right now, I'm sad to say, in most of the hospitals out there, the way they respond in that most crucial moment hasn't really evolved since the sixties."

"You mean with CPR and paddles?"

"Well, yes. We use them, of course—you have to, it's key. But it's not enough. See, most doctors out there, they'll do CPR for fifteen, twenty minutes tops, then they'll stop. It's like they've given up before they've even started. But this term, 'clinically dead' . . . it's nonsense. I don't know what that means, medically speaking. In those situations, the decision to declare someone dead is completely arbitrary. It doesn't reflect what we know about life, and how long after such a 'death' someone can be brought back. If you know what you're doing and you have the right tools to do it."

"How long are you talking about?"

"There's a girl in Japan who had been declared dead for three hours. Dead. Gone. They hooked her up and spent six hours resuscitating her." He smiled. "She's fine. In fact, she just had a baby." He moved closer to his prized machine. "We can work miracles with this thing. Well, maybe a combination of miracles and scientific wonders." He pointed out the various pumps, heat exchangers and oxygenators on the trolley. "We first cool down the body drastically and very quickly, in order to slow down any damage to brain cells. You need state-of-the-art machines to monitor and maintain oxygen levels to the brain, that's key. Then we siphon out the patient's blood, re-oxygenate it, warm it up and filter it and pump it around again. This buys us time to fix whatever caused the problem in the first place. We're doubling survival rates and when they come back, they're not brain damaged."

"Sounds like they should have them in every ER in the country," I said.

"From your lips," he replied.

I liked him. A lot. But I left there with a seething rage. Somehow, I was sure they'd killed Nick. Which, added to everything else, made me absolutely desperate to get my hands on these scumbags.

Forget about clearing my name—right now, it was only pure, primal revenge that was on my mind.

# MONDAY

# 39

*Cape Cod, Massachusetts*

It was inching up to noon by the time I was guiding Gigi's BMW down a winding lane, a parade of red oak trees looming over me from either side of the road like emaciated sentinels, still annoyed it had taken being a fugitive to motivate me to visit my mom and her husband for the first time in almost a year.

We'd never been as close as some mothers and sons. The combination of a career she frowned upon, my failure to find a wife—then finding one and not marrying her—plus the physical distance, meant we were only ever going to drift further apart as the years passed.

Across two decades, I'd probably spent no more than two weeks around her, and that was probably down to both of us. I guess I reminded her of my dad—like most sons, by the time I was thirty, I'd started to accumulate both physical traits and mannerisms that directly echoed his—and she reminded me of the first ten years of my life, which seemed near-perfect from my innocent perspective. Innocent till my dad blew his brains out.

I hadn't told my mom any of what was happening, both in the present and over the past six months, since I found out about Alex. All she knew was that I had a son who was now living with us, a grandson she was desperate to meet. Not involving her in the dramas of my life suited us both, since she didn't have to fret about things she had no way to influence, and I didn't have to worry that she was fretting.

Half a mile down the lane stood a classic Cape Cod house, perfectly symmetrical, white portico, sloped shingled roof and two dormer windows. Pastel-blue wooden slats covered the front of the house and all the windows had well-maintained, hung-back shutters. An equally well-maintained dark-green panel van with the words "Standish Tree & Landscaping Service—serving Cape Cod since 1972" stenciled in discrete letters on the side stood alongside the car port, in which sat my mom's Volvo SUV. The van belonged to Eric, my stepdad—though I never called him that.

My mom had remarried and moved out to Cape Cod while I was an FBI rookie in Chicago, so I'd never lived with him. He still co-owned and ran his own business, though most of the work was now done by his younger brother and nephews. As so often happens, my mom had chosen someone at the opposite end of the spectrum from her first husband. While Colin Reilly was an intense, self-contained intellectual who could easily spend sixteen hours a day alone in his study, Eric Standish was easygoing and warm and was happiest in nature when he wasn't with his extended family.

I parked Gigi's car behind the panel van, climbed out and stretched my legs.

The air was different here. Somehow sweeter than Mamaroneck, even though both places were bounded by the sea. It was also milder than New York, there having been only a couple of mild snow flurries in the past couple of weeks, neither of which had settled for longer than a few hours, though heavier snow was forecast.

As I rocked on my heels to get the blood flowing through my legs, I saw Eric walking toward me. He was wearing a thick woolen jacket and holding a small hand saw.

"Busy day?" I asked.

"Winter's the best time to prune," he said. "You can see the tree structure better without the leaves."

The area around the house had no lawn to speak of. Just neatly maintained areas of native trees and shrubs, the ones I remembered him pointing out being dogwood, hazelnut, black cherry, witch-hazel and pepperbush. As you'd expect, Eric could reel off the names of every single New England native, as well as an exhaustive list of non-native invasive varieties that he'd spent years encouraging his clients to eradicate.

He swapped the saw to his left hand and held out his right. Although he was the kind of guy who hugged men and women alike, we'd never got to the point where either of us felt comfortable enough to try it.

I shook his hand. "Sorry I didn't bring the kids."

He hadn't yet met Alex either, of course, but Kim had taken

rather a shine to Eric and the admiration went both ways. Even counting the weeks spent on her Aunt Hazel's Arizona ranch, Kim was fast becoming a staunch city girl, but she'd still enjoyed the couple of times Eric had taken her out on jobs and shared his love of the local habitat with her.

He smiled. "Sarah's going to be disappointed. She's dying to meet Alex, you know."

"I know, and I'm sorry. This wasn't planned. Next time, though. Soon."

"She'd like that," he said, his tone conveying that while she really would, he wasn't holding his breath while I made it happen. He thumbed a gesture at the house. "She's in the kitchen."

I nodded and stepped through the open front door, pausing to override a fleeting change of heart about my visit.

"Mom?"

She emerged from the kitchen, wiping her hands on an apron.

"Sean."

We hugged awkwardly.

"Come into the living room. I've got some fish pies in the oven. Eric will finish the vegetables."

That's something my dad would never have done. I don't think I saw him set foot in the kitchen once.

She untied her apron, slung it over a kitchen chair then led the way through to a cozy living area. A log fire was burning in the grate. Two perfect miniature pine trees stood at either end of the mantel, each of them adorned with shiny red wooden Christmas baubles. Tiny handcrafted anchors and ships' wheels also hung from the branches. On a varnished beech table sat a Christmas centerpiece, with snow-dusted pinecones and dried starfish.

Up here, the ocean got into everything, even Christmas.

I'd called ahead to see if my mom was around and to say that I needed to ask her a few things. I'd had to say it was about dad when she got all worried about what I needed to talk to her about, and it felt like she had asked Eric to give us space to talk uninterrupted, which meant he must have had some idea why I was here. Even me driving all the way out to talk to his wife about her first husband had zero effect on his positive mood or gracious demeanor. He was about as comfortable in his skin as it's possible to be. I admired him for that.

We sat opposite each other, Mom on a floral-patterned armchair and me on a brown leather sofa. We spent a few minutes on niceties, she asking how everyone was, about Alex in particular, chiding me for not having brought him up to see her already. I had to accept the blame sheepishly without being able to tell her what he'd been through. Then her whole body tensed up a bit and she asked, "So what did you want to ask me about regarding your dad?"

It was immediately clear she really didn't want to talk about him, but I could see she was ready to force herself, for which I was grateful.

"I need to know more about what was going on in his life in the months and weeks leading up to . . . you know."

I could see her trying to decide where to start.

She told me about how he'd become too caught up in his work, how it seemed to have taken over his life and pushed everything else aside. How his general mood had changed.

"He didn't seem there when we were together, most of the time," she said. "We'd be out having dinner with friends and it was like his mind was elsewhere. He'd stay at the office late, then spend hours in that damn study of his—you probably don't remember, but he'd come down sometimes, serve himself a plate and take it back up there and eat alone. It was like he'd lose all interest in family life. It wasn't until after that I found out he was clinically depressed."

"Yes, tell me more about that." While trying not to sound accusatory at all, I added, "I mean, how could you not have known? All that time?"

She shifted in her seat, her body language betraying some defensiveness. "He never talked. From time to time, when the moment was right, I'd ask, 'Are you OK? Are you happy? Are we good?' He'd just say, 'Yes, of course," give me a smile and a kiss—but I knew he was just avoiding something."

"But you never saw him take any pills, nothing like that?"

"No. He kept the diagnosis to himself."

"But, I mean—" I caught myself and took a breath. She was

going to clam up if I started accusing her. Funny how being with family makes you forget everything you've ever learned about how to interview someone. Not that Mom was a suspect, just that she knew so much that I didn't. Not yet, anyway. "Sorry," I said.

She smiled. "It's all right. This was never going to be easy. For either of us. It's why I'd hoped we'd never have to dig it up."

I nodded. "So how did you finally find out?"

"It was part of the coroner's report. The men investigating his death turned up the shrink he'd been seeing. Turns out he'd been diagnosed with clinical depression about nine months before . . . before he died."

"Did you ever meet this guy?"

"Oh, yes. I went to see him. He couldn't tell me much—you know, that ridiculous doctor-patient thing, even after death. I mean, how silly is that?" Her face relaxed with a bittersweet, faraway look. "He couldn't tell me much. He was just very sorry about what happened."

"Can you remember his name?"

"Oh, Lord." She thought about it. "Something like . . . Orwell? No . . ."

I could see her trying to retrieve the name from some burial ground deep inside her memory.

"Orford? Yes, Orford. That was his name. I can't recall his first name though."

I bookmarked it.

"Had he ever suffered with it before?"

"Not that I ever knew, and the psychiatrist said he didn't think there had been any previous history, but that there were aspects to his personality which were warning signs it could develop."

"Like what?"

"His insularity. Always wanting to be on his own. Focused on work to the point of obsession. Never really, truly happy. I mean, do you remember him smiling or laughing with a big, hearty, honest laugh?"

I thought about this and could only think of one time. When he unwrapped a parcel from a university publisher to find his first book inside, the title of which was so obscure I didn't remember it the next day, let alone almost thirty-five years later. His face had been beaming with pride—but she was right. He wasn't a font of joy.

She shook her head—the memories flooding in.

"Those last months, over a year really, he couldn't see the beauty in life and he had this broken smile . . . except with you. With you, I saw a different side of him. You lit him up like I never could. You made him forget about the heaviness of the world that he was immersed in. Then one day it stopped. Even you couldn't make him happy. No wonder . . ."

Her eyes had started to fill with tears. She took out a crisp, folded white handkerchief, shook it out, and dabbed at her eyes.

I made my voice as gentle as possible, hoping I was on the edge of a genuine revelation. "No wonder what?"

"No wonder I fell in love with Eric."

It was guilt, as much as sadness. Some small part of her must still have felt that falling for someone else was a betrayal. Both of her husband and of their son.

"He doesn't want to change the world," she added, "or stand up for justice." She gestured to the house. "This is enough for him. We spent more time together in our first six months than your father and I did in our last five years together. It must make me sound so very selfish . . ."

The tears started to flow again.

I shook my head.

"Not at all. And I'm happy you found him. You deserve this. You deserve to be happy. Everyone does."

We were both silent for a long moment as she shed a few more tears, dried her eyes and composed herself. Then she stood, refolded her handkerchief and placed it carefully back inside her pocket.

"Let's get some food."

Sitting in his rental car across from Flo Line Autos, Sandman studied his target with unerring concentration.

The high-performance car shop's owner, Marcus Siddle, was showing some guy and his girlfriend around a newly customized Chevy Impala low rider. The client oozed the testosterone and barely suppressed violence of a soldier in one of Miami's many drug gangs, while his girlfriend was a classic Florida muscle-car babe—apart from the ubiquitous tattoos scattered around her curvy body. She was, even in December, wearing denim micro-shorts the size of knickers and a midriff-baring, too-tight T-shirt. Her only concession to the weather was a pair of knee-high UGG boots and the extra coke she had to be snorting to ward off the goose pimples.

Siddle's outfit had gone the whole nine yards on the thug's car. The Impala was a deep purple color, its rear sitting barely an inch off the ground. The sound system was at full blast and was so loud it was making Sandman's car vibrate.

At the flick of a switch, the rear suspension jumped skyward, sending the rear of the car at least three feet off the tarmac. The owner clicked the fingers of one hand together, his gold bracelets fighting to stay on his wrist, grinning like the babe had just told him she'd invited her girlfriend over for a three-way.

As the guy climbed into the Impala to check out the interior, Siddle walked over to the babe, casually brushed his right palm against her ass and slipped a business card into a rear pocket of her shorts.

Sandman knew of Siddle's seductive abilities when it came to the opposite sex, but he still couldn't wrap his head around how the guy managed it with such ease. On top of being certain that his target would find him attractive, he had to be absolutely sure they wouldn't mention his approach to their husband or boyfriend, especially if it was someone who, by the looks of it, was far from averse to inflicting serious pain on anyone who crossed him. Sandman supposed it was all down to selection. Identifying a target, then choosing the right moment.

In that way, it was very much like Sandman's own line of work.

Timing was everything.

# 40

I said yes to the offer of coffee, which Eric went off to make, then thanked my mom for lunch—and for agreeing to talk about dad.

The meal had been accompanied by small talk—Kim, Alex, Eric's grandnephews, the snow, the appalling ignorance and downright negligence of people planting and even selling the wrong kind of viburnums—anything except mention of Colin Reilly. But with Eric out of the room, the mood changed, both of us lost in thought about a man neither of us had known as well as we wanted to, needed to, or thought we did.

She looked across the table at me. "He loved you."

I wanted to say, "He loved you too," but as the thought formed, something from a long-buried part of my brain made me wonder if, toward the end, maybe it wasn't true. Maybe he cared for her—I'm sure he did—but did he love her? I mean, he must have loved her once. I'd seen their wedding photos. Pictures of them with me as a baby. I was pretty sure that love had come through, loud and clear. Why had that changed? Was it a chemical imbalance that made it unavoidable? Was it simpler—his job, his introversion, his dedication to work at the exclusion of everything else? Or was there something else?

So I said the only other thing I could. "I know he did. And you loved him too. I know that."

She looked up, as if she'd find him floating there. "Yes. But too much and for too long, when I was nothing but the housekeeper who kept everything ticking over, a shadow he passed on the stairs."

I looked directly at her. "Thank you, though. Thank you for staying with him, throughout. I can't imagine it was fun, but I also can't imagine how my life would have gone if I'd lost you both."

She stood, unable to deal with this, some part of her still feeling guilt that she'd failed him somehow—maybe failed me too.

I realized that the way things were going with my life, I might not be able to see her again, so this time I stood up and I hugged her tight. I held her for a few seconds—past the point when she instinctively tried to pull away, all the way through to the moment when she gave in and let herself feel my embrace.

Finally, I let go and stepped back. There was the faintest smile on her face—a perfect memory.

So I waved, turned and headed for my car.

Eric followed me outside, holding a travel mug.

"Figured you'd be on your way."

I took it. "Thanks."

Then that thought again, but louder.

I knew Eric could keep his counsel; it was one of the things I respected about him. And, as if sensing my thoughts, he said, "It's tough for her, talking about that time. You know, things weren't great between them towards the end. And the last thing she'd want is to tarnish your memory of him."

The thought was now too loud to ignore.

I asked, "Was there someone else?"

He just looked at me for a moment, his expression neutral.

"I can't raise it with her, no matter the stakes. I just can't, knowing how she'd react," I added. "It's where I draw the line. And if you knew anything about what I've been through these past few days—weeks, even—you'd appreciate what that means."

He shook his head and smiled. "I don't need to know about it. You love her and you don't want to hurt her. That's where you and I climb the same tree."

He gestured for us to head over to the BMW, as far from the house as possible.

"I don't know," he said.

"But you know something?"

He shrugged, the discomfort apparent in the deepening furrows across his face. "It was years ago. Your mom and I, we were just flicking through the channels one night. We came across the remake of the *Thomas Crown Affair*. As we started watching it, I made some comment about how Rene Russo couldn't hold a candle to Faye Dunaway. I must have struck a nerve or something, cause your mom bristled at the mention of Dunaway and, after a while, she asked if we could watch something else. I didn't press it, but I was curious. And when I asked her about it later, she just shrugged it off and asked me to drop it. I couldn't help but want to know what was going on, and a few days later, I picked my moment and asked again. She just said she didn't care for the name much, said it reminded her of someone and that it had to do with your dad, and asked me to leave it at that. I did."

"Was that all she said?"

Eric hesitated, then added, "No. She did say it was an assistant of your dad's. One of his grad students. Another Faye." His look filled in any blanks I still had.

A grad student. Christ. Talk about tarnishing a memory.

I knew what I needed to do. "No last name?"

"No, sorry."

We got to the car, and I thanked him for his candor.

He held out his hand. "You'll bring the kids next time? She'll never tell you, you know how she can be, but she wishes she could see Kim more, meet Alex."

I shook his hand. "Sure. In the New Year. We'll all drive up."

I climbed into the BMW, started the engine and drove away, leaving Eric wondering why, despite some considerable effort, my expression had so totally contradicted what I'd just said.

I drove a bit, then pulled over and parked ten miles west of the house. I drank the coffee, then called Kurt and Gigi using a smartphone they'd given me. They were working on Rossetti and his editor's digital trails, as Gigi had suggested. I asked them to find a psychiatrist named Orford who'd been practicing since at least 1981, probably in DC, and I told them to keep working their way out from there till they found him. I also asked them to track down a postgraduate research assistant in jurisprudence at George Washington University at around that time with the first name Faye.

I then started making my way back to New York City, hovering just under the speed limit, with the radio turned up full blast to try and drown the armada of memories that had me under siege.

# 41

*Miami, Florida*

An onshore breeze had cleared the night sky of any lingering clouds as the customized Lamborghini Aventador blew north along the A1A, its growl echoing up to the heavens and scaring off any remnants that were stubbornly clinging to the velvet dome high above it.

As the supercar hit the Hillsboro Mile, its driver pressed down on the gas pedal, powering it past a hundred and forty miles per hour. The driver knew the route intimately. He knew this stretch of road was pretty much totally straight. He knew there were no traffic lights for three miles, and no speed traps either. He knew that at three in the morning, there would be no police cruisers or bikes around with uniforms that needed to be bribed, and that he could pass using the oncoming lane, though it was unlikely he would need to. There was nothing but empty road, a clear mind and a pleasantly aching groin from the award-worthy oral experience he'd enjoyed an hour earlier from the nineteen-year-old tattooed muscle-car babe, fringe benefits of owning one of Miami's top custom-car workshops.

Whenever he and his guys finished work on a vehicle, he'd take it out for a drive in the small hours and really open it up, before the owner came in to collect it. The Aventador was a truly glorious piece of machinery. It handled like the muscle-car babe—no complaints, zero hang-ups, nothing fatigued from overuse. It just did exactly what you wanted it to do and performed it with pulse-spiking gusto.

His team had taken the horsepower from the already monstrous seven hundred to seven fifty, reworked the rear apron completely around a new stainless steel exhaust tailpipe that was split into four, added a striking rear spoiler, changed the wheels into a light alloy that was forged and not cast, pimped the entertainment and communication system, then given the whole thing a matt black finish, which he wasn't crazy about and was the only thing he would have done differently. Still, Siddle hadn't argued and had kept his reservations to himself. In his customization business as well as in his work as an assassination contractor for the CIA, the client was always right.

Marcus Siddle looked about thirty-five, though he'd been on the planet exactly fifty-nine years and ten months, which he knew because in two months, to the day, it would be his sixtieth birthday. He had a tanned, clean-shaven face and a youthful body honed by thousands of hours in the gym. Contrary to what people thought when he removed his baseball hat to reveal hair cropped short enough to hide his almost total baldness, a state of denial about his age had not led him to try and look young, simply because he had never stopped feeling—and, in many cases, acting—like he was still in his mid-twenties.

Unlike many men his age and with his more-than-healthy bank balance, he abhorred the idea of Botox, surgery, or even a hair transplant. He was totally comfortable in his own skin, so comfortable that the thought of screwing with it made him almost physically sick. He knew several guys—at least three at his golf club alone—who'd spent tens of thousands of dollars trying to make themselves look younger. The psychology of it made no sense to him. If you really loved yourself, why would you change yourself into someone else? And Marcus Siddle loved every single part of himself, without exception or reservation. He never experienced self-loathing about the amount of money he'd made from customizing cars for people richer and stupider than himself, never felt regret that, as the years passed, he hadn't put his considerable talents to more constructive use, never felt sad that he'd never spent more than three months with a member of the opposite sex before becoming bored, and never felt guilt about the people he'd helped kill because his employers had told him to. It wasn't that life was too short, but that life was simply too much fun for any of that negative bullshit. And he enjoyed it all, from the fortnight he'd spent with the twin girlfriends of a Russian mobster after he'd sent the fat fuck and his brand new Harley into the Chicago River, to the satisfaction he experienced bringing down a large twin-jet helicopter en route to the Hamptons because he understood the on-board navigation systems better than the guys who built and designed them.

Surprisingly, despite all the deaths he'd caused, there was nothing in Siddle's past except love and kindness. His dad, an Air Force Colonel, had been supportive and often told him that he'd be proud of his son no matter what he did when he was older. His mom had often voiced how much she loved him. In high school, he'd excelled in math and science and been a social success. At college, he'd studied electrical engineering before joining the Air Force and training as a mechanical engineer.

He'd been shipped to Vietnam in the last months of the war to maintain an assortment of fatigued Phantom, Crusader and Super Sabre fighter-bombers. When he returned to the US, he'd been recruited by the DoD, moving to the CIA a couple of years later after being personally selected by Edward Tomblin, who was only a few months older than him. Then, in the 1990s, he'd gone private, continuing to work for the CIA as a contractor, but also starting his car business after a move to Miami.

He'd fallen in love with the city several years earlier after being dispatched there to sabotage a boat owned by an ex-agent of Cuba's *Direccíon de Inteligencia*. The guy and his family had relocated to the US under new identities, but only enjoyed a few weeks in the land of plenty before they'd all died in a massive fireball when the ex-agent's boat had exploded due to what was later assumed to be a faulty fuel line.

Siddle had quickly built up the shop to the point where he could leave his team to run the place and use an auto show, vehicle auction or consultation as cover for his more lethal pursuits.

He was watching the digital speed counter flicker higher when he felt a slight pull to the right.

His senses were so highly tuned to the smallest reaction coming through from the car that even with that barely noticeable move, his pulse spiked.

Just the new tires bedding down, he thought.

As he passed a line of five-story apartment blocks, the car jerked to the left, halfway across the oncoming lane, then swerved back again just as quickly.

Siddle lifted off, slowing the car right down. Perplexed, he turned the wheel carefully left and right, checking the steering's response.

Everything was fine.

He made a mental note to tell his crew the car needed more testing before it could be delivered to the waiting client. He could do without one of his customizations killing its occupant, something that had never happened up to that point, even though he specialized in extreme cars that were usually far too powerful for the limited talents and experience of those who ordered them.

He'd also have to bawl out the guys for letting him drive the car before it had been properly checked. Although his habit of taking out the finished vehicles had started as a way for him to personally check that everything was in order, it had become more than that—an opportunity to drive as many different cars as possible, to feel that while his clients might own that particular supercar, in a way he owned them all.

Once he was through Deerfield Beach he'd throttle the car back up to over a hundred, shoot past Lake Boca Raton, take Linton Boulevard west over the water, then turn south and take Route One back into the city, using the three-lane section through Boca to revel in some at-speed passing and lane changes.

Siddle eased off the gas and shifted down into second gear as he approached East Hillsboro Boulevard. The lights were red and he had no reason to jump them. As a matter of fact, he enjoyed taking the engine right down through the gears, enjoying the gurgles of each downshift all the way to a growling idle. Then, as the lights turned green, he'd be flooring the gas and feeling the gees and the kick of each gear shift.

Before the lights turned, the car lurched forward, hitting sixty in well under three seconds and continuing to accelerate.

As he struggled with the controls, Siddle's whole body iced over as he realized what was happening.

He was no longer driving the vehicle.

The vehicle hijack system he'd spent over a year developing was controlling the car.

There was no point him trying to do anything. His design was flawless. He knew all the car's safety features would already be disabled—no airbags, no emergency brakes, no pre-tensioned seatbelt.

And he knew what the inevitable outcome would be.

He'd watched it enough times before, never imagining that he'd ever experience it from the driving seat.

Sandman had waited until the Lamborghini he was trailing powered away down the Hillsboro Mile, checked the 3G signal for the final time and keyed in the passcode to make the system go live.

These days, most functions in most cars, from a mid-sized Toyota to a Bentley and beyond, were controlled by an onboard computer. Hack that computer using either a physical device connected to the on-board diagnostics port—the one car technicians use to investigate a fault in a car by plugging in a laptop computer under the dashboard—or wirelessly via a phone signal dialed into the car's telematics system, and you could control anything that the computer controlled, from the windscreen wipers to the cruise control, from headlights to steering and braking. Not only that, but such an attack code could also be programmed to erase any evidence of its existence on the device, complicating, or even preventing, a forensic examination of a crash scene.

And with each year, as the embedded systems in cars became more and more sophisticated, the opportunities for automotive cyberattacks grew.

The hack Sandman was using required nothing more in the field than a Netbook with a 3G SIM card. Siddle had designed it to bypass the car's firewall along with any proprietary security features specific to the target make and model. Although the list was certainly not exhaustive, Siddle had focused on expensive cars all the way through development, his argument being that not only would they have better security and therefore represent a sterner test of his expertise, but that it made sound operational sense seeing as many of their future targets would drive high-end vehicles.

Due to his personal taste, Lamborghini Aventadors were on that list.

Siddle was almost half a mile ahead of him when Sandman heard the collision.

He couldn't see the crash site clearly, but he didn't need to.

At that speed, there was simply no way that Siddle could have possibly survived the impact.

Helpless and only able to watch as the Lamborghini's speed increased, Siddle's thoughts darted across scattered memories of some of the people he'd already killed using the system: the Saudi diplomat and his gay lover; the congressman who kept refusing to do what he was being asked to do; the female college grad who was already one of China's top corporate spies. They would all have thought their cars had simply malfunctioned.

Siddle knew there was no malfunction in the Aventador.

It was simply that, right now, someone else was driving the car.

He saw the speedometer streak past one-twenty and keep climbing, and as the purple streak veered slightly to the right, Siddle swallowed hard as a large, sand-colored building in the distance grew very big, very quickly.

Hitting it at that speed would be like falling thirty stories onto the sidewalk. And although its creator had just been killed by unstoppable force meeting immovable object, he would have been proud that yet again, his system had worked perfectly. And, because of the way the system was designed, there would be no evidence of anything other than driver error, with every rogue command being logged as coming from the driver's own actions.

For the press, it would be yet another story about an entitled star or a reckless speed freak with no respect for the law—unless it was somebody everyone loved, in which case it would be a genuine tragedy that that person was taken from us all so young.

The only people who would miss Marcus Siddle, though, were the people who had ordered his death.

# TUESDAY

# 42

*Philadelphia, Pennsylvania*

After a troubled night tossing around Gigi's sofa bed I decided to make a very early start and it wasn't even eight o'clock by the time I found myself standing outside the Criminal Justice Center on Filbert Street, waiting for Faye Devane, hoping she'd be willing to talk about someone who died more than thirty years ago, someone she may not want to think about, let alone discuss.

Courtesy of Kurt and Gigi, I had a recent photo of her and a solid idea of where she'd be at this time of morning. I didn't feel great about Kurt having hacked her email account and credit card statements, but I couldn't risk either the delay or the point-blank rejection that would, in all likelihood, accompany a polite request.

Faye Devane was a Philly native. She'd grown up in Glenwood and won a scholarship to George Washington where she'd spent nine years that culminated in a doctorate in Judicial Science. After that, she'd moved back home and joined the Philadelphia Bar. She lived alone in a Brewerytown apartment, having never married nor had children. Her persona appeared to be reflected totally in her professional life as an assistant defender working exclusively for the Philadelphia Defenders Association, a not-for-profit whose members are barred from both private practice and partisan politics. From the snapshot of her that my indefatigable, if quirky, support staff had put together, I suspected she'd be a formidable opponent, both in court and as an interview subject.

Kurt had been tracking her cell phone since she'd left her apartment at six forty-five and had messaged me that she'd be arriving at some point within the next five minutes, her routine being to get in at least an hour before she was due in court.

After several minutes scanning the pedestrian traffic in both directions, I saw her approaching, briefcase in hand. She looked much younger than her fifty-six years. She wore a navy blue pants suit, which I assumed would highlight the blue eyes I'd already seen in her photos, and polished black loafers. Her raven-dark hair was short—almost boyish—and it didn't look like her slim figure had changed much over the past thirty years: easier to maintain given she'd never been at the mercy of pregnancy and childbirth and the hormones and physical changes that accompany them. It was still easy to guess how she would have looked when she knew my dad and just as easy to see why any man would have fallen for her. She had an agile grace and moved with total confidence—both regarding her professional status and her appearance.

As she approached, I intercepted her as gracefully and non-threateningly as I could managed.

"Faye?"

She paused and nodded, her face giving absolutely nothing away. I guess she'd had years to practice that skill.

"I'm Sean Reilly, Colin's son." I watched and saw her eyes fill with recognition, then surprise, before settling on a forced confusion. "Can we please talk? Just for a few minutes?"

She made a move to get past me. "I don't know who that is."

I put my arm out while giving her a relaxed, warm smile. "I hope you lie better in court."

She fixed me with a firm, no-nonsense look. "I never lie in court. I leave that to the cops." She scrutinized me more closely. "You're a cop yourself, aren't you?"

She tried to step around me again, but I blocked her. "Faye—"

"I'm expected in court."

I knew I had only one chance to get through to her.

"I'm not a cop," I told her. "I'm with the FBI. And from what I've read, you and I share something else with my dad. Your whole life is about fighting for justice in the face of huge odds. About the greater good rather than personal gain. He would have been proud of you. I hope he'd be proud of me, too."

She was quiet for a moment. "What do you want?"

"Just to talk. Give me ten minutes. Please."

Her eyes flicked down to her watch then back to me. She sighed. "OK. Ten minutes. This way."

She gestured east along the street and we headed in that direction. She eyed me as we walked, sizing me up, but more than that—like she was looking for something in me. It made me wonder if, somewhere in her mind, she was twenty-four again and walking with my dad.

"You're from here, aren't you?"

"Look, I know you probably know more about me than I remember about myself. Just do me a favor and don't tell me how, OK? 'Cause I'd really rather not know."

We covered the block in silence. I thought about the fine line between how a tragedy can either define your life—make everything about that one moment—or give your life crystal-clear definition, as it seemed to have done with Faye. The jury was still out on which applied to me, because although my life had had definition for many years, over the past few months everything had become defined by what had happened to Alex and by my father's suicide. I just hoped there was a way to get back to the other side.

I followed her across Twelfth Street and into the Reading Terminal Market, which occupied the lower levels of a nineteenth-century train shed. She led me through the market stalls—most of them only just open for the day—till we arrived at Old City Coffee.

I asked her what she wanted and ordered, then carried our coffees over to an empty table at the edge of the seating area where we took seats opposite each other. She sat in silence for a moment, then turned toward me.

"You look like him," she said as her gaze danced around my face. "Not just the eyes. The expression."

I nodded, half-smiling. "So I hear." I paused for a breath, then I asked her, "Were you together?"

Much as she tried to mask it, I could see her breath catch and her eyes flare. "You don't mince words, do you?"

"I'm sorry, but—I wouldn't be here if this wasn't important. And I'm not some troubled soul looking for some kind of closure related to his parents, believe me. This has to do with an investigation."

"Into what?"

"His death."

This time, she didn't try to hide her surprise. "What are you talking about? And why now, after all these years?"

"Tell me about you and him first," I said.

A solemn sadness spread across her face. "We were together," she said, averting her gaze. "Very much so."

Even though I suspected as much, the stark, unabashed confirmation still hollowed out my stomach. The idea of my dad, a dad I hardly got to know, someone I'd idealized despite the way he died, maybe even more so because of it, the idea of him, leading a double life, cheating on my mom—it was a tough image to accept, even after all this time.

I asked, "How long were you together?"

"Just over a year," she answered without hesitation. "I'm sorry if this is disappointing to you, but I feel you want the truth."

"I do. And I appreciate your candor."

She nodded and looked away, into the distance. "I never recovered, you know. He was very special. A big part of me died with him. I never forgave myself either."

"For what?"

She took a strengthening sip of coffee. "Your dad was drifting through life when I met him, Sean. He and your mother . . . they loved each other, but they weren't *in* love. Do you understand what that means? I mean, *really* understand?"

"Time affects all couples, married or not," I countered. "It's only human, right?"

"Yes, but your dad . . . he was a man of passion." She visibly blushed, then shook her head. "I don't mean it that way," she said. "Not that he wasn't—what I mean is, he expected a lot out of life. Big gulps of it. And, over time, his life with your mom had gone stale. A lot of it was her fault, he felt." She paused a bit, hesitated, then added, "You know she had a miscarriage?"

And the hits keep on coming. I had no idea. "No."

"I'm sorry . . . she did. A girl. Six months in. She would have been around four years younger than you." She took a breath, watching me, clearly judging whether to keep going. "It was bad. Colin said she was never the same after that. He said there was a sadness in her that was always there. And Colin couldn't blame her for it. It was just bad luck. But it took its toll on them. On him, too, first because of the miscarriage, then because of how your mom couldn't come out of it. I mean, he understood she'd feel devastated. He was too. But, year after year, she stayed that way. He could see it in her eyes. He ended up morose, dour. His spark was gone."

"And that changed when you came into his life?"

She seemed increasingly uncomfortable.

"Please, Faye," I said. "It's fine. I'm not judging you, not at all. I just need to know. It's important."

She nodded, willing herself to keep going. "He came back to life. He told me that's how he felt, but he couldn't bring himself to leave your mother. Or you. He said it was out of the question. He cared for you both too much. He couldn't do it."

"But you wanted him to?"

I watched as she allowed the memories to rise to the surface—feelings she maybe hadn't allowed herself for over three decades. "I'd be lying if I said I didn't want him all to myself. But, above all, I wanted him to be happy. And part of his appeal was about how good a person he was. I know it sounds perverse, but his firm commitment to you both—it just made me want him more. And then, a few weeks before he died, he told me he'd decided to leave your mom. He was worried about her—worried about you, even more—but he felt he only had one life to live and he'd done everything he could to try and make things better and that maybe she'd be happier having a fresh start with someone else, without that baggage. He asked if I'd wait for him to find the right moment to do it. I know, a lot of guys say that, right? It's like Meg Ryan's friend in *When Harry Met Sally*, the pathetic mistress who's totally delusional about her guy leaving his wife for her and they keep reminding her, 'He's never going to leave her for you.' But your dad wasn't like that. He wasn't lying about that. And I was in no rush." She dropped her eyes, and her voice broke a touch. "Afterwards, I felt so guilty about what happened. I thought that maybe if nothing had happened between us he wouldn't have . . . I never imagined it would make him do what he did."

Only then did I see the true sense of loss in her eyes. Maybe still as raw as the moment she heard Colin was dead. A bottomless chasm that could never be filled.

Still, something wasn't sitting right. "That's why you feel guilty? You think he killed himself because he couldn't handle his double life or the thought of leaving my mom?"

"Well, what else could I think? It was the only way I could make sense of it. I mean, he was a strong man. Clear-thinking. He seemed to be in control; he had two separate, parallel lives, and he seemed OK with how he was going to handle it. But I couldn't see any other reason why he'd do it, and I could never talk about it, not to anyone. No one knew. Isn't that why you're asking me all this?"

"You think that was the cause of his depression?"

"What depression?"

"He was seeing a shrink in the months before he died. He was diagnosed with clinical depression. He was being treated for it."

"Nonsense. Colin wasn't depressed. Conflicted, yes. Torn, maybe. But depressed? No way. Not at all." She said it with total conviction. "I would have known. He was at peace with it. I mean, he felt bad about what he was going to do and about me having to wait, but like I said, I was in no rush. I was very young. I wasn't thinking that far ahead. Little did I know how deeply he'd already affected me." She sat back, visibly relishing some lost memory. "He was happy when he was with me. We were happy." Emphasis on the "we."

Right then, I think she wished she'd been more tactful.

I looked away, gave her some space to recover her poise. "He certainly wasn't seeing any therapist," she added, her tone firm. "I would have known about it."

"My mother didn't know. I'm pretty sure she didn't know about you either. The man could keep secrets."

"Not from me, believe me. Not about something personal like that."

"Maybe he couldn't bring himself to tell the shrink about you, and since he couldn't find a reason for his being depressed, the shrink ascribed it to clinical depression. It's in the coroner's report. My mom met the shrink. I mean, he did kill himself—or that's what everyone accepted at the time."

"But you think otherwise?"

"I'm not sure."

Her eyes flared wide. "You think he was *murdered*?"

"I don't know."

I'd been thinking about this all night. If he had a lover and felt conflicted about it, it could explain a depression and maybe, maybe, the suicide. But if he'd been planning to leave my mom—and me—for her, then it underlined my suspicions. Someone with plans to make a new life with his lover doesn't go blow his brains out. And from what Faye was telling me, he didn't seem overly troubled by it. Certainly nowhere near enough to even begin to justify a suicide.

I asked, "What can you tell me about the days or weeks leading up to his death? Was there anything particular he was involved with?"

"Something that he'd kill himself about? Or that others would want to kill him for?"

"Maybe."

She finished her cup as she thought about it. "He was very focused on all the big issues facing the country, and it wasn't a good time," she said. "We were in a deep recession. Inflation, interest rates, oil prices—they were big problems. And that was the year of the presidential election, Reagan against Carter, a big showdown . . . they had opposing ideals, you were too young to really know about it. They were troubled times. Abroad, there was the hostage crisis in Iran."

"I remember watching it on the news with him and my mom," I said.

"Yeah, it was a big deal at the time." A wistful look brightened her face. "I thought of him when I saw *Argo*, you know. Poor Colin. It was like the whole country was under his watch, he took so much to heart."

"But nothing specific?"

"It was all on his radar. It was his nature."

"There had to be something out of the ordinary? Something that struck home more than the rest?"

"You've got to understand, his work involved a lot of confidential meetings, things he couldn't and wouldn't talk to me about. I mean, a few weeks before he died, an old college buddy of his got in touch and he wanted me to meet him. It was like a fresh part of his life that he could involve me in, a part of his past he didn't need to exclude me from. We could actually go out and socialize with him, he didn't need to hide me from him since the guy didn't even live in the US. And it was great to meet him, to be out with Colin openly. We went out for drinks. But it wasn't just a social call, they were working on something together, and I couldn't be part of that. Which was frustrating, because his friend was fun and I wanted to hear more about his life and his travels, especially with that accent. Then a couple of weeks later, Colin was dead. I didn't understand it then and I still don't understand it now, though it set me on a path. That's how life works."

Something about what she said pinged deep inside some crevasse in my brain. "What accent?"

"I'm sorry?"

"His friend. What accent did he have?"

"Oh," she recalled. "Portuguese. He was from Portugal. And I love the accent, it's like Brazilian, I've sung along to it for years without knowing what the words mean, salsa and bossa nova, Antonio Carlos Jobim and—"

The crevasse was lighting up like lava was about to burst out of it. "Portuguese? What was his name? Do you remember?"

Her nose crinkled under the effort of dredging her memory for a long-lost name, then I said, "Camacho? Octavio Camacho?"

Her face recoiled with surprise. "Yes, exactly. How do you know that?"

# 43

Camacho. The Portuguese investigative reporter whose name Kurt and Gigi had dug up in that Corrigan-linked CIA dossier and who died in a rock climbing accident the same year my dad did. I needed to check on the date of his death, but I was sure it was within weeks, if not days, of my dad's death.

They knew each other. More than that—they were old college buddies.

I was having trouble controlling my internal expletives. What the hell had they been discussing? And why did they both die? My gut was telling me they were both killed to silence them, but ever since that night at Nick's his warnings about finding out my dad was actually part of something bad were still gnawing at me.

Right now, though, I had to downplay it with Faye. I didn't want to expose her to any danger and so I really didn't need her getting all overzealous about finding out what really happened to my dad. One obsessed vigilante was enough.

"I just remember my parents talking about him," I said. "It's the kind of unusual name that stays with you." Moving her away from that, I asked, "You don't know what they were working on?"

"No. I just know it was grave. It consumed Colin for days, but he wouldn't tell me what was going on. All I know is that he was struggling with a major decision. Why not ask Octavio? I'm sure you could track him down?"

I was surprised that she didn't seem to know that Camacho was dead. If he'd died after my dad did—and given that it wasn't even noteworthy news in Portugal, she would have been oblivious to it here in the US. On the other hand, if he died before my dad, surely my dad would have known and told her about it? She would have known even if he hadn't told her—unless he didn't want her to know.

Nick's words again, like stubborn fleas, scratching away at me.

There was nothing more to learn here. I drained my mug and

we both got up to leave; I told her it was great to meet her, despite the circumstances and the bulk of our chat.

As we stepped outside, she asked, "Will you let me know what you find out?"

I wasn't sure, but I still said, "Absolutely."

As I walked away, I decided I would. I couldn't help feeling like I was trying to learn the truth for her as much as for my mom and myself.

I checked the clock on the dash as I got in the BMW and called Gigi and Kurt. I asked them to redouble their efforts on Camacho. Clearly, he was key to figuring out what happened to my dad.

Kurt said he had some news for me: he'd managed to hack into the computer in the office of Rossetti's boss and pull out his online search history for the days leading up to his death. There was a lot there, as you'd expect for a newspaper editor, one working for a top paper. I said we'd look at it together when I got back and I made myself comfortable as I set out on the two-and-a-half hour drive down to Bethesda, Maryland and the second ghost from a murky past that Kurt and Gigi had unearthed for me.

It was time to have a chat with Dr. Ralph Orford and see what he had to say about my dad's state of mind.

Sandman arrived at Reagan National at twenty past nine in the morning. He'd slept for almost the entire two hours and twenty-five minutes, waking only as the jet touched down. There was a car waiting for him at Garage A, key in the usual place, a field kit locked in the trunk.

He hadn't bothered waiting for the EMT, Fire Rescue and Miami PD to descend on the crash site, hadn't needed confirmation that Siddle was dead. The building that now housed the Lamborghini was so damaged by the collision that the senior Fire Rescue officer had immediately declared it unsafe and evacuated the apartments on the second and third floors. In terms of collateral damage, it was a less than fitting tribute to a man who had killed so many without blinking.

By the time Sandman had driven back to Miami International it was after four in the morning. He used the two hours before check in to read the file on his next assignment.

He knew the psychiatrist by reputation, if not personally. As he always did, Sandman would get inside the head of his target, but in this case it would be quite impossible to achieve this at a level anywhere approaching the capabilities of the target himself.

# 44

*Bethesda, Maryland*

My early start was paying off and it wasn't yet noon as I rode the ramp off I-495 and headed into Bethesda. Traffic was light and before long, I was rolling down Old Georgetown Road, which was where Ralph Orford had his office.

It was time for the third stop on my magical mystery tour of the past. Mother, lover, psychiatrist—it was like a three-card spread from the Woody Allen Tarot deck.

From what Kurt and Gigi had learned, Orford's life had barely altered across thirty years, the only adjustment being a reduction in the number of hours spent seeing patients, both at his office and across a short list of hospital psychiatric departments. As of five years ago Orford spent at least ten hours every Monday at Walter Reed where he took a strong interest in the more complex cases. Tuesday through Thursday he was at the office. He rotated around several private psychiatric hospitals on Fridays, keeping the weekend free for golf or hunting, a fact which sparked my interest in light of what Rossetti's editor had tried so hard to conceal.

In fact, I was still unsure about what Orford would turn out to be. Was he my dad's shrink, and had he genuinely diagnosed him as depressive and treated him before he died? Or was he a CIA plant who had been parachuted in after the fact to pad out the coroner's report and lay any suspicions about my dad's death to rest?

Of course, I was leaning toward the latter, and for someone I suspected of being a key part of whatever conspiracy I was starting to unravel, his public life had been an almost entirely open book—at least it was if you had a couple of talented hackers working with you who could follow the digital breadcrumbs and map out his movements as accurately as if he'd swallowed a tracker. There were gaps—sometimes lasting a few days—that were consistent with someone traveling under any number of cover identities, and Gigi hadn't managed to pinpoint any of them. If he had been working for Corrigan, then this made sense, because he would have had the full resources of the CIA at his disposal when it came to creating watertight legends.

As it had been in the 80s, his practice's client list included congressmen, lobbyists, journalists, Fortune 500 executives and university professors, and it struck me this was a source of confidential information that would just keep on giving. If Orford was indeed dirty, he and his handlers had clearly been careful about how they used what they discovered, evidenced by Orford not having so much as a question mark hanging over his entire professional life.

The small office building in which Orford's office suite had been located for the last twelve years also housed two dentists, an OB-GYN, a family doctor and a dietary nutritionist—all on the first and second floors above a high-end travel agent, pretty much the only kind that had survived the almost total exodus of the business from the real world to online.

I passed the row of cars parked on either side of his street and pulled in around the corner, behind the building. I got out and headed back and I had just reached the corner when my eyes snared something that froze me in place.

A man in a baseball cap and gloves was walking up to the building.

Sandman was parked fifty yards down the street from Orford's office. He'd been there since eleven, running over the plan in his head while he waited for the clock to hit something approaching an early lunch hour.

As he waited, he wondered where this crisis would take him next. If it all went according to plan, then only Roos and Tomblin would remain. Sandman wondered which of them would blink first—if indeed either of them did. They hadn't survived more than seventy-five years in the secret world between them without knowing how to stare down a threat, but Sandman had a strong feeling this was perhaps one of the most potentially catastrophic situations they had faced. In Sandman's experience, even the most battle-hardened soldier was capable of losing control when faced with something outside their operational experience, and although he trusted both men whose bidding he performed without question or complaint, he suspected that one of them was more likely to lose a game of chicken than the other.

He checked his watch—five to twelve—and pressed the dial button on his smartphone just as a white BMW drove past. He couldn't see the driver's head from the tinted windows and the fact that the driver had his head turned away from him, but it wasn't something that registered as a threat on Sandman's radar in any way.

After a couple of rings, Orford came on the line.

Sandman said, "The season's over for sika deer, but a limited cull will continue. Considering our mutual interests, we should discuss this at the earliest opportunity."

Sandman could hear Orford processing this in the silence that followed.

"I'll send Violet out for an early lunch." Orford's voice was calm but focused.

"Good."

Two minutes later, he watched as a young woman wearing a smart coat over a pencil skirt—hair, makeup and posture all perfect—exited the building and headed toward a strip of restaurants three blocks to the south.

Sandman checked his face in the mirror, climbed out and walked up the sidewalk toward Orford's office.

It was the baseball cap and gloves that gave him away.

As I held back and watched him approach the building, an instinctive memory meshed with what my eyes were sending to my brain. Although the man was clean-shaven and no longer wearing glasses—his face was half-obscured by the turned-up collar of an old-style waist-length coat—I instantly recognized him as the bearded man from Kirby's. And I figured the odds were pretty slim that he was here to buy an all-inclusive tour of Italy's opera houses.

I quickly pulled out my phone to snap a picture of him, but I was too late as he reached the entrance to the building and turned away to ring the buzzer.

I muttered a curse, pocketed the phone, and watched. The killer pulled the steel-and-glass door open and disappeared inside. I charged down the street and got there just as the door closer was doing its job, and just managed to catch the big glass door before its lock clicked in. Behind the glass, I glimpsed Kirby's killer before he disappeared through an internal fire door in one corner of the small lobby. It was no surprise he'd decided not to take the elevator, aiming to considerably reduce the risk of running into anyone.

I knew that if I followed him up the stairs, I'd be an easy target if he heard me, so I pressed the call button and waited for the elevator.

The bastard wasn't getting away this time.

## 45

Sandman arrived on the second floor, checked the corridor was empty, then exited the stairwell and made his way past a dentist's clinic toward Orford's office. A shared kitchen stood opposite the door to the dentist's suite. It was empty right now, but would surely start to get busy shortly.

Sandman only needed ten minutes, fifteen at the outside.

He found the door to the suite and entered, then locked the door behind him, crossed the reception area, and let himself into the psychiatrist's office, closing the door behind him.

Ralph Orford was sitting in a large leather chair behind a polished oak desk on which sat an open laptop, a pen set, a blotter and several golf trophies. The office was tastefully decorated—mostly with large black-and-white photographs of Maryland's national parks. A few personal photos sat on a lacquered filing cabinet beside a large window. There was an old-fashioned modular hi-fi on a side cabinet, with at least five hundred CDs arranged in tastefully designed wall shelves above. A leather sofa stood against the back wall beside a closet door.

Orford looked Sandman up and down. "This is completely against all protocol."

"Not all," Sandman replied. "We wouldn't be talking right now otherwise."

"But for you to come here? In broad daylight? That's not how we work."

Sandman sat in one of the two chairs facing the desk. He could see that the poor guy was trying to stay cool, but was clearly rattled.

"We need you," he told Orford. "There was no time to set up a meet at the blind."

The mere casual invocation caused a visible change in Orford's attitude. He let out a ragged breath, then asked, "What do you need?"

"There's a senator. He's like a stray dog with a juicy bone he can't stop chewing on. We need it to look like the guy's gone bananas. Like everything he's been doing for the past year is the delusion of an unhinged mind. It needs to be very public and as messy as possible. A total meltdown. Something that's a shoo-in for the top of the six o'clock news."

"Something like the Ukrainian ambassador?"

"Something exactly like that."

Orford's eyes widened. "You do know it's highly unpredictable? It's the nature of it. People react differently depending on what they've got tucked away in the folds of their brains."

"That'll be fine."

"Delivery?"

"Injection. He's diabetic, so the needle mark will be discounted as an insulin shot."

After a moment's consideration, Orford stood. "I have some in the fridge. You'll need the right syringe."

Sandman moved to one side as Orford walked over to a wall unit. He pulled out a key fob from his pocket and unlocked it. It led to a walk-in cupboard with a locked fridge, a fire safe, a set of golf clubs and floor-to-ceiling shelves of confidential patient notes.

"He'll need zero-point-four milliliters per pound of bodyweight. Intramuscular."

"The upper thigh. Yes, I know."

"How much does he weigh?"

"About the same as you, I'd guess," Sandman said.

Orford didn't register the significance of the remark as he unlocked the fridge and pulled out a small vial. He then opened a shallow metal drawer in a standing unit and carefully selected a small syringe.

I had the door to Orford's suite open in less than thirty seconds. There was no one at reception, but I could hear voices from inside Orford's office. I drew one of the confiscated FBI Glocks from my coat pocket and edged toward the door.

"I still think I need to look at his medical file. He could be taking something that'll react badly to the drug." I assumed it was Orford talking.

"Oh, I'm sure that won't be necessary." That voice I recognized.

And although the words were reassuring, his tone was full of thinly veiled menace. "Tell me, doc, are you on any medication?"

The room went quiet for a moment, then I heard Orford, his voice clearly imbued with fear. "What are you—no, wait. You can't!" Fear was quickly giving way to incredulity. "Dear God. Padley? That was you? You did that?"

"A fitting way for him to go, don't you think?"

"But . . . why?" Orford pleaded.

"Think of it as a tribute to his work—and, in this case, to yours."

"You're going to make it look like I injected myself? No one's going to believe it."

"Why not?" the killer said. "Hoffman, Lilly, Bob Wilson. All the great warriors of consciousness have wanted to dive off the deep end. They wanted to know what was there before they sent anyone else. And you're one of the greats, doc. You wouldn't want to go out any other way, would you?"

"But why?" he asked again

"We're just cleaning house. Think of it as the Janitors' work coming full circle."

"And Siddle?"

The killer didn't answer. I guess he didn't need to. Then it sounded like Orford knocked something over as he tried to back away. "No, please . . ."

"Come on, doc. Don't make this any harder than it needs to be."

It was time to intervene. I turned the handle as quietly as possible, then shouldered the door open and burst in, my gun leading me.

The killer already had his left arm around Orford's throat and the needle about to go into the doctor's neck when I leveled the gun at him.

I yelled, "Let him go," stepping in closer. "Let him go right now."

Orford screamed "No!" as the killer pushed the needle into his neck, his finger tight on the plunger.

I figured I could put a round through the bastard's hand before he got the drug into Orford's bloodstream, but even as I was thinking it, the guy adjusted his position so his hand was shielded by the psychiatrist's shoulder.

Involuntarily, I gave a micro-nod of appreciation.

This guy wasn't just good. He was exceptional.

For a second, I didn't move. Nor did he. I could see he was thinking fast about his next move. He looked right at me, his eyes, though they kept darting out from either side of Orford's head so quickly that I could only catch brief glimpses of them, so dark they were almost black.

"Really?" he said. "You want to save this guy? After everything he did to your son?"

Confusion gripped Orford's face, but all I saw was a solar flare of blinding truth. The logic of it was so unassailably elegant, yet so totally perverse. This was the guy who had programed Alex. The same guy who maybe, somehow, drove my father to kill himself.

It only seemed right that I should be the one to refresh his memory.

"Alex Martinez," I hissed at the doctor. "My four-year-old son, in San Diego. The job Corrigan asked you to do."

Orford couldn't hide his own flash of recognition.

The killer must have felt Orford's body momentarily tense—a crystal-clear tell that he knew exactly what I was talking about.

I could feel my finger tightening around the trigger before my brain had even sent a message to my hand. And just as the part of me that was still a reasonably clear-thinking FBI agent waged a split-second Armageddon with my raw hunger for revenge, the killer pressed down on the plunger and shoved his screaming victim toward me before pulling out his handgun with lightning agility.

My aim was blocked by Orford who was staggering toward me, his hands reaching desperately for the syringe. I ducked around him and fired twice just as three bullets from the killer's automatic cut through the space I'd occupied a split second earlier and drilled into the wall behind me in a perfect kill pattern. My own shots missed, though I didn't think by much.

Jesus, the guy could move.

I ducked left as the bastard unleashed more shots before crashing out the window and dropping from view.

We were on the second floor—there was simply no way he was going to walk away from that, I thought as I bolted to the window, but there he was, on the damp soil and rising out of a perfect roll.

He was already upright when I fired several rounds at him as he jagged one way, then the other, and sprinted off down the sidewalk.

"Fuck!"

I gritted my teeth so hard I could feel the roots grind into my jaw, and after an instant of raging frustration, I realized that Orford needed urgent medical attention if I was going to keep him alive long enough to answer my questions—but the door to his office was open and he'd vanished from sight.

Where the hell was he?

I rushed out into the suite's reception. No one was there, but the door was open. Raising my gun, I edged toward the door and peered out into the corridor. Down and across the corridor from the suite, Orford was standing in the kitchen, a large kitchen knife in each of his hands.

I moved toward him. Thankfully, the area was otherwise empty. "Orford, we need to talk. About my dad, Colin Reilly. Then I'll get you the help you need."

He was staring at me with manic eyes, his pupils dilated like he was staring into the darkest black hole, his face was all sweaty, his knife arm moving jerkily from side to side.

"Stay back," he hissed. "You're not getting me too."

My arms opened up in a calming gesture, my gun no longer aimed at him, my other palm wide open.

"Orford," I said. "Put the knife down and talk to me. That's all I need. Colin Reilly. 1981. I need to know what happened. I need to know what you did to him."

He was just eyeing me with sheer terror. "I know what you are. I know what you really are inside—*that*," he said with a mix of fear and disdain. "You don't fool me. Just—stay away from me. You're not getting inside me. Do you hear me? You're not getting me too!"

Whatever he'd been injected with was taking over and messing with his mind, big time. I realized I might not have much time. "Orford, calm down. Just talk to me. What did you do to my father?"

"Your father? How the hell should I know? Your people—they probably took him too. Like they took everyone. Everyone!"

"Orford, put the knife down," I said as I inched closer. "I'm with the FBI." I tried to talk as unthreateningly and soothingly as I could, but he was backing away, riven with fear, his eyes manically darting left and right—then they registered the window.

Our eyes met—then he just freaked and yelled, "You're not taking me, you fuckers!" and he threw the knife at me—a lousy throw, it just flew past harmlessly—before charging towards the window. I rushed after him but I couldn't cover the ground in time to grab him before he flung it open and just threw himself out.

His landing wasn't anywhere as graceful as the killer's. He was sprawled on the ground, his neck and arms twisted at odd angles.

I hurtled down the stairs and out of the building and reached him just as a few gawkers were hesitantly approaching his prone body. Blood was oozing out of his mouth and his eyes were just staring into the distance, unfocused.

"Someone call 911! Get an ambulance here," I yelled at the shocked faces as I tried to focus on what really mattered to me. I bent down, closer to Orford's face. He was still breathing. "Orford. Do you remember? You *must* remember! Colin Reilly? He shot himself?"

His eyes flickered, then glanced sideways at me with the look of a soul so lost, so haunted it was hard for me to not look away. "That's why you're here, right? To set us free. Ralph, Marcus, me, Reilly . . ."

I couldn't make sense of it. "What you do mean? Did you know my father? Did you know Colin Reilly?"

"Reilly . . . yes, he was . . . interesting."

I knelt down and took hold of Orford's head, knowing this was my very last chance. "Orford. Please. Tell me what happened."

His eyes locked onto mine, but there was little light behind them. Then it flickered out and he was gone.

The sound of distant sirens edged into my awareness.

*I have to get out of here.*

I stood, pocketed the gun, pulled my badge and spoke in the most authoritative voice I could muster.

"I need to go after the man who did this. Tell the police they'll find the murder weapon on the floor of Orford's office. Tell them there was another man here, a man sent to kill him. He jumped out of Orford's office window and escaped."

I was about to run off when I remembered the open laptop on Orford's desk. I decided I had to risk it. I raced back into the building and up the stairs to Orford's office where I grabbed the laptop and stuffed it into his own shoulder bag.

I was almost back at the stairs by the time the sirens were right outside.

I stopped, stepped across to the window of the kitchen, which was on another side of the building, and looked out.

Two Montgomery County PD cars and an EMS vehicle had pulled up outside. Four cops and two paramedics were rushing towards Orford.

I watched as the EMTs got to work and waited for the cops to disappear inside, then swung the bag across my shoulder and rushed back to Orford's office. I was going to have to follow the killer's route out. I grabbed the neatly folded blanket from the leather sofa and laid it over the base of the window frame. No way was I jumping out. I'd try to hang off the frame and drop down, reducing the distance to around fifteen feet.

As I lifted one leg over the empty window, I noticed something for the first time. The photo at the back of the framed pictures sitting on a lacquered cabinet, only now visible because of the angle at which I was looking at it.

It showed three guys in their forties on a hunting trip—Orford on the left. Behind them was some kind of hunting blind.

I swung my leg back inside, grabbed the picture and stuffed it into the laptop bag. Then I climbed out, took all my weight on both hands, hung for a moment, and dropped to the ground. A piercing shot of concentrated agony burst through my right ankle as I hit the sidewalk.

I pulled myself upright and hobbled away, parting a few rubberneckers as I picked up speed, ignoring the screaming pain accelerating up my right leg.

I climbed into the BMW, thankful that Gigi had explained the car's registration was tied to a fake ID and a derelict address, and charged off.

# 46

*Federal Plaza, Lower Manhattan*

Sitting at Aparo's desk, Deutsch was staring off into space, her mind and body so worn out that she was now totally dead to any emotion regarding what had happened over the past two days. Indeed, this impenetrable numbness was so oddly relaxing she feared what would happen once it wore off after she'd grabbed a good night's sleep and eaten properly.

As she sat there, both unable and unwilling to move, a junior agent she'd vaguely seen around the office walked over to her. He was waving a letter-sized manila envelope.

"Agent Deutsch? This arrived this morning; it's addressed to Agent Reilly. Since his calls are being rerouted to you, I figured you'd want to take care of this too?"

"Who's it from?"

"There's no name, no return address. Scan shows it's only got paper in it."

He held it out to her. She hesitated momentarily.

*Who the hell got mail these days?*

The thought was enough to pique her interest.

She levered herself out of her chair and reached for it. "I'll take it."

She did just that, waving the junior agent away, and glanced around her cubicle. Her immediate neighbors weren't at their desks. She knew they were locked in the main meeting room, trawling through Reilly's case files, looking for anyone he might go to for help. Satisfied she had a moment of privacy, she sat back down and examined the envelope.

As the junior agent had said, it bore no return address. It had Canadian stamps with an illegible postmark. Reilly's full name and the field office address were written in neat but overly small block capitals with an old-fashioned ink pen.

She carefully tore it open. Inside was a single brown folder, in which were two sheets of drawing paper from a pretty decent artist's sketchpad. On each sheet, portrait layout, someone had drawn the face of a male adult. Under the first face, written in the same block capitals, were the letters "F.F."

At first, the letters under the second face, "R.C.," didn't mean anything to her either. Then it suddenly hit her, and she couldn't help but gasp, though luckily there was no one around to hear her.

They were initials.

R.C. was Reed Corrigan.

The one guy who knew what the hell was going on. And why.

There was also a small note with them, written by the same hand, with the same pen. It said: "Hope these help. With eternal thanks, L+D."

She put the note aside and laid out the drawings side by side and stared at them for a few seconds, then she pulled out her personal cell phone and took full resolution, sixteen megapixel shots of each portrait and of the note. She then pulled out a large blank envelope from her desk, put the three documents back in their folder and the folder in the envelope. Then she folded the original envelope in half, hiding Reilly's name, and stuffed it at the bottom of a drawer in her desk.

Although it went against everything she'd said to Tess, everything she'd been tasked with by Gallo—along with every single shred of self-preservation and common sense—she'd already decided to find a way to get the drawings to Sean. He wasn't around to see that she was finally thinking of him as Sean, now that she'd gone over to his side. The change felt irreversible.

Someone had to help him. With Aparo dead and Tess willing but at risk, she was all he had left—but she couldn't tell anyone about it. She was fully aware that she'd be risking her career, not to mention potential prison time, if she contacted him without telling her superiors and passed on the drawings instead of handing them in. And even though it went against everything she believed in—the FBI, for her, staunchly stood for Fidelity, Bravery and Integrity, as it did for pretty much every agent she'd come across apart from Lendowski—and everything she fought for, she felt she had to do it. She sensed that his life, his career, even his family's future, could all hinge on it.

She couldn't hand the envelope over to Gallo. He'd either

dismiss its contents, or he'd share it with Henriksson, who in turn would quickly ensure that the drawings ceased to exist.

There was one small problem. She had no way of contacting Reilly. Tess, however, could. She was sure of it. She'd need to involve her, at least to get through to him, however queasy that made her in terms of Tess's wellbeing as well as that of the kids. But she had no choice. There was simply no other way she could think of to get the drawings to him, and she was convinced they would prove to be more than useful.

She grabbed her keys and, without bothering to inform anyone, hurried out.

# 47

*Chelsea, New York City*

It wasn't just the image of Orford and his possessed, terrified look that was haunting me.

It was his words.

*That's why you're here, right? To set us free. Ralph, Marcus, me, Reilly . . .*

Us.

That damn word.

Two small letters that were driving me nuts.

And yet, and yet . . . yes, the guy was under the influence of some monster drug. The killer in the baseball cap had talked about the "great warriors of consciousness," compared it to them pushing the envelope on mind trips. Who knew what was going through Orford's brain at the time he said these things. But still—what if the drug had actually taken away his inhibitions. What if it was an *in vino veritas* moment—the notion that being loosened up with alcohol frees us to say what we really mean?

What if my dad was part of them?

What if he'd killed himself out of guilt and remorse, or they'd bumped him off because he was about to blow the whistle on their activities?

And what the hell *were* they?

It was around five in the afternoon and we were sitting around the big island in Gigi's kitchen.

Orford's laptop was on the counter, taunting me. I'd told Kurt and Gigi I needed them to crack it open. It could tell us exactly what Orford had done to Alex, which could help fine tune his recovery and make sure he got the right therapy. They'd said it would take a bit of time for them to get past its password. Regardless, it wasn't the priority. We had something more pressing to figure out.

"We've got three names," I said to Kurt and Gigi as I finished telling them what had happened. "Ralph Orford, psychiatrist, killed off using some kind of psychoactive drug. Someone called

'Ralph,' who also died in some way that was a 'fitting tribute to his work.'"

"Poetic," Kurt said.

I shrugged. "We've got another guy, 'Marcus,' who was also recently bumped off. And they seem to be part of something called 'the Janitors,' and they're being wiped out to 'clean house.'"

Kurt flinched. "What did you say? 'Janitors?'"

He hunched over his laptop and started punching away at the keys like he was living in fast forward, then he turned the screen to face me. "Janitors. It's here. In the web history of Rossetti's editor."

I leaned in for a closer look.

"See, here," he pointed out. "He searched for 'janitors government secret,' 'CIA janitors,' 'janitors murder.' Followed some links from them. I had a quick look at them. They all led nowhere. Just random sites that had the words scattered in them, but not directly relevant to the kind of thing we're talking about."

I asked, "What about Rossetti's search history?"

"He worked from home, where he had a Version FiOS connection. They're harder to crack."

"We need to look at both their search histories more closely. And we need to ID these three Janitors," I said. "Which shouldn't be too hard. I mean, Marcus isn't exactly a widely used name. Male, adult. Died recently. We also know their skill sets. They do accidents—Rossetti's fire, the Portuguese reporter's climbing accident. They do heart attacks—Rossetti's editor, Nick. And they do mind games. My son Alex, Orford—"

"And maybe your dad," Gigi added.

"Maybe," I said.

Gigi had been studying the framed photo I'd snatched off Orford's desk. She set it down on the island. "And we've got this. Three guys in full mid-life crisis who decided they'd rather play *Deer Hunter* than *Deliverance.*"

"So these 'Janitors,' they clean things up by killing people?" Kurt asked while Gigi started tapping away at her keyboard. "You think the guy who called you was one of them?"

"I think so," I said. "Either 'Ralph' or 'Marcus.' Maybe he was a whistleblower. He contacts Rossetti first. They find out. They kill Rossetti and his editor. For some reason, they weren't able to figure out who he was. I guess neither Rossetti nor his editor knew who he was, and if they set a trap for him, he saw it and avoided it. He knows how they operate; he's one of them. He knows what to look out for. So he tries to get his story out again, with me. Only this time, they get to him."

"Before he could tell you what he knew or give you the evidence he said he had for you," Kurt said.

"He kick-started all this," I said. "And they decided to shut it all down. Clean house. Fewer people who know what was going on and who can talk about it if it all goes pear-shaped."

"Here we go," Gigi said as she looked up from her screen. She started reading off it. "Marcus Siddle. Fifty-nine years old. Died last night in Miami when his Lamborghini slammed into the side of a building. The guy owned and ran a high-end car shop. Souped-up all kinds of cars, a king of the road." She looked up from her screen. "Then he drives into the side of a building?"

"A mechanic," I said. "Maybe he's good with house electrics."

"And climbing gear," Kurt added.

Things were falling into place. "OK, which means our Ralph might be a heart guy if they truly have that capability." I turned to Gigi. "Look for—"

"Ralph Padley," she said, way ahead of me already. "A top cardiologist at Harvard. Died of a heart attack in a swimming pool in Boston on Tuesday. Sixty-nine years old."

"Jesus," Kurt said. "How many others of them are out there?"

I asked Gigi, "Do you have headshots for them?"

She tapped some more keys, then swiveled her screen around to face me.

I got out of my chair and moved in for a closer look. She had two faces up, a bit grainy from her having enlarged them, but clear enough. I moved the framed photo I'd snatched off Orford's desk closer to her screen and compared them.

They were all there. Orford, Padley and Siddle.

The three "Janitors."

Three middle-aged civilians—a psychiatrist, a cardiologist, and an upscale car mechanic—who were part of what seemed to be some top secret CIA hit squad. A hit squad that, by the looks of it, was operating not just outside our borders—which was already illegal enough—but on home ground too. We knew they'd committed a murder in Portugal over thirty years ago. The question was, how many other people had they killed over the years? How many of those were Americans and on American soil? And was this unit still active?

And—the biggest question of all—had my dad been working with them?

"I'm starting to understand why they're desperate to keep this under wraps," Kurt said.

"Padley said he had proof to show me. Evidence he needed me to make public," I said. "If it's still out there somewhere, if he managed to hide it before they got to him . . . maybe we can find it."

"Without ending up like the rest of them," Gigi added as a sense of gloom settled over the room.

I had a lot of questions, but the only guys who could give me the answers had been either wiped out, or—in the case of my ever-elusive bête noire, Reed Corrigan—untraceable.

And then Tess called and the dam burst wide open.

Deutsch angled a nervous glance at the Bureau cars parked outside Tess's house as she rang the doorbell.

She hadn't had any problem getting to Tess's front door. She just hadn't mentioned her little jaunt to Gallo or anyone else at Federal Plaza, and she knew she'd have some explaining to do when she got back. She had some time to come up with an excuse and knew she'd find a way through it, but that would wait. Right now, she needed to act fast.

She ducked inside as soon as Tess opened the door, then ushered her discreetly through the house and out onto the rear deck while asking her mundane questions about how she was and whether or not she'd heard from Reilly yet.

Once they were outside, she looked around, making sure she hadn't missed any part of the FBI's surveillance net, then turned to Tess.

"I can't stay long and it's not safe talking inside. You're under watch," she told Tess in a low voice.

"I assumed, but—"

"Tess, everything is being monitored," Deutsch told her. "Phones, emails, WiFi. Any connection you make with the world beyond this house or even within in for that matter, we're on top of. Even what you say. So you're going to have to be careful."

"Be careful?" Tess asked, her face tight with tension. "About what?"

"I need you to connect me with Sean."

"Annie, I told you—"

"Listen to me!" Deutsch interjected. "I know, I know—you don't know how to get through to him, you haven't heard from him. Tess, this is important. I know you can find a way to get in touch with him. He wouldn't disappear without telling you how. Not when you're under threat like this. And this is coming from me, personally—I'm sticking my neck out here for you. For him. Please."

She watched as Tess ran a deep scan up and down her face, clearly trying to decide whether to believe her. "Why? What's happened?"

Deutsch glanced around again, more out of paranoia then out of some credible threat, then leaned closer and dropped her voice even lower. "Someone sent Sean two drawings. Portraits, of two men. They were sent from Canada and just signed 'L+D.' I think they're important. I think they might be the guys that Sean's been trying to find."

She fished out her phone, pulled up the pictures she'd taken of the drawings, and showed them to Tess. She watched as Tess studied them.

"I've never seen these guys before," Tess said.

"Nor has he, I imagine. But I think they could help him zero in on them." She put her phone away, then asked, "You know who L and D are, don't you?"

Tess hesitated—it was enough of an answer for her.

"They're important, aren't they?" Deutsch asked. "You know they are. Come on, Tess."

Tess finally nodded. "They're a couple Reilly helped out. They owe him. A lot."

"And this is them paying him back. Come on, Tess. He needs this."

Tess hesitated some more, her face muscles tightening up visibly—then she nodded. "I have a phone number. A burner phone." She looked intensely worried. "God, let this not be a mistake. You can't lead them to him, Annie. How will you get them to him?"

"All I need is a smartphone number or an email address. Hell, even a Facebook account will do. I'll send them to him from my personal phone."

Tess held her gaze for a moment, then nodded.

Sandman knew his message would anger Roos and the others but, strictly speaking, he'd still achieved his immediate assignment. Orford was dead, even though it wasn't as clean a kill as he'd been aiming for. Still, if it was going to be considered more of a murder than a suicide, Reilly would be on the wanted poster. All of which, coming on the back of the successful dispatch of Siddle in Miami, wasn't too shabby.

Still, Roos's tone wasn't thrilled, even though from the sounds of it, he was calling with good news.

"We've had a hit," Roos told him. "Unexpected, and lucky, but I'll take it, given the recent fuck-ups."

Sandman let it slide and said nothing.

"We picked up Reilly on a surveillance cam at a nightclub in Manhattan Saturday night. The DEA had a Serbian drug dealer in their crosshairs and the face-recognition trawl picked up Reilly in its sweep. It looks like he had company, two of them. A guy and a girl. Face recog hasn't had a hit with them and the targets are in some weird get-up. They're sending you the file. Sandman . . ."

"Yes," he asked, knowing what was coming next.

"Finish this," Roos said. "While we're still young."

# 48

*Chelsea, New York City*

"So what the hell do we do with them?"

I leaned back against the back of the banquette, interlaced my fingers behind my head and blew out some of the frustration, anger and impatience festering inside of me.

The three of us were sitting around a corner table in the large brasserie-style restaurant across the street from Gigi's apartment, printouts of the hand-drawn sketches of Frank Fullerton and Reed Corrigan that Deutsch had emailed Kurt staring implacably up at us.

I couldn't take my eyes off Corrigan's face. I couldn't believe I finally knew what he looked like—well, thirty-odd years ago, but still. It was something. It was more than something.

It would lead me to him.

It had to.

Kurt and Gigi didn't know where the portraits had come from. Kurt hadn't been privy to that side of the story when I first roped him into helping me track down Corrigan. I had firewalled it off from him, just as I'd kept his involvement secret from all the others who'd been involved. Right now, though, given how much they'd stuck their necks out for me and how deeply enmeshed we were in everything that was going on, I felt I owed them the full story.

I told them "L+D" were Leo and Daphne Sokolov. Leo was a brilliant Russian scientist who'd invented an incredible, world-changing piece of technology while working for a secret lab in Russia back when the USSR was still intact. With commendable insight, he decided his invention was too dangerous to hand over to his Soviet minders. He contacted the CIA and arranged for his defection, promising to hand over his invention to our government instead. What he didn't tell them was that he'd already decided he didn't trust them with it any more than he did the Soviets. Once they'd whisked him and his wife, Daphne, safely out of the Russia and brought him onto US soil, he also gave his CIA minders the slip. Leo and Daphne had lived in Queens in anonymity for over thirty years until an unfortunate outburst at an anti-Russian demonstration outside the Russian Consulate in Manhattan a while back had blown Leo's cover.

I had been instrumental in rescuing him and Daphne from the Russian agents who wanted him and his technology. I also agreed that the technology was too dangerous to hand over to any government, even ours, and I got my connections at the Vatican to help me set them up with a new life outside the US. For that, Leo and Daphne were immensely grateful, and they hadn't failed in expressing it before we parted company. We had another connection, too. Their CIA minders had been none other than Reed Corrigan and Frank Fullerton.

Hence the drawings—portraits of what Corrigan and Fullerton looked like back in 1980, when Leo and Daphne last saw them. I didn't know who had drawn them up, but they were good, clean sketches showing two clearly identifiable faces.

Kurt shook his head. "Well, the obvious thing would have been to digitize them, then compare key features with the CIA employee database. But they closed that door."

"I doubt you could have got anywhere near the full roster anyway," I said. "And these guys are probably off the books."

Gigi threw up her hands. "I hate this. Ever since I got into their deep archive, they completely reconfigured the firewalls. I can't clone a valid authorization; I can't create a new one. I'll get in eventually, but I need more time."

"Which is not something we have," I said.

It was supremely frustrating. I had him, had as good a forensic sketch artist's rendition of a suspect I'd ever seen, but I had nothing against which to run it.

Kurt tapped the drawings with two fingers. "Why doesn't your friend at the Bureau run with them?" he asked. "She could give them to your boss, get him to show them to the CIA, say they're from a witness they've got in protective custody. That'll get them worked up."

"No," I said, "they've stonewalled every request I put through from day one. The party line is that Reed Corrigan does not exist. Period."

"Bastards."

"Yep," I said.

Gigi waved her favorite waiter over—Theo, an aspiring stand-up with a slightly psychotic gaze who, he gleefully informed us, was excited about an audition he'd just done for a part on *Louie*—and ordered us some fresh coffees and three slices of an apparently life-altering raspberry cheesecake.

I gave my face a good rub and looked across the restaurant. It was packed, as usual. Was there a single trendy eatery in Manhattan that wasn't? The morning espressos and croissants had long given way to after-work beers and mojitos. Watching the constant tide of people gliding by outside the restaurant, on their way home from work, maybe tired, maybe fulfilled, maybe looking forward to a nice meal and a cuddle in front of the TV, maybe about to spend an evening alone trawling through social media apps on their phones while eating cereal out of a box, I couldn't help but envy them, all of them. Normalcy of whatever kind felt like such an alien concept for me right now. This obsessive search had taken over my life and flipped it over and inside out.

I thought of my dad, of my mom and Faye, and of Tess. Whatever negative effects Dad's death had on me, it had also ensured that I didn't marry young. In fact, the more I thought about it, the more now felt like the right time to talk to Tess about tying the knot.

Though now would have to wait. Perhaps indefinitely.

As Theo brought the coffees and cake, I turned and noticed Gigi giving me a mischievous little self-satisfied grin. I looked at her curiously, but she just held my gaze and said, "Jake Daland."

Which totally threw me, since I'd never mentioned him to her or to Kurt. I almost did the full Kramer double-take—eyes popping, electrocuted limbs, the works.

She grinned. "What? Did you really think we wouldn't know about something like that?" Then, of my continuing surprise, she said, "Settle down, G-Boy, and lend me your ears. 'Cause Daland might just be the key to your salvation."

The velvet rope outside the nightclub's entrance had only just been set up and nobody was lining up as yet. It was still early for a Manhattan night spot, which suited Sandman fine. He wasn't there to party. At least, not in the traditional sense, and only if he couldn't avoid it.

There were two men milling around outside, two bouncers in black suits over black shirts and black ties to add a splash of black, the whole look accessorized with the ubiquitous clipboards and earbuds. One was beefy, the other supersized—easily two hundred and fifty pounds. Sandman was not in the least intimidated. Like any fighter worth his salt, he knew that size really didn't matter.

He noted the security cam over the club's entrance as he walked up to them and flicked a small gesture to the bigger of the two to come aside for a chat. The bouncer seemed put out and somewhat bemused by the request; he shuffled over on beefy, lumbering feet that couldn't have moved with less interest.

Sandman flashed him a Homeland Security ID card—a real one—then pulled out his phone and showed him a screen grab of the two targets that seemed to be accompanying Reilly as he left the club.

"I'm trying to ID these two," he told him. "They were here Saturday night. You know who they are?"

The bouncer tilted his face to one side and grimaced as he gave Sandman a once-over that was overflowing with disdain. "Dude, seriously. This club—it's like a church. Sacred ground, sanctuary. People who come here, they know they can be who they want or what they want without anyone giving them a hard time. You understand what I'm saying, brother?"

Sandman shrugged with a bored roll of his eyes. "I think you're saying you don't plan to be helpful in this matter."

The big man moved in closer and was suddenly right in his face. "I guess I'm saying you need to—"

His face froze on that syllable, then quickly morphed into a shock of wide eyes and round lips as he howled with pain from the testicle lock Sandman had him in. The assassin squeezed harder, almost sending the bouncer to his knees.

The big man tried to push Sandman off him, but Sandman had already calmly pocketed his phone and used his other hand to stab the bouncer's throat with a quick jab using the outstretched tips of his fingers, causing the bouncer to gasp for air and eliminating all resistance.

The other bouncer saw this and darted toward them to help his buddy. Sandman didn't react and waited until the man was within range before spinning around and whipping out a kick, catching him just above the knee. He didn't intend to cripple the man, he just needed to tame him, which was why he spared his fragile cartilage and tendons. The bouncer fell to the ground without realizing how much long-term suffering he'd been spared.

"Let's try this again, shall we?" Sandman asked. "I need to know if you and your friend here know these two. If you don't, I'd appreciate a friendly introduction to the joint's manager who might be able to help me with my inquiry. A copy of Saturday night's CCTV footage would also be useful as I imagine they grabbed a cab and it would help to know which one it was. Does that sound doable to you?"

He really didn't need him to reply.

"How do you know about Daland?" I asked, still stumped.

Gigi glanced at Kurt, then gave me a relaxed grin. "I like to know who I'm working with. And the CIA might have shut me out, but the FBI's servers . . . *pu-lease.*"

I was still trying to process the relevance. "You know about this guy?"

Gigi glanced at Kurt again, this time a bit less comfortably, then turned back to me. "He came on to me once. At Comic-Con. Back in his Hidden Lynx days. The guy's a total sleaze. I mean, he was dressed as Aquaman. Talk about lame. I had to pry his greasy claws off my hips."

I appreciated Gigi's honesty, but needed a cogent plan, not hacker crew reminiscences. "Again, Gigi—the point is?"

There was that grin again. "Oh, padawan, you still have so much to learn. You guys think you took him down? You only scratched the surface. They're not called onion networks for nothing. The top layers might have been peeled away and dropped in the trash compactor, but there are deeper layers underneath it, built from an entirely different architecture, and they're still fully functional. One of them's called Erebus and that's the one we need to get into."

I knew a little about Erebus. The name was from Greek

mythology, the god of darkness and shadows. It was a deep darknet site that had attained almost mythical status with our cyber geeks at the Bureau. As far as I knew, no one knew who'd built it or who ran it.

"Erebus?" I asked. "That's Daland?"

"Yes. It's the dark underbelly of Maxiplenty. The VIP area. We're talking deep, deep darknet. But neither of us can access it. No one from the outside can. It's so watertight it's genius. You need a personal invitation from a site maven. On top of that, they use a three-stage access sequence. Each and every access permission is generated by multi-level cryptography starting with an asymmetric keyset based on a one-time algorithm. The unencrypted code is then used as the key for a symmetric cypher which, when combined with a separate code sent via text message, results in a single-use, time-sensitive password. The network is impossible to hack using a brute force attack. There are no back doors. The virtual server hubs are constantly moving around the world—Estonia, Chile, Lebanon, you name it—mirroring themselves without trace then overwriting the origin server's code so it vanishes into thin air. Even if you could locate a server, the core code will have moved before you get a chance to clone it or get inside and upload a worm. It's a thing of beauty, really. Daland is one hell of a programmer."

I may have caught three words of it. Kurt didn't exactly look overjoyed either, but—I'm sure—that was for entirely different reasons.

"Don't worry, Snake. I appreciate relativity—in both its general and specific incarnations—but that doesn't mean I want to screw Einstein's brains out."

I wasn't following any of this. "Gigi, seriously. What the hell are you talking about? How does that help us?"

Gigi seemed to notice that Kurt's eyes were now alive with possibility.

"I swear to God, Snake, I thought you were dead," she told him, in a weird voice that I took to be some kind of fair approximation of one of the actors in that movie. Then, in her normal voice, she added, "Tell him, Sensei."

Kurt smiled. "We need to speak to Daland. He can tell us how to get into Erebus. Then we can post the sketches and ask if anyone recognizes them. Maybe offer a reward. Or just see if there's anyone there with a grudge against them. By the sounds of it, these assholes might have one or two out there."

"Why would anyone on Erebus know them?" I asked.

"Seriously, G-boy," Gigi said, "you don't know who hangs out in the deep levels of the darknet?"

"Drug dealers, hired guns, human traffickers, child porn sickos? Friends of yours?" I asked.

"Well, them too," Kurt said. "But it's also where you'll find retired Eastern Bloc spies with shitty pensions, wet-work contractors, ex-Special Forces operatives looking to monetize their antisocial skill sets, drug cartel lieutenants with an eye on climbing up the food chain, gallant security consultants for noble African dictators . . . you name it. And if there's one place where someone may have come across these two, it's in Erebus."

Gigi smiled. "That's my Snake."

I tried to let it all sink in. "You really think it's worth a shot?"

"You want to find rats like that," Gigi said, "where better than to look in the sewer?"

"OK, maybe," I said, "but you seem to have forgotten a tiny detail."

She deliberately played dumb. The girl really was enjoying this.

"Slight inconvenience," I said. "Daland might not be able to meet us here for a latté as he's currently in residence at the MCC while awaiting trial."

The Metropolitan Correctional Center is New York City's Federal jail, where prisoners are held pending, and during, trial, usually at the US District Court, which is directly opposite it. It's been home to some of the worst criminals the country's seen, some of whom have been there for years, awaiting a trial that would probably never happen.

Gigi leaned forward toward me. "So we go talk to him there."

I had to laugh. "Great idea. Shouldn't be a problem whatsoever that I'm a wanted man and that I'm not exactly a stranger to that building or that it's a literal stone's throw from FBI headquarters."

"So?" she pressed.

"So there are guards in there who might recognize me. Lawyers.

Judges. FBI agents going in and out of there. Not to mention maybe a dozen guys that I put there."

"Fine. So we change your look."

I shook my head. "What did you have in mind? One of the Avengers? How about Thor? I think I'd look cool with blond locks."

I thought I was doing well by talking their lingo, but she wasn't laughing. "We go in. Together. In disguise. You're his ultra-slick defense attorney. You're brash, brilliant and you tell it like it is, no matter who gets hurt. I'm the sexy paralegal who won't let you get inside her panties."

She was a couple of minutes from pitching the pilot.

Kurt's voice was unusually forceful. "No fucking way."

Gigi smiled, her voice gentle. "Down, tiger. Yes, way. And, in fact, only way."

Kurt was glaring at me, willing me to shoot the idea down, eyes already filling with dread for a decision made without him.

Problem was, we had nothing else.

I sent Kurt a sideways look of apologetic resignation.

"OK. Tell me how we do it."

# WEDNESDAY

# 49

*Park Row, New York City*

The brown wig and goatee that Kurt and Gigi's favorite costumier had selected in order to make me look like a fictional attorney from a genuine law practice were so itchy I had to keep reminding myself not to mess with them. Still, and despite the fact that I knew the MCC far better than was healthy right now, we survived the signing-in procedure, the ID checks, the scan and search and the roving eyes of several guards.

Gigi—who seemed to spend far more of her life in costume than she did as herself—looked alluringly sexy. Transformed in a long black wig set against blood-red lips, white blouse, coal-black pencil skirt, burgundy jacket, black stockings and high heels, she looked like a *femme fatale* from a 40s noir brought to life and selectively colored in.

Unlike the sirens from those films, though, I knew I could trust her.

Yet again, I had to hand it to Kurt. And to the universe in general. Maybe good things really could happen to good people.

Gigi had kindly admitted my fictional alter ego to the New York State Bar Association last night and first thing this morning Kurt had hacked into the law firm's phone system and, posing as one of the practice's senior law clerks, cleared my security permission with the MCC's legal department, which meant I required only the fake driver's license we'd procured late last night and not a Federal Bureau of Prisons Secure Pass Identification card, which would have been harder to get hold of.

I had filled out the Notification to Visitor form and we'd both walked through the metal detector. A young guard had been about to tell Gigi that he needed to search her—it was tough to argue with his obvious appreciation—when an older guard had waved him away. We'd had our hands stamped and signed the old-style bound logbook.

In the face of some pretty forceful objections from Kurt, we'd decided to leave our smartphones in Gigi's car—we wouldn't be allowed to use them, and that made them just one more thing to worry about. Kurt had prepared a stack of authentic-looking legal papers, half of which were the sole contents of a battered leather briefcase Gigi had found at a thrift store, while the other half was in a leather document wallet held by Gigi. Nothing more than props, but necessary ones. Both briefcase and wallet had been searched and passed through the fluoroscope.

I glanced at my watch. Forty minutes after two. We needed to start by three o'clock, which would give us half an hour before Daland had to return to his cell for the four o'clock count. We'd decided not to request that Daland be put on the "out count," which, although it would mean we could all remain in the interview room during the count, would also mean that Gigi and I would be subjected to an additional layer of scrutiny in addition to having to stress our way through the count itself without the right to leave till it was done.

We were admitted to Eleven North, the self-contained unit where Daland was being held, and led along a corridor toward an interview room.

Twenty yards up ahead, I tensed up at the sight of a couple of guards who were walking a detainee back to his cell. I knew exactly who it was: Vince Northwood, a white supremacist and homegrown terrorist who'd posted several death threats against African-American politicians before trying to blow up a community health center in Queens simply because it received federal funding. He'd failed—luckily—and the only reason he wasn't going to get a second chance was because we'd arrested him. He'd been here almost three years, the trial date having been put back so many times he probably now considered the MCC his home.

My blood turned to ice as the distance quickly closed between us. If he recognized me, we were screwed. Gigi must have noticed my body tense up because she immediately accentuated the swing of her hips and lasered a killer of a seductive curled lip on Northwood, giving him something he couldn't afford not to look at.

When they were within touching distance, Northwood gave Gigi a leer acidic enough to dissolve Kevlar. We drew level, which meant I was in Northwood's direct line of sight, even though Gigi was between us. His eyes flicked up from Gigi's ass and landed on my face. There was a moment of almost-recognition, then the guards nudged him forward. The three of them turned a corner before Northwood could look back.

We really couldn't afford another moment like that.

I gave Gigi a pointed, relieved glance as our guard unlocked the interview room and showed us inside. Gigi turned to the guard. "I'll give you a shout when we're done with our client."

The guard eyed her with bored indifference, then nodded and stepped out of the room, shutting the door behind him. It gave a disturbingly clean click.

She turned to me. "You OK, G-boy?"

"Loving every second," I said.

Barely a minute later, Daland—his silk kimono replaced by an orange jumpsuit—was led into the room by another guard, who walked the detainee to the far side of the table, then stepped back toward the wall. If Daland had noticed anything unusual about Gigi or me, he was keeping it to himself—for now.

I held out my hand. "Mr. Daland, Ben Burnham. And this is my paralegal, Polly Harris. I'll be representing you going forward. As you know, Simon had to move to another case, but we're fully briefed and up to speed on everything."

He took my hand in a firm grip, his eyes boring into mine. I could tell he *had* recognized me—and that he was using the time to decide how to react. I could see his thought processes so clearly it was obvious that he wanted me to. If he ratted us out, then he'd never find out what was going on. If he played along, then he might discover what was happening, but by the time he'd come up with his own plan, it might well be too late to save the deep network beneath Maxiplenty.

After a nerve-melting few seconds, he let go of my hand. "Sure. Simon told me about it. He says you're a cybercrime specialist."

I kept my immense relief in check and indicated for him to sit. "I have some experience that should be relevant, yes."

Gigi and I sat down opposite him.

I gestured to the guard. "Could you please make sure all the cameras and recording devices are switched off?"

He nodded. "I'll be outside."

The door snapped shut behind him.

Daland leaned back in his chair, waiting for us to make the first move.

"Polly" opened her leather document wallet, took out a single sheet of paper and laid it on the table.

Daland pretended not to look at it, but I could see he was quickly scrutinizing every inch. After a moment, he looked at Gigi.

"You look familiar."

This threw me. I'd expected him to tell me he knew exactly who *I* was.

Daland kept looking at Gigi. "Wonder Woman. New York Comic-Con."

Gigi smiled. "Wow. I'm impressed. But still, keep your paws to yourself."

He grinned and relaxed back in his seat. "How could I possibly forget that body?" He closed his eyes, enjoying the moment. "You made a damn fine Diana of Themyscira."

After savoring the memory, he finally turned to me, and all delight drained from his face. "What is this? You posing as a rogue agent to trick me into telling you more than I should? Seriously, dude. You Feds need to get over this infatuation you have for stings. Even if it did help you nab Ulbricht—a total fucking amateur, by the way—doesn't mean it'll work with me."

I knew all about Dread Pirate Roberts and Silk Road. Even if the FBI's Cyber Division hadn't found a backdoor into the Silk Road servers, Ulbricht—the man accused of creating it—had been so lax with his personal online security it was only a matter of time before the Bureau caught him.

Daland was a whole different order of pirate.

I tried a different tack. "Think about it. Would I really go to these lengths and risk you not hearing about me?"

"You could easily have paid someone in here to tell me you're a wanted man. Or threatened them. Northwood, for example. He and I shared some fond memories of you."

What was that I said about him being smart? He was so damn keyed-in it was scary.

Daland must have noticed my unease. He could have made me suffer for longer, but instead he gave another signature shrug.

"It wasn't him."

"But that's really what it hinges on," I said. "Who told you—outside or in here—and how much you trust them."

His face was completely impassive. I had no clue whether I was getting through to him or not.

I could hear the desperation seep into my voice as I continued. "And Polly, here. You must know how talented she is. I'm sure you're aware of her unequivocal respect for the law, and it's not like she needs money either, right? So how did I get her here, unless it's down to trust?" I paused, gauging his reaction, then leaned in. "Look, you have all the power here, no question. I'm suspected of killing a CIA analyst and there's a missing FBI agent out there they probably think I'm good for too. But you already know all that. Probably even more. But I still walked into the MCC like a lamb to the slaughterhouse."

I stopped for a moment and dialed down the anger. It was hot in there, and the back of my shirt was soaked. The edges of my moustache were also starting to peel back as the glue was assailed by a stream of sweat. I tried to regulate my breathing.

I could tell Daland was now reveling in my misery.

"Here's the thing, Jake. We all know you could have given us up when you first saw us. But you didn't, which means you're intrigued enough to hear us out. So hear us out."

He shrugged again. "Shoot."

"I've got two head shots. Drawings, to be precise. Like by a police sketch artist. They're black-ops guys. Seriously nasty. I think they're behind a whole bunch of deaths over the years. Assassinations. Reporters, you name it. I need to ID them. I only know them by their codenames—their Agency legends."

I waited to judge his reaction. He pursed his lips in a small whistle. "'Agency?'"

I nodded.

He shrugged. "Heavy. So what's this got to do with me?"

"I want to post their mugs on Erebus and see if anyone knows who they are."

I paused, studying his expression, looking for his reaction to the magic word.

He was good. More than good. He gave away nothing. I could

see him cleaning up in Vegas with that poker face without resorting to the black sunglasses and baseball caps.

"Never heard of it," he said.

"Look, I know what I'm asking you for here, OK? But you have my word, in front of a witness, that I'm not here as a cop and that this isn't some elaborate sting. This is just between you and me and no one else. I wouldn't be here if I had any other way of doing this. You consider yourself a crusader for openness and truth and justice, right? Well, something bad is going on here, something seriously nasty that's been going on for years and these guys are behind it. And if you get me into Erebus and someone gives me their names, I'll be able to do something about it."

He still sat there, dead-eyed, staring at me.

"Jake," Gigi added, "this in on the level. I wouldn't be here if it wasn't."

"I need the real names of these scumbags," I pressed. "All we need is for one user to have as good a memory as yours."

He remained Sphinx-like for a moment, then he smirked, his gaze panning across to Gigi. "When you want to get into someone's pants, you always remember." He let his subtle, seductive line linger for a moment before adding, "Hiring someone to pull a trigger? Or being paid to be the one who does it? I suppose you remember that too."

"It doesn't bother you?" Gigi asked him, her tone genuinely curious and not accusatory. "That people use your sites for stuff like that?"

I shot her a surprised look—I mean, I liked her blunt directness and all, but this was borderline Aspergeresque and it really wasn't the time for her to be bringing it up—but the damage was already done. Fortunately, it didn't seem to faze Daland.

"Do you blame Tim Berners-Lee for Internet porn? How's that any different? Sure, he advocates regulation; I've read the manifestos. But it was always going to be too late once he opened Pandora's browser. So should we blame him for an entire generation of teenagers who think a spit roast is perfectly normal sexual behavior? Or hold him accountable for cannibals grooming their next meal on Facebook or for ISIS recruitment videos? I just gave people a way to communicate without being spied on. By people like him."

He jabbed a forceful finger in my direction. "What people choose to do with it is up to them."

I shook my head. I didn't have the time or the headspace for a philosophical debate.

"OK, well, that's exactly what I need . . . to communicate without anyone listening in, because the guys I'm after are part of the listeners."

Gigi smiled and leaned in closer to him. "If you knew even ten percent of it, you'd help us." She gestured toward me. "He's about as far out on a limb as it's possible to be without dropping into an abyss of serious suffering."

Daland went quiet for a moment, his eyes tracking back and forth between Gigi and me.

"I get what *you* need, but what do *I* get? Are you going to stop the traffic on Pearl, drill down through thirty feet and spring me from the tunnel while I'm shuffling off to court shackled at the ankles, chained and cuffed at the wrists and sandwiched between four US Marshals, trapped between the remotely activated electronic doors at either end?"

I had to smile at that. The tunnel beneath Pearl Street that ran between the MCC and the Federal Courthouse was legendary, especially among the criminals and their associates on the outside who'd spent hours thinking up ways to breach it—all with zero success.

I looked straight at him. "When this is all over, when I've dealt with these bastards and cleared things up, I'll use everything in my power to help. And I mean everything, short of destroying evidence. You have my word. And believe me—when this breaks, a lot of big shots are going to owe me a lot of favors."

He studied me curiously. "Come on, Reilly. I know how fucked you are. The chances of you ever being able to do anything for me are so close to nothing as to be irrelevant."

"I have a favor or two I can pull from high up," I told him, wondering if the fact that I had saved president Yorke's life only weeks ago would ever count for anything.

"So why haven't you used them to help yourself?" He let me sweat it for a beat, then he grinned. "But don't worry about it. I'm in if it helps score a big one against those fascists."

Gigi shook her head and chortled. I don't know if she muttered something unsavory under her breath, but her lips were creased in a smile. "So how do we get in?"

I understood nothing of the conversation that followed. In fact, a couple of sentences in, I had totally zoned out as if I were having an out-of-body experience, watching the three of us like a silent observer. I found myself questioning what I was doing there, wondering what the odds were of someone on Daland's uber-darknet recognizing one of the two faces that had my mind under siege. Corrigan and Fullerton had both been field agents. They had been good at what they did—which meant they would have been extremely careful about who knew their true identities. They would have traveled extensively and met with a significant number of assets over the decades, but many of those would have never known who they were really dealing with. On the other hand, I expect their profiles at the Agency were visible enough that anyone reasonably senior who'd worked there sometime in the last two or three decades would know their real identities. I only needed one of those former colleagues or assets to remember one of them. Maybe it wasn't such a stretch after all.

Gigi put a hand on my shoulder. "We're done here, Ben. Time to go."

I blinked, no idea whether they'd been talking for five, or twenty-five minutes. "You got everything you need?"

She nodded. "Like I said, it's a thing of beauty."

Daland smiled. "I'll take that, seeing as how you don't seem too keen for me to take you."

Gigi couldn't help but laugh. "You really are a total dickwad, Jake. But hey, never say never, right?"

Daland's face reconfigured into a hopeful, curious leer.

I stood, walked over to the door and knocked.

No reply.

Knocked again.

Nothing.

I could feel the panic rising.

*They know who I am. They've been listening to everything. The only place I'm going from here is Florence supermax.*

"Guard? We're done now."

I looked at Gigi. She had her mouth right up against the door, but her poise was ice-cold. Like she was expecting a waitress to bring her a flute of champagne.

The door finally opened and the guard appeared. "Sorry about that, folks. Just stepped away for a few seconds."

I forced the relief off my face and turned back to Daland and shook his hand. "Hang tight, Jake. We'll let you know about the plea bargain very shortly."

He held my hand firmly. "You do that." He turned to Gigi and smiled. "Drop by any time."

She smiled back and followed me out of the interview room.

As we made our way down the hall, she leaned in close and whispered in my ear, "Jesus, I need to get back to Kurt pronto. Role playing like that, plus all the adrenaline—I'm like unbelievably horny."

I didn't reply as we continued along the corridor, starting to feel the relief that I wouldn't allow free reign till we were both back in her Beemer and had checked in with Kurt.

"I don't think Mrs. Burnham would appreciate you talking to her husband like that, Miss Harris. Pull your mind back to the case. You have a lot to do."

She grinned over her shoulder. "Don't worry, boss. I'll just multitask."

# 50

*Chelsea, New York*

I sat in the restaurant opposite Gigi's building, letting the time drift by without scrutiny, eyes unfocused, the steady snowfall outside creating a blur of white against the night's dark backdrop. I figured I'd hang out here at least another hour before I went back upstairs. There wasn't much for me to do there anyway. Corrigan and Fullerton's portraits were roaming the darkest corners of the Internet and until someone decided to let us in on who they were, all we could do was wait. And hope.

I didn't want to intrude on Gigi and Kurt's downtime either—not that I'd cramped their style in any way so far. After she'd finished uploading the sketches to Daland's online catacombs, Gigi had left me and Kurt in the large open plan area before returning not long after, fully decked out in a Wonder Woman costume—the classic outfit, she explained, not the new, post-modern black outfit she and the rest of fandom apparently hated. She'd been pretty vocal about how pumped up she'd felt after our incursion into the MCC and her digital stroll through Daland's blackest creation, which was why I thought her costume change probably had something to do with her wanting to show Kurt he had nothing to worry about when it came to Jake Daland. The lovable bear seemed seriously rattled that his girlfriend was so in awe of Daland's programing prowess and, even worse, that Daland had propositioned her—even if nothing had come of it—that he'd shrugged off at least two blatant attempts by Gigi at intimacy since our return from the MCC. The Wonder Woman outfit did the trick.

Kurt was also pissed off at me too, but once he'd seen Gigi in the outfit, any lingering resentment evaporated. With a huge grin on his face, he went looking for his Green Arrow costume, which was my cue to leave the apartment.

I was actually glad to have an excuse for a change of scene. I took a long walk, drifting aimlessly through the streets of Lower Manhattan as darkness swooped in overhead, gentle fluffy snowflakes peppering my face and my clothes, my mind still besieged by the idea that my dad could have been part of it all. I felt a cold hollowness inside me and I wondered if maybe I'd been wrong to pursue this so doggedly, maybe I should have left it alone and let sleeping dogs—especially rabid feral ones that sink their teeth into you and never let go, in this case—lie.

I ended up back at the trendy eatery across the street from Gigi's apartment, with more time to think, mull, grind, process—though all it did was put me in an even worse mood than when I first sat down an hour earlier.

Kurt had managed to hack into Rossetti's home broadband connection and pull up his online search history. He'd put both documents on a small Vaio laptop that now sat on the table in front of me, goading me. I hadn't yet taken a look. The coffee next to it—my third—was already stone cold, the life-altering cheesecake barely defaced. I'd been through everything in my mind, turning over each piece of information like it was part of some demonically unsolvable Rubik's Cube, hoping that with each turn, something new would reveal itself.

Nothing came. I had reached a dead end.

Every stream of information had turned to ice. We had three guys who all seemed to be part of some CIA covert assassination unit, but they were now all dead. We had the deeply unsettling notion that my dad was part of that noble group. And we had Corrigan and Fullerton's faces from thirty years ago, but no one who could ID them.

All I could do was wait and see if someone in Daland's underworld recognized either of them and stepped forward. Obviously, there was a strong chance that wouldn't happen at all. Then what?

Deflated, weary, and missing being home with my family—a lot—I powered up the laptop, clicked the browser open and pulled up Rossetti and his editor's web histories that Kurt had put on it.

They were long, running to several pages each. I suppose their careers made them use Google far more than your average Internet surfer.

I was trawling through it when Theo, Gigi's comedian-waiter friend, passed near me and noticed the untouched coffee. He pointed at it and said, "Call me psychic, but it seems to me like you're ready for something with a bit more of a kick, right?"

"What do you recommend?" I asked.

He picked my cup up off the table. "My barman has this amazing Reposada tequila he brings in from Mexico. Guaranteed to push those demons away."

I wasn't sure I was keen on the idea of a Mexican potion messing with my mind, not after my recent experiences down there, but I still said, "OK." Then I asked him, "Any news on that audition?"

His face beamed with pride, his crazy eyes taking on an even more manic look. "I got it. A bit part on *Louie*, can you believe it? I've got two small scenes with the man himself."

I nodded, bittersweet. "That's terrific news, man. Terrific."

Things were clearly working out for Theo. Maybe I'd catch a break too.

I halfheartedly dragged my eyes back to the screen to scan a second page of Rossetti's web search history when three words skewered my attention:

THE OCTOBER SURPRISE

My spine went ramrod straight as I clicked on the link and started reading.

Sandman eased himself soundlessly down the rope onto the small terrace at the back of the loft and quickly dropped to a crouch.

It was cold enough for the insubstantial but steady fall of snow to accumulate where it landed. Already there was at least an inch covering everything that didn't have traffic moving across it.

He took a moment to let his eyes adjust to the low light emanating from inside the loft, scanning the interior for any signs of activity. He saw none. He crept up to the French doors and, with gloved hands, pulled against the handle gently. They weren't locked, it being fair to assume that this high up there was little risk of any burglars gaining access that way. A stream of warm air hit him from inside the loft. Clearly, Miss Decker had no problem heating the huge space, given that both her checking and savings accounts had very healthy balances, and those were just the accounts in her name. Her sloth of a boyfriend seemed to have nabbed himself a pretty sweet catch.

Something else was drifting out into the freezing cold. The unmistakable sound of a woman reaching her climax. Sandman smiled inwardly. This was going to make things even easier. For a brief moment, he wondered about what he could hear. Was it at all possible that Reilly was scoring with his hostess behind her boyfriend's back? Unlikely. It had to be the costumed freaks that were at it. Which meant Reilly was elsewhere in the loft, if he was in at all.

The visit to the nightclub had paid off, big time. He hadn't needed CCTV footage to see them get into a taxi and have to trace the cab's number to find out where he'd dropped them off. The floor manager he'd spoken to didn't know who the guy in the blue cape was, but he knew Gigi Decker, who was a regular at the club and liked to splurge on good champagne. Sandman had left little doubt in the floor manager's mind that any attempt to forewarn Miss Decker of his inquiries would incur the harshest of consequences.

He slipped inside.

The overhead lights were off. A couple of oversized standing lamps that were replicas of old Hollywood searchlights cast a dim, warm hue over the space. The painted floorboards creaked slightly as he moved carefully through the loft, but he knew it was highly unlikely the pair in the bedroom would hear anything.

He focused his attention and ran it around the loft. The large living room was empty. Unless Reilly was asleep, he didn't think the FBI agent or anyone else was around. He advanced further and found a small stack of clothes and personal possessions beside a neatly made futon in one corner. They had to be Reilly's, so his target was—as he'd surmised—out.

Sandman systematically searched them for a sidearm and found the holdall with the Glocks in them. Which meant that Reilly had probably gone out unarmed. He hid them deep under the mattress and stepped back into the large space.

As he reached the closed bedroom door, there was a shriek of such intensity that he had to hover for a moment until it subsided. They were both laughing now, the woman giggling hysterically like a teenager. There was no way either of them was going to offer any kind of defense.

Sandman pulled out his handgun, suppressor already in place, turned the door handle and entered the bedroom.

Jaegers saw him first, eyes immediately filling with unfiltered terror as he recoiled upright and back against the headboard.

"Shit!"

Decker followed the boyfriend's alarmed look to Sandman and flinched, pulling the sheet up to cover her. "Kurt!"

Sandman just stood there, knowing there was no benefit in stepping further into the room and offering one of them a target.

"Get dressed. Move."

They both did, quickly. Jaegers pulled on a pair of dark green leather trousers and a matching hooded jerkin while the girl slipped on a pair of sweatpants and a T-shirt, which got caught on the gold diadem in her hair. She let out an annoyed groan and reached up, disentangled her hair and finished pulling on the tee.

Sandman waved his gun, herding them out of the room.

"Let's go."

He took a couple of steps back as Jaegers walked out of the bedroom first, obscuring the inside for the briefest of moments. The girl followed, holding out the diadem.

"Here, you have it. It's not fucking working anyway."

Just as Sandman instinctively stuck out his left hand to take the gold band, he knew she'd tricked him. The heavy lamp base she'd concealed behind her back under cover of Jaegers exiting the room was already arcing toward the side of his head. He moved fast, whipping his head away as the lamp slammed into his shoulder with surprising force, but before the pain hit him, he jabbed the butt of his gun into the girl's head and sent her crashing to the floor.

Jaegers was moving toward him—he'd spun around the second he heard the approach from behind—but Sandman was too quick, swinging his left elbow up and back into the guy's face. He heard Jaegers' nose break and the accompanying wail of agony as he turned and aimed a vicious kick just below the guy's knee—not enough to break more bone, but enough to open up an additional well of excruciating pain.

Jaegers bounced off the wall and crumpled to the floor.

"Enough of this bullshit," Sandman barked, his gun leveled at the hacker's head, his intention beyond doubt.

Jaegers removed the blood-covered hands from his nose and held them up, palms out. "OK, OK. Just—please, don't hurt her again."

His eyes, wide with fear and worry, bounced from Sandman to his girlfriend and back, then, hesitantly, his palms held open by his face, his lips quivering, his whole face pleading in silence for permission, he crawled over to Decker, slowly.

"Gigi? Gigi!"

She wasn't moving.

Sandman watched him lean in to listen to her breath, then turn to look at him. "She's breathing," he said, then he repeated it before he started to sob.

Sandman looked down on him. "Can I take it you're going to behave from here on?"

Jaegers just nodded as he wiped the blood and the snot that were streaming out of his nostrils.

# 51

The October Surprise.

I knew about it already, of course. Not just as a concept, but in terms of its most notorious occurrence—specifically, from the Reagan-Carter election year.

1980.

The expression referred to any major, unexpected news event that could—deliberately—affect the outcome of the presidential election, which takes place in early November. In the days before both the 1968 and 1972 elections, claims that the end of the war in Vietnam was in sight were used to boost popularity, but those were minor instances of it. The expression really referred to the conspiracy that was thought to have taken place in 1980 to secure Ronald Reagan's defeat of the incumbent, Jimmy Carter.

The facts were that, almost a year to the day before the election, fifty-two Americans had been taken hostage in Iran. This had been a major trauma for the nation and was on every voter's mind. Heavy negotiations were ongoing to win their release, with the Carter administration correctly hoping for their own "October Surprise": bringing the hostages home just before the election, which would provide an immense boost to Carter's re-election prospects. The hostages weren't released and Reagan won the election. They were eventually released, on the day of his inauguration. Not just on the day, but—literally—five minutes after Reagan took his oath of office.

Suspicions soon arose of a secret arms-for-hostages deal brokered by Reagan's men—a deal designed to delay the release of the hostages until after the election, to help ensure Carter's defeat.

The suspicions were dismissed until the Iran-Contra affair exploded five years later, during Reagan's second term. It transpired that senior administration officials had arranged for Iran to secretly receive American weapons—an illegal act, given that it was subject to an arms embargo. Iran would pay for the weapons in two ways: in cash, which would then be funneled to the Contras in Nicaragua—another illegal act, given that funding the Contras had been banned by Congress—and in influencing the release of seven American hostages who were being held in Lebanon.

The Iran-Contra affair firmly established the links between the Reagan administration and the Iranians and underlined the former's readiness to play dirty and break the law. This revived suspicions about what had happened during the 1980 campaign. After increased media scrutiny, both the Senate and Congress eventually held inquiries to look into the allegations. Both failed to produce an indictment. However, in the years since, several senior figures who were in positions of power at the time including Abulhassan Benisadr, the former President of Iran, Yitzhak Shamir, the former Israeli Prime Minister, and Barbara Honegger, a former Reagan campaign and White House staffer, have all confirmed the allegation.

My mind raced back to my chat with Faye, my dad's mistress. What had she said? That he felt the whole country was under his watch, that he took it all to heart.

Was there more to it than that?

Was he aware of what was going on in the shadows? Was he fretting about getting the hostages out in time—and did he know about some dirty tricks that were going on behind the scenes?

My dad was a registered Republican. He was a fan of Reagan's. Which could mean he might have been killed to stop him exposing the truth, if he'd found out about it and wanted to blow the whistle—or simply to keep him quiet, if he knew about it by virtue of being part of the dirty plot.

I knew I was grasping at straws—but something felt right, like gears that had meshed into position and were now propelling my mind forward.

I didn't have much time to dwell on it, though. I was slamming back a shot of that tequila Theo brought me when my phone buzzed in my pocket.

It was Kurt.

Kurt sat with his back slumped against the bedroom wall. Gigi lay on the floor in front of him, still out cold. The intruder had bound them both with plastic cuffs, wrists and ankles, and had just finished ensuring there was nothing within reach that they could use to free themselves. Apart from a soft glow from the bedroom and some faint ambient light from outside, the loft was dark.

His heart sank as he watched Gigi's chest rise and fall slightly as she breathed. At least they were both still alive, he thought, which meant there was hope. Separate from the throbbing pain, which had spread across the center of his face, he felt a piercing ache in his chest so intense that he knew it had to be what people referred to as love. It had taken Gigi being cold-cocked into unconsciousness to trigger the feeling, but he knew exactly what it meant—he would do anything, anything at all, to keep her alive.

The intruder stepped back, visibly satisfied that Kurt and Gigi were secure. "Reilly. Call him."

Even though he suspected it would be ultimately fruitless, he knew he had to try lying. "What? I don't know what you're talking about."

The intruder let out a cold, dry chortle. "You really want to play it that way?"

Kurt felt his chest cave in as the bastard just stared at him. "No," he said meekly.

"Good. Where's your phone?"

"I think—I'm not sure. Maybe in the bedroom?"

The intruder walked off and disappeared out of view, leaving Kurt to try and focus his mind.

He needed to buy some time. There was no way Reilly could help them unless he knew they were in trouble. Added to that, from what Reilly had told him and Gigi, the agent had already out-thought and out-gunned the sadistic motherfucker who held them captive. They'd helped Reilly at every turn, ignoring the risk to themselves. It was time for him to help them. But what if Reilly did come back? Wouldn't the guy just get what he needed and kill all three of them anyway?

The intruder was going to kill him and Gigi either way. And without them around to help Reilly, it was probably only a matter of time before he wound up dead himself. At least this way they had a chance, however small.

The intruder appeared again, holding two phones. "Which one's yours?"

Kurt pointed it out.

"It's one half of a secure pair, right?" the man asked.

"Yes. I hacked them. Reilly has the other."

"OK." He held out the phone, but before Kurt could take it, the intruder held it just out of reach. He aimed the gun that was in his other hand straight at Kurt's eyes. "Tell me exactly what you're going to say."

"What am I going to say? 'Reilly? It's Kurt. We just got a hit. You need to get back here.' That's it." Kurt said it without thinking, but as he said it, he knew it would work, even if it risked unraveling their plan to unmask Corrigan.

That wasn't the priority any more.

"'A hit?' On what?"

"We've been helping Reilly with something." He hesitated, then added, "We posted a couple of mug shots on some forums. Asked if anyone knew them. We haven't got anything back yet. And probably won't. But that's what he's waiting for."

The bastard nodded to himself, then smiled. "You mean the sketches?"

Kurt's mouth went dry. They'd known all along that it was just as likely that an ex-CIA agent or asset who recognized Corrigan or Fullerton would warn them as it was for someone with a grudge to give them up. There was little point in denying it.

"Yes. But we haven't had a hit."

"I know you haven't," the intruder said. "OK. Make the call".

"Reilly?" he said. "It's Kurt." He paused for a moment, then said, "We just got a hit. You need to get back here."

A rush of elation consumed me—then it was instantly flushed away by the feeling that a yawning chasm had blown open beneath me.

Something was wrong.

Very wrong.

Kurt had never, ever referred to himself as Kurt in any of our communications. It was part of his extreme paranoia about the heavily surveilled world we lived in. He'd used Mrs. Takahashi,

Cid Raines, Green Arrow, Snake of course, Crown Prince Arthas Menethil and even once, when he was particularly excited, Lord Humungus, his hacker name from before he got himself onto the FBI's cybercrime watch list in a commendable seventh spot.

But never Kurt.

I needed to buy some time. Fast.

"Fantastic, man. I'll head on back, I've walked all the way up the park."

"Central Park?" Kurt asked.

"Yeah. I lost track of time. I'll hop in a cab. Should be back in twenty minutes or so." I tried to sound as enthused as possible. "Great work, Curtis. Really great."

I hung up, pretty sure that I'd managed to keep the doubt from my voice and hoping he'd got my little hidden counter-message, but as I ended the call, the rush of elation had been replaced by a crushing avalanche of dread.

Kurt's brilliantly hidden-in-plain-sight message could only mean one thing. Baseball Cap was there—and he had Kurt and Gigi.

At least I'd bought some time.

Now I needed to make use of it.

## 52

I churned through a few desperate ideas before quickly settling on the one I thought had the least chance of turning into a disaster. I quickly put it through the wringer a few times, made sure I hadn't missed anything, and decided I had to go for it.

I pulled out the burner phone and called Deutsch's personal phone. She answered immediately.

"It's me."

Her voice jumped, even as it went lower. "Where are you?"

"I'm close. Listen, Annie. I've got a hostile holding two friends hostage here in the city. Not far from Twenty-Six Fed. It's the same motherfucker who killed Kirby and I think he killed Nick too—"

"What?" she interrupted, in shock.

"I'm convinced they killed him, Annie. And a bunch of other people too. And this guy wants me, and you can imagine how badly I want him, but I can't take him alone. Not with him holding them. The guy's a pro. A black ops pro. And he's sanctioned. I need your help, but we have to do it my way. My friends' lives are at stake."

"Jesus, Sean—"

I didn't have time for any kind of debate. "Annie, are you in or out? I need to know right now."

Even as I said it, I knew she would help. She'd already gone out on a major limb for me by getting me the drawings instead of handing them in to the Bureau. For reasons only Deutsch could explain, I guess—and in spite of my inflicting the worst kind of humiliation on her when I escaped from her custody—it was clear she believed my version of events.

I heard her take a steadying breath. "I'm in."

"OK. I need to get a SWAT team to West Twenty-third, between Seventh and Eighth.'

"A SWAT team?"

"Yes. And I need them there in the next fifteen minutes. The guy's good, I can't take him alone, not when he's got my people in there with him."

"How am I going to get them to push the button, Sean? It can't be a tip-off from you."

"I know. Here's how we'll play it. A call will come in from one of the informants me and Nick had with the Joint Terrorism Task Force. A Lebanese guy, Ramsey Salman. He's in the database, works at a deli in Brooklyn. He was keeping tabs on a couple of preachers for us. He's been dark for a while, but he'll say there are a couple of guys in that apartment about to launch a hit on the city. It'll justify a red alert about a credible incoming threat."

"Hang on, hang on." She thought about it fast. "OK, but I can't just say I got the call. I need an actual call to come in to the Bureau switchboard, a call for you or Nick. And it can't come from you, obviously."

Obviously—since it would be taped, and Deutsch needed it to stand up to scrutiny after the fact. I'd thought about this. If I made the call, there was the very real possibility that my voice print would be recognized, which would put her in a serious jam. My eyes wandered aimlessly across the joint as I looked at my solution. He was wiping down a table in the far corner.

I waved Theo over to my table. "I know. I've got it covered."

"You've got someone who can make the call?"

I watched as Theo walked over, hoping he'd be up for it—and that he'd be as good as he'd been in that audition. "Yes."

"OK, let's get going. But better he ask for Nick. They're routing all his calls to my BlackBerry."

Gigi's head felt like it had after her one and only time at Coachella. She'd fulfilled a bucket-list ambition by seeing Portishead live—their first two albums had been the soundtrack to her teens—but it had taken her a full week to recover from the experience. By the time Roger Waters had finished his trip back to *The Dark Side Of The Moon*, she'd felt like someone had drilled a hole in her cranium, filled it with silly putty and razor wire and left her on the cold lump of rock. The putty felt comfortably numb, but the second she moved—even a micron—the blades would score the inside of her skull and she'd want to die.

As she blinked her eyes open and tried to pull focus, the situation that had put her on the floor of her own apartment came cascading back.

*Fuck.*

That pretty much summed it up.

"Gigi," she heard Kurt whisper. "You OK?"

She pushed herself up on her elbows, ignoring the screaming anguish that was quickly filling the left side of her head. Kurt was turning toward her from a slump against the bedroom wall, eyes locked on hers. They were full of a chaotic storm of relief, terror, confusion and—she'd seen it only once before but knew she'd recognize it again—genuine care.

"What's happening?" she asked with a groan.

"It's going to be OK," Kurt told her.

"OK how?"

"Reilly's on his way."

This didn't sit well. "What do you mean? How?"

"I called him." Kurt paused, seemingly embarrassed, then said, "He made me call him. Tell him we had a hit."

Gigi thought it through quickly and groaned. "You fucking pinhead!" she hissed. "Jesus Christ, Jaegers. Don't you realize the bastard is going to kill us anyway?"

She heard the intruder say, "Shut up. Both of you."

She turned and spotted him sitting in the living room, defiling her sleek Italian sofa, the one that had taken four months from order to delivery, and watching over them. Her expression soured with disdain. "Whatever, dickhead." She twisted her face back at Kurt, shaking her head slowly, trying to block out the despair.

She looked at Kurt. He just looked like he wanted to weep. Right then, she thought of how she loved the pinhead and how it would be nice to hear and say the words—she never had, not once—but first they needed to survive the night.

The bastard checked his watch. "You two should kiss and make up. You don't want to go out like this, do you?"

"Up yours," she spat back as she slithered backward toward the wall, closer to Kurt. She reached out and squeezed his forearm in what she hoped was a gesture of support, finishing up slumped right next to him.

She inclined her head toward him and whispered, "Reilly'll get him."

The movement was so painful she felt like she was going to puke. And she wasn't sure she even believed what she'd just said.

# 53

From my vantage point in a sheltered doorway on Twenty-third Street up the block from Gigi's building I watched as some NYPD uniforms quietly cordoned off the street and set up their perimeter.

I could barely make out a couple of cops going in to the eatery, where they would herd everyone to the back of the place and tell them to stay clear of the windows until further notice. Another team would be doing the same on the opposite sidewalk.

I'd spoken to Theo before I slipped out, needing to make sure he understood how important it was for him to keep our little secret. He was a bit nervous, rightfully worried about the call I'd asked him to make, which he'd pulled off with a very convincing foreign accent—not necessarily Lebanese, but it did the trick. I'd already assured him as strongly as I could that it was all under control and that he had nothing to worry about. I genuinely didn't think he did. We'd made the call from my burner phone, which was untraceable. They didn't have his voice on record, and I sure as hell wasn't going to tell them who'd made that call if it ever came down to it.

Through the light snowfall that was drifting down from the darkness, I watched and waited, knowing I needed to move quickly once my window of opportunity opened up. I wouldn't have much time if I was going to capitalize on the confusion and make my move undetected while the situation was still fluid.

I was also wondering if my target would spot the forces moving in on him, and—mostly—I was hoping I hadn't miscalculated and sealed Kurt and Gigi's fate.

Sandman walked over to one of the large windows and carefully peered outside. The snow was still falling—light, but steady. There was nothing going on out there. Except . . . the street was quiet.

Too quiet. No cars driving down. No pedestrians on the sidewalks. Nothing.

He noticed the slightest of movements on the roof opposite. He pulled back and retrieved his night-vision scope, then he moved tight against one of the thick vertical columns of exposed brick that provided the loft's skeleton and looked out through the scope. A sniper and a spotter were taking up position. He recognized the gear and the edges of the big letters on their ballistic vests.

He swung the scope down toward the street, though the angle obscured the sidewalk immediately outside. He adjusted his position and looked down along the front of the building in time to catch two cops disappearing from view inside the restaurant across from him.

They'd tricked him. The sloth and his slut girlfriend had found a way to alert Reilly and he'd called in the troops.

Sandman pulled out his gun, took quick strides over to his hostages and pushed the suppressor hard into the side of Kurt's head.

"What did you tell him?" he barked.

"What? Why? Nothing. You heard me. I didn't—"

"What did you tell him?" he repeated, seething with controlled anger.

Sandman leaned his foot against Kurt and shoved him to one side before swinging the suppressor around to Gigi's forehead. He kept his eyes locked on Kurt.

"I want you to watch her die," he hissed at Kurt. "I want you to watch it, knowing it's your fault. In fact, I want you so close to her you'll actually feel her die."

Sandman could see both defiance and fear in the girl's eyes and knew that both were genuine. She wasn't trying to hide her feelings, or mask one emotion with another. There were no prayers, pleading or promises. Like Sandman himself, she was completely in the moment and, at some level, he admired her for that. He'd need to kill them both eventually, once they'd outlived their usefulness. Based on what he had seen and heard, he'd already decided that a staged sex game with tragic unintended consequences would be an appropriate way to dispatch them both. It would simply be two more "deaths-by-misadventure" to add to all the others, but he had to deal with the nuisance of Reilly's little counterpunch first.

For now, he still needed them alive, so he pulled the gun away from the girl's head. He stepped back a few paces, took out his encrypted cellphone and dialed.

Roos answered quickly, evidently waiting for the update.

"I've got a SWAT team getting ready to move in on me," he told Roos. "It's got to be Reilly."

"Can you get out clean?"

"I could, but it would probably mean inflicting multiple casualties on friendlies, and our agreed mission protocol is for minimal collateral harm. Unless you want to sanction an override."

There was a moment of silence as Roos considered this. "No. Current parameters remain in force."

Sandman had assumed that would be the case. You don't expend seemingly bottomless resources to keep your work off the radar, only to blow it all when things get more difficult than you'd ideally like. "Then get them off my back. It'll force Reilly's hand."

"We're already plugged in. They're saying an informant called in a suspected terrorist cell with plans for an imminent attack."

"The guy's no slouch."

"We're telling them the Agency has someone on the inside and that we need to let it play out."

"Will that fly? The FBI won't want to be left with major egg on its face if there's any chance of it happening."

"Let us worry about that. You take care of your end."

"Copy that."

As Sandman ended the call, he realized he'd never taken quite that tone with his current employer. Of course they'd let it slide, but it told Sandman the extent to which Reilly had got under his skin. It certainly wasn't personal—even the most relentlessly intractable and obdurate target would always fail to push a top operative toward emotion of any kind—but it had certainly become a matter of professional pride. On top of the sheer necessity of his current task, it would be immensely satisfying to take the guy down.

No meticulous plan. No elaborate "accident."

Just a bullet in the brain and the body incinerated.

It would be as if Agent Reilly had simply disappeared from the world, never to return.

# 54

I watched as the sedan reversed into the parking spot on Twenty-third and even before its sole occupant got out and walked to the back of the car I'd already decided he'd be the one.

Ops like the one that I'd instigated around Gigi's apartment would be JTTF efforts—Joint Terrorist Task Force, a combined effort of both the Bureau and the NYPD. The SWAT team that was converging on us wasn't being dispatched from some bat cave. It consisted of all kinds of highly trained cops and agents with day jobs at CT or CI or any other division who, when they got the call, would make their own way to the staging location, somewhere safe outside the perimeter that was set up around Gigi's building. Deutsch had called to tell me where that was, and I knew that if I waited within close reach of it, I'd get my chance.

The big boys—the command post and the special weapons truck—hadn't yet arrived, but they'd soon be here. I had to move quickly.

With light snow dropping around me, I approached him as he popped the trunk, glancing inside it to make sure he had what I needed and somewhat relieved that he wasn't anyone I knew. I mean, I'd been on many ops with these guys, guys I'd entrusted my life to while they'd done the same with me, and the fact that I didn't know him made what I needed to do somewhat easier—not by much, though.

"Hey," I said in as friendly and harmless a tone as I could manage, "what's going on down there?"

He glanced around, but before he could answer, I swooped in and hit him with a big punch to the chest. He staggered back, winded, and I moved in quick with him and pulled his gun out of his holster and pressed it against him while my other hand grabbed his cuffs and handed them to him.

"Turn around. Quickly."

He grudgingly did as I asked. I cuffed his hands behind his back.

"Flat on the ground. Right now."

He went down.

I tucked the gun away and turned to pillage his trunk. I slipped on his navy blue field jacket, cap, and level three ballistic vest. He was FBI, not NYPD ESU—Emergency Services Unit—and the letters on the vest reflected it. I took out the Remington pump-action shotgun, checked that it was loaded and chambered, then I saw something else. A battering ram. This, I hadn't expected—but it opened up a safer option, so I slung the shotgun over my shoulder and grabbed the ram.

"In the trunk," I told him. "Let's go."

He was climbing in when my phone rang.

I slammed the trunk shut and started trotting back towards Gigi's building as I answered the call. It was Deutsch.

The radio broke into several pieces as Deutsch hurled it against the inside of the Bureau SUV.

Gallo hadn't even had a chance to sign off after telling her that he'd been ordered to shut down the operation due to express orders from Homeland Security. Up until that moment her head had been lagging behind her heart—the former already totally sold on Reilly's innocence, the latter still harboring reservations. Now the two were in perfect synchrony. The bastards clearly had some staggering reach.

She pulled out her personal cell phone and dialed Reilly's burner phone, already anticipating that what the SWAT team was supposed to take care of would come down to her and Reilly on their own.

Deutsch wasn't happy. "I'm really sorry, Sean, I can't do anything about this."

"About what? What's going on?"

"We just got the order to pull back."

I had guessed right. "Langley?"

"Yep. They're saying they've got someone on the inside and that it's under control, that there's no imminent attack and we're jeopardizing an op they've been working on for months."

I had to chortle at their brazenness, given that there was no "inside" for them to have anyone in.

"It's out of my hands. Out of Gallo's, out of the Director's and everyone else who matters, bar the president himself by the looks of it."

I told her, "Don't worry about it." Which she clearly wasn't expecting.

"What?"

"You've got your orders, Annie. Stand down and pull out."

"Sean—"

"Annie. It's not your fight. Just get out of here and make sure you still have a job tomorrow. I might need you again."

And with that, I ended the call, not giving Deutsch a chance to object further.

I had work to do.

## 55

I hugged the shadows as I quick-walked down the sidewalk towards the entrance to Gigi's building, trying to look like I was moving with clear purpose on a set task.

I made it to the entrance without encountering anyone, and I guessed I could thank my shooter and his handlers for that. The chaos they'd triggered by getting the op called off was giving me an opening.

I looked around, made sure no one was watching, then I gave the frame of the building's front door a little jab with the battering ram and the glass door popped open.

I slipped inside, found the stairs, and climbed up.

Sandman watched the spotter team on the roof across from him fall back and disappear into the night.

Somewhat relieved that he wasn't going to have to shoot his way through a SWAT deployment, he stepped back into the apartment, away from the windows, and hovered over his captives, thinking things through.

"You two are lucky that at least someone can do what the fuck they're told," he said to Kurt and Gigi.

Neither of them moved or responded.

Something had changed about the pair, though he couldn't quite identify it. It was like they were now offering him a single reaction instead of two—as though they were somehow inside each other's thoughts.

He could feel Reilly's presence now, not only in his mind but also in his gut. Maybe they felt it too.

The agent would be coming. And Sandman would be ready.

Deutsch was in turmoil as she watched the cops pull back from their positions, but it wasn't so much the sight of them that was causing it as it was Reilly's words.

She knew he was going to make a move on his own and felt wracked with frustration about it. She had to do something, couldn't let him deal with the situation on his own. She thought of calling it in, saying something, anything, to get the SWAT op reinstated, and pulled out her radio—and hesitated.

Reilly was probably already making his way into the target apartment. Calling in the troops might jeopardize whatever crazy plan he'd concocted. If he didn't know SWAT was moving in again, her call might put him—and his friends—at risk. Furthermore, he was still a wanted man. She didn't want him to end up in custody because of her, even if the move could save his life.

She struggled with the decision, torn by savage tugs from both directions—then she muttered a sharp curse and hurried up the sidewalk towards the target building.

She found its door busted open and pulled out her handgun as she stepped inside. She gave the lobby a quick scan. She saw the elevator and a couple of doors to one side of it. The elevator was on the sixth floor. She hit the call button, then thought better of it and opened one of the doors to find the stairs.

She headed up.

The noise speared Sandman's attention.

It was barely audible; the faintest of disturbances skirting the edge of his consciousness, but it was definitely there.

He froze.

He concentrated his listening and identified the source: the low rumble of the elevator, announcing it was in motion.

He moved stealthily across to the apartment's front door, giving the suppressor on his handgun a quick tug to make sure it was firmly in place.

He crept closer to the door, listened for a moment, then leaned across it to look through the peephole. He barely caught a glimpse of what looked like a SWAT guy swinging a battering ram before the door blew in and slammed against him.

# 56

I flung the battering ram aside as the door burst inward and followed it right in with the Remington in both hands.

It was dark inside, but in the light coming in from the outside hallway, I caught sight of my shooter regaining his footing from being hit by the door. I spun around and swung the shotgun towards him, but he was already charging at me and grabbed its barrel before I fired, using my turning momentum to fling me around and slam me into the wall just as I pulled the trigger.

The explosion was deafening, but the shot was wasted. My shooter was clear of it and all it did was blast a framed art print and the wall around it into confetti. I held onto the shotgun as I hit the wall sideways, hard, barely having time to recover before he flicked it up ferociously, its stock connecting with my jaw like an expertly placed uppercut. I yelped as he then drove a boot into my shin, an instant before his right hand reigned several quick blows into my ribcage, sending me recoiling back, though not far enough to avoid feeling the full brunt of his left landing a hammer blow to the side of my head. I somehow managed to keep hold of the shotgun throughout this onslaught, but it was impossible to take aim. I tried twisting my entire body and stepping back, swinging the shotgun around toward his head, but he grabbed my wrist with his left hand and sent my aim down at the floor before slamming my hand against the wall and sending the shotgun to the ground.

He shoved me off to one side and dived for it, but I launched myself back and stomped on his hand just as it reached it, kicking the shotgun away and sending it skittering off to some far corner of the room at the same time as I heard some snapping tendons and his sharp grunt. He span around and sent a hammer of a punch with his left hand at my kidneys, winding me and causing me to go light-headed for an instant—enough for him to move in with his injured hand, aiming it right at my throat.

I saw it in time and ducked it, grabbing his arm and flinging him past me and spinning him around so I had him from behind, my arms now tight against him, one around his chest, the other around his neck—and I tightened my grip. He couldn't move. I had my legs planted firmly and out of range and I could feel the momentum had shifted—I was choking the life out of him and he was waning. He was strong, though, and it was still taking everything I had to keep him locked in. He tried kicks, elbows, and punches, but nothing connected, and each one was getting less potent than the last.

I had him—at least, I thought so—his right arm stopped trying to pull me off his neck or pound me off him, and weirdly, his hand went down and he seemed to be doing a frenzied rummage through his pocket, and before I realized what was happening, I felt it: a stab, deep and sharp, like a bite—the bite of an injection, some kind of pressurized delivery, deep into my thigh.

My senses went haywire—I instantly knew what he'd done to me.

I was already dead.

Every neuron in my body went into hyperdrive, acutely aware of the poison that I knew was coursing through my veins, winding and weaving its way from my thigh across my torso and all the way up to my heart, where it would soon wreak havoc and cause some catastrophic failure that would kill me right there and then, in Gigi's loft, in mid-fight, with my own killer in my hands.

I could feel odd sensations happening all over me—my arms going a bit numb, a tightening in my chest, a heaviness in my head, though I couldn't tell if they were real or if I was imagining them. Either way, I knew I didn't have much time left.

I had to end it here, right now.

I couldn't let him walk away. Not after he'd killed me.

I wouldn't be able to save myself, but at least Kurt and Gigi would walk away from this. Maybe.

I summoned every ounce of strength I could muster and went for the kill—I tightened my grip around his neck, then I quickly brought up my other arm, took his head in a vice-like hold and twisted it as brutally as I could. One move, the most unflinchingly savage and rage-filled act of my life. I just wanted him dead. I knew how hard it was to pull off, but I also knew enough about the body to know which vertebrae I needed to break in order to sever the spinal cord so as to kill him almost instantly and not just cause him slow respiratory failure or some kind of survivable paralysis. I haven't killed that many people—my career is about locking people up, not playing judge and jury—and those I have killed, usually in self-defense, I've dispatched with the help of some kind of weapon. I'd never killed anyone with my bare hands, though right now I could think of nothing I wanted more.

I saw Deutsch appear in the doorway, saw her aiming her gun at us in a two-handed stance as her mouth formed the words "Stop! Hands in the air," but I was oblivious to her presence and her voice; all I could feel were the muscles, bones and tendons between my hands as I heard the telltale crack and felt his body twitch before it went limp in my arms.

I let go of him and he dropped to the ground like a rag doll, lifeless—just as I soon would be.

I spun around for a three-sixty, my eyes not really registering anything, unsure about whether Kurt or Gigi were still alive, unable to see much in the darkness and through the haze shrouding my senses, then my eyes settled again on Deutsch, and I staggered towards her.

Her face was locked in shock as I told her, "He hit me with a . . . Alami. Get me to Alami, fast."

Then I hit the ground and all sight and sound faded to nothingness.

# FRIDAY

# 57

*NewYork-Presbyterian Hospital, Manhattan*

Much later, when we'd talk about it, I'd often get asked if I saw the "white light" or some kind of tunnel. To everybody's disappointment and contrary to what Alami had told me many of his patients had experienced in those hours and days when they were technically—in the traditional, loose sense of the word—dead, I could only say I didn't see anything like that. No lighted tunnel, no angel to guide me, no heaven either. It was simply the deepest sleep I'd ever had. Twenty-seven hours of it, I was told.

I didn't hear the panicked shouts between Deutsch, Kurt and Gigi at the apartment after I lost consciousness. I didn't remember or feel the ten minutes of relentless chest compressions Deutsch gave me or any of the six defibrillator shocks the paramedics hit me with before resuming the CPR as they rushed me to NewYork-Presbyterian. I have no memory of everything Alami and his team did to me during those long hours: shoving the hose down my throat to intubate me, cutting into my veins to siphon out my blood, cool it down and re-oxygenate it, hitting me with more shocks, injecting me with all kinds of intravenous drugs and plugging various monitors into me to bring me back to life. But they did. Those brilliant, dedicated human beings—my real-life angels, I guess—all of them brought me back, and I'll forever be grateful and humbled by their actions.

The first thing I became aware of was the blurred face of Tess hovering over me. Deutsch had driven up and escorted her out of the house, past the FBI and local cops who were watching it, saying she needed to ask her some things down at Federal Plaza. Tess later told me my fingers had twitched unexpectedly and she'd jumped out of her seat by the bed and looked down on my face, willing me to wake up. Within seconds, other familiar faces came into focus: Kurt and Gigi, someone I eventually remembered to be Alami, and some other people I didn't know but who I'd soon realize were doctors and nurses. They all had faces intensely contorted by worry and relief, which confused me. It would take me a while to understand what was going on. I couldn't remember what happened, I didn't even know what I was doing in the hospital. I couldn't speak because of the tube down my throat, and when I tried writing out a question, I was shocked to see my penmanship looking far more like that of a toddler than my own.

I spent most of that second night asleep again. The next morning, Tess wasn't around. It was too risky to have her come down here on her own or to have Deutsch bring her over again. Instead, Deutsch had promised to keep her appraised using Viber VOIP calls to Kim's laptop, which wouldn't be picked up by any taps on Tess or Kim's phones. Still, one thing helped make up for her absence: they took out the tracheal tube they'd shoved down my throat. I could speak again—more of a croak, really, but still. It was a huge relief.

Deutsch came by early, long before going into work. She, Kurt, and Gigi filled me in on what had happened, starting with Deutsch's surprise at seeing the couple shouting to her from deeper inside the loft space and finding a guy dressed entirely in green leather and a striking-looking but bruised redhead struggling to work their way free of flex-cuffs.

In the heat of the moment, Deutsch had made a couple of quick decisions to keep me off the radar. She'd asked Gigi to call in the emergency services and say Kurt had had a heart attack. When a couple of cops who'd been part of the aborted SWAT raid had taken an interest as they wheeled me into the ambulance, she'd used her FBI creds to defuse their interest and say it was an unrelated matter, some random guy in the building who'd had one hamburger too many. At the hospital, she'd also used her shield to register me under a false name, saying it was a matter of national security, two words that wield huge power these days.

The downside of her decisions was that my shooter's body had remained in Gigi's apartment and Deutsch couldn't call it in, get the body taken to the coroner's lab and trigger an investigation into finding out who he was. It wasn't a great loss, in that I didn't think he would show up on any of our databanks. I imagined he was part of that same invisible group of spooks that officially didn't exist. It was a problem for Gigi and Kurt, though, because it wouldn't be long before the busted door to the lobby would attract attention, as would the one to Gigi's apartment. Deutsch had made Kurt drag the shooter's body away from its highly visible position and hide him in the bedroom to avoid letting the paramedics spot him. The people who sent him—Corrigan and his CIA ally or allies—had to know where he was when he went missing, and if they hadn't done it already, they'd soon have someone there to find out why he'd gone dark. Deutsch didn't know if that had happened already, since she wasn't about to go asking and they weren't about to announce it. Either way, Gigi and Kurt would be the obvious candidates to finger for his death, if his body ever made it into the system, but so far Deutsch had seen no sign of it. Perhaps they'd make his body disappear and that would be the end of it. Deutsch was still struggling to figure out what she could do to defuse things for them if things got heated, without landing behind bars herself.

For the time being, though, what was clear was that Gigi's apartment was off limits. She had checked herself and Kurt into a small hotel close to the hospital using a fake ID. Gigi had planned for the day she'd need to hit the eject button and get out of there quickly, and while the paramedics were busy working on me, she'd hit the kill switch she'd built into her systems and purged them. Anything of importance, though, was still contained in a four terabyte hard drive the size of a paperback novel and accessible by her beefy laptop, both of which were still in her possession.

Which was critical to me because the next day, a message would land on her laptop, a message that would finally break down the walls of secrecy that I'd been bashing my head against for months.

Someone responded to the anonymous posting Gigi and Kurt had uploaded onto Daland's Darknet site.

And we were game on again.

# 58

*CIA Headquarters, Langley, Virginia*

Edward Tomblin had been through major crises before. He'd been shot, even tortured, and he'd had field ops go bad on him. The worst were two occasions when he and Roos had been undercover on foreign soil and had contacts sell them out, one for material gain while they were in Sudan, and the other under torture in Nicaragua. Both times they'd had to exfiltrate themselves out of hostile territory with only the thinnest of margins separating them from extreme unpleasantness.

Tomblin was never fazed by crisis. He had the reputation as one of the calmest tacticians in the business, a man who could face down calamities with a sangfroid that bordered on unsettling.

He wasn't calm now. Not after one of his inner circle of trusted OSINT geeks had informed him that portraits of him and someone else—who Tomblin knew to be Roos, even before the Open-Source Intelligence analyst had messaged him a copy of the drawings—had popped up on an underground Darknet marketplace, offering a reward for anyone who could identify them.

Tomblin hadn't been out in the field for years. As the current head of the CIA's National Clandestine Service, physical danger wasn't on his radar, not any more. He'd done his time, and he now left the dirty business up to others. Sure, he still had to negotiate tricky political situations himself and maneuver to keep certain secrets from threatening his career. But physical threats? A thing of the past—until now.

This was different.

This was a left-field attack from an unhinged, obsessed man who possessed a highly dangerous skill set and seemed like he'd never give up. And for the first time since the crisis started, Tomblin wasn't only worried about the possibility of exposure and prison time. He was worried about his life.

"So what are you waiting for?" Tomblin asked the analyst. "Take them down. Take them down or just kill the whole damn site."

"We can't," the analyst replied. "That's not how this thing works."

"What do you mean, we can't? It's running on Tor, isn't it? We own the damn thing."

Which was, in some ways, true.

As an anonymity online network, Tor—the name came out of its initial incarnation as The Onion Router—was Shakespearean in its origin. It was a privacy tool, free software that was supposed to shield Internet users from being spied on by the US government's intelligence agencies—a somewhat unrealistic expectation, given that they were the very people who had created it.

Not that most Tor users were aware of that.

It was developed, funded and built by the US government—specifically, the Office of Naval Research and DARPA, the Defense Advanced Research Projects Agency—to allow its agents to work online undercover without leaving a trace of government IP addresses that could unmask them. It was then released as free software and today, millions of people used it. Using "onion routing," which consisted of bouncing traffic randomly through a parallel peer-to-peer network that was wrapped in layers of encryption to confuse and disconnect its origin and destination, dissidents and activists in countries with restricted Internet reach could use Tor to publish out of their governments' reach. At the same time, illegal child porn and drug marketplaces could also thrive in its supposedly untraceable cloud.

What most of its users didn't know, however—not until Edward Snowden's leaks, that is—was that Tor actually provided the very opposite of anonymity. It helped red-flag targets for NSA and law enforcement surveillance and gave the watchers access to all of those users' online activity.

"Not in this case," the analyst said. "It's not a pure Tor play. Whoever built Erebus knew we had our claws all over Tor, so they built it to use Tor in a way we didn't foresee. A couple of our guys at Fort Meade and me have been working on it since I spotted the post with your face on it, but we can't find a way into its core. We can see the sketches, but we can't take them down."

Tomblin was standing by the floor-to-ceiling glass wall of this office on the northwest corner of the sixth floor of the New

Headquarters Building, facing the courtyard and the white triple vault that housed the dining rooms beyond it.

"Of course you can," he said as his eyes roamed across the Kryptos sculpture that sat alone and undisturbed in a quiet corner of the courtyard. A ten-foot-tall, curving verdigris scroll that contained an 865-character coded message, it seemed to flow out from a petrified tree near a water-filled basin that was bordered by a stone garden.

"I'm sorry, sir, but right now—we can't."

Tomblin stared through the sculpture as he contemplated the analyst's words. It had taken another Agency analyst more than seven years to crack its code and reveal the hidden message inside it—although one of its sections, consisting of ninety-seven characters, still waited deciphering. He'd done it in his spare time, during his lunch breaks, using nothing more than pencil and paper and a brilliant mind. Over seven hundred hours of quiet contemplation and brain gymnastics to uncover what another inspired mind had created in the privacy of his studio.

Such was the caliber of the analysts Tomblin had gotten to know at the Agency.

Tomblin wondered if the Erebus darknet site would prove as stubborn in giving up its secrets. He had full confidence in his team's abilities to break down any barriers that prevented them from achieving what needed to be done. Now, more than ever, he needed that same determination, that same dogged pursuit of a solution—he needed a result, only he needed it fast.

"Shut it down," he told the analyst. "I need this done quickly. Am I making myself clear?"

"We're trying, sir. But even when we use the source's login credentials, the most we can do is create a fresh account using our plant as a nominator. Given enough time, we might be able to identify regular users and their locations by analyzing entry and exit patterns, but that will take days—if not longer. And if they're smart, whoever uploaded the sketches will only log in once more when they get the alert—and that's if someone recognizes you and decides to take up that offer to sell you out."

Tomblin closed his eyes and pinched the bridge of his nose. "That's not good enough."

"I know, sir. I can tell you, whoever built it wasn't some DoD contractor or a Naval Research brainiac out to make a fast buck. This came from true motivation, one of these crusaders who thinks protecting the Internet from Big Brother is like Orwell going to Spain to fight Franco's fascists and managed to create a site layer which is as close to artificially intelligent as anyone's come. The site's servers are totally virtual and self-perpetuating—they behave exactly like a virus. They move around the world from server farm to server farm, overwriting their trail as they move along. The guys over at the Bureau found Silk Road because it was physically hosted somewhere. The cyber crimes team found the server with a little help from the NSA, they cloned it, they combed through the transaction records and used what they found as evidence to indict the guy who set it up. Whoever built this learned from that—this baby's a couple of generations up on it. It has no physical location, no owner in law, no administrator logging into it to keep it running. It's the ghost in the machine—literally—though in this case, we didn't kill the victim."

"Find a way," Tomblin insisted, his tone, though calm, leaving no doubt about his resolve. "And keep it contained. No one outside your immediate team is to breathe a word of this to anyone. And I mean, anyone."

"Understood."

Tomblin hung up and looked up from the sculpture at the bleak December sky hanging over him.

He had a decision to make.

The portraits were good. Anyone who knew him and Roos would easily recognize them. It was as if they were done in a professional sitting, and they looked younger in them. They'd been aged a bit, but Tomblin's expert eye could tell it had just been layered on. They were from someone from their past. From decades earlier, maybe.

He knew it had to be Reilly. The FBI agent had found a way to get his hands on their likenesses, and given Reilly's recent collision with Tomblin and Roos's past, Tomblin knew exactly who Reilly's benefactor had to be.

Sokolov. The slippery Russian scientist had given them up to Reilly.

Tomblin was seething inside.

This was all Roos's fault. This whole mess had started after Roos had gone and helped his old buddy at the DEA with his cockamamie scheme to flush out a drug baron by brainwashing Reilly's son—without consulting with Tomblin. A reckless, unwarranted, unilateral act that had ignited Reilly and turned him into a rabid bloodhound.

A bloodhound who, by the looks of it, had his teeth in them already and wasn't about to let go.

Tomblin's discontent intensified further when he thought about Sandman. If their assassin had done his job and finished Reilly off when he'd had the chance, none of them—not Tomblin, not Roos, not Viking—would be in this predicament. But that ship had sailed. Tomblin's men had recovered Sandman's body from Gigi Decker's apartment and spirited it out unnoticed. No one would ever find a trace of the dead assassin. Not the way they'd had it disposed of. Alerts and facial recognition surveillance trawls were quickly put in place for both Gigi Decker and Kurt Jaegers, but so far, nothing had come up.

Tomblin had a tough decision to make, and his mind was already homing in on one of the two options open to him.

He knew Reilly's family was still off limits to them, due to round-the-clock FBI and police surveillance in case Reilly made contact with them. He couldn't get to them without attracting attention.

Which left him with one strategy—but two different variants of it. He played them out in his mind, then settled on the one that seemed more logical.

He couldn't not tell Roos. There was a chance Roos would get a similar call from someone who was on Erebus. Tomblin didn't think it would come from within the CIA—Roos had been working on the outside long enough that the new analysts, like the one who had alerted Tomblin, didn't know him. Furthermore, they were under strict instructions not to inform anyone about it. Still, a lot of ghosts from their past were skulking around Erebus. Tomblin knew that.

He picked up his encrypted cell phone and called Roos.

His old partner was, not unexpectedly, livid. He said he hadn't yet heard about the drawings, which was probably true, although given how high the stakes had reached and how good Roos was at dissembling, Tomblin couldn't be sure.

Either way, he brought him up to speed with the analyst's assessment.

Roos asked, "So . . . options?"

"I don't know," Tomblin said. "There's a chance no one will sell us out."

"You want to count on that?"

"Not really. And I don't want it hanging over me like that, not knowing if and when someone does sell us out."

"I don't either. So it's only a question of time before Reilly knows who at least one of us is."

"That's a fair assumption," Tomblin replied.

Roos didn't say anything for a moment. Tomblin knew he was letting the thought play itself out, allowing competing scenarios to unfurl in his mind's eye.

"He's gonna come after us, Gordo," Tomblin added, his tone somber and resolved. "Sooner or later, unannounced, and unforgiving. It's gonna happen. And I think we need to kill off that uncertainty and make it happen."

"You want to flush him out?"

"Yes," Tomblin said, already visualizing the endgame that would get rid of his problem once and for all. "On our terms. With a home-court advantage."

"The blind," Roos said.

Tomblin wasn't surprised that his old partner had come to the conclusion he'd expected of him. "Exactly," he told him. "I'll set it up."

# SATURDAY

# 59

*NewYork-Presbyterian Hospital, Manhattan*

Gordon Roos.

My nemesis was called Gordon Roos.

It didn't even end up costing me any money. The anonymous informant on the other end of Gigi's fiber-optic Internet link only seemed too happy to rat him out without bothering with the ten thousand dollars we'd offered. This guy just said he owed Roos some payback without specifying what it concerned, and said that if fingering him caused Roos grief, that was reward enough. He told us where we were likely to find him, then he disappeared. Given the way Erebus was set up, if he didn't want us to be able to contact him or trace him, we wouldn't be able to. He'd popped up, given us his good cheer, and sunk back into the murky bowels of Daland's creation.

Kurt and Gigi had run a check on his name, of course, to see if it was genuine. They had to dig a bit deeper than they would have with your average Joe, but they tracked him down to a house in Ocracoke, North Carolina through, of all things, a pilot's license. They didn't turn up the cabin up in the Blue Mountains that our mystery informant had told us about, but that didn't surprise me. It probably wasn't registered in his name. Which made perfect sense—given what they intended to use it for.

I looked around the hospital room at my assembled avengers and I've got to say that we didn't exactly look invincible. There was me, just barely back from the dead, still with a couple of IV lines pumping magic potions into my veins and monitors giving out reassuring little beeps that I was still alive. Kurt, who looked like he'd sprinted into a brick wall, what with the broken nose in splints and the black eyes. Although the splints and the strips across his brow and over his upper lip did have something vaguely superhero-esque about them and he did wield some potent superpowers at his computer, he was far from a lethal weapon out in the field, which is what this was going to turn into to, without a doubt. Gigi, also damaged and still nursing the aftershocks of a concussion and a noticeable bulge on her skull. Deutsch was intact—so far. I was determined to keep it that way.

Deutsch said, "It's a trap."

The light outside was fading fast, courtesy of us being just two days away from the winter solstice, and the encroaching darkness was mirroring the somber mood on her face.

"Of course it's a trap," I said. "That's what I was hoping for."

"You were hoping for a trap?" Kurt asked, his emotive range limited by the gauze socks stuffed up his nostrils.

"They're watching," I told him. "They're watching everything. Even Erebus. Especially Erebus. This was bound to generate a rise in them. It had to. It was always going to be more likely than getting a shout from someone real who knows them."

Kurt, despite his cloaked face, still managed to convey deep concern. "So . . . you're not going to go, obviously?"

I looked at him like he was speaking Urdu.

"You're going to go?" he asked, incredulous.

"There's a difference between going in blind and going in prepared," I told him. "I don't intend to go in blind."

"But surely you don't need to." He swung his look over at Deutsch. "Why don't you call it in and get a SWAT team up there and arrest the guy? You're FBI. You know what's going on. You know the whole story. You're a witness to all this. That's got to count for something, doesn't it?"

"Calm down, Snake" Gigi said. "She may know the whole story, but it doesn't mean it counts for squat in terms of evidence. Which, from what I gather, is nonexistent," she said, turning to Deutsch.

"Correct," Deutsch said. "All they have right now is Reilly," she told Kurt, "wanted for murder, with a lot of evidence to support that."

"Everything else, everything about Roos," I added, "it's just a story, a fairy tale—my overactive imagination. Any court-appointed defense attorney with a mail-order law degree would walk all over it in the opening seconds of a preliminary hearing, assuming we ever got that far. Assuming they let any of us live that long."

"So you're going to go after him," Kurt said. "In your current condition. Knowing it's a trap."

"Like I said, I don't plan on going in blind." I looked over at Deutsch. "And I think we have a couple of surprises we can use to our advantage."

"You're nuts," Kurt protested. He flicked an outraged glance at Deutsch. "He's nuts, right? And you're OK with that? You need to do something." He turned back to me, gesticulating wildly now. "I mean, look at you. You just had a heart attack, for Christ's sake."

"'Sudden cardiac arrest,'" I corrected him with a half-smile. I straightened up. "Look. I didn't start this. Hell, I didn't even know I had a son until they came after him and maybe, in some perverse sense, I can actually be grateful for that. But I'm not. He was living happily with his mom and they took that away from him. Then they killed a lot of people, ending with my own partner. So I don't care if Annie here said she had enough evidence to bring Roos in. We're past that. Besides, even if we had a halfway decent case, there's no jail that's going to hold these people. They're connected enough to make some kind of deal or get some kind of pressure applied and they'll be back out there in no time, with us all in their crosshairs. Which I'm not comfortable with. No, there's only one way this is ending, and that's with me making sure they get what they deserve and they don't live to bother any of us, or anyone else for that matter, any more."

I glanced around the room.

Deutsch's expression was focused and grim. She held my gaze and looked like she was about to say something, then seemed to decide against it and just gave me a slight, reluctant nod. Kurt and Gigi didn't have anything to add either. They just looked at me with settled eyes and even expressions that told me they understood what I had to do. It also told me they were prepared to do what they could to help me.

I pulled the sensors off my chest. The monitors started beeping. Then I reached over to the IV bags, and slipped them off their stand. "Let's go."

I swung my feet off the bed and pushed myself to my feet. I felt dizzy—I'd been laid out for more than two days. I steadied myself against the bedside table, shut my eyes, and sucked in a few deep gulps of air. I let it go deep into my chest, and again, several big lungfuls, enjoying the sensation despite the tingling around my rib cage. Then I opened my eyes and padded over to the electrical socket and unplugged the monitor just as the nurse came rushing in.

"What are you doing?" she asked, her shocked eyes like saucers.

"National Security," I told her, using Deutsch's new favorite catch-all, get-out-of-jail-free card. I gave the nurse a dead serious look to make sure it sunk in, then I gestured at the IV bags that I was now holding. "I'll keep these in as long as I can, but I'll need whatever else you can give me as pills or injections to keep me going. Enough for forty-eight hours, tops. Then I'll be back here and I'll stay as long as you need me to. Deal?"

# 60

*Nelson County, Virginia*

Almost four hundred miles southwest of the hospital the Cessna Skyhawk broke through the low cloud cover and banked left as it positioned itself for a landing.

There was no tower here at Oakridge Field Airport. In fact, there was no airport either. It was just a privately owned tract of farmland on which an eighteen-hundred-foot landing strip had been fashioned out of the flat turf, and nothing else. To get to his hunting cabin, Roos normally flew in and out of the Eagle's Nest Airport in Waynesboro, which was fifteen miles south of there. That was more of an actual airport than Oakridge, with an asphalt runway—cracked, but still more of a runway than the trail he was about to land on. It was also just as near, by road, as Oakridge was to the remote corner of mountain that was home to Roos's retreat. Eagle's Nest had no tower either, of course, but at least it offered hangars and tie-downs if the weather turned nasty. It also had a wind indicator, which would have been useful at Oakridge, given the crosswind that was currently buffeting the small prop plane. For today's purposes though, Roos preferred a more discreet arrival. He knew the owner of the Oakridge strip and had called him to make the arrangements. He knew no other aircraft would be there and knew the man was solid enough to keep Roos's being there that day a secret. If all went well, he'd soon be flying out of there without incident very soon, in time to settle back in and enjoy a quiet Christmas Day's fishing out in the Gulf Stream.

If all went well.

As he approached the strip, he could feel the crosswind coming from the northwest and he scanned the ground to look for clues that would tell him if the wind direction on the ground was the same as it was up there. He spotted a thicket of trees swaying under the wind's influence and quickly compared it to what the dial on his instrument panel was showing. They were more or less similar.

He drew on his considerable experience to maintain his wing level while keeping the plane's nose facing the wind at a skewed angle to the runway's centerline. It was disconcerting to watch—an aircraft crabbing its way down to a runway with its nose pointed off to one side, almost like it was flying sideways. The runway, he could see, looked like it was mostly clear of snow. The field's owner had cleared enough of it to allow him to land. It looked like someone had run a razor down the white field that surrounded it.

Just before the flare, Roos applied opposite rudder to correct the crab while using opposite ailerons to keep the wings level. The plane aligned itself just as its wheels touched down with a barely audible squeal.

He taxied to a stop by the old farming warehouse where three black SUVs and eleven hard men were waiting for him. He killed the aircraft's single engine and, without more than a nod, he got out, walked over, and climbed into the back of one of the cars.

If all went well he'd soon be driven back to his Cessna with one less major worry on his mind. He'd greet the New Year in a state of calm, his mind free to focus on new opportunities.

If all went well.

Which, given that it concerned Reilly, was—Roos knew—not at all a given.

# SUNDAY

# 61

*New York City*

We had shopping to do.

Some of it was Kurt and Gigi's doing. They had some ideas—good ideas, ones that would help us. They went out to stock up, mainly at the B&H Superstore by Penn Station, and came back to Deutsch's place with a couple of large bags. Given what I knew about them in terms of their love of tech toys I was surprised they didn't bring back a GoPro and a selfie stick. But what they did bring back would come in handy, no doubt. We needed all the help we could get.

Deutsch, on the other hand, went to a different kind of superstore: the armory at Federal Plaza. She finessed her way into signing out a small arsenal for me, which was now stored in the trunk of her car. When she got back I followed her down to the parking garage of her building to check out her haul, and that's when I noticed the problem.

She'd managed to bring all the items we'd talked about: helmet, vest, gloves, night vision goggles, stun grenades, M4 carbine with suppressor, CCO optical gunsight, Springfield .45, extra mags for both weapons, spike strip, Smith & Wesson folding knife, comms package. Everything, in fact, short of an MRAP truck—a heavy armored Mine-Resistant Ambush Protected vehicle, which would have been ideal, given what I imagined I'd be facing—though it might have raised eyebrows if she'd requisitioned one.

What she'd chosen wasn't a problem.

The problem was that she'd brought two of each.

Standing there in the garage, I turned to her quizzically a second after she'd popped the trunk.

She cut me off before I spoke. "I'm going in with you."

"No, you're not."

"Sean. I'm coming."

I felt my insides contract. "Annie. I've had enough people

around me die because of these pricks. I'm not letting that happen again. It's not your fight."

She didn't flinch. "It is."

"Annie, this isn't Bureau business any more—"

"Screw the Bureau, Sean. This is about me. And you. And Nick."

She held my gaze, and for a second there, my eyes scoured her face for a better understanding of what she meant—then it sank in. Nick's Tinder booty call had been nothing of the kind.

"You . . . and Nick?"

She didn't react for a breath, then she nodded.

"The night I ended up at his place, after the shooting," I asked. "He was with you?"

She nodded again. "He was going to spend the night, but he'd messed up his shirt with some pasta sauce and, well, you know how the guys at Twenty-six Fed can be total dicks."

I pictured him walking in, his surprise at seeing me that night. "So you and—"

"Two months," she said, anticipating my read, given Nick's dating history. "We'd been seeing each other for two months. No one knew. Once we both got comfortable with what we were doing, with being together, he said he was going to tell you. I guess he never got the chance."

All I could say was, "I wish he had." I flashed back to Nick and I outside Daland's house, all those long nights, and how he hadn't spent those hours swiping through his Tinder, and I felt bad that I'd missed it, that I hadn't realized he and Annie had a thing going and that we hadn't had a chance to talk about it.

"It doesn't matter, Annie. I can't have you do this."

"And I can't have you do it alone. It's that simple, Sean. It really is."

We just stood there for a moment, in the dim light of the garage, face to face, a trunk-load of SWAT weaponry at our disposal.

I couldn't object. I had no right to object.

She was in.

I waited till we were all set to go, then I called Tess using the safe Viber protocol. It was killing me not to have her here, not to be able to see her and hold her tight against me and kiss her before setting off, knowing the dangers ahead, what we were going up against—but it was better this way. It would have been hugely tough on us both to say goodbye face to face and it was still too risky to have her come down here again, for both of us. It was also better to keep her at a distance from it all, knowing she'd have serious objections over what my makeshift crew and me were about to do. Which, sure enough, didn't take long to materialize once I had her on the line.

"Sean, you know who these people are," she said, her exasperation growing with every word since the beginning of the call. "You know what they're capable of, you know what resources they have to draw on. This is nuts."

"Tess, please. Like I said—"

"Just take a night to sleep on it," she interjected forcefully, "to think it all through again. Maybe you'll see something you missed."

"We've been over it, Tess. I know what I'm doing. And this is the way it has to be."

"It's a trap, you said so yourself."

"Yes. A trap *we* instigated. They're playing into our hands, Tess. We've got to strike before they have too much time to think things through."

She went quiet for a moment, just a long, leaden exhale. I could just picture the way her face would be all crunched up with frustration, the way her eyes would be set, all fierce and fired up.

"I won't be able to talk to you until it's done," I added, breaking the heavy silence.

"I know," she said, subdued now.

"It's going to be fine. I know what I'm doing, Tess."

"I damn well hope so."

We'd said all that needed to be said. It was time to go.

"I love you," I said.

"I damn well hope so too," she said, her tone cracking a bit. "Give the kids a kiss from me. And I'll see you . . . soon."

"OK."

Then I hung up.

*

We drove out of New York City that evening after putting the finishing touches to the plan of action I had proposed while cleaning out some takeaway Chinese at Deutsch's place.

Four of us, in Deutsch's Crown Vic: me, her, Kurt and Gigi. Our minds were all busy playing out what we imagined the next day would bring. We'd already gone over what we were about to do several times and the fact that, during the whole drive down, the only time one of us spoke up was to question some aspect of our plan aloud just showed how it was all any of us was thinking about.

The traffic was fluid heading out of the city on a Sunday night, and with no major roadworks to impede our progress and the snow not strong enough to cause problems, we passed the signs to Philadelphia around two hours later and skirted Baltimore an hour after that. An hour more, and we were checking into a Marriott at Tysons Corner, west of Washington DC and almost exactly halfway between Vienna, Virginia and the CIA's headquarters at Langley. Two rooms, one for Deutsch and me, the other for Kurt and Gigi.

We all needed a good night's rest, although I wasn't sure we'd be sleeping sound.

We had an early start tomorrow if we were going to catch the first of our worms.

# MONDAY

# 62

*Vienna, Virginia*

It hadn't been Tomblin's best weekend.

He didn't like this—playing a waiting game. Not this type, anyway. A lot of the intelligence work he oversaw involved waiting and often felt like watching slow, ponderous moves on a chess board: you put something in play, you hoped your counterpart reacted the way you wanted him to, then you made your next move and so on, in the hope of getting the result you wanted. A result on which lives, often many lives, depended. Then there was the other type of waiting: the nail-biting, pulse-racing wait while an op was underway, monitoring it from hundreds or thousands of miles away in the comfort of a windowless, climate-controlled Langley room, hoping a radio confirmation of a successful outcome would come through.

This was different. They'd planted the seed on Erebus late Friday night. He'd sat with his analyst and watched as the brief, typed exchanges had popped up on the monitor facing them. The message had been received and understood. The question was now about when Reilly would act, when he'd show up at Roos's lodge, and what the outcome of that confrontation would be.

Until Reilly showed up there, Tomblin was uneasy. The agent had shown himself to be an unpredictable bastard and a loose cannon. Tomblin wasn't comfortable having him out in the wind. Even though he'd fed him Roos's name and location, he still felt vulnerable. It had been on his mind all weekend—the wait for the call from Roos telling him it was over—and was still on his mind as he slipped on his coat, grabbed his briefcase, and made his way to the garage that abutted his six-bedroom house.

Moments later, the garage door glided open and he pulled out in his car, an imposing dark grey Lincoln Navigator. He paused at the end of the drive as he always did, glanced in the rearview mirror to make sure the garage door shut properly, then he stepped off the brake pedal and motored away.

As he drove in the cossetted comfort of the large SUV, he felt good about going to work. There would be a lot going on to distract him from the discomfort that was gnawing away at him. Before long, he'd be immersed in situations and strategies that required his decisions. And the call from Roos would come. Tomblin knew Reilly would not be able to resist going after him, even knowing the odds were stacked against him.

The snow was still falling, and an inch or so of it had settled on the quiet residential lane, not enough to worry the big tires of his four-wheel drive. He was adjusting his climate control as he reached the stop sign at the T-junction with Wolftrap Road where an attractive, full-figured redhead was waiting to cross the street.

He brought the Navigator to a complete stop and found himself staring at her, his attention sucked in by the alluring woman who turned and gave him a warm smile to acknowledge his having stopped. His eyes studied her as she started to cross the road, trying to divine the exact contours of what looked like a fetchingly curvaceous body that lay cloaked under her flowing coat. His imagination basked in the moment, transforming her into someone he fantasized about, a broadly similar female actor from a television drama series that was set in the advertising world of the 60s. The show bored him, its machinations far too simplistic for his taste—but he still watched it with his wife in an effort to find more common ground in their increasingly diverging tastes, and enjoyed every second she was on screen. He pictured her as the woman who was now mere feet from his bumper, taking it slow, using careful, elegant steps to avoid slipping, glancing around again to jolt him with her smile—and he was relishing the moment until he sensed a shadow rushing right up to his side window a split second before the window exploded inward and showered him with shards.

He didn't even have time to react before a balled fist rocketed in and punched him in the jaw, rattling his brain and sending him flying sideways against the seat belt. From the corner of his eye, he glimpsed a hand reaching in and yanking the door handle open, then Reilly was stuffing a gun in his face while his other hand hit the start/stop button and killed the engine.

"Get out, quick," Reilly ordered as his free hand fiddled with Tomblin's seat belt and unhooked it.

Tomblin was too stunned to react. That, his rattled brain, and the handgun pressed against his cheek, made him obey. He climbed out of the car, which was when he saw someone else standing by the back door, also holding a gun, though that one wasn't aimed at his face. It was a woman he didn't recognize.

"Get in," she said as she opened the rear door.

He did, hoping a neighbor was watching and was calling it in or that another car would drive by and do the same. Neither seemed to be happening.

The woman clambered in after him. Reilly was already in the driver's seat.

Eleven seconds after the car had come to a halt, it was off again, trailed by an unmarked Crown Vic with the seductive redhead in the passenger seat and headed for the Blue Ridge Mountains.

# 63

*Nelson County, Virginia*

Despite the clear plastic sheeting I'd duct-taped in place of the shattered window, it was still pretty cold in Tomblin's beefy SUV as I drove it down Route Twenty-nine. The snow was intermittent and the temperature gauge was reading minus two, but that wasn't counting the effect of the wind. I wasn't too bothered by the cold. It helped keep me alert, especially given what my body had been through, juicing me up with adrenaline and kick-starting any parts of me that were still a bit sluggish. It also helped prepare my esteemed guest for what was to come. I was more worried about the plastic sheeting, and the fact that I had two passengers in the back and no one next to me, attracting the attention of some bored state trooper. I had Deutsch in the car, though, and her badge would come in handy if that were to happen. The flex-cuffs around the wrists of the guy sitting next to her, and the duct tape over his mouth, would probably be less of a help.

I didn't want to listen to him, and I didn't want to talk to him either. We had a two-hour plus drive, and I wanted him shut out and seriously rattled by the time we got to our destination. I imagined the panic that had to be building inside him. CIA big shot, head of the National Clandestine Service—I don't care who you are—getting grabbed like that by someone with my skill set who you know to be out to settle a score and who looks like he has nothing to lose is going to trigger some major panic in you. I imagined he was also wondering how we got him, how we even knew who he was. After all, he'd tried to subvert our efforts by stepping in quick and having one of his minions log into Erebus and hand me Roos on a silver platter. I was sure he was behind it. According to Tomblin's plan, I was supposed to be hightailing it straight to where Roos was holed up—where I would no doubt have a few determined heavies and a sniper or two waiting for me—instead of coming after him with the help of a buxom redhead. And yet, we'd found him. His name had risen out of the sewer, courtesy of another anonymous poster on Erebus, one Tomblin's minions couldn't have—and clearly hadn't—seen.

Kudos to Daland and his programing genius.

The genuine mystery informant, whoever he was—assuming it was a "he"—hadn't elaborated on why he was selling them out, and although he hadn't said—typed—much, I was pretty sure his native language wasn't English. Still, he got me the name I was missing, one Edward Tomblin of the CIA, the "Frank Fullerton" to Roos's "Reed Corrigan."

Kurt and Gigi had had a hard time fleshing out his persona beyond the broadest of strokes of his career. The guy clearly valued his privacy and hadn't exactly embraced social media either. They were helped, though, by the fact that Tomblin wasn't a particularly common name, and they ended up getting his home address pretty easily. His wife was one of a hundred and forty-five million eBay users whose personal details were on a database that had been hacked from the site a few months back, the only Tomblin within commuting range of Langley.

We'd disabled the trackers on both cars before setting off, and I'd removed the battery from Tomblin's phone and the SIM card from his car phone. It wouldn't be long before they realized he was missing. We had a limited time in which to act. So we set off as quickly as we could and, a little over two hours out of the DC metro area, we were skirting Charlottesville before continuing on south.

The landscape got progressively more dramatic around us as the traces of human settlement receded—forests of tall trees, both bare and evergreen, cushioning the parallel two-lane strips of blacktop that hardly had any cars on them, and glimpses of the Blue Ridge mountains beyond, all filtered through a glaze of light snow and set against a white-grey backdrop.

It wasn't long before we were cutting through some glorious Virginia country. Abundant mature hardwoods on either side blanketed rolling hills that climbed up to the mountains, nature's full majesty gone wild over centuries and millennia, an outstanding corner of the planet within a stone's throw from several big cities. This country was truly blessed in that sense. Tess and I had driven through these parts a couple of years back, one of those idyllic road trips through Shenandoah National Park and the Blue Ridge Parkway. We'd timed it perfectly, cruising down in the full glory of fall, visually drunk on a surreal palette of blazing reds, russets and gold of the ridges and the smell of woodsmoke in the air. The landscape was no less heart-stirring this time of year, but I felt it for entirely different reasons. What we were doing here was obviously far from idyllic.

We reached the area we had reconnoitered online and I veered off onto a narrow, single-lane road. I guided the Navigator a couple of miles up into the Miran Forest, then turned into a dirt track that didn't seem like it had seen much traffic lately. It felt as if the mountain was preparing to swallow us up. We followed the narrow, winding trail for about a mile and a half until we reached the strategically placed small clearing we'd chosen.

I pulled into it and killed the engine.

Gigi, driving the Crown Vic, tucked in behind me and did the same.

Leaving Tomblin in his SUV, the four of us got out and walked up the clearing. We checked our location using Gigi's tablet, confirmed we were in the right place, and got a visual sighting of the direction our target was in.

Then we got to work.

"Eddy?" Roos asked as he answered the phone.

He hadn't expected to hear from Tomblin. It was more Tomblin who was waiting to hear from him, once it was done.

He knew something was wrong the second he heard the caller's voice.

It wasn't Tomblin.

"Try again, Gordo."

Roos's grip tightened around his phone. He'd never spoken to Reilly, but—besides the fact that he'd heard his voice on surveillance tapes—he knew it wouldn't be anyone else. "You do know how to ruin a party, I'll give you that."

"Next time, maybe you should draw up your invitations more carefully. And put an RSVP to avoid disappointments."

"Oh, I'm not disappointed," Roos said. "I'm looking forward to meeting you. That's what this call is about, isn't it?"

"You know me so well," Reilly said. "Hang up. I'm going to call you from another phone. This one could be a bit hot right now."

Clever bastard, Roos thought. He hung up. Seconds later, his phone rang again. "So what's on your mind?"

"I've got your boy here," Reilly said. "And I've got this decision to make."

"What's that?"

"The reasonable, rational side of me is thinking: why take any more risks? Why not just make Eddy here tell me all he knows about everything you two have been up to all these years—everything about the Janitors, the heart attacks, the accidents, all those deaths . . . and everything about my dad. Get him to clear my name while he's at it, for the record, and throw in everything he knows about you too. Get it all on video, hand it over to the DA, and be done with it. Then I can come back for you with a warrant and a SWAT team to back me up. That sounds like the sensible move, don't you think?"

"Yeah, sounds reasonable to me," Roos said without missing a beat. "I mean, Eddy's a high-ranking intelligence officer. Hell, he could be running the whole Agency before long. People would believe what he says."

"I think they would," Reilly said. "He's a respectable pillar of the community. And even if there happened to be a few cuts and bruises on him, which I would hope we could avoid—he'd give us a pretty compelling testimony. There's only one problem with that."

"And what's that?"

"I'm not in a reasonable mood."

Roos smiled. He hadn't expected anything less from Reilly. Not after everything the agent had gone through to find him. "No?"

"Not really," Reilly said. "Besides, to be frank with you, I don't really trust the system any more."

"You should," Roos said. "You've fought for it all your life. It's a sad day when an agent of justice loses his faith in it. It's almost like you're saying you've devoted your whole life to something worthless."

"I wouldn't go so far, Gordo. But it's true that lately, it's been letting me down. And I'm not fully convinced that you and Eddy here wouldn't manage to pull a few strings or do a dirty and use some kind of leverage to make that tape disappear and ride back into town on your high horses. With all the nasty implications for my friends and me. We could put it on the Internet, but that wouldn't work either. You'd just spin it off as another hoax from some conspiracy nut jobs."

"I know what you mean," Roos said. "It's tough to beat the system sometimes."

"So you see my dilemma."

"I empathize. I do. But you said you had a decision to make. What's option two?"

"Option two is: justice can wait."

Roos wasn't sure what Reilly meant. "I'm not sure I follow."

"It means, let someone else deal with the big picture and the crimes of the past. Me, I'm a simple guy. I've got more focus."

"And that focus is?"

"Beating the truth out of you with my bare hands."

Ross chortled. He'd read a lot about Reilly—surveillance reports, case files—but he'd never spoken to him until now. He was actually starting to like Reilly, though it wouldn't have any effect on what he had in store for the agent.

"Well, you know," Roos said, "focus is good. And you and I—we've had this coming for a long time. From way back, in fact. Around the time you were ten, right?" He paused, knowing the words would have the intended effect on Reilly. "Why involve anyone else?"

Roos heard the slight pause, the one the agent would have loved to snuff out entirely, before Reilly said, "Exactly."

"So what do you propose? I'd invite you up here for a chat and an Irish coffee, but something tells me you have something else in mind."

"No, that sounds great. A sandwich would be nice too—I haven't had lunch yet. But you did say we shouldn't involve anyone else."

"That I did."

"Then I need you to send those boys away."

"What boys?"

"I need to see at least six guys leave your place before I come up."

Roos snorted. "All six of them?"

"Actually, make that eight."

"Eight? I think you overestimate my importance here. Or maybe you're overestimating yourself."

"Eight guys, Gordo. I want to see eight of them leave your cabin or I'm going to work on Eddy."

Roos was curious. He wanted to *see* them leave?

Reilly was nearby. Had to be.

"Ah, well. Let's say I could rustle up eight of my boys. How am I going to prove to you that they're gone?"

"Have them drive down to the bottom of the mountain. Tell them to get out of their cars once they get to the main road, then get back in their cars and head back where they came from."

Roos needed more information about where Reilly was. "And you'll be watching?"

"I'll see them, don't worry. I've also got a spotter some ways up on Route Twenty-nine, on the way to Charlottesville. When he calls to say your boys have passed him, I'll come to you. Just to make sure they don't decide to double back 'cause they forgot something."

"How do I know you'll come alone?"

"It was my idea, wasn't it?"

"What about Eddy?"

"I cut him loose."

Roos thought about it. "OK," he said. "I'll need proof that you really have him."

"Hang on."

Roos heard some buffeting from the wind, then Tomblin's voice came on. "Gordo?"

"You OK, Eddy?"

"I'm fine. Listen—"

More abrupt buffeting, like a phone being snatched, then Reilly's voice came back. "We good to go?"

"Sure. When are we doing this?"

"No time like the present," Reilly said. "We've waited long enough, right? Ten minutes enough for them to hit the road?"

"Make it fifteen."

"OK. I'll see you soon," Reilly said.

He clicked off before Roos could reply.

# 64

We had lift off.

On several levels.

The most literal, however, concerned the drone Kurt had brought with him.

I'd never seen one of these, but apparently they were all the rage, a brilliant piece of playful technology that was as much as a game changer as the original iPhone and the Oculus Rift.

I hadn't been entirely facetious with Roos. Yes, I had Tomblin. Yes, he was Roos's partner back in the day, which meant he probably knew a lot of what I wanted to know, maybe even about my dad. Yes, I could have made him talk and got the whole thing on video. But I really did think they would find a way to bury it. And I wasn't sure we'd survive long enough to suffer that disappointment. I was holding the head of the National Clandestine Service, the CIA's most secret department. You don't just walk away from that. No, it really was about Roos and me. Any answers I wanted had to come from him and nobody else. What I'd do once I got them—well, I'd figure that out if I made it that far.

I was stunned by how easy it was to get the drone airborne. Kurt had brought a DJI Phantom, the Vision 2+ model, he explained, which had a built-in full HD camera hanging underneath it. It had only taken him a couple minutes to get it prepped, which involved taking it out of the box, manually screwing in the four plastic propellers, snapping the battery in place, doing a quick compass calibration and getting a GPS lock on our position by spinning it around itself on both axes, and syncing up the drone to the remote control unit he'd use to fly it. Easy enough, although we were lucky he'd done it before and knew how to pilot it with ease—he had one back at his place, but since that was a no-go zone, he had to buy a new one. It was small, a sleek white X-shape made out of plastic, with each of its arms not even a foot long. It was also light, weighing less than three pounds. It still managed to pack enough clever technology in that compact package to justify its thirteen-hundred-dollar price tag.

Our present location had been chosen to allow three things: we needed it to be close enough to Roos's cabin so that it was within the flight range of the Phantom, which was about a mile; we needed it to also allow the drone to monitor the departure of his goon squad, follow them until they were well on their way out of here, and make sure they didn't double back; and we needed it to give us the privacy to get on with our work.

We sent the drone up the first time before my call to Roos to get a closer, real-time picture of the situation. The weather was borderline—not so much the snow as the temperature, but the Phantom didn't seem fazed by it. Kurt sent it up to around five hundred feet. It was so small that we stopped seeing it long before that, and its buzz was so discreet anyway that we stopped hearing it even longer before that. I was confident that Roos and his entourage wouldn't know it was there.

Kurt had flown it across the hill toward Roos's property, its remote-controlled camera relaying what it was seeing to the remote control unit in Kurt's hands, which in turn beamed the footage by Bluetooth to Gigi's laptop. The image was surprisingly stable thanks to the three-way brushless gimbal that held the camera, and it gave me a great aerial view of what I'd be facing.

Roos's cabin sat at the end of a long dirt trail that snaked its way from the main road up the mountain, carving a path through his eighty acres of land. Kurt flew the drone in a big circle to see what else was around, which was basically rolling hills of forest, forest, and more forest. At one point, the camera caught the mountains at an angle that looked familiar, and I was pretty sure it was the same mountain range that was behind Orford, Padley and Siddle in that picture of them in full hunting gear, the one I'd snatched from Orford's office.

This was a hunting lodge, pure and simple, a secluded retreat to escape to and stalk black bear, whitetail deer and turkey, as well as predators like coyote and fox. It was also, it seemed, a lodge where far deadlier kinds of predator roamed around, no doubt plotting their own special brand of hunt.

Kurt had brought the drone around again and put it in a fixed hover so as to give us a clear view of the front of the lodge. It was a rustic log cabin, about a thousand feet in footprint, two floors with a couple of dormers on the roof, a wraparound porch, screened deck at the side. There were three cars out front, parked haphazardly in the small clearing that faced the house, large black SUVs, standard issue for hard-asses with attitudes. I couldn't see them cramming more than four men per car, given the gear they had to be lugging. So it was likely Roos had eleven hired guns up there. We could see two guys standing outside, by the cars. The others weren't visible. I'd decided the most I could ask Roos was to ship off two of the three vehicles, hence my request for eight men. I'd be left with Roos and three others to deal with. Twelve-to-one didn't sound promising. Four-to-one I could live with.

I'd asked Kurt to give me another look at the road up to the cabin and I tried to memorize its turns by matching the visual with the satellite picture on Google Maps. Then he'd brought it back and swapped its battery for a fully charged one while I'd prepared the car for my drive up to the cabin.

Once everything was ready, I'd called Roos just after Kurt had sent the quadcopter back up. I'd made sure Tomblin hadn't seen the drone—we had his eyes covered with duct tape too, and we flew it away from the car so he didn't hear it. I didn't want him telling Roos we had a bird up. It was amazing to be able to do this with something anyone could pick up at any halfway-decent electronics store or just buy online for next-day delivery. We had live coverage of the cabin all while I spoke to Roos. There was no action to watch, though. He was obviously inside, and the men outside were just standing there, waiting for orders.

Things changed after I hung up.

After a couple of minutes, three men came out of the house and joined the two who were already outside. The drone was too far for us to get a look at any of their faces. They just looked like small, dark figures against a dirty-white background. Then three others came outside, followed by two more.

They all held position for a moment, the first eight clustered close to each other, the last two closer to the house, facing them. I moved nearer to the screen, sensing one of the two was Roos—the general addressing his troops. Then the eight men climbed into two of the SUVs, which drove away and took the long trail down the mountain.

"Where do I go?" Kurt asked. "You want the cars, or you want me to stay on the cabin?"

Ideally, I needed both. The guys at the cabin would be setting up whatever ambush they had planned, while the guys in the departing SUVs might be putting in place a trap of their own. And there were many more of them to worry about.

"Stay on the cars," I told Kurt. "Let's make sure they're really gone."

He nudged the two joysticks expertly to control the drone's flight, and I took one last look at the tiny figure on the screen that I imagined to be Roos, burning his image into my memory before he headed back in and the cabin disappeared from the picture.

We watched as the two black SUVs snaked their way down the dirt road. They hung left when they hit the main road, pulled over, and the eight men got out. Kurt had moved the drone well up to make sure they wouldn't see or hear it. The eight tiny figures stood there aimlessly for a moment, like they were stumped, then they got back in the cars and headed north. Kurt brought down the drone and had it follow them as long as it could, to the limit of its range. Once it reached it, its return-to-home feature kicked in automatically and it just reversed direction and started flying straight back to us. Kurt stopped it after a few seconds and held it in a stationary hover to monitor the road and make sure they weren't coming up yet. We watched the road for about ten minutes and nothing showed up. I doubted Roos believed my story about a spotter, but it was worth a shot anyway. I figured they'd pull over somewhere within reach and wait for the call that would tell them I'd arrived at the cabin, then they'd rush back. Which meant I wouldn't have much time up there.

Kurt brought the drone back while I got the Navigator and Tomblin ready. He swapped the battery for another fresh one and we were set. I'd have a guardian angel in the sky and a comms piece in my ear. Deutsch would have the other one. She'd be monitoring the situation and giving me some live updates, for which I was grateful. Assuming I made it up to the cabin alive.

I glanced at my watch. Almost an hour had passed since I'd spoken with Roos.

It was high noon on the shortest day of the year. I didn't know whether to take that as a good sign or not.

Either way, it was time to go.

# 65

The black Lincoln Navigator stormed up the mountain, making mincemeat of the narrow trail and swallowing up the slushy bends in its stride.

From behind an open window inside the cabin, Roos waited, scanning the tree line for any sign of movement. The mountain was entirely still, with nothing but the distant sound of water cascading over rocks to disturb it. The snow was still falling lightly, the sky behind the carpet of hardwoods a dull grey. Then he became aware of a growl at the edge of his hearing, the throaty gurgle of a large engine. Its noise grew and grew, sending his pulse spiking up with every added decibel, and then the black SUV appeared from behind the trees as it rounded the last bend eighty-five yards downslope from the lodge.

Roos looked through his binoculars. Straining to get a clear picture through the irregular reflections bouncing off the SUV's windshield, he was able to make out one solitary figure inside it, behind the wheel: male, as expected, in a black baseball cap, sitting straight up. There could be others ducking low inside there, but it wouldn't really matter anyway. If anyone else was in there with Reilly they'd also soon be just as dead as he was.

He watched as the Navigator rushed up to the mouth of the clearing outside the cabin—and didn't slow down. It kept going, accelerating now and heading straight at the cabin.

Roos gave the signal, and a barrage of high-powered rounds erupted out of the trees.

The relentless feed of bullets, coming from outside on both sides of his cabin, drilled through the SUV. Roos watched as the 7.62mm NATO rounds rained down on the charging car, obliterating its windshield, side windows, body panels, as well as its driver, whose body was visibly shaking around violently with each impact. It was less than forty yards from the cabin when its wheels exploded from the gunfire, which hobbled it until more rounds ate into its engine and crippled it three car lengths away from the cabin's front steps.

The gunfire stopped. The stillness returned to the mountain, apart from a light hiss and some irregular clinks from the crippled car.

Roos wasn't smiling.

Something was wrong.

Reilly wasn't suicidal. He had consistently shown himself to be way too clever to attempt a blind charge like that. Roos looked again through his binoculars, focusing on the head of the driver. Too many rounds had found their target—and even though the man was a pulped, bloodied mess, his head was still upright. Which wasn't natural. And the man wasn't damaged enough for Roos to recoil when he saw enough to recognize the dead driver.

It sure as hell wasn't Reilly.

I struggled to keep the car properly aligned as I guided it up the mountain.

It wasn't easy, given that I wasn't sitting in the driver's seat. Nor was I driving it by remote control. I was crouched in the footwell of the passenger seat, wearing a helmet and goggles and a vest, surrounded by body armor panels, with one hand on the selfie stick that I'd taped to the gas pedal and the other on the steering wheel.

Above and to my left, Tomblin was in the driver's seat, held in position with enough duct tape to ensure he couldn't move an inch. I'd even made sure Tomblin's head would stay upright by running some tape around his neck and the headrest. His mouth was also taped shut. Only his eyes were free to roam, and they were darting back and forth between the road ahead and an intense, terrorised scowl directed right at me.

Kurt and Gigi had set up the visual aids for me: a smartphone taped to the big Lincoln's front bumper, linked by video call to a 4G tablet they'd taped under the dashboard, where I could see it. It was cramped and awkward, but it was the only way I could see myself even getting close to the cabin in one piece.

The gunfire erupted the second the cabin appeared clearly on the monitor, remorseless large-caliber rounds raining down on the SUV from somewhere up ahead. I crouched lower and floored the pedal, aiming at the house as bits of the car and of Tomblin exploded all around me, showering me with all kinds of debris, hard and soft. Some rounds found their way to the Kevlar panels and punched into them, hard, kicking them back onto me, but I kept the pedal floored and kept it moving until the car shuddered and plowed into the ground for a full stop. Then the shooting stopped.

A panicked voice in my earbud blurted, "Reilly? Reilly! Jesus, are you OK?" It was Kurt, back at the clearing, at the controls of the Phantom.

The plan had worked in the sense that I'd made it up to the door of the cabin in one piece, but I needed to stay that way, which meant I needed to take one of those big guns out. Given the sound they made, the cycling rate and the damage they'd caused, I figured it was something like one of the M240 family of machine guns, positioned under cover outside rather than inside the house to allow for a quick repositioning and a bigger playing field.

"I'm fine, relax," I whispered into my throat mike. "What do you see?"

"You've got two gunmen—on either side of the cabin." He was flying it lower now, although I didn't think it was visible or within earshot yet.

"The one to my right. I need a lock on him. Where is he, off the car's nose?"

"I'd say, two o'clock."

"I need more precision than that, Kurt. Give it to me in minutes. And be accurate, for God's sake. I'm only going to get one shot at this."

"OK, OK, hang on. I think, uh, thirteen."

"You sure?"

"Yes, yes. Thirteen."

I quickly asked, "Distance?"

"OK, uh, it's around, uh, thirty yards. Yeah, I think that's about right, I'm measuring off the length of the car. He's behind what looks like some fallen logs."

"OK. Hang on."

I focused on my positioning, imagining the front-to-back axis of the car and locking it in my mind relative to everything around me. Then I closed my eyes and conjured up a mental picture of what Kurt had told me about my position relative to the shooter. I'd only get one shot at him and it had to count.

I adjusted my position and got the M4 ready, then I pulled out a stun grenade, pulled out its pin, focused my concentration, and lobbed it out the opening where the front windshield used to be, to the left of the car, the opposite side of the shooter I was going for. Flashbangs had very short fuses, two seconds in this case, so the small, perforated cylinder had barely left my hand when it went off in a deafening bang and a blinding flash. I knew its effects wouldn't be as disorientating as they would if this were inside a room, but the blast was so powerful that, even inside the car, I was rocked by its concussion wave. It instantly created the desired result as more rounds erupted from the trees, but were directed away from the car. With my eyes closed, I spun around and came up from my crouch, M4 ready and already aimed in the direction and at the distance Kurt had spotted for me—and I opened my eye, looked through the scope, and there he was, for a second, the top of his head and the barrel of the gun barely visible through the light snowfall, the red dot inside the optic aligned on his forehead.

I squeezed the trigger and saw his head snap back in a burst of crimson.

One down, maybe two—and Roos—to go.

"Guide me out of here, quick," I rasped.

"OK, I'm looking at your side of the car. There's that large rock to your right that we saw before, at one o'clock," he added, "and the trees are just beyond that, about ten yards farther."

"Got it."

The belts these guns used held a couple of hundred rounds at best, and given that they fired at upward of six hundred rounds per minute and seeing as how many hits the car had taken before this last onslaught, I figured whoever was manning them should be needing to restock their feeding tray by now. Regardless, I had to move fast. They now knew I was alive and in the car. I sucked in a couple of quick, deep breaths, then I pulled on the door handle and kicked the door out, following it out in the same frenzied move. I rolled on the ground before coming up in a crouch and I sprinted towards the rock, bullets kicking up the slush around my feet. I didn't shoot back, saving the rounds of my M4 until I had something viable to shoot at. I made it to the rock just as more bullets ate into it, sending shards of it flicking around me. The shooter was on the other side of the house from me now and I knew the rock would protect me. I had no idea where the third guy, if there was one, was, nor if Roos was in the cabin or elsewhere.

I figured I couldn't stay where I was for too long and I couldn't cut across in the open, so the best option seemed to be to get to the cabin and work my way around it or through it to take out the guy with the big gun on its opposite side. I peeked out, took in my position. I couldn't see any movement. I figured that if I took the direct route to the cabin, I'd be exposed longer than if I went parallel to its side initially, then cut across to it—longer, but safer, unless there was a shooter in one of its side windows. It had three—two on the ground floor that gave on to the porch and a third on the floor above. I debated going the extra ten yards away and using the edge of the tree line, but the soil there would be less even than the clearing I was in; more snow would have settled there under the bare branches, and I'd be moving less confidently while risking a fall.

I steeled myself for the move, then sprinted out from behind the large rock, running parallel to the side of the house. Snowflakes licked my face as gunfire erupted immediately from the same shooter but, surprisingly, nothing came from the cabin. I ran as fast as I could and, within seconds, the shooting stopped as the gunner lost his bead on me. I cut across the field, headed straight for the cabin now, and hurdled onto the porch before slamming to a stop against the log wall.

Everything went silent again.

I didn't like it. Playing cat and mouse like this, facing an unknown number of shooters who'd brought major firepower to the fight. Then Kurt's voice came through my comms, and his words only made things worse.

“Reilly! Reilly,” he hissed.

“What?” I whispered.

“I just sent the drone on a quick perimeter swoop. The two SUVs, the ones with the heavies? They’re back.”

# 66

I couldn't worry about that right now. I had enough to deal with here. And the sooner I cleared this kill zone, the sooner I could start figuring out how to deal with the new threat.

I used the stock of my carbine to smash through the window closest to me, then I chucked in another flashbang. Between four walls, its effect was much more potent this time and I charged in after it, loosing quick bursts left and right. And hitting nothing.

The space was empty. My eyes quickly adjusted to the darkness. I was in a large, open area, typical of an old log cabin, with a large fireplace as its central focal point and six-point buck heads staring down from the bare wood walls. I scanned around, looking for signs of life, but saw and heard nothing. I sensed the cabin was empty—it didn't offer enough cover to make tactical sense to remain in it. The forest outside was a much better option. Still, I advanced cautiously, if quickly, swinging my weapon from side to side, my senses alert to any disturbance. I was all the way across to the opposite side of the cabin, the side of the other shooter, when I heard a rustling outside. I rushed to the side of the window and slammed against the wall just as something crashed through the glass and flew into the room.

They'd wanted to draw me into the cabin all along. That was their kill zone. And now that I was inside, one of the bastards had just fired a grenade launcher at me.

The lead SUV veered off the main road and bounced onto the trail that led up to the cabin, its big tires kicking up a spray of slush onto the windshield of the second vehicle, which was right on its tail.

It accelerated uphill, its powerful engine propelling it up the gentle slope with ease, and about twenty yards before the trail veered right around a large rock outcropping, its tires suddenly hit something and shredded to bits, causing the heavy car to crater into the ground and come to a shuddering halt.

The driver of the SUV behind it, his vision already hampered by the slush flying onto his windshield, didn't have enough time to react and just plowed into the back of the lead vehicle, hard.

Which was about when the gunfire started.

I didn't think. I just reacted.

Pure instinct, zero lag time. Just neurons firing an instantaneous reflexive order and muscles reacting without hesitation.

I launched myself through the glass of the window shoulder first and was airborne when the blast tore through the space behind me.

I hit the porch hard, curled into a roll, my ears and my skull reeling from the explosion, but I couldn't let it affect me just yet—I needed my senses to function for just a second or two more; I needed to push away the heaviness and the ringing and the blurred vision and just focus every nerve ending I could muster to lock onto my target while he was within striking range and before he could get a shot off at me.

I caught him at the edge of my perception, a wraith with a white face and dark camo gear, and my arms somehow managed to bring the carbine up and line it up on him and my finger pulled back on the trigger as I aligned the red dot of the CCO sight on his chest. He staggered back as my three-round burst punched into him and dropped out of sight just as I rolled onto my back and shut my eyes to try and recalibrate my senses.

The whine in my ears was manageable—I'd had worse—and I guess the helmet had helped dampen the full brunt of the blast on the insides of my skull. I stayed like that for a few long seconds, breathing in, letting the blood rush around and reboot my shocked operating system.

I hit my comms and said, "Kurt?" but there was no answer.

I called out again, but nothing came back.

I pulled the transmitter out of its shoulder pouch and checked it. It was cracked. I switched it on and off, tried again, and got nothing. My heavy landing must have busted it.

I was on my own.

I pushed myself back on my feet and, hugging the log wall, I crept to the back of the cabin and the forest beyond.

I still had maybe one shooter out there, then there was Roos.

I scanned left, right, couldn't see any movement. The ground rose away from the cabin in undulating hillocks and the tree cover was dense, some of it with good visibility in the case of the deciduous oaks and maples, other parts much darker under the evergreen firs, spruces and beeches. The snow cover was accordingly irregular and patchy: thicker and whiter where the branches above were bare, and thin to nonexistent where the canopy was forbidding. More flakes were falling, though, and they were getting meatier.

Then I spotted something: tracks, in the messy scree around the base of the porch. Boot prints, one pair, leading away from the cabin, into the forest.

Maybe I was wrong. Maybe Roos had only brought ten men with him and not eleven.

Ten, a round number. An excessive one, if you asked me. I mean, I really didn't think I merited that much of an effort. Eleven—that was just overkill.

I checked my carbine, slammed in a fresh clip just in case, and headed out.

I'd barely taken a step when distant machine gun bursts cut through the silence, angry, intense volleys echoing out from behind me. In that split second, I noticed a flash of movement, a shift of tones, a silhouette that was darker than its backdrop of leaves and branches, about thirty yards ahead of me, high up. I dropped to one knee and brought the M4 up just as several bullets cut through the space my upper body had been occupying and slammed into the logs behind me.

I squeezed the trigger, and the silhouette jerked before dropping thirty feet to the ground. He'd been waiting for me, up in a tree stand.

There had been eleven after all.

I was pretty sure Roos was now on his own.

And I was coming for him.

Deutsch let rip with full dedication.

She'd set up the spike strips at the end of the first relatively straight stretch of trail, before it swept gently right around a large rock outcropping that served to shield her parked Crown Vic and to offer her a great vantage point from which to unleash her assault.

She knew what she was facing, but it didn't worry her. She was committed, and she was ready. She was kitted out in helmet, ballistic vest, comms; she had the M4 carbine with its suppressor in place and its laser sight ready and she'd laid out her gear within easy reach around: five extra magazines, flashbangs, a fully loaded handgun, even the big knife.

Everything she needed to maximize the kill.

She started firing mere seconds after the long metal barbs of spike strips had shredded the SUV's tires, just as the vehicles were immobile, before the doors even cracked open. She wasn't off to one side but was almost in front of the cars, at a slight angle perhaps, which allowed her to cover both sides of the vehicles. Anyone trying to get out from either side would be within her reach.

She started with the two men in the front seats of the front car, moved to the two in the front of the rear vehicle, then came back to the front car and its back seat passengers before returning to the rear vehicle and the final two targets.

Thirty rounds per clip, three-round bursts, ten bursts per clip. Ten different targets, ten chances to take out an enemy. Six clips, one hundred and eighty rounds, sixty chances to take out the eight targets. If she connected with one out of seven bursts, if one out of twenty-one bullets managed to find its mark, they were all out of play.

Her mind was clear, her focus full, her aim true. With each red dot aligning on a target, with each pull of her trigger, she thought of Nick Aparo and nothing else. With each splatter of blood, she thought about what men like these had done to him. She allowed no other thought any breathing space, none whatsoever. She was just fully, totally, exclusively committed to wiping out each and every one of those sons of bitches that appeared in her sights.

The last two required a little more effort. She had to use stun grenades to rattle and tame them, had to come out from her cover and climb down to the kill zone and execute them at closer range. She didn't mind it, though. It was what she was there to do. And after it was all done, after all eight of them had taken their last breath, a voice cut in and intruded on her serenity.

Kurt was hailing her through her earbud. "Annie?"

He needed to call for her twice before she responded. "What?"

"Annie, I can't reach Reilly. I can't see him either."

Her mind folded itself back into reality and she started moving toward her car. "When did you last hear from him?"

"About ten minutes ago. Then we heard that explosion."

"I know," she said as she reached her car. "I heard it too."

"He might need help," Kurt said.

"I'm heading up there now," Deutsch said as she slammed the car into gear and floored it.

# 67

It was eerie and uncomfortable.

It was also slow going. Very, very slow going.

Making my way up the mountain wasn't easy. Loose footings, boulder fields, slippery rock outcroppings, and the snow, heavy and damp on the ground, in patches of irregular thickness and consistency. It wasn't too easy to see either, what with the continuous snowfall layering a ghostly veil on it all.

It was desolate and quiet, the bare trees and the rough terrain giving it a grim, otherworldly feel, the dense evergreens then changing it into one that was brooding and mysterious. I knew the area was teeming with wildlife, and the multiple tree rubbings I saw confirmed it. But I didn't see any bears, deer or elk. Not even a turkey. The only wildlife up here right now seemed to be two predators who were out hunting each other. It was as if the rest of the animal kingdom had vacated the mountain to give our confrontation plenty of room to play itself out. Maybe the blasts and the gunfire had just scared them off. Or maybe they knew better and didn't want to get caught in the crossfire.

My senses, still jarred by the grenade's blast, were doing their best to cut through the haze and stay focused, to try and pick out the tiniest movement, the smallest sound.

Roos was out here, somewhere.

This was his territory.

It was where he hunted, and the realization made every step I took more hesitant.

He knew these woods. I didn't. But I wasn't leaving here till I found him.

Roos huddled under the blind he'd built at the mouth of the rock tunnel, listening intently as he scanned ahead for any sign of Reilly.

He didn't have to worry about his back. He knew Reilly would be coming up the mountain. All he had to do was wait. Then he'd just pick him off and make his way back to civilization.

Waiting for a kill wasn't new to Roos. Far from it. He was a natural hunter, a talent his father had spotted and helped nurture ever since Roos was a young boy. Stalking prey, whether on land or at sea, was a feeling he was very familiar with, a hobby he enjoyed greatly, and one he'd been able to indulge to his heart's delight ever since his father, a successful dentist who'd ridden the popularity surge of orthodontics in the mid-70s, had bought that huge piece of land for a song after Hurricane Camille had savagely devastated the area in 1969. An only child, Roos had inherited the lodge from his father after the man had died prematurely from a heart attack almost ten years to the day after buying it.

He'd put it to good use, for all kinds of hunts.

Over the years, Roos had built many blinds across his property. Nature provided a lot of the materials that made the best blinds: trees torn down during heavy storms, densely leaved branches from conifers, large boulders to tuck in against. He'd build them early in the season, give the animals time to get used to them. Then he'd go up and spend hours huddled inside them, watching, waiting—making sure no noise and no smell scared off his prey. Then they would appear, out of the trees, oblivious to the danger he posed. There was nothing more satisfying than watching a bull elk or a white-tailed doe walk by, mere feet way, so close he could reach out and touch them. Observing them at eye level, stretching out the time before the kill as long as he could, toying with their lives before he took them away.

Those same emotions were channeling through him now, only it wasn't a bear or a buck he was waiting for.

He sensed something in the distance and slunk lower, slowly, carefully.

Movement, through the thin, white haze down the mountain.

He flattened himself completely and calmed his breathing. He knew from hunting hungry bucks how crucial it was to remain quiet and immobile. The smallest sound, the minutest movement, could spook his prey.

He looked out intently through the light snowfall, then adjusted his rifle and peered through its scope.

A lone figure was making its way closer to him, headed in his direction. Taking slow, hesitant steps. A dark silhouette against the white backdrop, disappearing in and out from behind the army of bare chestnut oaks that dotted the hillside.

As the figure got nearer, his concentration deepened. He could sense the imminent kill, intoxicated by the endorphins that were rushing through him in anticipation. God, he loved a good hunt, and this one would cap them all.

And then he got a glimpse of his quarry's face and his pulse spiked and flushed his euphoria away.

It wasn't Reilly.

It was a woman.

Annie Deutsch advanced cautiously as she made her way up the mountain.

She hadn't found Reilly in the charred cabin, hadn't seen any sign of him outside. She'd seen Tomblin's body in his chewed-up SUV before stumbling upon a dead shooter by the side of the cabin and she figured Reilly had gone up the mountain, tracking his prey. She also figured two guns would be better than one.

She wasn't comfortable out here. She was a city girl through and through and hadn't spent much time out in the wilderness. She'd skied in Vermont a couple of times, years ago, at the insistence of a college boyfriend, but apart from that she couldn't remember the last time she'd been in such an alien landscape.

It was a shame, she thought. It did possess undeniable beauty, and she could understand why people made the effort to get away to places like this. But right now, that appeal was completely wasted. All she could see around her was suffering and death.

She stopped for a moment, looked around. Nothing but bare trees, boulder fields, a couple of large rock outcroppings, and snow. A cold, bleak canvas of white and various shades of grey, punctuated by the occasional dash of dark green from some mountain laurel or a huckleberry shrub.

She couldn't see any sign of life. She wished she could call out to Reilly, make sure he was still alive—make sure she wasn't the one being stalked. But she couldn't.

Instead, she just panned left and right, made sure she wasn't missing anything, and continued on up, her mind picking out the large outcropping on the ridge to her right as a heading to follow.

Roos watched the woman get closer and closer.

She was fifteen yards away and closing. He had her in his crosshairs now. One gentle pull on his trigger and she'd drop to the ground without knowing what hit her.

He held his breath, adjusted his aim. At this distance, in these conditions, it was an easy shot. Almost unsportsmanlike. No challenge whatsoever. It was also almost unfair. Does and bucks had highly tuned senses. They could see, hear and smell even the slightest of clues. This woman was, by comparison, like an astronaut in full gear. Slow, lumbering, strained. Incomparable. He'd be able to call out to her, wave at her and ask for her name before he pulled the trigger, and he'd still drop her.

But then, he didn't think killing her would be a wise move.

She'd be dead, no question. But the shot would ring out across the woods, and Reilly would know where he was. He'd need to try and make his way to another blind before Reilly spotted him. Staying in this one and using the dead woman as bait was too dangerous. Reilly would anticipate that move. And no matter what, he'd still have Reilly out there, on the loose, stalking him.

No, killing her now would be a mistake. He had a far better use for her. Much simpler, much more straightforward, but knowing how righteous Reilly was, it was bound to work.

He watched her climb up, seemingly drawn to the outcropping that shielded him. He knew he was perfectly camouflaged, knew she wouldn't spot him until it was too late.

She kept coming. Slowly, but inevitably.

He waited until she was a few feet away, then, in one swift move, he launched himself up at her and slammed the stock of his rifle into her back.

She grunted heavily and stumbled forward, falling to her knees, her carbine tumbling out of her hands.

She turned around slowly, groaning with pain, but he was already on top of her, his rifle right in her face.

"Shh," he said. "No noise. Not yet. Now turn around."

# 68

I was tired. Exhausted, actually.

My body was starting to flag. I hadn't been too kind to it lately. It had been a pretty intense couple of weeks that had included hours when I was technically dead. But I couldn't give up now.

I kept advancing, my legs moving on their own, carrying me up further and further into the mountain, trying to avoid a fall or even a slip. Up here, right now, a damaged ankle or a busted knee would be fatal. And there'd be no Frankenstein machine to bring me back this time.

I heard the air move above me and glanced up to see a turkey vulture glide by. It banked, made a full circle over me, then with a flick of his wings, it was gone again, disappearing into the white mist. I wondered if that was a good omen. It had to be—for one of us, anyway.

There were more than a few blowdowns up here, maybe casualties from some recent hurricane. I either climbed over them or made my way around them, long bare trunks that were just making my advance more difficult.

And then I heard her, a call that echoed through the trees.

"Reilly! Reilly?"

It was Deutsch.

I almost shouted back, then I held back.

*He had her.*

Shit.

What was she doing up here?

I gritted my teeth to swallow my anger, then I summoned up more resolve and increased my pace, heading in the direction I thought her shout came from.

She hadn't sounded too far—a hundred, hundred and fifty yards, tops, I figured. I was moving faster now, breathing hard, eyes focused intently ahead of me, acutely aware of a potential ambush.

"Reilly!"

Her voice rang out again, acting like a compass heading.

I kept going, my fingers tighter against the carbine. And after a long climb that left me almost breathless, something appeared out of the haze that was shrouding the mountain, something foreign to this desolate landscape.

It was Deutsch, standing in front of a large rock outcropping at the top of the ridge. Only she wasn't alone. A figure was standing behind her, and he was holding a handgun to her head.

Roos.

I slowed my pace, swung my gun slowly so it was pointed in their direction, and kept moving until I was about ten yards away from them.

There he was. Gordon Roos. After all these months—after all these deaths, I was finally face to face with him.

I have to say, in the flesh, he was a disappointment. Mid-sixties, I imagined. Nothing noteworthy, nothing particularly vile or evil in his features. No glass eye, no scarred face, no deformed fingers. His face looked very similar to the drawing Leo and Daphne had sent me. They had really done a phenomenal job. I couldn't see his build to ascertain what shape he was in, but he seemed fit enough. He was up here, after all, and he wasn't panting like I was.

"Nice to put a face to the voice," I said, trying to play down the fact that Deutsch and I were truly and genuinely screwed.

"I figured it was about time we met," Roos said. "You've put enough time and effort into it."

I wasn't in the mood for games. "Let her go," I said. "This is between you and me."

"You're such a Boy Scout, you know that? Like someone from a Norman Rockwell painting. 'This is between you and me?' Really? What are you—Shane? When did that ever work in the real world? You think I'm going to roll around in the snow with you when I can just shoot you? Jesus, I could have picked you off minutes ago, while you were still coming up here. But I wanted to see the look in your eyes when you realized you were fucked. When you realized you and this little bitch of yours were both fucked. That look you have on your face right now? That'll keep me company for years to come. It's moments like these . . . when they come around, you've got to grab them. Which I now have."

And just like that, he calmly, matter-of-factly, raised his gun at me from behind Deutsch. I thought of shooting first, swinging my gun up quickly as I dived off to one side, but there was no way I was getting a clean shot off at him, not with Deutsch there in the way, not on the move and given how weary I was and how my hands were shaking.

Still, I couldn't just stand there, and in that instant of deciding whether to duck left or right or charge ahead, something rushed down out of nowhere, a buzzing white flash that came out of the sky and smashed itself against the large boulders next to them. Roos wasn't expecting it—none of us were. But the split second of distraction from the kamikaze drone was all we needed.

Deutsch moved fast as lightning, grabbing his gun hand with both hands and just yanking him forward, almost over her shoulders, causing him to spin and topple over and slam into the ground. I was already charging at them and I covered the ground between us and got there as Deutsch was wrangling the gun out of his hand. I dove in, giving him a massive downward punch that just planted him in place and loosened his hold on the gun. I gave him another—unnecessary, but what the hell?—then Deutsch and I stepped back and took in our captured prey.

Gordon Roos was finally mine.

Now I had to decide what to do with him.

# 69

We marched Roos down the mountain.

He tried talking a couple of times, but I shut him down, first with a couple of words, then with another punch. I wasn't ready to listen to him. I was still gathering up my thoughts and playing things out in my head.

We kept going until we got to a small clearing that was dotted with ghostly birch trees, within sight of the cabin. More snow had settled up here—two, maybe three inches. I knew the temperature was still hovering just below zero, but there was a mild wind blowing, which was what I needed.

I told Roos to sit down by the base of one of the trees. He did as told. I walked over and cuffed his hands around it.

I stepped back and turned to Deutsch. "Is the Crown Vic down there?"

She nodded. "Yes."

"And the jerrycan? Still in the trunk?"

"Yep."

"You're wasting your time," Roos called out. "I'm not telling you anything."

I walked over to him. "I'd bet otherwise."

"Fuck you," he said. "You're going to kill me anyway. At least this way I'll enjoy knowing you'll never clear your name and you'll never know the full story about your dad."

"I really think differently." I turned to Deutsch. "I'll be right back. If he makes trouble—try not to kill him."

"I can't promise."

I left them and made my way to the cabin. The place looked like a war zone. The charred cabin, Tomblin's shot-up Navigator, his mangled body still inside it. It looked, and smelled, like death.

I popped the trunk on the Crown Vic, got what I needed, then headed back up to the clearing.

Roos was still where I'd left him. He was fixing me with a long scowl, his defiant attitude coming through loud and clear. Still, you didn't need to be the Amazing Kreskin to know what he was thinking. A desolate place where no one would hear you, a guy intent on revenge. If he had any sense, some very uncomfortable images had to be spooling through his mind right now. Especially since my left hand was holding a five-gallon jerrycan.

I set it down and stepped across to him. Then, without saying a word, I bent down and yanked his shoes off his feet.

He started kicking around. "Hey, what the—"

I punched him hard to calm him down. "Shut up!"

Then I got back to it. I pulled his socks off, undid his belt, and yanked his pants and his shorts off too, in one go. Then I pulled out the tactical knife and held it in front of me for a couple of seconds, visibly fueling more uncertainty in Roos. His eyes were just locked on the drop point blade, his forehead now bursting with sweat beads despite the bitter cold.

"I was in California last summer," I told him. "An ex-girlfriend of mine called me up, asking for help. She was ex-DEA. Some guys were after her. When I got there, I found out I had a kid. A four-year-old boy. Turned out they were really after him, and she died trying to keep him safe." I jabbed the blade in his direction. "She died in my arms. Because of you."

"I wasn't part of that—"

I held up the knife to silence him. He piped down.

"I know. It wasn't your deal. But it wouldn't have happened if you hadn't stepped in to make it happen. To do what you and your people—Orford would be my guess—did to my boy."

I studied him for a moment, then I continued. "Still . . . the guy you were all after? Maybe you know this, maybe you don't. He thought these bikers were dicking him around, so he came after them with his men. Shot them all up. All except their leader. What he did to get the truth out of him . . . I was there and I saw the result. It wasn't pretty. He started with the fingers. After two of them, he got bored. So he moved on to somewhere different. The coroner said he bled out, and let me tell you, when you bleed out from down there? Not the best way to go. But at least the cut was clean. One go. He had the benefit of using garden shears."

I let that simmer for a moment while I tapped the blade on my open palm, then I added, "I don't have any garden shears. But I have this." I held up the knife. "It'll have to do."

I stopped talking for a moment, just staring him down, giving his imagination time to generate all kinds of horrific visions. Then, with Deutsch standing guard and aiming her M4 at him, I stepped forward.

He flinched and kicked back, like he thought I was going for it. I wasn't. Instead, I used the knife to cut through his sleeves and the back of his jacket and a minute later he was totally naked.

In the snow.

With a light wind blowing.

He was shivering now. Probably from a combination of cold and fear.

I moved back to join Deutsch.

"What?" he asked her, a disturbing leer on his face. "You see something you like?"

She ignored it as I glanced up at the sky, looked around the trees—then set my gaze back on him.

"I want to know *everything*. I want to know *who* the Janitors were. *What* they were. What they did. I know about Padley, Orford, and Siddle. I want to know about the others. I want to know what your role was in it, what Tomblin's role was. I want to know who else knew about it. I want to know who you killed and who you had killed. I want to know who the guy you sent after me was, the guy who killed Kirby and Nick. And I want to know about my dad."

I stopped there, letting him process it for a moment. His eyes were locked on me, the defiance still there, but now I could see some cracks in it. He wasn't going to break easy. I knew that going in. But we were getting there.

"You're going to tell me everything I want to know," I continued. "That's a given. No way around that, trust me. I won't kill you before I get what I'm after, and we both have enough training to know that it's going to happen. The only question is what condition you'll be in when we're done. If you're still in decent enough shape, I'll hand you over to my friend here and she'll take you in. I'll need to make sure she doesn't shoot you herself, because my partner, the one you had killed? That was her boyfriend. But we talked about it, and I think she'll get more pleasure out of seeing you go through the humiliation of a trial before marching you into prison. Maybe. Or maybe you're connected enough that your people will cut some kind of deal or find some kind of loophole and let you walk free. Me, I'd take prison. You wouldn't want to be out here. Not with my friend and me here knowing what we do. So that's option one. Option two is, you play hard-ass and I have to cut the truth out of you one piece at a time. In which case it'll be hard for me to send you back without getting myself into trouble. Sensible move would then be to finish you off here and leave you for bear food. So it's up to you, really. Crunch time. And just so you don't feel rushed, I'm going to give you time to consider it. To think about what I said. To see if you reach the reasonable conclusion I hope you'll reach. But, in the interest of speeding things up . . ."

I turned, picked up the jerrycan, and undid its top. Then I held it over him, watching him stare up at it in terror, shaking his head, mouthing, "No, don't—" for me to stop, and I emptied its contents all over him, drenching him top to toe.

He went fetal and curled into himself defensively and shut his eyes tight and sputtered, then he stopped suddenly and shook it off his face and looked up at me with burning, angry surprise.

It wasn't gasoline. It was just water.

Water, which, on naked skin, in snowy weather, would accelerate his hypothermia.

Dramatically.

"I think we've had some of the same training," I told him. "I don't know how much you remember about this stuff, but . . . I figure it's about minus two or three out here, tops. And the wind is, what—ten, twelve miles per hour? Call it ten. Minus two degrees and a ten mile-per-hour wind gives us a wind-chill temperature of minus twelve degrees or so. Add the water and I'm betting you're not feeling too comfortable right now."

I stepped back and took in the sight of him there, tied to that tree. I don't think I've ever seen anyone in such a pathetic, vulnerable state. Normally, I'd be the guy walking in to save someone like that. Here, I was responsible for it.

"That shivering you're doing?" I said. "That's stage one. Mild hypothermia. Your body's trying to generate more heat to warm itself up. Soon, your hands and feet will start feeling numb. You'll feel tired, and even the smallest effort will feel difficult. Another couple of degrees and you'll be in moderate hypothermia. You'll experience violent shivering and a loss of coordination in your muscles until that shivering stops because there's no energy left to keep it going, which will make your temperature drop even further until you lose consciousness at around thirty degrees and slip into stage three: profound hypothermia. Which is around the time frostbite should start setting in. I'd give it half an hour, tops."

I looked around again, taking in the conditions. I figured it wasn't far past midday, but the sun was very low this time of year, making the setting feel even bleaker.

"I'll leave you to think things over."

Then I nodded to Deutsch, and without another word, we headed down towards the cabin, Roos's curses fading with each step.

We left him to stew there for twenty minutes, which was pushing it. I certainly didn't want him dead. But I knew he was a tough son of a bitch, and I wanted this over today. Before the sun set.

We didn't say much as we waited. I asked Deutsch about the gunfight down the mountain. She said it had been all right. And that was about it.

She could see I'd never done anything like this before.

I wasn't a fan of "enhanced interrogation" or any other euphemism people came up with for torture. I wasn't raised that way. It ran against everything I believed in, everything I thought our nation stood for. But I wanted him to talk, and I needed to scare the bejeezus out of him. I can't say I was enjoying it, but to be perfectly honest with you, I wasn't uneasy about it either. It had to be done, which, I know, is not a politically acceptable excuse. It's the excuse everyone gives. But there was no way around it and all I needed to do to brush away the first semblance of a qualm, if it arose, was to picture any one of the people that I knew had died because of a few callous words that bastard and his cronies had said to his hired gun.

No qualms showed up.

We went back up there twice.

The first time, he was still playing tough even though he looked like shit. He was going through violent shivering and had lost a lot of his muscular coordination. He'd also peed himself. Exposure to this much cold reduces the blood flow to the skin's surface. The body can only hold so much liquid and responds by ditching whatever it can. That's usually the first to go.

At this stage, you'd expect him to lose the ability to make rational decisions. Mountaineers suffering from hypothermia sometimes just laid down in the snow to sleep, or failed to fasten the most basic of harnesses properly. I'm not sure whether spilling his guts to me constituted a rational or an irrational decision as far as he was concerned. I was hoping for rational: it might help him survive, even if he only thought that had a small chance of happening. When we've got our backs right up against the wall, our survival instincts take over. I hoped his would, before it was too late.

But he was still fighting it. So I left him again, for fifteen minutes this time.

When I got back, he was in really bad shape. His body had stopped shivering, having lost any energy to keep itself warm. His limbs were stiff, his heart rate and his breathing barely there. His skin was pale and icy cold to the touch. More importantly, his resolve had also frittered away. His mind was weakened, he was disorientated, and his speech was slurry. And he was in pain. Lots of pain. His body had also decided his internal organs were more important that his extremities, which were red and hurting. All of them. Frostbite was settling in, fast.

If I left him there, he'd start dying soon. A long, painful death. Eventually, he'd start having hallucinations, then he'd lose consciousness and drift off into oblivion.

He didn't want that.

I didn't either.

On my haunches close to him, I asked, "Are you ready to talk?"

To the extent that he could answer, he did.

He wanted to talk.

It wouldn't just be for my own ears. This would be saved for posterity.

I pulled out the GoPro Kurt had bought in New York, turned it on, and aimed it at Roos. For added safety, Deutsch also took out her phone, switched its camera to video, and started filming too.

# 70

With the GoPro blinking red as it recorded his words, Roos talked.

A lot.

The Janitors weren't born out of some evil master plan, he told us. They didn't come about by design. They just grew out of necessity and took shape gradually, with each new assignment.

It was all about getting rid of liabilities. Eliminating threats. Silencing whistleblowers. Whether they were abroad—or at home.

"All this fuss about JSoc," he said with a weak, wheezy chortle, his words struggling to come out. He was referring to the Joint Special Operations Command, a present-day network of highly trained paramilitary assassins who operated outside the traditional chain of command in executing the kill lists they were handed. They'd been the subject of exposés and debates in the news lately. JSoc combined the secretive, unaccountable world of mercenaries with the intel and firepower of the military, and its officials reported directly to the president. Its budget was secret. JSoc was, for all intents and purposes, the president's personal hit team.

"It makes me laugh," Roos continued slowly after a dry, pained cough. "People think this is something new. It's not. We've been doing it for decades. Only difference is—everyone's now for it. Hell, JSoc got bin Laden, didn't they? They ran team six. Back then, things were different. The Cold War, Eastern Europe and Central America, South-East Asia, back in the day—it wasn't as sexy. They were too far away for people to really care. It wasn't the 'War on Terror.' We had to stay in the shadows."

"But the people you were killing weren't terrorists who were responsible for the deaths of innocent civilians," I said. "They *were* innocent civilians."

He wagged an angry, trembling finger at me. "We never killed anyone who didn't pose a direct threat to the nation. And that's a fact. We just did the dirty work no one dared talk about. People out there—they have no idea. And they owe us. Because it's not just about military threats. It's not just about bringing down the towers or blowing up an embassy somewhere. It's also about the bigger picture. About our place in the world. About how other countries see us. And it's about economic power. Making sure we stay on top. I mean, look. You *know* the damage Woodward and Bernstein did. That whole Watergate mess—that should have never been allowed to happen."

"You call it damage," I said. "I call it what makes us strong. What makes us the best."

"Such a god damn Boy Scout," Roos spat. "That's what makes us the best? To have our own president humiliated like that? To get him impeached, watch him crawl away from the White House with his tail between his legs while the rest of the world is laughing at us? How does that make us the best, exactly?"

He shook his head with disdain. I wasn't about to argue with him. I wasn't here for a debate. I was here to listen.

"It shook us, I tell you. Shook us all. I was still starting out, but for everyone around me, it was a massive failure. And I can tell you this—had my team been in place, that story would have never come out. Woodward and Bernstein wouldn't have been around long enough to get the story out. And if we were still around today, you would have never heard of that cocksucker Edward Snowden either. Or any of those other Wikileaks faggots. That would have never been allowed to happen under our watch."

We were getting off track. I had to reel him back.

I asked, "How did it start?"

He paused, gathering more strength, catching his breath. "We were at the CIA. Me, Eddy . . . we had an op going on in London with a Dutch contact. We were arranging some cocaine shipments to him in exchange for some favors in East Germany. And this fucking reporter for the *Telegraph*," he said, "he got wind of it, cornered the guy, and got the whole story. And he was going to put it out there. Well, we found out in time. We talked to him, asked him to back down, explained the bigger picture. Explained that lives and careers were at stake. He wouldn't. We tried threatening him. That only made things worse."

"So you killed him?" I said.

"You're damn right we did," he said. "Made it look like an accident. No one suspected a thing. The guy rode a motorcycle, one of those crappy English models, not a Harley or even a Jap one. Piece of cake. And we got all his notes, everything. It was easier back then, before email and all that. Physical, paper, you know? Photographs and negatives and audiotape. Things that, once they were gone—they were gone for good." He shrugged. "The op went through without a hitch."

"Then you did it again?"

"We got asked to take care of another problem the agency had in Istanbul. We did that. Then another in Zurich. Pretty soon, it became our sole focus. We were the go-to guys if anyone had a problem."

"And you operated outside our borders *and* on home soil," I added.

"We took care of any threat, anywhere. No one knew about us, so it didn't really make any difference to us. An enemy's an enemy, I don't care what passport they're carrying. And we had a pretty good unit set up, too. Small. Covert. No leaks."

"You and Tomblin—you ran it."

"Yes. We had three whiz kids, each of them with their own specialty, to figure out the best way to do it without raising suspicion. We'd meet up to discuss the situation. We'd do it here when we could—it was within easy reach for everybody. Come up with the best option. Then we had an operative go out and execute what we came up with."

"The specialists. Padley, and the other two," I said.

"That's right. Padley, for the medical option. Siddle for anything technical. And Orford for mental breakdowns."

"Mental breakdowns. Like my dad," I asked, feeling my blood boil over.

He looked up at me with tired, desensitized eyes. I tensed up. It was now or never. He'd either talk—or he'd leave me hanging forever.

"Yeah," he slurred a bit. "Your dad. Stubborn man, he was."

I didn't know if that was good or bad. "Keep going. What happened?"

He studied me, the manipulative wheels of his mind still

managing to spin despite his battered body. "You *would* like to know, wouldn't you?"

"I would."

He said "Hmm," and nodded slowly. Then it was as if he came to some kind of realization, something that gave him some inner satisfaction. And he raised his tired eyes at me again.

"You know about the October Surprise, don't you?"

I told him I did. The US embassy hostages in Tehran during the Reagan-Carter election year, their release within minutes of Reagan's inauguration, the allegations of foul play.

"Iran was under a weapons embargo, right?" he said. "But they needed guns. They were about to have an eight-year war with Iraq. They were already in talks with Carter's people. They had a deal, the hostages were coming out. In October. Which would have got Carter re-elected. Then Reagan's people stepped in behind the scenes, made them a better offer, and bullied them into accepting it. They didn't want the hostages released until after he won the election. And in return, Reagan would give them what they really wanted: weapons. Five billion dollars worth. But it had to be done under the table. Because of the embargo."

"What's that got to do with my dad?"

"Your dad," he said, quite matter-of-factly, "he had this friend, this old college buddy of his. A Portuguese guy."

"Octavio Camacho," I offered.

Roos looked at me, a little surprised. "Exactly. Well, it seemed Camacho had done pretty well for himself back home in Portugal. He'd turned into this hot little reporter. And he came to see your dad because he had some documents. Some information."

"About the October Surprise?" I asked. "It was already out there. People were talking about it already."

"Well, true," Roos said. "But they didn't know the whole story."

"And Camacho did," I said.

Roos nodded.

"But—you said he was in Portugal? What did that have to do with Iran and us?"

"The guns had to come from somewhere. Some of them were shipped out from Israel, like with Contra. But the rest—they came from us. And they went through Lisbon airport and a couple of others, smuggled through with the help of the Portuguese military."

"And Camacho found this out?"

"No. He found out what happened after that."

"What?"

"The Portuguese defense minister, Da Costa—he found out. He wasn't happy about it. He was their first civilian defense minister and he had an idealist crusader's view of the world, much like yourself. So he dug around and he got himself all the evidence he needed."

I could see where this was going.

"He was going to take it to the UN. We had to move fast. He'd chartered a small Cessna to go to an election rally. It was three days before their own presidential election. Then, at the last minute, his buddy who'd given him that post, the prime minister, Sá Carneiro—he decides to hop on board too. The plane crashed just after take off. The investigation decided it was an accident."

"Siddle?" I asked.

He nodded. "One of his first gigs. High-pressure job, though. A lot at stake."

I couldn't believe what I was hearing. "You murdered the Portuguese prime minister and their defense minister?"

He shrugged. "Their military weren't unhappy to see him go. The defense minister, I mean. He wasn't one of them. And he was going to put a lot of them in jail."

"But you had them killed?"

"Hey, I would have done it again," he said. "This would have devastated the country worse than Watergate. Reagan was a massively popular guy. A man of the people. Carter had screwed things up and we needed to get the country back on track. To hear that he had fifty-two American diplomats and civilians kept in chains in some Tehran cell for three extra months just so he could win the election . . . how do you think the country would have reacted to that?"

I was trying to keep my anger in check and stay focused. "So Camacho found out? And he came to see my dad?"

"He was scared. The military in Portugal had eyes and ears everywhere. He thought the safer way to go about it would be to put the story out there first. So he got in touch with your dad. He told him what happened and asked him to find a way to go wide with it. Your dad had a solid reputation. He wasn't someone you could bend."

"He was a threat to the nation?"

Roos shrugged. "We knew about his affair. We tried to lean on him that way but he didn't care. He didn't leave us a choice."

An immense weight had lifted off my shoulders, but it was coupled with a profound sadness for this noble man that I never really got a chance to know. A profound sadness—and a raging anger at the animal sitting in front of me.

"Orford?" I asked.

"No, actually. We staged it. But we needed a real shrink to convince the coroner and your mom that it was a real suicide. Orford did that. He was a practicing psychiatrist. The three of them had real jobs. Worked better for cover."

I asked, "Who made the decision?"

"It was mine and Eddy's call. We made the threat assessment, decided on what action to take."

"Who pulled the trigger?"

"Eddy," he said. "Tomblin did it. We were both in there together."

Images of Tomblin getting shredded to bits while taped to the car seat next to me flashed through my mind. I guess it couldn't have happened to a nicer guy.

I got Roos to reel off the names of their victims. Whatever he could remember. Places. Dates. A brief summary. For the record. I'm sure there were more, but the ones he gave me were already shocking enough. Murder victims that no one realized had been murdered.

Throughout, something was gnawing at me. He was being too open, too helpful. I know he was doing it to survive, but still—he could have held a lot back and I wouldn't have realized it. But I was getting the sense that he was telling me everything. Which worried me. I didn't think his brain was *that* battered by the cold.

No, he had something up his sleeve. And it wasn't long before it became apparent.

"I'm glad we had this little chat," he said when we were done.

"Because now I can fill you in on one last thing you don't know. See, now you feel good. You think you have the truth, you've got it all on tape on that silly little camera. You think you're going to go back home, be a big hero and live happily ever after with that woman of yours."

"That's the plan," I told him.

He laughed. Weakly, barely—he was still in bad shape. "You have no idea. All this, everything that happened? It's not us. It's bigger than me, bigger than Eddy and the others. You really have no idea. But I can tell you one thing. You're not even gonna make it to breakfast tomorrow. And if not tomorrow, the next day. That tape of yours? No one's going to see it. Go on, put it out on the Internet. Upload it right now. No one's going to take it seriously. You'll see. Well, you won't—you won't be around that long." He turned to look at Deutsch. "You neither, honey."

"You mean there were others?"

"Of course. Others who can't possibly let this come out. Not now. Not ever. But especially not now."

"Who?"

He chuckled his wheezy, grotesque chuckle again. "Now that is the brass ring you're not going to get."

I nodded to myself, knowing what was ahead of us. "I wish you hadn't said that. I really do, Gordo. For your sake."

It took another hour.

The cold, more water. And other stuff.

And then he talked.

And he was right.

It was going to be a problem.

I thought about it for a minute or two. Deutsch was standing back, in the cold, watching me in silence.

"Reilly," she finally called out. "We have him. We have it all on tape. It's done. Let's take him in. It's over. Let's go home."

It wasn't over. Not with what he'd just told me.

"You heard what he said," I told her. "He's too connected. This thing's too big. They'll work out a deal."

"We have enough to make sure they don't."

I thought about it some more.

Then I said, "I can't take that chance." I turned to her. "If not for you, or for me, then . . . for Nick. And all the others."

I went over to the camera, made sure it was off. Then I pulled out my gun, went right up to Roos, and put a bullet through his head.

## 71

The next two days were intense.

Deutsch and I hadn't gone public with the tape. We'd shared it with our boss, and he'd shared it upstream. Needless to say, it kicked up quite a shitstorm. The immediate result was that the FBI and the CIA got Arlington PD to drop any inquiries about me regarding Kirby's murder and cleared my name, for the record. The rest—well, they all needed to figure out how they'd handle it. There was a potential political, legal and public relations tsunami brewing, and I had little doubt a whole bunch of national security honchos and a few select politicos were having long, heated debates about what to do with Roos's revelations.

What they ultimately decided wasn't really up to me, nor would I be able to influence it. To be honest, I didn't really care. Roos and Tomblin were dead, and I was just happy to be reunited with my family. It felt awesome to be back home with Tess, Kim and Alex. I was ready to sleep for a week, and the bureau obviously had no problem with me taking the next couple of weeks off. It was going to be a great Christmas of hanging out at home, enjoying my family. Doing the things life's best at.

Kurt and Gigi had managed to hack into Orford's computer and had found his notes relating to Alex. They made for some pretty shocking reading. I'd be passing it all on to Alex's shrink in the New Year, right after the holidays, certain that it would help finally eradicate any lingering traces of everything they did to him.

All of which, of course, left one last thing to deal with. The thing we hadn't shared with Gallo: the video recording we'd kept for ourselves.

The last part of Roos's testimony.

I told Tess about it, of course. We'd spent hours talking about it, after I'd had the whole house swept twice for any hidden mikes or cameras. And the simple conclusion was that I couldn't leave it alone.

For one thing, it wasn't safe to do so. I didn't want to spend the rest of my time looking over my shoulder. Or needing a taster to check anything I was about to put in my mouth, for that matter.

Besides, I couldn't let it lie. No way.

I had to tackle this head on.

Which was why I was now being ushered into the Oval Office for a private audience with the president.

Yorke greeted me with a big handshake and a slap on the shoulder. "My God, Reilly, I knew it had to be important for you to miss out on dinner with us like that, but my Lord—from what I hear, you've been through a real wringer."

"It's been . . . intense," I said flatly.

"Sit down, sit," he said as he guided me to one of the armchairs by the twin sofas.

I wasn't in the mood to sit down, but I felt I might as well. This wasn't going to be easy.

"Tess, the kids—everyone excited about Christmas? Have you had time to do your shopping yet?"

"I'm not here to talk about that, sir."

"No, of course you're not. Well, let's get right to it, then, shall we?"

I just nodded.

"Obviously, what you've uncovered . . . I'm still having a hard time processing it. We all are. And I've got to say, you did a great job getting to the bottom of it, a great job. It's one hell of an achievement, son. But at the same time, it's a huge headache. A monster of a migraine, in fact. We're going to have to think about what we do with it very, very carefully. Revelations like that—they could cause the kind of damage a country like ours might never recover from."

I didn't say anything back. I just fixed him squarely, trying to get a read of the man.

The problem was, I liked him. Up until that miserable evening in the Blue Ridge Mountains, up until I'd heard what Roos had to say about him, I liked our president. I'd always thought Hank Yorke was a good guy. He'd guided our country through four decent years. He wasn't a polarizing figure and the raging wars of partisanship had calmed down under him. I was proud to have saved his life and I would have been voting for him next year.

Not any more.

"It'll take a while," he continued. "In the meantime, I hope you're going to take some time off and enjoy the holiday season with your family. God knows, you deserve it."

"That's the plan," I finally offered. "But before we do that, there's something else we need to deal with."

"Yes, of course," he said, leaning forward. "You asked for this meeting. What can I do for you, Reilly?"

"I think it's more about what I can do for you."

He looked perplexed. "What do you mean?"

"There was a second part of Roos's testimony. One I haven't shared with the Bureau." I paused, gauging him.

His eyes narrowed just slightly, but it was there. "Oh?"

I nodded. "Roos told me about Viking. About you and the Janitors. I know everything there is to know about that."

His expression clouded, but being the consummate, gregarious politician that he was, it wasn't the meltdown you would expect to follow me saying something like that.

"And I've got to say," I added, "whoever came up with your code name—they should have been fired."

The city of York, in England, was captured by the Vikings late in the ninth century. It became a Norse kingdom for over fifty years, and the city became known as Jorvik.

"Yes, well," Yorke said with a shrug, "those were the days before Wikipedia. And the obvious can also work as misdirection. But I take your point."

"I know what you did, sir. I know you were Roos and Tomblin's boss. I know you ran the Janitors for all that time and I have the names of all the people you had them take out."

Yorke exhaled lengthily and sat quiet for a long moment. Then he got up and walked around his desk and looked out the big windows.

It was a gorgeous day outside. Blue sky, perfect sun, a crisp bite to the air. Not a great day to accuse the President of the United States of having run a secret assassination squad that had targeted Americans. On home soil, at that.

"It was a different time," he finally said. "The guys we're dealing with now . . . Al Qaeda, ISIS? They're pissants compared to the threat we were facing back then."

"I don't care—"

"We had nukes, Reilly," he blurted angrily. "Thousands of nukes aimed at us and a serious enemy that was deadly serious about wanting to take over the world."

"Desperate times, desperate measures, right?" I replied evenly. "Keeping the country safe, making the hard decisions so people can sleep safely at night? Yeah, I've heard it all before. Roos gave me the same speech. Still doesn't make it OK to do what you guys did. Which was murder, plain and simple."

That really riled him up. "You don't know what the hell you're talking about," he growled. "You didn't live through it like we did. You didn't know what we knew, what the intel was telling us on a daily basis. You have no idea how thin the ice was under us and you think you can just stand there, all smug and righteous, and pass judgment on us when you weren't around to see what we were up against?"

"You had people killed. Civilians, Americans, foreigners—"

"And you think it was easy?" he fired back, slamming the desk with his palm. "You think we took it lightly? You think we didn't do everything possible to try to find another way every time we had to make one of those terrible decisions? You think each one of them didn't haunt me?"

"I don't know if they did," I shot back. "I'd like to think so, but either way, it doesn't change what happened. It doesn't change what you did."

"And you think you would have done things differently? Knowing what it could mean, knowing the risk of what could happen? How do you know you wouldn't have done what we did?"

"I would have found another way. Because there's always another way. Maybe you just didn't look hard enough. Maybe it just got easier with each one."

Yorke kept his gaze locked on me, his mouth tightly clenched. Then he looked away, nodding in silence, deep in thought.

After an interminable pause, he muttered, "Why are you here, Reilly?" He turned to face me. His face was all shriveled up. "Why are you here? You're telling me you know what you know. Presumably, you're sitting on some compelling evidence or you wouldn't be here, right?"

"I have enough, sir. Enough to cause you some very serious problems."

His expression darkened, and his voice went sharp. "So what do you want?"

It was a question I'd been wrestling with ever since Roos had finally talked.

"To be frank with you, I'm not really sure. Because you're right about one thing. If this came out, and if your part in it came out, it would be a huge catastrophe for the country. The country I love, the country I'm sworn to protect. But I know two things. I know I don't want to live looking over my shoulder. And I know I can't let you get away with it. You and your people had my father killed."

Yorke stared at me, then he pursed his lips and he looked away. His head was bowed down a little. "It won't change anything to say I'm sorry, but for what it's worth, I am. Some decisions are . . . impossible. But the outcomes of not taking them are even worse."

Maybe he was a great actor, or maybe it was my own wish fulfillment, but I sensed some genuine remorse. Regardless, I said, "I know all about how the good of the many outweighs the good of the few, but we're still talking about murder. *Multiple* murder."

He nodded. "So we have a problem."

"Yes, we do."

Yorke breathed out again with frustration. His shoulders stooped as he padded back over to me and sat down in the armchair facing me. "I'm not going to insult you by saying I could make things very, very comfortable for you, career-wise. We're talking a fast lane like no one's ever seen before."

"I'll pass."

He nodded to himself. "So where does that leave us?"

"I've been racking my brain trying to come up with a solution for this. Because, until now, I've had nothing but respect and admiration for you. I think you've been good for this country. Someone handed you responsibility for more than three hundred million people and you've done them good. And I can't ignore that."

"Thank you for saying that."

"But it doesn't change the fact that you're a murdering son of a bitch who should be rotting away on death row."

I took a breath. Part of me wanted to just walk up to him and strangle him with my bare hands, but I obviously needed to control myself.

"I can't overlook what you did," I continued. "Regardless of whether it involved my father or not. But I've been trying to think of what he would do if he were in my shoes, not that I knew him well enough, but I knew his values. I know how much he loved this country, what he was about. And I could only think of one thing."

"What's that?"

"You give it all up. You drop out of the re-election campaign."

His face crumpled with confusion. "You want me to walk away from the presidency?"

"Yes."

I could see the wheels spinning away inside his brain. "You'd be satisfied with that?"

"Right now, and hard as that is, I think I just might be able to live with that, yes. Because the alternative would rip the country apart at the seams. Political meltdown, markets crashing, international standing down the toilet . . . Just massive pain, maybe for generations. And much as part of me feels, well, that's justice, that's what needs to happen, the truth will set us free and all that bullshit . . . maybe the country's better off living with that lie. So I'll keep my mouth shut if you walk away, leave DC and devote the rest of your life to trying to atone for what you did. Just remember, the evidence I have . . . that's not going away. I'm not hitting any 'delete' buttons on anything."

Yorke took a moment to reflect on it. As he looked out the window I could see that his eyes had taken on a faraway, doomed stare. The consummate politician, having to walk away from . . . this room. Maybe I wasn't sending him to death row, but I was certainly condemning him to a life of hard labor, if only in terms of coping with what he'd had taken away from him.

Not my preferred outcome, but maybe it was the right one.

He finally asked, "How do you know the next guy won't have even worse skeletons in his cupboard?"

"I don't. But I know you do. And I can't ignore them."

He nodded, then frowned and shook his head. "Well, we'll need to come up with something else," he said with firm resolve. "That can't happen. You don't just walk away from the Oval Office. It's not that easy."

I wasn't biting. "Of course it is. You'll find an excuse. Family priorities. Health issues. Make something up. Happens all the time. We live in a world of spin, remember?"

He thought some more, then he said, "Let me think about it. I'm sure I can come up with something else that'll satisfy you. Some other solution that'll work for us both. How about that? Will you let me do that?"

For all I knew, he'd be giving the order to have me shipped off to Guantanamo or set into the concrete foundations of some highway overpass the second I stepped out of his office. But somehow, and despite everything I now knew about his past, I didn't think Hank Yorke, the president, would do that.

"No," I told him, firmly. "There are only two possible ways this plays out. You do as I ask. Or it all comes out. And FYI . . . Janitors or anyone else comes after me? The whole thing goes live. Big time. The cork pops and there's no way of putting it back in. You really don't want to go there. Trust me."

"Oh, I don't doubt that for a moment, Reilly."

We didn't shake hands.

I walked out of there, hoping I hadn't unleashed a trunkload of pain on myself.

I didn't think I had.

But I guess only time will tell.